# Bad
# Neighbors

# Also available by Maia Chance

## Agnes and Effie Mysteries
*Bad Housekeeping*

## Discreet Retrieval Agency Mysteries
*Gin and Panic*

*Teetotaled*

*Come Hell or Highball*

## Fairy Tale Fatal Mysteries
*Beauty, Beast, and Belladonna*

*Cinderella Six Feet Under*

*Snow White Red-Handed*

# Bad Neighbors

## AN AGNES AND EFFIE MYSTERY

Maia Chance

CROOKED
LANE

NEW YORK

Copyright © 2018 by Maia Chance.

Published in the United States by Crooked Lane Books, an imprint of The Quick Brown Fox & Company LLC.

Crooked Lane Books and its logo are trademarks of The Quick Brown Fox & Company LLC.

Library of Congress Catalog-in-Publication data available upon request.

ISBN (hardcover): 978-1-68331-541-4
ISBN (ePub): 978-1-68331-542-1
ISBN (ePDF): 978-1-68331-543-8

Cover illustration by Teresa Fasolino
Book design by Jennifer Canzone

Printed in the United States.

www.crookedlanebooks.com

Crooked Lane Books
34 West 27th St., 10th Floor
New York, NY 10001

First Edition: April 2018

10 9 8 7 6 5 4 3 2 1

For my inventive, steadfast Zach.

# Chapter 1

My name is Agnes Blythe, I'm twenty-eight years old, and I'm not going to lie: I'm a nerd. We nerds do our research. We think outside the box. We know how to buck up and keep going, even when the popular kids are calling us eraser breath and using us as a dodgeball target.

So, I don't know. I guess I was just thinking that somehow Aunt Effie, Cousin Chester, and I were going to restore the Stagecoach Inn all by ourselves. Using nerd superpowers.

YouTube toilet installation tutorials, *POW!* HGTV house-flipping marathon, *ZING!* This Old House *Essential Home Repair, SLAM!* Maybe a little gold-and-red spandex?

Or something.

But on that sunny, mid-October afternoon when Quinn Jones, architect, stood with Chester and me outside the inn, showing us the proposal he'd drawn up, I realized that the whole process was going to be more elaborate, expensive, and time-consuming than I'd thought. This meant (a) the dozens of hours I had spent worshipping Bob Vila had possibly been wasted, and (b) I was going to be living in my hometown of Naneda, New York, waaaaaaaaay longer than I'd planned.

Which was fine. I mean, I was dating (I think?) the guy I'd

been in love with *forever*, I had a free place to live (yes, in the inn's attic with the spiders, but FREE), and I had a job helping restore the inn—a job that, unlike my post-college gigs as barista, hotel receptionist, and library barcode drudge, I actually *cared* about.

And I belonged in Naneda, even though I had spent the last decade away. Of *course* I belonged. I mean, what kind of weirdo doesn't feel totally awesome, at ease, and not-like-an-outsider in their own hometown? *Snort.*

"Picture it," Quinn Jones was saying, tucking his binder of plans under his arm and spreading his hands like a frame around the inn. "Stabilize the foundations. Completely rebuild the porch—rot has set in pretty bad, and I saw some carpenter ants over on the far side. New front door, maybe a glossy black with brass hardware. Paint the shutters—well, first *replace* the shutters, and then paint them. All new windows, of course—you can get some stunning historic replicas with multipanes and real working sashes, just like the originals, except that, well, they won't be broken. Oh—and you'll need a new roof, and one of the chimneys looks like it's about to topple over."

"Yeah," I said, trying to add up the time and cost of basically rebuilding the entire inn piecemeal. "New roof. New chimney. Check and check."

Quinn, dapper and plump, gave me a hard look. "You guys want to do this the right way, don't you?"

"Of course!"

Chester nodded, flipped a Cheezy Puff into his mouth, and crunched.

"Just checking," Quinn said. "You're looking a little sick, Agnes."

"Me? Sick? *Pfft.*"

"She always looks like that," Chester said.

I shot Chester a glare.

A warm smile wreathed his round, pleasant face (well, pleasant minus the creepy little smudge of a mustache he was growing).

"Okay," Quinn said. "Because your aunt—"

"*Great* aunt." Chester crunched another Cheezy Puff.

"—she said that your budget is more than adequate."

"It is," I said. This was the truth. Aunt Effie had finagled her wealthy elderly boyfriend Paul Duncan into underwriting the entire renovation. I wasn't sure why he had agreed to do it, especially since he lived in Florida, but I wasn't going to argue. No Paul, no renovation. Case closed.

"The Stagecoach Inn, as you must be aware," Quinn said, "is a historic landmark—"

"Treasure." Chester was rummaging noisily in the Cheezy Puff bag. "It's a historic *treasure*."

Quinn gave a stiff smile. "Then you know how important it is not to cut corners or"—he made one-handed air quotes—" 'do it yourself.' "

*Was* the inn a landmark and a treasure? Well, sure. You just couldn't tell by looking at it.

My Great Uncle Herman had recently left the inn to Aunt Effie, his cousin, in his will. It had been condemned, but now it had brand-spankin'-new wiring and was off the Naneda code compliance officer's hit list. Built in 1848 on the site of the burned-down Chester Stagecoach Company headquarters, it had flourished as a hotel even as stagecoaches were supplanted by the railroads and the railroads by automobiles. Why? Because it was in the prettiest spot imaginable, on the shores of gentle Lake Naneda in the Finger Lakes region of upstate New York.

Offering wholesome family fun like canoeing, fishing, and swimming, the Stagecoach Inn became a summer holiday destination for generations of families. Then something happened in the 1960s (someone told me that's when the ghost showed up, but I don't buy it), and it slipped into a decline. It was a boarding house for a while, and then sometime in the late eighties Great Uncle Herman and his wife gave up on it. The place fell vacant.

If, that is, you don't count the mice, squirrels, spiders, and, apparently, carpenter ants who called the place home.

"Of course we know how important it is to do it right," I said to Quinn. "This building has been in our family for a hundred and seventy-odd years, and the land way longer than that. This is our heritage. That's actually why we're looking for an architect who understands that we want to help with the restoration—"

"You?" Quinn said. "*Help?*"

"Is that a problem?"

"Do you have any experience restoring old buildings?"

"Well, no, but we want to learn."

"We've been reading up on the subject," Chester said. "And we watch a lot of HGTV."

"Reading?" Quinn's eyelids drooped with disdain. "HGTV? That's not going to cut it. If you decide to hire me as your architect, I'm afraid I'm going to insist upon a professionals-only policy. This property is too special to be destroyed by dabblers."

"Okay," I said. "Sure." I'm pretty sure Quinn missed my "We hire this guy as our architect when hell freezes" tone.

Also, there was the little matter of how Chester and I had already started demolition on the attic bathroom. We'd gotten all pumped up watching *This Old House* reruns the previous week and plunged right in. The toilet had been removed and the claw-foot bathtub sat in the hallway. Next up was removing the sink. But no way was I sharing this with Quinn.

"All righty then, I'll keep going," Quinn said. "The garage? I was thinking we could tear it down and rebuild it with two additional guest rooms above—"

"Tear it down?" I said.

"Didn't you notice the way it's sagging? The foundations are shot, and anyway, it was probably built in the 1930s or '40s. It's not really a 'heritage' "—more air quotes—"building. What's in there, anyway? It's so crammed full of junk, it looks like a fire hazard."

"Junk?" Chester said. "Hardly." He stuffed four Cheezy Puffs in his mouth at once.

As if on cue, a U-Haul truck came growling down the inn's drive, overgrown bushes scratching along its sides, potholes making it jounce. Some burly guy I didn't recognize was behind the wheel, and Aunt Effie sat in the passenger seat. She saw us and made twiddly fingers.

"More?" Chester whispered to me. "*Seriously?*"

"More what?" Quinn asked, looking back and forth between Chester and me.

"You'll see," I said.

Chester, Quinn, and I watched as the burly guy maneuvered the truck, with lots of bumps and back-up beeping, so that the rear cargo door was lined up with the garage doors. Then he parked, and he and tall, thin, silver-bobbed Aunt Effie climbed out.

"Hello-o!" Effie cried merrily to us. "Come and see what Auntie-Claus has brought, children! You'll just *drool*."

Quinn, Chester, and I walked across the leaf-covered lawn toward the U-Haul. The cargo door rumbled as the burly guy shoved it open.

"Happy birthday to me!" Effie said.

Her birthday wasn't for three more months. By my calculations, she was going to be turning seventy-two for the fourth or fifth time.

The U-Haul was crammed full of what I knew to be furniture—expensive, antique furniture—all wrapped up in quilted moving pads.

"What did you get?" I asked. "Dining room set for thirty-five?"

"Better. Two armoires for the guest rooms, and—you're not going to *believe* this—they're *Chippendale*—"

Chester opened his mouth.

"—no need for crass jokes, Chester—"

Chester shut his mouth.

"—and I got them for an absolute *song* because the estate sale was almost impossible to find—the address practically made Google Maps go up in flames—and hardly anyone showed. I also found two pristine claw-foot bathtubs that'll look perfect in the en suite bathrooms we'll be putting in. Those will arrive tomorrow." Aunt Effie beamed her white, youthful, one hundred percent porcelain–veneered smile at Quinn. "But how rude of me—hello, Quinn. I adore those brogues you're wearing!—so very autumnal. I'm simply dying to see your proposal—" Effie's phone chirruped inside her orange suede purse. "Hang on, darlings—I'm expecting a call from Paul—boring old money things, you know—Chester, why don't you use those big muscles of yours to help Boyd start unloading the goodies?" Digging her phone out of her purse, she wandered away.

"Big muscles, huh?" I said to Chester.

He popped one last Cheezy Puff in his mouth and tossed the bag on a rusty lawn chair. "Just call me Beefcake of the Year."

Chester and I wage halfhearted battle with the same doughy Blythe genes. The genes are winning. It's not that we're bad-looking, but there will be no bouncing dimes off our biceps. Chester is short and thick, with a mop of curly brown hair, intelligent hazel eyes, and great skin. I'm five foot five and no gazelle, but I've also been blessed with good skin, and I have shiny, straightish, shoulder-length brown hair and hazel eyes. I have been called "really pretty." I have also been called a clone of Velma Dinkley in *Scooby-Doo*. I figure the reality falls somewhere in between.

"Welp," burly Boyd said, "let's get to it."

I dragged open the double garage doors. Golden sunbeams illuminated the interior, which was crammed, Jenga-style, with furniture in protective coverings.

"Wow," Quinn said, lifting his eyebrows.

"Someone has a hoarding problem," Chester said.

"Someone also gets really competitive at estate sales," I said.

"But if that's all Chippendale and the like," Quinn said, his eyes glowing, "then someone's inn is going to be *gorgeous* when it's furnished."

"Is there even *room* for this new stuff?" I said. "Wait—" I walked into the garage. "I'll scooch this table over to the side, and then stack those two armchairs on top . . ."

Quinn put down his binder and helped me scooch and stack, and then Boyd and Chester started unloading.

Aunt Effie, meanwhile, was over on the lawn talking on the phone. The orange-striped cat who lived on the premises—he had grown too sleek with the organic free-range cat food Aunt Effie fed him to be called a stray—twined around her ankles.

Boyd and Chester were nudging one of the armoires down the U-Haul ramp when—

"Yoo-hoo!" came Aunt Effie's voice. She was mincing toward us in her too-high-for-a-seventy-something heels. The cat—I called him Tiger Boy—strode away into the bushes.

I was thinking, *Crud.* Because Aunt Effie's yoo-hooing *never* bodes well.

She came over, phone pressed facedown against her shoulder, bottle-glass blue eyes glittering.

*Double crud.* When her eyes glittered like that . . .

"Who's on the phone?" I whispered.

"Potential guests."

"Great—for, like, next July?"

"No, for tonight."

"Oh, my," Quinn murmured.

Boyd said, "You guys have any Gatorade?"

"What?" I yelped. "*Tonight?* Are you insane, Aunt Effie?"

Chester and Boyd, panting for breath, eased the armoire the rest of the way down the ramp and parked it. Chester grabbed his Cheezy Puffs.

"I *feel* perfectly sane," Effie said, "but so many people have suggested otherwise that I suppose I should—"

"Let me get this straight," Chester said. "On the phone, right now, waiting for your response, are guests for *this place*"—he swept a hand toward the inn, which suddenly looked extra-dilapidated—"for *tonight*? Aunt Effie, they might as well check into Castle Dracula."

"Or a dog kennel," I said.

Chester laughed. "Or the dumpster behind the Chinese restaurant."

"Or—"

"*Children,*" Effie whispered, massaging her temple with short, black-lacquered fingernails. "Please *focus.* It's a bit of an emergency, you see. A motor coach carrying a leaf-peeping tour group broke down, and the guests are stranded here in Naneda until the bus is fixed. Most of them will be situated at other inns and hotels in town that just happened to have cancellations, but other than that, because of the Harvest Festival, the entire area is booked solid. They're desperate. They're senior citizens. We can make do."

The person on the line must've heard, because a faint squawking seeped from Effie's phone.

"How many guests?" I whispered.

"Only four."

"Um, four guests plus one—*one!*—guest bathroom equals—"

"Don't panic, Agnes. We have a dozen brand-new mattresses right up there in the garage loft"—Mattress Barn had had a going-out-of-business sale the previous week—"and I could pop over to Bella's Bedding Boutique to purchase sheets and blankets and pillows. The place *is* spotless."

This was actually true. The entire rambling inn was spick-and-span and smelled, literally, like Spic and Span. Maybe a touch of Windex.

But that didn't negate the empty rooms, the expanses of hardwood floors yearning to be refinished, the crackly gray, stained plaster walls stripped of their layers of antique wallpaper, the saggy linoleum in the kitchen and bathrooms, and the gross purplish mahogany-effect stain (circa 1975?) on every last bit of intricate millwork.

"It should be only one night," Effie said. "It turns out that the driver—it's Golden Vistas Motor Coach Tours—managed to drive the last few miles to Hatch Automotive before breaking down entirely—"

"Hatch Automotive?" I said.

"Oooh," Chester said. "*Otis.*"

"Please," I said, rolling my eyes.

"Better get gussied up, kiddo."

"Give me those!" I snatched the bag of Cheezy Puffs from Chester and stress-ate a handful.

Hatch Automotive is owned and run by Otis Hatch—the guy I may or may not have been dating—and his grandpa Harlan. Otis didn't usually work on Sundays, but if the motor coach was being deposited there, that meant he had likely been called in. He's the head mechanic. His grandpa is mostly retired, and I happened to know he was away deep-sea fishing with an old buddy from Nam.

Oh—and after I had told Otis I was in love with him weeks earlier, he had NEVER SAID I LOVE YOU TOO. Hence the stress-eating.

"Agnes?" Effie said. "What do you say?"

"Okay," I said with a weird sense of doom. "Sure. Let's bring 'em on in."

"Chester?"

"Why not?" Chester said, snatching back the Cheezy Puffs from me. "What could possibly go wrong?"

# Chapter 2

Fifteen minutes later I was hairbrushed, tinted lipbalmed, lightly eyelinered, and driving toward Hatch Automotive in my "new" car. This was a fifteen-year-old whitish minivan that looked like a cross between a handheld Dustbuster and the Space Shuttle. Its undercarriage was about two inches from the ground and bumped and scraped on every last pebble. At speeds over forty-five miles per hour, it felt in danger of disintegration. I had bought it off a high school student for five hundred bucks— easy on my savings account but no boon to my ego.

Hatch Automotive was about four miles from the inn, out on a crossroads a mile from the main highway. It was one of those retro concrete boxes from the 1950s with an auto shop on one side and a small office on the other. Autumn-gold fields sprawled around it. On the far edge of the rear field stood an old white farmhouse that belonged to Otis's Grandpa Harlan. Otis lived in his own little bungalow in town.

As I rolled closer to Hatch Automotive, my heart kicked up. Something was going on over there, and it didn't look good. Two police cruisers flashed their disco-in-hell blue and red lights. Milling people, a huge glossy motor coach, and—oh, no—an ambulance.

Maybe one of the motor coach passengers had had a minor accident . . .

Because Otis, my beautiful Otis, *could not be hurt.*

The entire lot around the automotive shop was in chaos— omigosh, was that a *body* under that white sheet, being loaded into the ambulance?—so I slammed the Dustbuster into park at the side of the road, scrambled out, and jogged over.

I stopped at the first person I came to, a small, wizened man in a travel vest. "What's going on?" I asked, sounding a little shrill.

"A mechanic has been murdered. Head smashed in."

My heart shriveled to a raisin. *Otis.* Otis was a mechanic.

"*What?* Who . . . ? Where is—?"

"And the *other* mechanic's being taken in by the police. I guess he did it."

I looked to where the man was pointing. My mouth fell open.

Otis wasn't dead. Otis was stepping into the back of a police car, with a cop holding the door.

A gargling noise escaped my mouth.

"This is awful," the wizened guy said. "Our tour is going to be hopelessly behind schedule now."

I commanded my feet to move. Nothing.

Across the parking lot, the cop slammed the car door shut.

My feet stumbled into motion, and I zigged and zagged through milling senior citizens and paramedics and police with squawking walkie-talkies.

"Otis!" I cried. I knocked on his window. "*Otis.*"

"Hey!" someone yelled. "Get away from the car, miss!"

Inside the car, Otis turned his head. Through the hectic flashing lights bouncing off the window, I saw his wide eyes and hitched shoulders. He was surprised to see me, but also shocked and . . . *afraid?*

I'd never seen Otis afraid of anything before.

He mouthed "Agnes," and then the police car turned onto the road, gravel crunching, and accelerated in the direction of town.

Well, in the direction of the police station and the town jail, to be more precise.

I stared after the squad car, the relief I'd felt at seeing Otis unharmed lost in a blizzard of confusion.

Then, a thought: *Wait . . . then who died?*

I swung around. A paramedic was latching the ambulance's back doors shut. Over by one of the remaining police cars, a cop appeared to be taking a statement from a stout older woman in a tweed jacket. Three seniors were loading up, suitcases and all, into a van marked LAKESIDE MOTEL. Three more seniors were getting into the back seat of the Subaru station wagon I knew belonged to Clifford and Belinda Prentiss, the proprietors of Birch Grove Bed and Breakfast.

I hurried to the Subaru. "Clifford," I said breathlessly, stopping beside him. "Hey."

Clifford Prentiss is only an inch or two taller than me. He always wears a uniform of loafers, wrinkle-free khakis cinched with a braided leather belt, and a plaid shirt. In warm weather, it's short sleeve cotton, and in cooler weather it's long sleeve flannel or wool. But *always plaid*. He has neat, sandy hair and a bland, boyish face. He was probably pushing fifty. The *bad* kind of fifty that happens to some people when they start getting bitter about their crappy life choices. Calculation hardened his yellowish-green eyes, and his cheeks were sliding into a permanent scowl.

Okay, so sue me. I didn't like Clifford.

He rammed a suitcase into place and straightened. "Hello, Agnes. Don't tell me you and your crazy auntie are taking some of these stranded motor coach passengers into your rattrap?"

"It's not a *rattrap*, but, well, yeah, actually—"

"Need I remind you that you don't have your innkeeping license?"

"How do you know that?" I mean, we *didn't* have our innkeeping license yet, but the way private info infiltrates Naneda—jeez. It's like syrup on waffles.

"Everyone in the Chamber of Commerce knows," Clifford said.

"Why are we even *talking* about this? Someone—who?—is dead, and Otis was just hauled off to the police station! Who is dead, Clifford? Omigosh—it isn't Harlan Hatch, is it?" What an awful thought. Otis arrested for murdering his beloved grandpa? No. Wait. Grandpa Harlan was away fishing—

"Mikey Brown," Clifford said.

"Mikey! *Mikey.* Of course."

Mikey Brown had been hired by Otis about a month back to help out in the garage. He was a bachelor, looked like he was about forty, and the one time I'd met him he'd told me *allllll* about some touchdown he'd made as the star quarterback on the Naneda High football team. He'd been eating a foot-long meatball sub, and each bite had sent tomato sauce squooshing and meatballs bouncing down his mechanic's overalls.

"And good riddance to him." Clifford slammed the Subaru's hatchback shut.

"Good ridd—*what?* How can you *say* that?"

"Clearly you didn't know Mikey if you have to ask."

"Did you . . . see the body?" *Body.* My stomach went *bloop.* Why, oh, why had I stress-eaten those Cheezy Puffs?

"Good luck, Agnes. You're going to need it." Clifford circled around the Subaru, got into the driver's seat, and, with his passengers gawking out at me, drove away.

*   *   *

Without really thinking it over, I walked closer to the garage.

Yellow crime scene tape hung across the open doors of the shop. Inside, police were taking photographs, their camera flashes blinding white. A blue Toyota Camry was parked on the repair lift. The cops, however, didn't seem to care about the Camry. They were photographing dark splashes and a big wrench on the concrete floor. The wrench seemed cartoonishly outsized and too shiny . . . and I'd seen it more than once in Otis's hands.

"Hey," a policewoman barked at me. "Stay out."

I backed away.

More tape fluttered on stakes around a maroon minivan parked about six yards from the garage, one of a row of vehicles waiting to be fixed. The minivan's hatchback was up, and I glimpsed—*urk*—reddish-brown splotches on the gray carpeting.

Yeah. *Blood.*

I knew—I *knew*, with every cell in my body—that Otis would never hurt anyone. But was the ground swaying, or was I?

"Excuse me," an imperious voice said behind me.

I started, and turned to find myself face-to-face with the stout older woman in the tweed coat who had been speaking with the police officer earlier.

"Are you from the Stagecoach Inn?" she asked. The accent

was British, with the plummy tones I associated with BBC costume dramas. An *upstairs* voice. Not a downstairs one. She wore a silk scarf over her gray bun, and her face was long and makeup-free, with one of those puckered, judgy mouths.

"Yeah," I said. "How did you know?"

"Because you are wearing a sweatshirt that says 'The Stagecoach Inn.'"

"Oh. Right."

"What are you waiting for? All of us are simply beaten down by this hideous experience—I saw the body, you realize—and we'd all very much like to have a nice cup of tea and put our feet up. Poor Dr. Li's feet swell like Cornish game hens, and Mrs. Berman requires a nap. We *all* must take our pills. But where are my manners? I am Miss Bulstrode—call me Dorothea—the tour guide for Golden Vistas Motor Coach Tours. I spoke to someone on the telephone to arrange things, and she said she was sending her niece and assistant, Agnes. That is you, I presume?"

"Yes. Agnes Blythe." Just the idea of showing this woman the wreck that was the inn was curdling my stomach. "The, uh, minivan is just across the road"—I pointed—"so just show me where your luggage is, and then you can go and get settled while I take care of the rest." I had never played bellhop before, but Clifford had been loading *his* guests' luggage into *his* car.

"Good," Dorothea said. "The bags remaining beside the motor coach are ours. Mind that you brush off the dust."

\* \* \*

Once I'd finished stuffing the mountain of luggage into the back of the Dustbuster, four stranded leaf-peepers were buckled into my three rows of seats. In a daze, I sank into the driver's seat, found my keys, and—even though my hands were shaking and my brain was blabbering *Otis, Otis, what the heck?*—stuck them in the ignition.

"Where's the baby?" someone called from the third row.

"What?" I glanced in the rearview mirror. The dark eyes of a withered, gray-haired man peered back. He was the guy I'd spoken to first thing, the one with the travel vest with all the little zippered pockets.

"There's a BABY ON BOARD sign on the rear window, but I don't see a baby."

"Oh. That." How could I explain that Aunt Effie had put up that sign not for the safety of any child, actual or inner, but because she thought it kept people from tailgating? "I'm not sure. Ask my boss."

I picked up my phone, which was sitting on the console between the front seats, and tapped out a quick text message to Otis: ARE YOU OK? WORRIED!

"I'm *so* glad you aren't one of those young people who are always in a hurry," Dorothea said in a sarcastic voice. "Mm, a nice hot cup of tea is just what we all need, isn't it, my dears? Perhaps with just a *splash* of brandy for the shock."

"I think we might have some brandy at the inn." I dumped my phone on the console and started the engine. "We definitely have vodka." Aunt Effie loathes gin martinis.

I took the few miles back to the Stagecoach Inn slowly. Not because I was trying to impress my passengers with my ultrasafe driving (although I didn't hear any complaints) but because of the quivery rippling inside my chest and stomach.

Otis. Otis, what the *heck*?

He had somehow embroiled himself in a really bizarre situation. That wasn't like him. Otis is the wholesome, small-town, straight-shooting, superhot, corn-fed type.

"Would you mind speeding up?" the other male passenger said. I stole a peek. Heavyset, gray comb-over, no neck, black polyester track jacket zipped to triple chins. Big, alert, kind-looking brown eyes. "I gotta use the john."

"Myron!" the woman beside him whispered, elbowing him. Her reprimanding tone and pink polyester track jacket clued me in that she was his wife. A sculptural cloud of baby-blonde hair was hairsprayed firmly around her plump, pretty, juicily lipsticked, slightly jowly face. She had one of those reassuring figures where nothing but a horizontal groove separates the belly from the bust, and big, gold-tone clip-on earrings.

"You oughta be happy I didn't go on myself right then and there when I found that corpse, Lorraine," Myron said.

Another elbow jab from his wife. "Sorry," she said to me. "I can't take him anywhere. And call me Lo—Myron only calls me Lorraine when he's annoyed."

"Wait," I said. "*You* found the body, Myron?" I forced myself to keep my eyes on the road.

"Yup," he said with relish. "Sure did."

"In the back of that maroon minivan?" I said.

"Dodge Caravan, to be exact," Myron said. "Yup."

"Why was the hatchback open?" I asked.

"It *wasn't* open," Lo said in a scolding tone. It sounded like they'd already gone over this. "Myron was snooping. Oy vey, how I wish he would've just left it *alone* already! We could've been spared all that craziness, and someone else would've had to deal with the corpse!"

"It could've started to decay if I hadn't found it," Myron

said. "It could've started stinking, and then that van would be ruined for good."

"It's already ruined for good!" Lo yelled. "It'll be haunted forever!"

The man in the third row piped up. "Those bloodstains will come out easily with a little peroxide."

"Dr. Li is a retired physician," Dorothea said to me. "He goes by Hank."

"So *why* were you looking in that minivan?" I asked Myron.

Lo answered for him. "Because we're supposedly shopping for a minivan, and every last minivan we come across he's gotta go and check out. He's set off I don't know how many car alarms in about six states—"

Myron said, "I believe in comparison shopping—"

"For two *years*?" Lo wailed.

"—and right now I'm comparing trunk sizes. So when I saw that maroon Caravan, I thought, heck, if it's unlocked, I'll just take a quick look. It was unlocked, all right. And when I lifted the door, I saw the guy in there, kinda stuffed in, and with blood just *everywhere*."

"Head wound," Hank said in his clinical, retired-physician's voice.

"You can say *that* again," Myron said. "Whoever killed him was one angry—"

"Do we *have* to talk about this?" Lo cried.

Myron continued as though he hadn't heard her. Maybe he hadn't. Lots of people tune out their spouses after a decade or five. "He was killed inside the garage, and then his body was dragged to the minivan. I saw the drag marks in the gravel, before the cops came and messed everything up."

"Myron is a retired carpet salesman," Dorothea said to me in a confiding voice. "He always notices what's underfoot . . . I *do* hope the Stagecoach Inn's floors are clean."

"You could eat off of them."

"Well, I hope it doesn't come to *that*."

"Then that other mechanic came strolling out from the office, cool as a cucumber," Myron said, "and said he'd like to take a look at the motor coach, and I said, 'Motor coach? You wanna take a look at the motor coach when there's a dead body on the premises?' And that's when I saw it." He paused for dramatic effect.

"Saw what?" I noticed that my knuckles, clenching the steering wheel, were white.

"The blood on his shirt."

"On *Otis's* shirt?" I said.

"Goodness me," Dorothea said. "That nice cup of tea with brandy won't arrive soon enough."

"That's his name? Otis?" Myron asked.

"He looked more like a *Bruiser* to me," Hank said.

Myron said, "The blood on his shirt, and the fact that the body was found in his own business—well, that was enough for the police to haul him in for questioning."

"You mean he wasn't arrested?" I asked. It was true that Otis hadn't been handcuffed . . .

"Not yet," Hank said in a sour voice.

Lo said, "*I* thought he looked suspicious the moment I clapped eyes on him. He's just too handsome—you can't trust handsome men. That's why I married Myron here."

"Hey," Myron said.

Hank snickered.

"*And*," Lo continued, "did you see those biceps on him? Only men who've been in prison have muscles like that."

"Otis has never been in prison!" I cried.

"Wait a minute," Myron said, "is that murderer your . . . you aren't saying he's your fella, are you?"

Smearing tears from my eyes, I rolled through a stop sign. "He's not a murderer!"

"A nice, comfy, pretty girl like you, mixed up with a criminal?" Lo said.

Wait. What did *comfy* mean?

Lo leaned forward and patted my shoulder. "There, there, bubbeleh. You deserve better. I'll have you know, I come from a long line of matchmakers. I'll fix you up with some nice husband prospects in no time."

"We're only stopping here in Naneda for one night," Hank called.

"Well . . ." Dorothea made a delicate cough. "The mechanic I enlisted to fix the motor coach *has* been taken in for questioning, so there could be a *slight* . . . delay."

"We've got to stick to the schedule," Hank cried. "I have to see everything on the schedule."

"Simmer down, Hank," Myron said over his shoulder. "You oughta be happy. This is a *real* adventure, not a pretend one planned out by a tour guide."

"That's precisely the problem," Hank said. "*Precisely.*"

"We almost there?" Myron asked me.

I was braking at another stop sign. "Yes."

My phone buzzed. Otis! I kept my foot on the brake and grabbed my phone.

"Goodness!" Dorothea cried, hand to heart.

I peered at my phone. It wasn't Otis; it was a text from Aunt Effie: Keep them busy until six o'clock. Rooms will be ready then.

Great.

I tapped out a message to Effie: OK. FYI THERE WAS A MUR-
DER AT THE AUTO SHOP.

I put away my phone and cleared my throat. "Um, okay,
slight change of plans. Your rooms won't be ready for a couple
hours, so what I'm going to do—"

"We're exhausted!" Dorothea cried.

"My feet are swelling up," Hank said. "They need to be
elevated."

"I'm really sorry, you guys, but you know that our inn wasn't
officially open for business yet, right?"

"You're supposed to be hospitality professionals," Hank said,
"and this is *not* hospitable."

"Listen, it's a beautiful afternoon," I said. "Why don't I show
you downtown Naneda? We can go have a cup of tea or coffee—
you can put your feet up, Dr. Li—and then we can have
dinner—you'll love the Cup 'n' Clatter diner; it's a classic—and
*then* go to the inn."

"It's not really as though we have a choice in the matter,"
Dorothea said through a tight smile. "Is it?"

Someone pulled up behind me at the stop sign and honked.

"I wouldn't mind seeing the downtown, honey," Lo said,
patting my shoulder again. "Let's go."

# Chapter 3

O ur first stop would be Flour Girl Bakery, since Dorothea had been dropping hints about "nice cups of tea" and Flour Girl has an extensive inventory of loose leaf varieties from around the world. Hank could prop up his feet by the fireplace, they could all take their pills, and I could quietly freak out about Otis. Then at five o'clock, we'd mosey across the street to the Cup 'n' Clatter for something chicken-fried, french-fried, and/or bathed in gravy.

"We haven't done much leaf-peeping yet," Lo said from the back seat as I drove. "Believe it or not, this is Myron's and my first time upstate, even though we've lived in Jersey forever."

"Our first stop was Lakewinds Casino," Dorothea said to me.

"Had a great time at the Texas Hold'em tables," Myron said.

"I stick to the Wild Cash scratch cards," Lo told me in a confiding tone. "Forget the casinos. My cousin Frances won twenty grand with a Wild Cash scratch card from the corner store."

"Not long after pulling out of the casino's parking garage, the motor coach starting handling in a peculiar way," Dorothea said to me.

"Uh-huh," I said.

"Isn't there quality foliage in Jersey?" Hank asked Lo from the third row.

"Well, sure," Lo said. "But no *leaf-peeping*. Leaf-peeping is an art, honey. Haven't you read any of the brochures?"

"It's more like a sport," Myron said. "The brochures go on and on about 'bicycling along idyllic country lanes'—"

"Ha!" Lo laughed. "I'd like to see you idyllically bicycling, Myron!"

"—and hiking in state parks tinted with—how did they phrase it?—'shades of copper and rose gold.'"

"I hope you packed supportive walking shoes," Hank said.

"I did. *And* my orthotic insoles."

"There are also the winery tours," Dorothea said. "Don't forget those. We need plenty of arch support just to climb off and on those shuttle buses."

"I don't drink," Hank said in a dismal voice.

"Not even wine?" Dorothea called back to him.

"No."

Softly, so only I could hear, Dorothea said, "That man needs a woman's touch."

And then—really?—she blushed.

I pulled the Dustbuster into one of the angled parking spaces on Main Street, and we all got out. I led my leaf-peepers like a gaggle of goslings past quaint stone and brick shop fronts, cute painted signs, tempting shop windows, lots of weekend shoppers, and more decorative gourds than you can possibly imagine.

In the bakery, we all purchased hot beverages and scored the primo seats, the sofa and chairs by the glowy gas fireplace.

I was taking my very first sip of pumpkin spice latte when Lo plopped down beside me and said, "So, Agnes, are you from Naneda?"

"Yeah. I mean, I grew up here. I lived out of state for about ten years and just moved back this summer."

"Do you have family here?"

"Yeah. My dad lives here—he's actually the mayor—"

"Wow!"

"Trust me, it's not glamorous. I have cousins and aunts and uncles in the area, too. The Stagecoach Inn project is actually my Great Aunt Effie's thing, and my cousin Chester and I are helping her out."

"Then you're really family-oriented."

"Oh. I guess." *Am I?*

"Wonderful. And do you plan to settle down in Naneda?"

*Good question.* "I don't know. I'm not sure if—"

"If you belong?"

"Well, yeah, actually."

"It's always hard, coming back. You have to make it your home all over again . . . sometimes from the ground up."

*Make it your home all over again.* Yikes. How the heck was I supposed to do that? Surely not by camping out in the attic of my zany great aunt's derelict property. What if I was destined never to have a settled home anywhere? What if—

"And this boyfriend of yours," Lo said, interrupting my too-familiar train of thought, "the one who was arrested—just how serious is that?"

"He wasn't arrested, remember?"

Lo waggled her fruit punch fingernails. "You know what I mean."

"And I guess he's not . . . not really my boyfriend." I took a gulp of latte. "Yet."

"Wonderful."

"Why is that wonderful?"

"How did you meet him? Not at a *bar*, I hope?"

"I've known Otis since high school. We were lab partners in chemistry." *Where I fell in love with him on the first day, before the dismissal bell even rang.*

"High school sweethearts never last. Everyone knows that."

"We weren't high school sweethearts. We were just . . . friends. We only started dating about a month ago." I *refused* to tell Lo how I'd been engaged to my longtime boyfriend Roger— aka Professor Pompous—and subsequently dumped for the town Pilates instructor, a fiasco that had prompted me to change my plans to attend graduate school. I was still getting my act together after all that. I didn't miss Roger one iota, trust me. But I sure as heck missed having a Life Plan.

"You've been dating Otis only a month?"

"Uh-huh."

"How many dates?"

"I don't know—five? Six? Mostly we just . . . hang out, but we've gone to dinner, the movies, that sort of thing."

"Do you kiss?"

"That's personal!" *Heck, yeah, we kissed.*

"But you don't know if you're going steady?"

*No, I don't know, and I'd really like to find out.* "We're just, you know, taking it slowly."

Why was I even *telling* Lo all this stuff?

"Did you discuss going steady?"

"I don't really want to talk about this," I mumbled into my cup.

Lo picked up a worn copy of *Woman's Day* magazine from the table, opened it, leafed through a few pages, and then said, "Did you go to college, honey?"

*Oh, jeez.* "Yeah. I have a bachelor's degree—"

"Great!"

"—in anthropology."

"Oh." Lo's plump shoulders sagged. "That's okay. You can always go back and get a useful degree. Dental school is always a good investment."

"Dental school?"

"You do have nice teeth."

"What does that have to do with—"

"Which means your children will have nice teeth. How many children would you like to have, Agnes?"

"Um—"

"Three? Or maybe four?"

"I haven't really—" My phone buzzed.

Thank goodness.

I fumbled it out of my shoulder bag.

Lo flicked over a page of *Woman's Day*. "Is it him?"

"I don't know who you're talking about," I lied.

"You know, I have a nephew in Buffalo whose divorce is almost finalized. He's a podiatrist, and he's just *wonderful* with kids—he has three, so if you wanted to save yourself the stretch marks—"

"No, thanks." I looked at the screen and my heart leapt. I had a text from Otis: I'M OKAY.

Relief surged through me.

Otis: BUT MIKEY BROWN WAS KILLED AT MY SHOP. MURDERED.

Me: I KNOW. HORRIBLE. SCARY.

Otis: YEAH. WHERE ARE YOU?

Me: DOWNTOWN WITH INN GUESTS.

Otis: GUESTS?

Me: FROM THE BROKEN-DOWN MOTOR COACH.

Otis: OH, RIGHT.

Me: CAN YOU MEET ME FOR DINNER? WILL BE AT CUP 'N' CLATTER AT 5 WITH MY GAGGLE.

Otis: GAGGLE?

Me: YOU'LL SEE.

Otis: OK, SEE YOU THERE.

I turned my phone over in my hands, wrestling with the urge to pepper Otis with text-questions about what had happened. I decided to wait until I saw him in person. He wasn't in jail, which meant he hadn't been arrested, so everything was going to be *fine*.

Right?

\* \* \*

Heading toward the Cup 'n' Clatter at five, the gaggle and I passed Angel's Antiques & Devil's Junk, Harries Stationery (in the window: a display of Halloween costumes, including a half-dozen Headless Horseman pumpkinhead masks), the Pottery Guild Shop, the movie theater (now playing: *Headless Horseman III*—are you sensing a theme?), Country Mouse Yarns, Retro Rags (my best friend Lauren's vintage clothing shop), Lilting Waves Day Spa, and, next door to the spa, the new cupcake shop, Crumble + Fluff.

"Ooooh, cupcakes," Lo said, stopping in her tracks to gape into the window, which displayed tiered trays of pillowy-looking cupcakes.

"What an enticing display," Dorothea said. "I cannot resist cake."

"Anyone who doesn't like cupcakes might as well be Godzilla," Lo said, hitching up her purse and pushing into the shop.

The rest of us followed. We didn't really have a choice. Lo seemed like a woman on a mission.

It smelled amazing inside, all vanilla and cocoa with faint hints of fruity and spice. I looked around the tiny, pretty shop with interest. When I was growing up, the shop had been Ryder's Candies, but old Greg Ryder had retired and the place had passed through a couple unsuccessful incarnations (including, for a few awful months, a "healthful" sweet shop peddling date-and-nut rolls and—shudder—*carob*).

The new owner, Delilah Fortune, had come to town and opened for business sometime the summer before. Aunt Effie, Chester, and I had joined the Naneda Chamber of Commerce and attended their monthly breakfast a few weeks back. Delilah and I had been introduced there, but I hadn't been into her shop yet. I knew that she lived in the apartment above the shop and that she was running the place single-handedly. That was impressive.

The shop floor was the same vintage black-and-white tile I remembered, but the gold-and-crystal chandeliers were new. Pink-and-gold floral wallpaper hung on the walls—another new touch. The old-fashioned counter cases that had always been there displayed trays of perfect cupcakes, each mounded with icing, some garnished with sprinkles, gumdrops, or chocolate shavings.

"What a precious little shop!" Lo said. She dinged the bell on the counter. "I think just breathing the air in here has gone straight to my hips."

"Good thing those track pants have some stretch," Myron said teasingly.

Delilah emerged from the doorway behind the counters and gave us all a game-show-hostess smile. "Welcome!" she said. She was as chubby as I am, but she made her chub look perfect in her 1950s-style flared dress with tiny yellow and orange oak leaves printed all over, a white ruffly apron, and bouncy, golden, curling-iron curls. She was about my age, but she seemed at once younger—the cutesy voice and the dimples, maybe?—*and* older. Maybe that was her red matte lipstick. That stuff could make even a tween look ready for the early-bird buffet.

"Hey, Delilah," I said. "I'm Agnes Blythe—we met at the Chamber of Commerce breakfast?"

"Of course! *Agnes*." Delilah smiled at me, but I thought her big blue eyes looked a little . . . flinty. "Family reunion?"

"Family reunion?" I frowned. "No. These are my guests for a few days—their motor coach broke down, so they're staying in town while it gets fixed."

"Oops! I thought I saw a family resemblance." Delilah looked pointedly at my tummy and then *at Myron's gut*. I am not making this up.

I edged my shoulder bag over my tummy which, yes, has more in common with an inflatable pool toy than a washboard. But still.

"I want a plain vanilla cupcake," Hank said stonily. "No sprinkles."

"You betcha," Delilah said, flashing her dimple. "But let me get you all some samples before you come to any final decisions. I whipped up a few special batches for the Harvest Festival that'll make you think you've died and gone to heaven." She got to work, slipping on a fresh pair of food service gloves (to Hank's visible approval) and cutting up her new seasonal cupcake flavors: maple sugar, hot cocoa with marshmallow buttercream, candy corn, pumpkin velvet, and apple cinnamon. "I used fresh apples from Naneda Orchards—Honeycrisps."

"I just love Honeycrisps!" Lo said, stuffing a sample into her mouth.

"It's a good thing I got my apples in yesterday, since Randy who owns the orchard is probably *so* torn up about Mikey. I'll bet he won't be making any deliveries for a couple days."

"Is he family?" I asked. I had briefly met Randy Rice at the Chamber of Commerce breakfast, too. He was a short, fortyish man with bushy dark hair and pitted acne scars on his cheeks. He had seemed angry about something.

"No. But Mikey and Randy were friends. When they were younger, anyway." Delilah looked as if she wanted to say more.

"And . . . they stopped being friends?" I asked.

"Let's just call them 'best frenemies.' At least, according to Randy's wife, Alexa. Do you know her? She's *such* a sweetheart. We hang out a lot."

I remembered Alexa from the Chamber breakfast. She had been dressed like one of the Real Housewives, possibly tipsy, and clapping a little too enthusiastically for the announcement about the new waste bins installed in the city park.

"So, Agnes," Delilah said to me, softly so the others couldn't hear. They were arguing about the difference between frosting and icing. "I heard your friend Otis was taken in for questioning about that murder at his automotive shop."

Marshmallow buttercream went bitter on my tongue. "How do you know that?"

"How could I *not* know? There were so many sirens, I thought the whole town was burning down. A customer came in a few minutes ago and filled me in on all the details. I'm sure Otis didn't do anything wrong—he is *such* a nice guy—but it sure is weird that something like that happened. A *wrench* . . ." Delilah shivered. "There are a lot of creeps out there." She laughed. "Gosh, I've dated a few myself. Poor Mikey."

"Wait—did you know Mikey?" I asked.

"Well, sure! He came in a lot. He just loves—I mean, *loved*— my strawberry cupcakes." Delilah tossed her sideswept bangs out of her eyes.

"Did you date Mikey?" I asked.

"Me, date Mikey? How can I put this? I was . . . out of his league. Which may be hard for you to understand, because it seems like lots of people date out of their league in this town." Delilah looked me down and up.

I suddenly felt lumpy and ungainly in my jeans and hoodie.

"But hey!" Delilah said. "I'm new here. Maybe that's how things are done in Naneda." She turned to the gaggle. "Okily-dokily, folks, what's everyone's favorite cupcake flavor?"

Myron, Lo, Hank, and Dorothea purchased a few dozen cupcakes between them, and I bought one coconut lemon. I paid with a five-dollar bill and zipped the change into the empty coin pouch in my wallet. I don't like to carry change. Too much exercise. I routinely empty my coins into a jam jar on my bedroom windowsill.

The gaggle and I continued on our way to the Cup 'n' Clatter.

*Poor Otis.* The subject of wagging tongues. But I was completely sure his popularity—among his customers, friends, old ladies, babies, dogs, cats, and yes, even cupcake bakers—would help him ride out the storm.

# Chapter 4

One perk of being on the Senior Schedule was that the Cup 'n' Clatter diner wasn't crammed yet when we got there. The waitress settled Dorothea, Myron, Lo, and Hank into a window booth, and, since I was expecting Otis, I sat alone in the next booth over. While the gaggle argued about homeowner's insurance plans, I sipped Diet Coke and watched out the window for Otis.

And . . . here he came down the sidewalk, lean, lanky, and muscly in broken-in work boots, faded jeans, and a green sweater over a T-shirt. His straight, medium-brown hair was in need of a cut, which he made look like a good thing. Something about the way he moved—the self-assurance, that sort of loping, unselfconscious masculine grace you see in authentic cowboys—made my heart stutter.

*I loved him.* Omigosh did I love him. And I'd told him as much, so why, for the love of cookies *why*, hadn't he responded?

Was it because, as Delilah Fortune had hinted, he was out of my league?

Just as Otis was crossing the street, motion in the door of Crumble+Fluff caught my eye. Delilah was flipping the sign in the door from OPEN to CLOSED, stepping outside, locking the door. She had removed her apron and put on a denim jacket over her dress. Her movements were as twitchy as a squirrel's.

Then Otis was pushing into the Cup 'n' Clatter, grinning at the waitress (who, naturally, gave him her cutest smile, even though she was about sixty-five and wearing compression stockings), and weaving through the tables toward me.

Delilah was forgotten.

"Hey," Otis said, kissing the top of my head. He slid into the red vinyl seat across from me. "How are you?"

Was it just me, or had he gotten even better looking since the last time I'd seen him? Tawny skin, brown eyes, straight dark eyebrows, prominent nose, and square, slightly stubbly chin . . . just your average dreamboat.

"Agnes?"

"Huh? Oh. Fine," I said. "The more important question is, how are you? What is going on? Did the police . . . ? What the heck happened to Mikey?"

Otis rubbed his eyes. "I can't believe someone *killed* him."

"Start at the beginning," I said, glancing around to see if we had an audience. No one sat at the tables nearby, but the gaggle in the next booth had fallen suspiciously silent. "You were called in to look at the motor coach."

"Uh-huh. The tour director who's sitting in the next booth and listening to this conversation—Dorothy I think her name is—"

"Dorothea," came Dorothea's voice from the other side of the booth.

"That's right, Dorothea—she called and asked if I could come in and take a look at their motor coach, which has a blown-out tire—"

"Shredded like a piñata!" came Myron's voice.

"—and I said sure, I'd meet them there. I got there before they did, so I was doing some stuff in the office when the motor coach pulled up. Grandpa usually takes care of the books, but since he's been gone for the last few weeks, I've been going through them. They're a mess. I'm going to have to take over the books permanently. I guess he's just too old for all those numbers anymore. It's high time we started using a computer for all that stuff, anyway."

"Why don't you fast-forward to the exciting part?" This was Lo.

"Let the man talk!" That was Myron.

"Well, if I wanted to hear about bookkeeping, I'd call up my brother in Jersey," Lo said.

Otis's lips twitched, and he whispered to me, "You sure have a fun crowd here."

"I heard that," Hank called in his flat voice. "And I have never in my life been described as *fun*."

"Anyway," Otis said, "I saw the motor coach pull up, but I was organizing a huge pile of receipts and I dropped them, so it took a few minutes to pick those all up, and by the time I went outside to greet the motor coach passengers, Mikey's body had been discovered and they were all looking at me like I was—I was—"

"A cold-blooded killer?" Myron said.

"Yeah." Otis scratched his eyebrow. "That about sums it up."

I said, "They, um, told me you had blood on your shirt . . ."

"Are you—" Otis's eyes widened, and then his brows shot down. "Are you seriously thinking that *I*—"

"No! It's just that—"

Dorothea spoke. "Tell us, where did that blood come from?"

"From *my nose*," Otis said.

36

*Ohhhh.* He *did* get bloody noses with some regularity.

"Which, I might add," Otis said, "I told the police, and they took my shirt for DNA testing, which, whenever that's completed, will prove beyond a shadow of a doubt that it's my blood. Not Mikey's."

"Why was Mikey even there on a Saturday?" I asked. "I mean, the shop was closed, right?"

"Yeah. And I have no idea why he was there. He shouldn't have been."

"Was he in his work clothes? His mechanic's overalls?"

"No. Jeans, T-shirt, and this black leather moto jacket he always wore."

"Was his car there?"

"Yeah."

"And . . . it looked like he died inside the shop, and then his body was dragged to that minivan."

"Yeah, but, uh, could we not talk about this, Agnes?"

"Sorry." I fiddled with my Diet Coke glass. "So . . . the police know you're innocent, right?"

"They *should*, except . . ."

I leaned in. "Except what?"

Otis sighed. "I dunno. It seems like the detective—Detective Albright?—*wants* to believe I'm guilty. But they couldn't hold me or make an arrest, because obviously they don't have the evidence to do that." He shook his head. "This is so surreal."

"The police will find a more realistic suspect soon," I said, "and then you'll be off the hook. And it's not like you had a motive to kill your own employee. I mean, give me a break!"

"Actually . . ."

My stomach went into free fall. "What?"

"Never mind. It's nothing."

"Don't mind us, dear," Lo called. "We're from out of town anyway, so what does it matter what we hear?"

Otis sighed, leaned back, and folded his arms.

I tried not to ogle the way his biceps pressed against his sleeves. I am in love with Otis's heart, mind, and soul, but I am not going to pretend I have a problem with his bod.

"The point is, until the police find a better suspect, I'm all they've got," he said, "and that means I can't leave town, and *that* means we may not be able to go up to the Adirondacks next week like we planned. I'm sorry, Agnes. I know you were really looking forward to it. So was I. The mountains are beautiful this time of year."

*Nooooooooo!* The trip to my dad's lake cabin was to be Otis's and my first getaway together. It was where I'd planned to squeeze an "I love you" out of him. Not to mention go canoeing, cozy up in front of a fire, stroll through the crisp, sunlit forest hand-in-hand, and snuggle under a pile of crocheted afghans.

Right then and there, I knew what I had to do. Since Detective Albright had put Otis at the top of his murder suspect list, I had to find *better* suspects.

"So," I said in what I hoped was a nonchalant voice, "who do you think would want to kill Mikey?"

"Why do you sound so *professional* all of a sudden?"

"Professional?" I sipped my Diet Coke.

"Yeah. Almost like you're planning on . . . sleuthing."

"What is this, a Nancy Drew novel?"

"You tell me, Agnes."

"Okay, *fine.* Would it be so bad to ask a few questions around town to see if I can dig up some real suspects for the police? Then I can clue them in on the more viable alternatives, and they'll let you off the hook, and, um—" I swallowed. "—and we'll be able to go to the Adirondacks."

"Detective Albright has to be looking into other suspects already, Agnes."

"I wouldn't be so sure. The dude fixates on things."

"You mean, he fixates on *you*."

"No." *Yes.* My ears burned.

"Hey, I'm not jealous, Agnes. I can tell Albright has a thing for you. When we ran into him at the bowling alley last week, he couldn't tear his eyes away from your Doctor Who T-shirt, and I can't blame him. But just because you and your Aunt Effie solved one murder doesn't mean you should make a hobby of it. You didn't see Mikey's body, but I did—"

"So did we," Hank called from the other booth.

"—and it was really . . ." Otis's eyes glazed over. "It was *brutal*. Whoever did that to him isn't in their right mind. If they're capable of doing that once, they're capable of doing it again. Poking into things would be really, really dangerous, Agnes, and I'm asking you—begging you—not to do it. Okay?"

I didn't want to lie to Otis. And honestly, the prospect of asking around about a violent killer gave me the creeps.

Foremost in my mind, however, were all the instances I'd heard about in the news of people being imprisoned—or worse—when they were actually innocent. It happens. I wasn't about to let it happen to the love of my life.

So, I was opening my mouth to lie to Otis and say "Okay" when blonde curling-iron curls swung into view, right beside Otis.

Well, well, well. If it wasn't Delilah Fortune from Crumble + Fluff, peeking around from the next booth over. "Hi, you guys!" she said. "I happened to overhear your little convo. You know what? *I'm* going to sleuth, too. It's just so *mean* that the police are treating you like a criminal, Otis."

"Delilah," Otis said. "Hi."

They knew each other? And—I watched Otis smiling at Delilah—should I be concerned about that?

"Like I was telling Agnes," Otis said to Delilah, "sleuthing isn't a good idea. It could be really dangerous."

"How long have you been eavesdropping on us?" I asked Delilah.

"Long enough to know you're into Doctor Who. So. I guess we'll just have to see which one of us is the better detective, right Agnes?"

That settled it. I was going to figure out who killed Mikey Brown before Delilah did or die trying.

Delilah stood and smiled down at Otis and me. "Oh, and I read *every single* Nancy Drew book when I was a kid. Twice. See you guys later—it looks like my takeout salad is up."

She swished away toward the hostess desk, where a takeout bag sat.

Otis raked his hand through his hair. "Now *two* of you are going to sleuth?" he said with a groan. "This is not going to end well. Don't do it, Agnes."

"Wouldn't dream of it." I slurped up the last drops of Diet Coke.

* * *

After that, dinner was a little stilted. I was pretty sure Otis knew I *was* going to sleuth, but he didn't bring it up because he's a nice a guy and bringing it up would entail calling me a liar. Then there were all the looks Otis was getting as the Cup 'n' Clatter filled up with patrons. The news of Mikey's death and Otis having been questioned—maybe even Otis's bloodstained shirt—was in full, super-deluxe circulation. That Otis had not been arrested didn't seem to matter.

"I'm really, really wiped out," Otis said when he had finished his burger. "I feel like I could sleep for a year."

"The aftermath of adrenaline," I said.

"That must be it." A shadow flickered across Otis's face.

"Is there . . . is there more to the story?"

"Nope." This was clipped, too cheerful, and Otis wasn't exactly meeting my eye.

Crud. He wasn't telling me everything about what had happened out there at Hatch Automotive. This was like a kung fu kick to the love handles. Didn't he trust me?

*Excuse me?* A snotty little voice in the back of my mind said. This was my conscience, I guess. For some reason I always picture it like a cartoon bug in a waistcoat. *You're not being honest with him, either!*

I told the little voice to stuff it.

"I'm going to swing by and visit Mikey's brother and sister-in-law who live here in town," Otis said. "Make sure they're okay, see if they need anything. I don't think he had any other local relatives. Then I'm going home to get some sleep."

I waited for him to ask me to come over and, I don't know, tuck him in or something.

Nothing.

"Who are Mikey's brother and sister-in-law?" I asked.

"Mark and Karen Brown. Mark is some kind of technical freelance writer. Works at home. Karen runs that day spa across the str—wait." Otis narrowed his eyes. "Why do you want to know?"

Fantastic. My plan to clear Otis's name was making him suspicious of me.

"Why do I want to know? No reason," I said. "Just curious. I know Mikey was a bachelor, but I didn't think about whether or not he had family in town."

"Mark and Mikey grew up in Naneda, but their parents moved to Phoenix or someplace."

"Did Mikey have a girlfriend?"

"Not that I know of. Any more questions?"

"Oh. Um. Nope. Hope you feel better."

"Thanks. Good luck with your guests. Call me." Otis peeled some cash from his wallet and left it on the tabletop. He stood, kissed the top of my head again, and then he was gone.

Lo maneuvered herself into the seat across from me. "I saw that, honey. He kissed *the top of your head*. I don't care *what* you do behind closed doors—he certainly isn't your boyfriend if that's how he kisses you out in public."

Dessert. I needed dessert.

# Chapter 5

The sky was dissolving into orange and pink over the hills when I turned the Dustbuster off the far end of Main Street. Here, businesses gave way to large home lots and, further along, open countryside. I steered through a gap in a bushy laurel hedge and bounced down the shadowy drive.

"This is it?" Hank said when I reached the end of the drive and braked in front of the Stagecoach Inn. "*This?*"

I'll be totally honest about the condition of the Stagecoach Inn. It was bipolar. On the one hand, you had this hulking grayish building with peeling paint and a few boarded-up windows that looked like it could be a horror movie set. The hanging pots of yellow chrysanthemums on the porch were as out of place as lip gloss on a pig.

On the other hand, you had the lawn sweeping from the long porch down to the shores of Lake Naneda and the huge old trees that seemed to anchor the property in time and place. Aunt Effie had put together an album of black-and-white photographs of the inn during its heyday—kids splashing in the lake, laughing diners in the restaurant, a whole row of shiny old-time cars lined up in the drive—and I knew it was something worth trying to revive. Like, with a defibrillator.

I told myself my motivations were about preserving an important artifact of Naneda's history, because hey, I *had* majored in anthropology. More confusing was the weird heartstring tug the ramshackle place gave me. What *was* that?

Effie was there to meet us at the front door, swinging it wide and treating everyone to gushy, bony hugs and a flurry of Euro-style air kisses. "Hello, hello! Oh, it's simply fabulous to have our very first guests! What a delight! You must be Dorothea, who I spoke to on the telephone—yes? What a lovely coat! And you are—? Hank! Delightful! And Myron, and—? Lo! Is that short for something? Oh, Lorraine, of course! Come in, come in—I was hoping you would all join me in the library for an after-dinner drink—I heard all about the murder on Shore 7 news; you poor dears must have been *terrified*—this way, just through here . . ."

Wow. She was a natural.

I, meanwhile, was playing bellhop again, which felt totally *un*natural. I set two suitcases in a corner of the entry hall and went outside for more.

Chester joined me at the back of the Dustbuster, chewing on something. "What are you, Agnes Blythe, Slayer of Suitcases?"

"Hey," I said, dropping a duffle bag at his feet. "Are the rooms all ready?"

"More or less. It's not the Four Seasons, but it should be okay for one night. It's not like anybody can leave us a bad review, since we're not even registered on any of the inn review or booking sites."

"True."

Chester told me what he and Aunt Effie had been up to while I'd been gone. First, they had vacuumed and dusted the upstairs hallway, the three best bedrooms overlooking the lake, and the bathroom. The guests would have to share the one bathroom with its rust-stained claw-foot tub, marble sink, and guacamole-hued linoleum floor. Next, Chester and burly Boyd—they had hired him to help—had dragged three of the new mattresses from the garage loft and removed their plastic wrappings. Then they'd installed antique dressers and armchairs—from Aunt Effie's hoard in the garage—in each of the rooms. In the meantime, Effie had driven to Bella's Bedding Boutique to stock up on sheets, pillows, blankets, and towels for the three rooms.

"The rooms are spotless," Chester said, "and naturally Aunt Effie splurged on the most expensive bedding imaginable, woven from unicorn silk or something. Yes, the guests will be sleeping on mattresses on the floor since Aunt Effie hasn't yet managed to buy priceless antique bedframes, but they'll be doing it in style. Oh—and she also stopped by the liquor store while she was out and came back with *cases* of liquor. The bar in the library is stocked."

Just last week Effie had purchased a beautiful mirrored sideboard at an estate sale, which had been installed in the library to serve as the bar. Little had we known that we'd be using it so soon.

"So the strategy is to keep the guests tipsy twenty-four/seven," I said.

"Of course." Chester bent and grabbed the duffel bag handles. "This is Aunt Effie we're talking about."

"Is it legal to serve them booze? I mean, we don't have a liquor license."

"Sure. They're private, nonpaying guests. It's like serving alcohol to friends in your home."

Chester and I hauled all the luggage inside and placed it in the prepared upstairs bedrooms.

I had to admit that Effie and Chester had done a nice job

making the rooms pretty and comfortable in such short order. There were even white gauzy curtains on suspension rods in the windows, and all three rooms had big, fragrant bouquets of fresh flowers. Stacks of milky-white towels sat on antique chairs, and brand-new cotton spa slippers were arranged on the floor beside them. Heck, *I* wanted to move in.

"About the attic bathroom that we started gutting," I said.

"Press the pause button until these folks are gone," Chester said. "We can't deal with that on top of everything else."

* * *

A few hours later, Dorothea, Hank, Myron, and Lo had gone upstairs tipsy and exuding well-being, having been treated to Effie's strong cocktails and a string of anecdotes from her careers as fashion model, trophy wife, and globe-trotting alimony recipient. Even Hank had submitted to a small glass of red wine, saying its antioxidants would be good for his heart.

I helped Effie clean up the bar and carry the glasses, shaker, discarded fruit, and jiggers to the inn's big old kitchen at the back of the building. We loaded the dishwasher—a brand-new, industrial quality stainless steel number that looked totally out of place amid the 1950s salmon-pink cabinetry and sparkly Formica countertops. Then Effie sat down at the kitchen table for a cigarette. Tiger Boy, who had barged into the kitchen through his newly installed cat flap, leapt onto her lap and commenced purring.

I rinsed out the sink, gave the garbage disposal a whirl (another new addition), and then, drying my hands on a dish towel, turned to Effie. "So . . . I know I have to squeeze it in around work at the inn, but . . . I'm going to investigate Mikey Brown's murder."

"How exciting. Any particular reason?"

"Because, as of earlier this evening, anyway, Otis is Detective Albright's favorite suspect."

"Ah." Effie blew smoke. "And I suppose Otis can't leave town, which is bringing your weekend in the Adirondacks crashing down?"

How was she so annoyingly astute? Was it the vitamin B shots she got every Thursday?

"Yeah," I said. "There is that, but that's not the main reason. I can't bear seeing Otis wrongfully accused. He's too good of a person. And what if he *were* arrested, down the line? No. I mean, believe in—in *justice*, Aunt Effie. I have to nip this in the bud."

"Mm. Detective Albright *is* sweet on you, Agnes. That can't help matters. Every time he sees you, he—"

"I do *not* want to discuss this! Should you be smoking with the cat on your lap? You're going to kill him with secondhand smoke."

"I'll help you."

"What?"

"I'll help you catch the murderer. How fun! Where do we begin?"

Why had I mentioned this to her, again?

"Well, we begin with trying to figure out who might have wanted Mikey Brown dead," I said.

"Any leads?"

"Yeah, actually. A couple. First of all, Clifford Prentiss was there at Hatch Automotive picking up guests when the crime scene was in full swing—"

"Wearing plaid and that putrid braided leather belt?"

"As always. And he said 'Good riddance' about Mikey's death."

"Monstrous!"

"So we could try to find out what's going on there. And then Delilah Fortune at the cupcake shop acted a little weird about the whole thing, suggesting that Mikey was madly in love with her or something." *Also, she is trying to steal my not-quite-boyfriend by out-sleuthing me.* "So it may not be a bad idea to look into her a little. And then Otis mentioned that the lady who owns some spa on Main Street is Mikey's sister-in-law, so I thought I'd pay her a visit."

"Karen Brown. She owns Lilting Waves Day Spa on Main."

"Do you know her?"

"We both met her at the Chamber of Commerce breakfast. Curvy blonde with amazing skin and tired eyes?"

"Oh, yeah. Now I remember. Okay. I have to turn in. Good night, Aunt Effie."

"Good night, Agnes."

\* \* \*

I climbed the steep back stairs to the third floor.

This was my domain. Aunt Effie had claimed a couple of rooms and a private bathroom on the second floor, in the wing opposite that in which our guests were staying. (*Guests.* Can you believe it?) Chester didn't live at the inn, preferring to keep both his night shift job as custodian at the middle school (benefits!) and the tiny basement-level apartment his salary afforded.

I, on the other hand, having being kicked out of the apartment I shared with my ex-fiancé Roger, had lived for a spell at my dad's house. But Dad and his housekeeper/girlfriend Cordelia had made me feel as if I were crashing their love nest, so when the inn's electricity and plumbing were given the seal of okayness, I had moved in. Hey, it was rent free.

The inn supposedly had a ghost. Lucky for me, my days of floor scrubbing, wallpaper stripping, and junk hauling were so exhausting, I always slept like a baby. Also, I don't believe in ghosts.

Picking my way around the claw-foot tub sitting in the hall-way, I went into the bathroom. The lone, bare lightbulb flickered. A balled-up rag protruding from a hole in the floor was the only clue as to where the toilet had been a few days ago. Crackled, dog barf–green linoleum curled up at the edges of the room. Decades of foot traffic had faded most of the linoleum's design, but where the bathtub had stood, the faux-Mexican-tile motif was pristine. *Blech.*

Chester and I had left the wall-mount sink intact so I could at least wash up here. For other bathroom activities, I had to trudge down to the second floor. I removed my contacts, washed and moisturized, flossed and brushed. I had every intention of changing into my coziest pajamas and hitting the hay, but instead . . . I just stood there, staring at the dog barf–green linoleum.

Okay, maybe I was *glaring* at it.

What had they been thinking, installing that stuff in a dignified nineteenth-century building?

The next step in the project would be ripping out the linoleum, and I'd been looking forward to it like Christmas morning, but Chester and I had agreed to put the project on hold until the leaf-peepers were gone.

But . . . suddenly that linoleum seemed like just one more expanse of grossness that was getting in the way of what I wanted.

So I went over to the far corner where the linoleum was curled up like an invitation, and *peeeeeeled.* And man, it was satisfying. Before it broke off in the squishy-snappy way that old linoleum breaks, I had peeled up an irregular piece the size of a bath towel.

*Fist pump!*

A musty odor was released into the air, and there were the grayish wood floorboards beneath, blooming with generations of layered water stains and mold.

My pulse got all kicky. Original wood floors! I hadn't known what to expect, since Chester's and my explorations in the lino-leumed kitchen had revealed a definitely *not* original plywood subfloor. What if this bathroom floor could be refinished?

Fueled by hope, I tossed the piece of linoleum into the bath-tub in the hallway, then peeled up another piece, then another and another. I got grimy. I broke a sweat. Time stood still. I should've been wearing work gloves, because my fingertips went raw from gripping the torn edges and I snagged my thumbnail.

But this was like eating potato chips. I. Couldn't. Stop.

By the time I'd torn up all but an assortment of bits that were mysteriously cemented to the floorboards, it was almost two o'clock in the morning.

Did I feel slightly insane? Well, yeah, but that was overshad-owed by smooth, smug satisfaction. *No more dog barf floor.*

I tiptoed down to the second floor and took a shower in Aunt Effie's bathroom, with its cornucopia of high-end shampoos, conditioners, scrubs, and body gels. Then, exhausted beyond belief, I went back up to my attic bedroom with its thrift-store bed tucked under the sloping eaves.

An open suitcase on the floor held the few outfits I kept washing and rewearing. Boxes full of the *rest* of my life hulked on the other side of the room. I had been so busy, I hadn't gotten around to unpacking them.

Or maybe for some reason it just felt good to keep reality sealed up safely inside cardboard and duct tape.

I plugged in my phone—no messages from anyone, not even Otis—set the alarm for five thirty, and was asleep seconds after my head hit the pillow.

*  *  *

The next morning, Aunt Effie and I were already setting out a breakfast buffet when the sun emerged over the lake. Napkins, cutlery, juice glasses, and coffee cups were arranged neatly on the dining room table. A vase of cream and green flowers and foliage burst from a pottery vase. We had texted Chester to have him pick up juice, eggs, and breakfast sausage at the Green Apple Supermarket and then stop at Flour Girl Bakery downtown for a large assortment of pastries and cinnamon rolls. Aunt Effie was footing the bill for everything. I didn't ask questions; she was always flippantly evasive about finances.

"Oh, Agnes, would you fetch some champagne flutes from the butler's pantry?" Effie said. "And bring out that gorgeous silver wine bucket we found at that antique store in Skaneateles."

"Champagne bucket?"

"For the *champagne*, darling."

"Still drawing a blank. This is breakfast?"

"Mimosas." Effie click-clicked away, dressed to the nines as usual in a slim black pantsuit, hot-pink blouse, high-heeled booties, and makeup I was pretty sure she'd airbrushed on.

Right. I'd almost forgotten that the strategy was keeping our guests carefree and buzzing so they didn't notice the spiders or the way the bathwater was tinged with rust.

I was setting the wine bucket on the table when Dorothea

walked in carrying a smartphone. "Good morning, Agnes. Bad news. I've heard from the mechanic at Hatch Automotive."

"Otis?" My fingers, still sore from Adventures in Linoleum Removal, clenched around the edge of the wine bucket. "What sort of bad news?"

"You look like you've seen a ghost, dearie. It's only about the motor coach."

"Oh." I put down the wine bucket. "Right. The motor coach."

"He said he can very easily replace the tire, but he must order a special one, which will take a day or two to get here. The alternative is to have the motor coach towed to another garage, but that would be frightfully expensive. Thus, my only other option is to send my clients home early. Which will unfortunately entail issuing complete refunds."

"Can't Golden Vistas Motor Coach Tours just send another bus?"

Dorothea's neck blotched pink. "Well, no, you see . . . there's only the one motor coach. It's—this business is all I have. It's just the driver and me. Surely you can sympathize with having your eggs all in one basket?"

"I definitely can."

"I'll be issuing refunds to most of the other passengers, but the Bermans and Dr. Li have indicated to me that they'd like to stay on—if you are able to have us. It will save me from utter financial disaster if I need not refund everyone."

"I completely understand," I said. "Listen, I'll need to run it by my, um, business partners, but as far as I'm concerned, you're welcome to stay as long as you—"

"Stay?" Aunt Effie said, sailing in with a bottle of champagne. "Who?"

"Everyone," I said. "If you're game."

"Game? I'm ecstatic! And not only can we continue to put up Dr. Li and the Bermans—and you too, of course, Dorothea— we can also show them everything Naneda has to offer. You couldn't have picked a better time to break down, Dorothea—"

"I didn't precisely *pick*—"

"—because this is the week of the Harvest Festival, and there isn't a drop of rain in the weather forecast. You needn't pay a cent, of course—you can be our guinea pigs. Oh! You can go to the Lake Club Masquerade on Wednesday—I'm running the bachelorette auction, and there will be dancing. This will be *fabulous*."

It's hard to believe, but I'm certain Aunt Effie totally meant that.

Inwardly, I was groaning. Yes, I felt good about being hospitable. But my plan to do a little discreet detective work had just gone *kaboom*. Sure, I could sleuth . . . in the noisy company of four senior citizens plus Aunt Effie (whom I would never dare call a senior citizen for fear of repercussions).

"Thank you," Dorothea said. "You're a lifesaver."

I brewed coffee and tea, and by the time that was finished, Chester had arrived with two big white bakery boxes and a bag of groceries.

"What's with the outfit?" I asked him, glancing up from pouring half-and-half into a cream pitcher. "You look like an off-brand Richard Simmons."

"Didn't Aunt Effie tell you? Lakeside calisthenics." Chester set the boxes and bag on the counter. He was wearing red sweatpants and a matching sweatshirt, sneakers, and a terry cloth sweatband across his forehead. "For the guests."

"What?" I laughed. "That's weird!"

"It was her idea. She said every five-star hotel she's ever been to offers exercise classes taught by really, really good-looking, astoundingly fit instructors, so—" Chester swept his hands down and up his squat frame. "—here you go." He opened one of the bakery boxes and bit into a cinnamon roll.

"So," I said casually, "I ripped up all the linoleum in the attic bathroom last night."

"And *I'm* weird?"

"There are original floorboards underneath!"

"Cool. I'll take a look." Chester wiped icing off his mustache.

* * *

By around ten o'clock, I had vacuumed the dining room, guest rooms, and upstairs hallway, cleaned the bathroom, made the beds, and hauled the torn-up linoleum pieces, one bucket at a time, from the attic to the rent-a-dumpster in back of the inn. It was time to start sleuthing—I mean (*cough, cough*)—to show the gaggle a good time, Naneda style.

Woo-hoo.

The Harvest Festival Kick-Off wasn't until three o'clock—during which Dad always made a little speech, and downtown businesses had sidewalk sales, games, food vendors, and live music—so we had hours to kill. Dorothea was going to stay at the inn to work. She had to help make travel arrangements and issue refunds to all the motor coach passengers who were going home early. She did not look happy. I told her to help herself to tea in the kitchen. Aunt Effie added that there was a full bottle of brandy in the library.

First stop? Mikey Brown's sister's spa.

Lilting Waves Day Spa occupied a sweet, three-story brick storefront on Main. Gauzy pink curtains in the windows obscured the interior. A pink sandwich board on the sidewalk read THIS WEEK'S SPECIALS: PUMPKIN PEEL FACIAL, APPLE PIE BODY SCRUB, VANILLA SPICE HOT STONE MASSAGE.

"Too bad I already had that second cinnamon roll," I said, angle-parking the Dustbuster out front. "That sign is making me hungry."

"A day spa?" Hank said in a shocked voice.

Effie adjusted her enormous sunglasses, which made her look like an underweight lemur. "We're just popping in to ask a quick question."

"Good," Hank said, "because I've never been to a spa in my life."

"Well, there's a first time for everything, honey," Lo said. "And your skin does look a little dehydrated."

"This is about what your boyfriend said at the diner last night, isn't it?" Myron said to me.

"What?" I asked, all innocence. I switched off the engine.

"How he said Mikey's sister-in-law owns the day spa. You want to talk to her, don't you? Ask a few questions about who might've wanted him dead? Hey, I sound just like one of those guys on *Law and Order*, don't I?"

"Ooh!" Lo clapped her hands. "You're going to take us sleuthing? Like a sort of murder tour of Naneda?"

Effie said, "I don't know if—"

"No," I said. "No murder tour."

"It'll be *to die for*, honey." Lo caught my eye in the rearview mirror and gave me the least subtle wink in the history of winks.

# Chapter 6

I had envisioned Aunt Effie and myself going into Lilting Waves Day Spa to ask a few hard-boiled PI-worthy questions while the gaggle waited in the Dustbuster.

No dice. Everyone scrambled out. Okay, not scrambled so much as gingerly winched themselves. Apparently Myron had pulled a muscle during Chester's lakeside calisthenics class, but I had been assured by both Lo and Aunt Effie that I did *not* want to hear the details.

Inside the spa, we were enfolded by delicious scents and soothing new age music. A college-aged guy sat behind the reception desk. No one sat in the waiting area.

"Hi," the receptionist said. His glossy skin had been rid of every single expired skin cell. His name tag said MASON. "Do you have an appointment?"

"No," I said, "we'd like to make some appointments, but . . . is, um, Karen around?"

"Karen?" Mason's eyes widened. "No. She's at home. She's . . . there was a death in her family." His eyes flicked left and right, and then he leaned closer. "That auto mechanic who was killed yesterday? That was her brother-in-law."

"Omigosh, that's *awful*," I breathed. "Karen's really sweet—she must be devastated!"

Mason looked a little confused. I figured Karen wasn't often described as sweet.

"You know what, I'd *love* to send her some flowers," I said. "Could you jot down her address?"

"Sure."

I don't want to brag or anything, but . . . *booyah*.

Mason jotted an address on the back of an appointment card and slid it over. I glanced at it—*171 Adams Street . . . now why does that ring a bell?*—and tucked it into my shoulder bag.

Then we all made appointments for spa treatments the next day. That would kill two-plus hours of "showing the gaggle a good time."

"How fortunate you have all those openings," Effie said to Mason. "I would have thought you'd be booked solid during Harvest Festival week."

"Yeah, it's weird," Mason said. "Karen's a little worried about . . . never mind." His eyes darted down and away. "I shouldn't—"

"Not to worry," Effie said. "I think I understand. See you tomorrow."

We went back out to the Dustbuster.

\* \* \*

"Wait." My hand froze in the act of sliding the key into the ignition. "We need some kind of pretense for visiting Karen."

"Offering our condolences, of course." Effie said.

"Friends and family make visits after deaths," Lo said in the back seat. "Not random acquaintances. You should at least bring some flowers and food."

57

"Good thinking." I started backing out.

A few minutes later we were wheeling into the parking lot of the Green Apple Supermarket. Inside, Effie grabbed a pre-wrapped bouquet of white roses and I found a boxed apple pie in the bakery section.

Then we stalled for several minutes while Lo used the super-market bathroom and Hank took his sweet time (a) selecting denture-cleaner tablets in aisle two and (b) haggling with the checker over an expired coupon.

At last, we were on the road again.

"This still feels really weird," I whispered to Effie. "We have only met Karen once, at the Chamber of Commerce breakfast, and I have only the vaguest memory of—"

"There you go, then," Myron said. "Tell her you're visiting her in the capacity of concerned comembers of the Chamber."

Not a half-bad idea, actually.

"Thanks," I said.

One seventy-one Adams Street was a large white farmhouse with a wraparound porch and big trees. Fallen rust-colored leaves blanketed the front walk and uncarved pumpkins flanked the front door.

It also happened to be right across the street from Otis's Grandma Bee's immaculate ranch house, where only last week I had gone to dinner for the first time and been roundly beaten at Clue. That's why Karen's address had rung a bell.

A white Buick LeSabre sat pristine in Grandma Bee's drive-way, but that didn't mean she was home. She didn't like to drive. Otis took her to the grocery store and the beauty parlor, and her friends picked her up for church, bingo, funerals, and the movies.

Grandma Bee is Otis's maternal grandmother, a widow.

Grandpa Harlan, the guy who runs the automotive shop with Otis, is his paternal grandfather. He is a widower, but before you start getting any matchmaking ideas, let me tell you that Grandma Bee and Grandpa Harlan *hate* each other. Long story.

I pulled up to the curb and parked.

"What a lovely home this Karen has," Lo said.

"Yeah," I said, instantly alarmed by the wistful note in my own voice. There had been a time when I'd almost *assumed* that one of these charming old houses in Naneda's historical district would be mine. Back when I had a professor fiancé, plans for grad school, a newish Prius, and a George Foreman grill.

I wasn't grieving my plans, mostly because those plans entailed being with Roger, and now I had Otis. Undeniable upgrade. But since Otis and I were evidently still in the top-of-head-kissing phase, we weren't exactly talking about the future.

"Wait here, darlings," Effie said to the gaggle. "Back in a tick."

Effie and I went to the front door, carrying our roses and apple pie, while the Bermans and Hank waited in the Dust-buster. I felt their eyes boring into my back.

Effie rang the doorbell, and after thirty seconds or so, the door swung open.

"Hi!" I said in a cheery voice. "Karen?"

"Have we met?" Karen asked. She was stocky like a semi-pro softball player, with dark blonde hair pulled up into a sloppy bun. She wore a baggy Rochester Red Wings T-shirt, gray sweatpants with what looked like dried coffee on one thigh, and beaten-down Hello Kitty slippers. She looked pretty much the opposite of the proprietor of a not-cheap day spa, except that she had really glowy skin and movie star eyebrows.

"Sure we've met," I said. "I'm Agnes Blythe—"

"Oh, right. The mayor's daughter."

"—and this is my aunt, Mrs. Winters. We're getting the old Stagecoach Inn ready for operation again, and we met at the Chamber of Commerce breakfast a few weeks back."

"That's right, now I remember." Karen regarded me. "You were in the table at the front and taking notes like there were going to be midterms"—she turned to Effie—"and you were flirting with old Mr. Solomon, the lawyer."

Effie laughed. "If *that* was flirting, darling—"

"That's us!" I said quickly. "Anyway, we're here to extend our deepest sympathies about your brother-in-law. Mikey. And to ask if there is anything at all we can do to help."

"Wow," Karen said in a flat voice. "For people who just joined the Chamber a couple weeks ago, you sure are enthusiastic."

"That's just it," Effie said, smiling. "We're eager to learn, and eager to participate."

"*And* we're terribly sorry for your loss, Karen," I said. Good gravy, did I feel like a jerk. What the heck were we doing? This woman had just lost a relative.

"May we come in?" Effie said, and, not waiting for an answer, stepped into the entry hall.

Welp, we were going in.

The interior of Karen's house was just as perfect as the exterior, with a "fresh farmhouse" vibe straight out of a magazine: glossy pine floors, white walls and woodwork, wrought-iron knick-knacks, and beige jute rugs.

Effie led the way through a wide doorway into the living room. A laptop computer sat open and glowing on the coffee table.

"Have a seat, I guess," Karen said. She slapped the computer shut, but not before I had seen she was on eBay. "I'll go grab a vase."

Upstairs, someone turned on what sounded like a vacuum cleaner. It droned, the wheels bumping back and forth over floorboards. Who was vacuuming? A friend? A relative?

Effie and I sat down side by side on a white slip-covered couch. I placed the boxed apple pie on the coffee table, noticing with dismay that the top had caved in. We both eyed the huge, hand-lettered wooden sign hanging over the fireplace, which read FAMILY RULES: BE NICE.

"Nauseating," Effie murmured.

"What are you, Cruella de Vil?" I whispered back. "That's a cute sign!"

"And not a speck of dust anywhere, yet those sweatpants . . ."

"*She's in mourning!*"

Karen came back with a large white enamel jug, which she set on the coffee table. Without unwrapping the cellophane, Effie stuck the roses unceremoniously in the jug. A red REDUCED sticker was on full display. Karen was looking at it.

Crud.

"Is there any news on the—" I cleared my throat. "—on the police investigation?"

"No. They brought in Mikey's boss at the shop—Otis Hatch?—but they released him. Mark is starting to freak out."

"Your husband," Effie said.

"Yeah. Mikey is—was—his little brother, and even though they weren't super close, a death in the family is a death in the family. Plus, this was—" Karen swallowed. "This was murder. Honestly, I'm a little scared. What the heck did Mikey get himself mixed up in? He was always such an *idiot*."

"What do you mean?" I asked.

"He was incapable of making good choices. He had *zero* common sense. He was like a thirteen-year-old boy trapped in a forty-year-old body. Put him within a ten-yard radius of a dirt bike, a chainsaw, or a wasp's nest, and someone was going to get hurt. Although, the funny thing was, up until yesterday, Mikey seemed to always get out of these stupid situations he created unscathed. It was the people *around* him who got hurt." Karen's eyes flashed.

Effie and I exchanged a look—*red alert*—and then Effie said, "Did Mikey ever hurt *you*, Karen?"

She snorted. "No. I always had the good sense to steer clear of him. Growing up, Mikey got Mark into plenty of trouble. Bowie knife scars, concussions, a broken arm from falling out of some crappily built tree house. *Pfft*. And I wasn't too happy about the way my son Scootch was starting to think Mikey was all that and a bag of chips. Mikey would take Scootch dirt biking, or have him over to play video games. Mark said it was nephew–uncle bonding, but I knew it was just a matter of time before something bad happened to Scootch."

"*Did* something bad happen to him?" I asked. Karen's bitterness was making my skin crawl.

"Nope!" She made a weird bark of laughter. "And now it never will."

"Did Mikey have a girlfriend?" I asked.

"Mikey? *Girlfriend?* Ha!"

"He wasn't popular with the ladies?" Effie asked.

"Well, he *was*, back in high school when he was the town football hero and before all those Hostess Ding Dongs caught up with his gut. Before the rest of us grew up and left him behind."

"So . . . no recent dating or anything?" I asked.

"Well, no one I ever met, although the last time I saw him, which was when he came over to mooch dinner a few weeks back because apparently he was out of frozen burritos, he claimed he was seeing someone."

*Oh-ho.*

"But I didn't believe it. I thought it was just one of the stupid things he said to try and impress Scootch, like how he was going to buy a Chevrolet Camaro. *That* one got Scootch pretty worked up, until I had to break it to him that no way could his Uncle Mikey afford a Camaro."

Upstairs, the vacuum switched off. "Sweetheart?" a man shouted down the stairs. "For the millionth time, could you *please* put your dirty towels in the bathroom hamper, not the one in the closet?"

"Sure thing, Mark," Karen called back. She rolled her eyes at Effie and me. "My husband is a clean freak," she said softly. "This weekend, Mark took Scootch camping in Canada, and I felt like I was on a freaking vacation not having someone nagging me all day. I swear to God, he's going to kill me."

I shifted on the sofa cushions.

Karen laughed without humor. "I guess I shouldn't be saying stuff like that when there's been a murder, huh?"

Upstairs, the vacuum swooshed back on.

Effie said, "Karen, dear, who could possibly have wanted Mikey dead?"

Karen's eyebrows shot up in surprise, and then she looked away. "Honestly? Probably lots of people."

"He had . . . enemies?" Effie said.

"Not *enemies* exactly. He was too much of a doofus for that. More like people he messed things up for."

"Like who?" I asked. Yesterday, Delilah had hinted at something similar, saying that Randy from Naneda Orchards had been "best frenemies" with Mikey.

"Well, like his next-door neighbors, Clifford and Belinda at the Birch Grove Bed and Breakfast."

*Clifford.* Clifford of the "good riddance" comment.

"Why?" I asked.

"Listen, I'm not comfortable with gossiping, okay? Why don't you ask Clifford and Belinda about Mikey? Basically, all I'm trying to say is that Mikey was one of those people who screw things up for other people, not totally intentionally, just thoughtlessly. But then if you pointed out how he was screwing things up, he'd get all belligerent and hurt. He said he meant well, but how could he possibly mean well if he kept doing things over and over again after you told him to stop?"

At that moment, I heard the front door burst open, stomping, and then a teenage boy appeared in the living room doorway. "Hi, Mom," he said. He had blond hair and a fresh crop of pimples, and he wore a red plaid hunting jacket. His eyes looked a little pink, as if he'd been crying or maybe smoking something he shouldn't have been. He kept going.

"Hi, Scootch baby," Karen called after him. "I made you a snack! It's in the fridge!"

No answer.

Karen sighed. "I let Scootch skip school today. He's pretty broken up about Mikey. It makes me feel so *guilty*. Why should I have to feel guilty all the time?"

Effie and I both leaned forward fractionally on the couch.

"Yes," Effie said in a soothing voice, "why *should* you, Karen?"

Karen's expression shuttered. "Well, anyway. Thanks for the visit and the—" She looked at the dented pie and the "reduced" roses with distaste. "—for the gifts, but I really have to go and spend time with Scootch."

"Okay," I said, standing. Effie stood, too. "Just let us know if there's anything we can do to help."

"Here's our card," Effie said. She handed over one of our Stagecoach Inn business cards, which had my phone number, Chester's, and her own.

"Actually, there *is* something you could do," Karen said. "If, that is, you really want to get involved with the Chamber."

"Oh, we *do*," Effie said.

"Okay, well, as you probably know, the Harvest Festival Kick-Off is this afternoon at three o'clock, when the Peeper Prize judge will be introduced and all that hoopla—you know what the Peeper Prize is, right?"

"Yeah," I said. Effie nodded.

Every year Naneda entered to win the Peeper Prize, a trophy awarded to the most delightful leaf-peeping town in the northeastern United States, sponsored by VitaGrain Breakfast Cereals. The winning town won bragging rights and a spread in the American Association of Retirees' *My Turn* magazine.

Naneda never won.

"Since you're new to the Chamber, you may not realize what a huge deal the Peeper Prize is," Karen said. "Winning would mean more tourism for Naneda, and more tourism obviously means more business, and *that* means—"

"Ka-ching," Effie said.

"Uh-huh." Karen's eyes glittered. "We have to win this year. We *have* to."

I thought of how the receptionist at the Lilting Waves Day Spa had hinted that business was slow. Could Karen be hurting for money? Her house was certainly in good repair.

Karen said, "I was supposed to be the one to introduce the Peeper Prize judge on behalf of the Chamber—I'm the

Chamber's official liaison to the contest's judge—but . . ." She looked down at her stained sweatpants.

"No one could *possibly* expect you to do such a thing while in the midst of a family tragedy," Effie said.

"Great." Karen turned to me. "All you have to do—"

"Why me?" I said.

"Agnes, darling, no one wants to see an old lady strutting on a stage," Effie purred, not sounding as if she meant a word of it. No, she sounded as if she had ulterior motives. "We'll just have to get something suitable for you to wear."

Great. Effie was forever looking for reasons to give me little makeovers. I knew it irked her that no matter how many cute dresses or pairs of Spanx she treated me to, in the end I always defaulted back to jeans, T-shirts, sneakers, and a small yet unrestrained pooch above the waistband.

"All you have to do is make a little speech welcoming the Peeper Prize judge on behalf of the Naneda Chamber of Commerce," Karen said to me. "Try to sound warm and inviting, and don't forget to smile. Oh—and do you have contact lenses? And maybe a dress? Because those glasses won't look good in the newspaper photographs. Too much glare. Not, of course, that you need to look *glamorous*. Your homegrown look will be okay. It's just the *Naneda Gazer*." She stole a look at my orange sneakers. "Not *Star* magazine."

"Newspaper photographs?" I pictured myself standing onstage with hundreds of townspeople gawking. My belly trout-flopped.

"She'll do it," Effie said.

"Aside from the speech today," Karen said, "there isn't much the liaison needs to do. Unless, of course, we win the Peeper. The judge—he's just one of several who are deployed in the towns that entered the contest—will spend the week here, visiting local businesses and events and tallying up a score. He's staying in one of those lakeside rental cottages, I heard, but we should just leave him alone. We don't want to look like we're trying to cheat by currying favor."

"Um, okay," I said.

"Let me go get the card." Karen padded out of the living room in her Hello Kitty slippers.

"Thanks a *lot*," I whispered to Aunt Effie. "Why did you volunteer me to humiliate myself?"

"To put her off the scent," Effie whispered back. "We're posing as overenthusiastic newbie members of the Chamber. If we didn't agree to this liaison thing, it would've roused her suspicions. All in the name of staying undercover, darling."

"More like all in the name of giving me another makeover."

"That's merely an added bonus."

Karen reappeared with an orange greeting card–sized envelope and passed it to me. A yellow Post-it note stuck to it said HUGH SIMONIAN VITAGRAIN PEEPER PRIZE. "That's the judge's name. Hugh Simonian. And make sure you mention VitaGrain. There should be a bouquet of flowers for the judge waiting next to the stage. Floral Poetry is donating them. After you make a little speech of welcome, give him the bouquet and this card." She was leading us to the front door. "Thanks. The idea of going out in public was just . . . too much. You know?"

"Oh, we do," Effie said.

Karen herded us onto the porch.

"Please let us know if there is *anything* else," Effie said.

"Uh-huh," Karen said, starting to shut the door.

Just then, a champagne-pink sedan stopped across the street. Otis's Grandma Bee got out of the passenger seat, said something to the driver, and shut the door. She waved the sedan off and then, catching sight of us on Karen's porch, waved at us, too, before heading to her kitchen door.

Effie and I waved back.

Karen didn't wave. She narrowed her eyes. "Crazy old bat," she muttered.

"*What?*" I said, incredulous. In my opinion, Grandma Bee definitely had all her marbles. She had whupped me at Clue.

Karen gave me a sharp look. "Do you know her?"

"Oh." My instincts screamed, *Lie, Agnes, for the love of Pop-Tarts, lie!* "No. She just looks . . . nice?"

"Nope. She's crazy. Delusional."

*Hmm. I should probably mention this to Otis.*

As Effie and I headed down the leaf-crunchy front walk, we heard Karen shut her front door hard.

# Chapter 7

"Did you unearth any clues?" Lo asked as Effie and I climbed into the Dustbuster.

"Yes," Effie said, putting on her sunglasses. "And a new lead."

"Fun!" Lo clapped her hands.

"What's in the envelope?" Myron asked me.

"This?" I tucked the orange envelope with the Post-it note in the console. "Something for the Harvest Festival Kick-Off this afternoon."

"I need to use the restroom," Hank droned from the third row.

"What kind of clue?" Myron asked. "Direct or circumstantial?"

I was digging my keys from my shoulder bag. "Circumstantial, I guess. A potential murder motive for Karen—"

"Ooh, what is it?" Lo asked. "Revenge? Money?"

"More like . . . protecting her teenage son from harm, I guess."

"That sounds like an unconvincing motive," Hank said.

Yeah. Said aloud, killing someone just to prevent their teenage son from getting a dirt-biking concussion sounded . . . improbable. I mean, Karen could've simply forbidden Scootch to hang out with Mikey, right?

"How would you like to make a little visit to Birch Grove

Bed and Breakfast?" Effie asked. "In the capacity of potential future guests, of course."

"Absotootly!" Lo said.

"When is lunch?" Hank asked. "I need to take my pills with food."

"Right after the B and B," I said.

Myron said, "If I hadn't gone into carpet sales, my second choice would've been working for the FBI."

"I'll take that as a yes," Effie said. She peered at Hank through the rearview mirror. "Dr. Li?"

"As long as I can use their restroom," he said.

\* \* \*

Birch Grove B and B was in a pretty section of Naneda where the historic residential district gave way to one-acre lots and, after a few blocks of that, farmland. It had always been one of my favorite areas of town, the kind of neighborhood where the yards had room for tire swings, big dogs, and greenhouses.

"Before we stop at the B and B," I said, "let's try to figure out which house was Mikey's. Karen said he lived right next door."

"Good idea," Myron said.

Effie nodded.

We cruised past Birch Grove B and B, a gingerbreaded Queen Anne Victorian amid trees heavy with bronze foliage. Tall hedges separated the yard from the neighboring properties. On one side was a cottage with late-blooming rosebushes, a porch swing, and lace curtains.

"Uh—that's probably not Mikey's house," I said, recalling the meatball sub exploding on his mechanic's overalls.

On the other side of the B and B was a saggy one-story house shaped like a shoebox, with asbestos siding, a boarded-up window, and a lot of miscellaneous junk on the front porch. The lawn was shin-high. The one tree in the yard looked diseased.

I braked at the curb, and we all stared.

"I suppose we can't go in there and poke around," Effie said.

"Aunt Effie! Do you want to get arrested?"

"Not in these pants."

"What?"

"Being arrested means a lot of sitting around, and these pants have no *stretch*."

"That's why I like my leisure suits," Lo said. "I'm always prepared for *anything*. You can even get sequined ones for fancy occasions."

Effie shuddered slightly.

We stared at the house some more. Then I said, "It *would* be pretty interesting to see what's in there."

"A lot of empty beer bottles and pizza boxes, would be my guess," Myron said. "Girlie magazines, too."

"And video game systems," Effie said. "Karen mentioned video games. But there would *also* have to be some kind of clue about who killed him, right?"

"Unless it was a random violent act," Hank said. "Some nut job who came in from the Thruway."

"Yikes," I said. "I hadn't even thought of that. But seriously, you guys—we can't *break into a house*. Let's go talk to Clifford and Belinda."

I circled around the block and parked in front of Birch Grove B and B. As we all walked up the long front walk, it became apparent that the B and B wasn't exactly in tip-top shape. Paint peeled here and there. A section of the porch roof looked as if it could've used new shingles. The leaf-blanketed lawn needed raking, and the picket fence slumped. Still, it was a beautiful house, and the front door had original-looking beveled glass and an amazing ornate brass doorknob and key plate.

Yup. I was picking up some vintage expertise. I had once loathed secondhand shops—the grime, that stale odor that clings to your hair, the hyperawareness that eighty percent of household dust is said to be human skin. But the allure of old house-pieces—vent covers, light fixtures, doorknobs, salvaged decorative moldings—was twining around my soul. For one thing, the craftsmanship. People don't make stuff the way they used to. Second, I loved the idea of each vintage thing having a secret history of its own. Old stuff has *personality*.

I rang the (vintage!) doorbell, and Clifford opened the door.

"What," he said—or, rather, grunted—eyeing Hank, Lo, and Myron behind Effie and me on the porch. "We're sold out, so if you're looking for a place to dump the guests you're not equipped for in your rattrap inn, you're out of luck."

"Oh, no, honey!" Lo cried. "We just love the Stagecoach Inn!"

"*Love* is a strong word," Hank said.

"We were actually here to see if you'd give our guests a tour of your B and B," I said to Clifford. "For future reference, I mean. We're trying to give them a nice big taste of Naneda's highlights and, um, hidden gems."

"Because we just love Naneda!" Lo said, squeezing between Effie and me.

"And because I need to use your restroom," Hank added in a dismal voice.

"*And*," Effie added, "because we, as fellow Chamber of Commerce members, have something we would like to discuss with you in private."

Clifford had his hand on the edge of the door. He clenched it so hard his fingernails turned white. "The . . . Chamber?"

"Yeah," I said. *Why was he freaked out about the Chamber?*

Clifford glanced over his shoulder, then lowered his voice. "Okay, fine. But not in front of our guests. I'll give everyone a quick tour, and then your guests can stay for the midmorning tea in the solarium, ten dollars a head. There isn't enough"—he glared at Effie and me in turn—"for you two."

"My treat, darlings," Effie said over her shoulder.

Clifford opened the door wider, and we all trooped inside.

The entry hall was admittedly gorgeous, all high ceilings and stunning trim, although badly lit and lightly cobwebbed. The smell of musty potpourri made my nose itch.

Oh—and on a ledge built around the perimeter of the hall, about eight feet up, an electric train was buzzing by. It made a tinny *choo-choo* before disappearing through a little hole in the wall.

We were all gawking.

Effie spoke first. "Clifford! How cute. I didn't know you were an electric train aficionado."

"I have been for years." Clifford gave us all a stern look. "And please, if you feel the need to touch the trains—*don't*. Okay? They're not toys."

"Sure look like toys," Myron said.

"They are highly detailed and fully functioning miniature vehicles."

"*Otherwise known as toys*," Myron stage-whispered to Lo.

"Where is the restroom, for heaven's sake?" Hank said.

Clifford directed Hank to the restroom and then led the rest of us to a set of open pocket doors. "This is the front parlor," he droned in a tour-guide voice. Way too many dried flowers, dusty thrift store knickknacks, and framed photographs of dead people for my taste. Not to mention the three-foot-high model

73

mountain with—here it came—another electric train whirring along.

An older couple sat side by side on a high-backed Victorian sofa, both reading copies of the same Tom Clancy novel. They both looked up.

"Myron! Lo!" the woman exclaimed. "Well, I'll be!"

"Tilly Grace!" Lo cried. "Patrick! I *wondered* where you two were staying. In all that awful commotion at the auto shop yesterday, I never thought to ask."

Myron and Lo went into the parlor to visit with their friends from, evidently, the motor coach tour.

Clifford heaved an annoyed sigh. "What about showing you the inn?"

"The customer is always right," Effie said to him.

"What do *you* know about customers?"

"Oh, lots," Effie said with a warm smile. "My very first job was cigarette girl in a nightclub."

Clifford led us through a formal dining room—featuring miniature train trestle bridges and the dustiest chandelier I'd ever seen—into a large kitchen with circa-1980s relief tiles of fruits and vegetables all over the place.

And yes, in case you were wondering, I *did* itch to knock them out with a chisel. The eighties were not a happy era for décor.

"Hello," said Belinda Prentiss, standing at the work island, chopping cantaloupe. She was birdlike, with a narrow, pale face, a thick, long, henna-red braid, and a gauzy dress with beadwork and fringes and a vaguely Indian print. She was one of those people I knew by sight—in a town as small as Naneda, there are a lot of those—but we had never been introduced. "What do *you* want?" Her voice was as wispy as the rest of her, but her glance was sharp.

Clifford said, "They said they needed to discuss something about the Chamber—"

"Ouch!" Belinda's knife clattered to the floor, and she held out a delicate finger. Bright blood seeped from a tiny cut.

"Darling, are you all right?" Clifford asked—I thought a little halfheartedly.

"Do I *look* like I'm all right?" Belinda shrieked.

"Please." Clifford fluttered his eyelids. "Not with guests in the house, Belinda."

"Just get me a Band-Aid," Belinda said. She tore a paper towel from a roll and squeezed it around her finger.

Clifford scurried out of the kitchen.

"*Useless*," Belinda snarled under her breath.

All righty then. I guess you don't need to be BFFs to run a B and B.

"Not Flour Girl Bakery?" Effie asked Belinda, eyeing the jumbo boxes of scones and muffins from the wholesale warehouse club in Rochester.

"With *their* prices?" Belinda said. "No way. These guests would eat us out of house and home if we let them. Sometimes I feel like my house has been infested by huge, voracious rats. Rats that love to carbo-load. Anyway, what about the Chamber?"

"Oh. It's not really a big deal," I said, watching the little red spot blooming on Belinda's paper towel. "It's just that, with there having been a murder in town, Naneda's shot at winning the Peeper Prize is possibly in jeopardy. Tourism and murder don't really mix."

"Your point?"

"Well, those of us in the Chamber of Commerce really need to step up our game to win this thing," I said.

"And how do you propose to do that? *Cheat?*"

"Of course not."

Effie said to Belinda, "Agnes and I could personally escort the judge—what is the judge's name?"

"Hugh Simonian."

"We could personally escort Mr. Simonian to the highlights of the Harvest Festival," Effie said.

"*And* downplay the murder," I said.

"There are a million problems with this little scheme of yours," Belinda said, "foremost that it's breaking the contest rules to try to interfere with, bribe, consort with, or fraternize with a Peeper Prize judge."

"No consorting *or* fraternizing?" Effie said. "Those poor dears don't have a bit of fun, do they?"

"So there's nothing we can do to make sure the judge doesn't hold the murder against us?" I said. "Just sit back and relax?"

"What we *do* is strive for excellence," Belinda said. "Obviously."

I stole a peek around the messy kitchen. If that was excellence, I'd pass.

Belinda caught me looking. "Our maid quit suddenly last month," she said, "and we haven't found a suitable replacement, so *I've* been doing all the cleaning myself. It's running me into the ground. Where is that idiot with my Band-Aid?"

"Speaking of cleaning," I said, "whew, Mikey's place next door sure is a pit."

"A dump like *that* next door can't be good for business," Effie said, ruining my attempt at subtlety. "Too bad you couldn't just buy it yourself and tear it down. Then you could put in a swimming pool."

"*Buy* it?" Belinda snapped. "*Swimming pool?* I don't have that kind of money. Every time I turn around, I have someone trying to get me to pay for something! If it isn't the roofer, it's Clifford—just this morning he said he wants to travel to California to see the San Diego Model Railroad Museum. Can you *believe* that? I married a five-year-old."

"I suppose, in a way, you're a bit glad Mikey is gone," Effie said, studying her manicure. "I know *I* would be."

"*What is this?*" Belinda's voice sank to an I'm-possessed-by-demons hiss. "Are you suggesting that *I*—"

"Goodness, no." Effie pressed a hand to her heart.

"If you want to know how to make Naneda look better in the eyes of the Peeper Prize judge, then I suggest you quit trying to stir up—" Belinda was interrupted by a peeping *choo-chooooo*. An electric train burst from a hole in the wall and proceeded to chug along a shelf near the ceiling. Belinda's eyes fell shut and her lips pinched to a razor slash. She sucked a few noisy breaths in through her nose and out through her mouth. Then her eyes flew open. "God, I hate those things. Charming—he calls them *charming*! Honestly, I'm just waiting for him to die."

*Whoa.*

"You know what?" I said. "We have to—um, do something—and don't worry, we can find the door."

"And I think our guests will probably skip tea in the solarium," Effie said as she and I hurried to the door. "It sounds lovely, but we have lunch plans—"

"Don't let the door hit you on the way out," Belinda said. Then she yelled, "*Cliffie!*"

# Chapter 8

Aunt Effie and I found Hank and the Bermans in the front
parlor just as my phone chimed. I fished it out of my bag
and looked at the unfamiliar number on the screen, with an area
code I didn't recognize.

"I'm going to take this," I said to Effie, and went out to the
front porch and down the steps. "Hello?" I said into the phone.
I wandered onto a narrow paved walk leading around the side of
the house.

"Agnes?" a woman chirped. "Is that you?"

"Yes."

"Just checking! You sounded like a disgruntled postal worker
for a second there."

"That's funny, Delilah, because for a second I thought *you*
were a squeaky dog toy."

"Now, now. No need to get icky. I get it. You do the wry,
adorable thing really well, but you need to learn when to turn
it off. No one likes a Debbie Downer."

I unclamped my teeth just enough to say, "To what do I owe
the infinite pleasure of your call, Delilah?"

"I'm calling to ask if you wanted to share leads on the case."

"Leads?"

"Unless, of course, you don't *have* any leads—"

"I have leads. Tons." Why did I sound so *defensive*? Argh.

"Okay, well, I thought it would be fun if we traded."

"Why would I do that?"

"I don't know, maybe because you care about Otis?"

"Of course I care about him." I paused, running through the stuff Aunt Effie and I had learned so far. It wasn't a shabby list—Karen, Clifford, and Belinda all seemed pretty sketchy—although I couldn't make heads or tails of their behavior. "What do you have?"

"Check out the negative reviews of Birch Grove B and B on countryinns.net."

"Wait—Birch Grove B and B? How do you know where I am?" I looked up and down the street, seeing nothing but a few unoccupied parked cars and a terrier sniffing a rosebush. Still, a chill slithered through me. *Was Delilah following me?*

"You're at Birch Grove right *now*?" she said. "Wow, what a coinkidink! I guess great minds think alike. I'm obviously at my shop, baking up a batch of German chocolate cupcakes. Okay, now give me something."

"How about . . . how about that Mikey Brown was seeing someone?"

"Mikey? Seeing a *woman*? No way."

"Yes way."

"I think someone's pulling your leg on that one, Agnes, but okay. Sure. Stellar tip. This was great! We should do it again. Oh, and want me to say hi to Otis for you when he comes over to help me move some shelving? He is *so* strong."

"Uh—"

"Bye!" Delilah hung up.

I stared at the phone screen, my belly churning. I'd figured out the real reason for Delilah's call: she wanted my man, and she was out to crush my confidence, one little dig at a time. It's called psychological warfare, kids.

Oh, and you know what kind of cake is Otis's favorite? German chocolate.

While talking to Delilah, I had wandered along the paved walk to the side of the house, ending up next to the garbage can and recycling bins.

A breeze stirred papers in one of the bins, catching my eye. Most of them were newspapers, but there were several white envelopes in there, too.

I looked closer.

Those were unmistakably bills. And they were unopened.

Huh.

If you pay your bills online, you don't need to open your paper copies, of course. But here were a bunch of bills—credit cards, electric company, dentist, cable. Unless Clifford and Belinda had signed up for paperless billing for *everything*, and all at once, this didn't make sense.

Or they simply couldn't pay their bills.

*Maybe I should just take a peek and—*

No. I couldn't take any chances opening the bills. The last thing I needed was Clifford and Belinda reporting me to the cops.

\* \* \*

I went back inside the B and B. After the Bermans made plans to meet their friends for dinner later, we all left.

"Clifford and Belinda's maid quit last month and they *still* haven't found a replacement?" Effie said to me as we drove away.

"Either they're holding out for Mr. Clean, or Clifford was lying. Maids aren't that hard to come by."

Hank said, "The bathroom was *not* clean. I found a hair on the soap. And who uses bar soap, anyway? You might as well wash your hands with raw chicken."

"Well, *I* thought the place was just darling," Lo said. "I just loved all the little tchotchkes! It was like being in a museum."

"A museum?" Myron said. "Of what? Kitsch?"

"Of allergens," Hank said with a sniffle.

"Clifford was definitely lying," I said to Effie. "I saw a bunch of unopened bills in their recycling bin. They're broke."

"I can tell your mind is whirring, Agnes dear."

"Do you have your phone handy?"

"Always."

"Pull up countryinns.net—it's one of those inn booking and review websites—and check out the reviews for Birch Grove."

"I'm on it."

While I drove toward Main Street, Effie fiddled with her smartphone. After a few minutes she said, "Oh-ho. What have we here, darlings? Listen to this review, from just last month: 'I wish I could give this place zero stars! The next-door neighbor was practicing the drum set in the middle of the night, and we could see and hear this same Neanderthal clearly from our bedroom window, picking his belly button lint while he argued with a credit collector. Our twentieth wedding anniversary was ruined.'"

"Whoa," I said.

"Here's another: 'Dust, dust everywhere, bad-tempered host, everything they served for breakfast tasted stale. What is up with all the potpourri? It smells like a funeral home. And then there's the neighbor next door who was blaring Green Day on his front porch. I do NOT recommend this place.' There are good reviews too, of course—because evidently some people really *do* like dusty little soaps shaped like roses—but there are enough terrible reviews to bring their star rating, at least on this website, down to a two point five."

"Dang," I said. "That's an awful average. I guess Clifford and Belinda really *do* have a plausible motive, just like Karen was hinting: get rid of Mikey before he ruins their B and B business. There's a lot on the line for them."

"Enough to *kill*?" Lo asked.

"If they're desperate enough, sure," I said.

Yes, I realize it was probably inappropriate to be discussing this stuff with the gaggle. Heck, it was inappropriate to be discussing it *period*.

"The question is," I said, "can I figure out just how desperate Clifford and Belinda really are without doing anything drastic?"

"You could go back when it's dark and get those bills you're talking about," Myron said.

"Like I said, *without doing anything drastic*."

"Where are we going now?" Hank whined from the third row.

"How about a little lunch?" Effie asked. "There's a wonderful sandwich-and-salad shop on Oak—everything is locally sourced—and then after that we should go back to the inn and relax for a bit so we're all fresh as daisies for the Harvest Festival Kick-Off. Oh—and I must be at the inn to meet Boyd when he delivers the bathtubs—"

"I almost forgot about those," I said.

"—and the billiards table."

"The—? No, never mind. Fine. Why not? The billiards table."

\* \* \*

Counting out money to pay for my turkey-and-Swiss in the sandwich shop, I noticed something on one of the quarters I had dug out of my wallet. Along the edge of the quarter, gray stringy material clung, sort of like the stuff that's produced when you erase pencil, only a little stickier.

What *was* it? I mean, sure, coins get funky. But the thing was, I was one hundred percent sure this quarter had come from the till at Crumble+Fluff. The zippered coin pouch in my wallet had been empty until I'd put my change for that coconut lemon cupcake in there yesterday.

"Miss?" the cashier said.

"Oh. Sorry. Here." I slid my money across the counter.

Whatever. It was probably nothing. And jeez, it wasn't like Delilah was required to wash the money that passed through her till.

\* \* \*

Back at the inn, Chester was cracking open a Diet Coke when I walked into the kitchen.

"Hey," I said.

"Need some caffeine?" he asked.

"I need a nap. In an isolation tank."

"Okay, well, I have some good news for you, and I have some bad news."

"What?" I sank into a chair.

"The floorboards up in the attic bathroom are original—"

"I knew it!"

"—but they're rotten. Wet rot, not dry rot, which is good."

"How is that good?"

"Well, both types are fungus—"

"Gross."

"Yeah. But if it was dry rot, the entire building could be in jeopardy. Wet rot will just be concentrated around where there's been some water leakage. Which there was. The floor is completely rotten all around the bathtub and toilet. The leaking happened a while ago, of course. The boards are dry, now, but the damage is done."

"So what does that mean? Can we sand the floors down or something?"

Chester snorted. "No way. They have to be ripped out."

"Ripped out?"

"Uh-huh. Serious grunt work. Trust me, Agnes, save it until our guests are gone and this stuff with Otis and the murder has blown over. You don't want to be knee-deep in wood fungus at a time like this."

I blinked away the hot sting of moisture in my eyes. What, now I was going to cry? About *floorboards*? What the heck was wrong with me?

"Here comes Boyd with the U-Haul," Chester said, peering out the window over the sink. He swigged Diet Coke. "I don't know where we're going to put this stuff Aunt Effie keeps buying. The garage is full, and we can't have it inside the inn. Not when we're about to start a major renovation project."

"Well, no way is she going to stop buying," I said. "I know. I'll call and have one of those storage pods sent over. We can load it up as needed."

"Good idea."

I looked up a nearby storage pod company on my smartphone and gave them a call. They said they'd deliver one to the inn the day after tomorrow. After that, I checked my email. Phone bill, an invitation to a friend's baby shower, assorted spam, and a message from my friend from college, Charlotte. We had both been anthropology majors, but after graduation she had gone off for a few stints in the Peace Corps while I had done hard time as a barista and hotel clerk. She had just started graduate school in anthropology in Seattle, and her email was raving about the program. I KNOW YOUR PLANS HAVE CHANGED, she wrote, AND I KNOW YOU'D LOVE THIS PROGRAM. THIS YEAR'S APPLICATION DEADLINE IS NOVEMBER 1ST. THINK ABOUT IT!

Reapply to grad school? How the heck could I do that? That would mean leaving Otis behind. Leaving the Stagecoach Inn behind. And I wasn't sure if I even *wanted* to go to grad school anymore. It was so, I don't know, *elbow-patchy*.

I wrote Charlotte a quick note—basically saying thanks, but no thanks—and deleted her email.

* * *

Hours later, I pulled the Dustbuster into a parking spot downtown. The Bermans sat in the back seat, and Chester was beside me. Aunt Effie lurched her Cadillac into the next spot over, with Hank and Dorothea, who needed a break from working, on board.

"Ready?" I said.

"Can't wait!" Lo said.

"I'm hungry," Hank said.

"You could enter the pie-eating contest," Chester said. "I'm going to."

I stuck the orange envelope Karen had given me into my shoulder bag, and we got out, joined the others on the sidewalk, and headed toward Main Street.

I had submitted to Aunt Effie doing my hair. There had been a few touch-and-go moments when the close proximity of the Aqua Net, the searing hair dryer, and the cigarette in Effie's lips had made me fear for my life.

I had survived. My hair was a voluminous mass of artfully hairsprayed waves. They didn't really go with my nearly makeup-free face, but oh well.

Now my problem was the vintage rust-colored dress with a belt cinched so tight I could barely breathe. My best friend Lauren, having been tipped off about my speech by Aunt Effie, had brought it over from her shop. She had also brought knee-high brown leather boots with three-inch heels. She said they were from the seventies. They pinched.

The first thing we noticed when we reached Main Street was a slowly revolving orange metal pumpkin on a stand in front of Dickens New and Used Books.

"What in the world is that?" Myron asked.

"That's obvious," Hank said. "It's a broken finger waiting to happen."

"Good thing you're here, Dr. Li," Dorothea said with a blush. "Ready to spring to people's aid like a knight in shining armor. Goodness, I hope *my* fingers don't get caught in a dangerous pumpkin."

Hank looked confused.

"There's a sign," Lo said, speed-walking to the pumpkin. She had changed into a bright red velour tracksuit and a large sun visor. "Oh, how cute—it's a ballot box for the Gourd Queen contest!"

Sure enough, the revolving metal pumpkin was set into a large wooden box with a padlock and a slot to accept paper ballots.

"Gourd Queen?" Myron stopped beside Lo.

"Don't you remember *anything*, Myronie? We read all about it in the *Naneda Gazer* just this morning. The Gourd Queen will ride on a big, beautiful float during the parade."

"Then she's a beauty queen," Myron said.

"It's just a popularity contest," I said.

"I suppose it's a real boon to a lady's social life, being the Gourd Queen," Lo said.

"I guess, if she likes wearing a puffy orange dress and doing the royal wave," I said with a shrug.

"Is there a tiara?"

"The Pumpkin Princess wears a tiara," I said. "That's the second-place winner. The Gourd Queen wears a golden crown."

"Golden?" Lo said, eyes shining.

"Well, *spray-painted* gold." Was Lo picturing herself as Gourd Queen? Was she even qualified, since she was an out-of-towner? I decided not to burst her bubble.

I split up with them to go figure out the whole Peeper Prize judge–greeting thingy. They were going to shop, their plan being to show up at the ceremony in Fountain Square at three to see me greet the Peeper Prize judge.

I passed sidewalk sales, decorations, and games. People were setting up the pie-eating contest at tables in the blocked-off street. In Fountain Square, a stage and sound equipment were going up, and a red tent with a BOBBING FOR APPLES! sign stood in the far corner. The outdoor gear store was getting ready to raffle off a pair of binoculars that were, evidently, great for looking at distant foliage. Harries Stationery had piled their stock of

Headless Horseman masks onto a sidewalk table. The Army Navy Surplus had a long rack of 20-percent-off plaid hunting jackets. A kids' bouncy house was slowly inflating over by the Cup 'n' Clatter, the bank had set up scarecrows and dried cornstalks outside their door, and Lauren was arranging a rack of colorful vintage garments in front of Retro Rags.

"Hi," I said, pulling up next to her.

"Hey!" She straightened. "Wow, Agnes, you look . . . fantastic in that dress."

"Why do you sound so surprised?"

"Don't take this the wrong way, but everyone's used to seeing you in sneakers and T-shirts. Sometimes we forget how cute you are."

Lauren isn't classically pretty with her long face, sizable nose, and bony figure. And yet she is amazingly glamorous. That day she was wearing cat-eye glasses and a vintage argyle sweater dress. Her straight brown hair was in a French twist.

"It's not like I wear muumuus and a paper sack over my head," I said.

"Well, actually, you practically do."

"I'm going to grab a coffee. Want me to bring you anything?"

"Nope, I'm fully caffeinated. Thanks. I'll try to pop over to see your speech. If you hear whooping, that'll be me."

I said good-bye to Lauren and then crossed over Main Street to the Black Drop, which, in my humble opinion, frothed up the best pumpkin spice lattes in town. I had been making an exhaustive comparative study since pumpkin spice latte season officially began a few weeks earlier.

Main Street was filling up with people, dogs, and strollers. The mood was festive. Lots of tourists. Some tourists were the Romantic Getaway variety—holding hands, relaxed smiles, leisurely. Others were the Family FUN type (grit your teeth determinedly when you say *FUN*), which usually included one whining kid and one flushed, pissed-off parent.

Amid the stream of people, I noticed a rangy guy with a potbelly, in black jeans and a black Adidas track jacket.

He was striding down the sidewalk and swinging his head left and right, as though looking for something. Or someone.

He wasn't a tourist. Too businesslike. And I didn't recognize him as a Nanedan, either. Something about his hostile intensity, his dark sunglasses, and the down-slash of his eyebrows made my skin crawl.

He disappeared into Harries Stationery.

# Chapter 9

I was loitering by the coffee pickup area in the Black Drop when the cashier guy called, "Hi, Alexa."

Alexa? As in, Randy Rice's wife Alexa?

Trying not to be too obvious, I turned.

Yup. That was her, all right. The tipsy train wreck from the Chamber breakfast, wearing tall black boots over tight jeans with slashed-at-the-factory knees and a fitted black leather moto jacket. She went up to the PLACE ORDER HERE counter in a self-conscious way, tossed her high-and-lo-lighted blonde ponytail, and ordered a sixteen-ounce skinny latte, extra hot. When she said *extra hot*, she giggled at the cashier, which was kinda ooky since she appeared to be staving off forty, and the cashier was obviously a college student.

After Alexa paid for her coffee, she came over to where I was waiting.

I gave her a big smile. "Alexa Rice, right? I'm Agnes Blythe—I'm a new member of the Chamber of Commerce. I think we met briefly at the Chamber breakfast."

"We did?" Smudgy black eyeliner ringed Alexa's baby blues, already settling in the delicate fan of wrinkles on their outer corners. "I don't remember, but I'm always so bored at those things."

"How is Randy holding up?" I asked in a concerned-yet-casual voice.

Alexa almost . . . flinched. "He's . . . okay. You mean about Mikey?"

"Uh-huh." I swallowed. "Weren't they, um, friends?" Delilah had actually said *frenemies*, but I needed to get Alexa talking.

Her eyes welled with tears. "Poor Mikey. They said he . . ."

"I know," I said. "You don't need to . . . were you and Mikey close?"

"What?"

"You're crying."

"For *Randy*."

"Oh."

*Why so defensive, Alexa?*

"Randy and Mikey knew each other since they were babies," Alexa said. "Their moms were best friends, so even though Randy and Mikey might not have chosen to be friends with each other, they ended up being together, like, constantly. They even went on family vacations together and stuff . . ." A sniffle. "Randy is just *sick* with all this. He got so drunk last night. He has the worst hangover. I haven't seen him like this since he had his little midlife crisis a few years back and bought that stupid sports car that he never even drives." Alexa's voice took on a sharp, almost vindictive edge. "I told him a lot is riding on this week, with the Peeper Prize judge here and everything. Jeez. He has no self-control. None!"

*Oh really.*

"All of us in the Chamber feel the great importance of this

week," I said. Ugh. Who had I *become*, saying stuff like that? I felt as phony as Cheez Whiz. "Does, um, Randy have any idea who might've wanted to kill Mikey? Since they knew each other so well, I mean?"

Alexa glanced over her shoulder. The only other customers were busy chatting on the other side of the coffee shop. A man stood at the ORDER HERE counter, talking with the cashier, and the barista was frothing milk with such a loud hiss that there was no way she could eavesdrop. Alexa turned back to me, eyes wide, and lowered her voice. "Randy, doesn't have any idea, but . . ."

*Please-oh-please give me something good! Drop theories. Name names! I NEED this.*

"About two weeks ago, Mikey suddenly had—" Alexa swallowed. "—all this cash."

For some reason, it was at the precise moment that Alexa said *cash* that I noticed her large, sparkling stud earrings. Diamond? Cubic zirconia? I had no idea. Aunt Effie would've been able to tell in a second.

"How do you know about the cash?" I asked.

"Mikey was sort of flashing it, you know. Buying stuff. Bragging about the stuff he was planning on buying."

"To . . . you and Randy?"

"Yeah."

"Delilah Fortune—you, know, the owner of the new cupcake shop?—"

"Yeah. I know."

"—she said Randy and Mikey were actually *frenemies*, not friends, so—"

"You've been talking to Delilah." This was deadpan.

"Well, yeah. Just in passing, of course." I swallowed. "You know, Chamber of Commerce stuff."

Alexa was blinking faster than usual.

Were more tears coming? Or was it because I had mentioned the Chamber? Clifford and Belinda Prentiss, too, had gotten twitchy when I had mentioned it.

"Delilah and I are good friends," Alexa said. "We were actually together when we found out the news about . . . Mikey. We were up in Brighton, visiting my grandpa in his nursing home—"

Brighton was a pleasant suburb of Rochester.

"—he has dementia—and Randy called me and . . ." Alexa didn't continue. She was too choked up.

"Delilah goes with you to visit your grandpa?" I asked, trying not to sound incredulous. I mean, I could picture Delilah playing coy with a young guy, but not playing gin rummy with an oldster.

"She's been really supportive. Of course, we always go shopping at the mall afterward. To cheer ourselves up, you know. Visiting Grandpa is depressing. God, I can't stand the thought of getting old." Alexa's eyes welled with more tears. "I'm about to-to-to turn *forty.*"

Aunt Effie would've just advised her to stay thirty-nine till she went toes-up.

"What did Mikey buy with the cash?" I asked.

"Some totally ridiculous gold chains, for starters. I told him they made him look like a gigolo, the way he had them nestled in his hairy chest . . ."

"Real gold?" I asked.

"Yeah. I'm sure of it. And he bought video game stuff—he was addicted to video games. He bought his nephew some super-expensive sneakers."

"Scootch."

"Yeah. You know him?"

"Sort of."

"I already told this to the police, and I couldn't tell if they thought it was important, but *I* think it is. Maybe the police always act like that, to play it cool. I know they do on *Law and Order*."

Did *everyone* watch that show? Jeez.

"All I know is that Mikey was pretty broke," Alexa said, "and then boom! Cash. And then, two weeks later, he's dead, and no one knows where the cash is."

"What do you mean, no one knows where it is?"

"Well, the police said they never saw any big money. Like, in his house or in his wallet, or in his bank account."

"Wait," I said. "Hold on. Are you saying that you think Mikey was *murdered* over this cash?"

"Uh-huh."

"Like, because he stole it from someone, and they wanted it back?"

"Uh-huh." Alexa leaned in and whispered, "I'm scared."

"Alexa!" someone roared.

Alexa and I both started, and turned to see Randy, Alexa's husband, poking his head through the coffee shop door. He was wiry, with a surprisingly lush head of chestnut hair on his oversized head, and sunglasses. His face was puce. Even from a distance, I could see the pitted acne scars on his cheeks.

"Coming, Randy," Alexa said in a meek voice.

"Could you *take* any longer?" Randy slammed the door. The bells jingled.

Alexa didn't meet my eye. "Randy gets bored waiting."

"Oh." What else could I say?

Then my pumpkin latte was up. I gave Alexa one of the Stagecoach Inn business cards and told her to call if she needed someone to talk to. It felt pretty inadequate, considering she had to go out and contend with Angry Randy.

On the other hand . . . *whoa*. Mikey Brown's boatload of cash. Can you say *Pivotal Clue?*

When I stepped out of the Black Drop, latte in hand, Randy was sitting on a sidewalk bench, arms folded tight, joggling one of his small legs up and down. A bright-eyed corgi sat on the bench beside him, panting. The two of them made *the* most bewildering contrast of creepy and cute.

Despite my pinching seventies boots, I powerwalked away.

\* \* \*

At three o'clock sharp, Dad lumbered up onto the stage in Fountain Square to clamorous applause from the crowd.

Dad has been the mayor longer than I've been alive, and he'll probably be the mayor until he retires. I'm guessing his approval rating would be somewhere in the 90s if the *Naneda Gazer* did a poll. He's like a cross between a teddy bear and Perry Mason, and he exudes this fatherly warmth that makes every last person in town feel reassured and heard. No, he's not perfect, and neither is his cholesterol. That sometimes keeps me up at night.

While Dad was giving his speech—it was all about community and how lucky we were to live in such a magical place; obviously no mention of murder—I wove my way through the crowd to the area beside the stage.

To say I had butterflies in my stomach is an understatement. It felt as if I had pterodactyls swooping around in there.

"Hi," I whispered to a lady with a clipboard who looked In Charge of Everything.

"You're the Chamber's Peeper Prize liaison?" she whispered.

"Yeah."

Just then, Dad finished his speech to more applause.

"Well, it's show time," the clipboard lady said to me. "You're late."

"Oh. Sorry." I set down my coffee, took out the orange envelope Karen had given me, and dropped my shoulder bag on a folding chair.

Clipboard Lady dumped a bouquet of orange and yellow chrysanthemums into my arms and gave me a push. "Make it snappy."

The crowd fell silent as I climbed the stairs onto the stage. I felt as if I was wearing stilts, not three-inch heels. I stopped behind the microphone.

Right in the front row stood Aunt Effie, Chester, Hank, Lo, Dorothea, and Myron. They all smiled and waved. In the very back, the rangy, Adidas track jacket–wearing out-of-towner stood, his sunglasses turned in my direction.

Eek.

I cleared my throat, and the resulting rumble in the microphone was deafening.

"Get *on* with it," Clipboard Lady whispered.

"Good afternoon, Naneda," I said. My words boomed through the speakers. "I'm Agnes Blythe. Most of you may know me simply as the mayor's daughter, but I am also, along with my aunt, Euphemia Winters, and my cousin, Chester Blythe, one of the newest members of the Naneda Chamber of Commerce."

"She'd make a great Gourd Queen!" Lo shouted.

Next to Lo, Chester tossed a piece of caramel corn into his mouth and waved.

Lo went on, "And she's basically single, too!"

At that precise second, I saw Otis. He was off to the side,

standing with his arms folded, in worn jeans and a red-and-blue plaid shirt. Our eyes briefly met. I saw the hurt in his eyes. I had to look away.

"Um." I peeled the Post-it note off the envelope in my hands and held it up. "And it is on behalf of the Chamber of Commerce that I would like to extend a warm welcome to Hugh Simonian, the esteemed judge of the VitaGrain Peeper Prize!"

Lots of applause, and then a man trotted up the stage steps.

Hugh Simonian wasn't the three-piece-suited balding guy I'd pictured. Nope, he was youngish—about my age—built like a jockey, and dressed in skinny jeans, a plaid shirt, lace-up logger boots, and black-framed hipster glasses. He clutched a smartphone the same way a baby holds a binky.

"Um, welcome," I said, plastering on what I hoped was a Miss America smile. I extended the bouquet and the orange envelope.

"Yeah, thanks," Hugh said, grabbing the bouquet and the envelope. He edged me out of the way to get to the microphone. "Hi. I'm Hugh Simonian, the judge of the VitaGrain Peeper Prize." He spoke in a brisk, nasal monotone. "I just want everyone to know that although in past years, Peeper Prize judges may have gotten a little too cozy with the business owners of their towns, that's not the way I do things. Everything is going to be aboveboard with me, okay? So if you see me around, sure, say hi, but don't go offering me free meals at your restaurants, or"—he pulled a grimace—"for the love of Pete, *no more free maple fudge*. Okay?"

Crickets. This guy had as much charisma as a graphing calculator.

"Oh," Hugh said, as though in an afterthought, waving his smartphone, "and if you're at all interested, check out the app I developed, PrimoLeafPeep. Only two dollars and ninety-nine cents will get you all the latest information, including foliage maps, weather forecasts, and the best places to eat, drink, and stay. Hands down, it's the number one leaf-peeping app in North America. *Ciao.*" He made a limp wave and left the stage.

Dad stepped forward to the microphone. "Well, folks, I think that about sums it up, so without further ado—let the twenty-fourth annual Naneda Harvest Festival begin!"

Cheers, orange and yellow confetti. Festive fiddle music from the sound system. The crowd began to disperse.

"You did a great job, honey," Dad said, patting my shoulder. "Who knows, maybe someday you'll follow in my footsteps as mayor."

"Me? *Mayor?*" I was looking around, distracted, searching for Otis. I needed to tell him how Lo's yelling to the crowd that I was single had not been my idea.

"Can you come to dinner tonight?" Dad asked. "Cordelia said she's making your favorite dessert—sugar-free Jell-O."

In my opinion, sugar-free Jell-O is a preschool craft supply, not a food, and furthermore, Cordelia knew it. But Dad couldn't see Cordelia's passive aggression. Love goggles. "I'd love to, but we have some guests staying at the inn—"

"Without an innkeeping license?"

"We're not charging them. It's more like a Good Samaritan type of situation."

"Oh, okay. Stranded folks from that motor coach?"

"Exactly."

"By the way, how is Otis holding up? With the, uh, the—"

"Mikey Brown's death? I'm not . . . I'm actually not sure how he's holding up." *Maybe you should ask Delilah Fortune.*

"And who was that lady yelling about you being single and making a good Gourd Queen?"

"One of our guests."

"What a character."

"Tell me about it."

Dad's attention was sucked away by other people, so I walked down the stage steps and looked around for my shoulder bag and coffee.

I was intercepted by Hugh, the Peeper judge.

"So," he said, "you're the liaison for the Chamber of Commerce?"

"Um, yeah?" Hadn't I just announced that?

"What's your name?"

"Agnes." Hadn't he been listening?

"Agnes," he said. "I went to a Catholic school where there was a Sister Agnes. She taught PE. Doesn't it mean 'little lamb' or something?"

"Yeah." I hate it when people know this awful fact.

"So, Agnes, these flowers are really great, but they're not really my style."

"What kind of monster doesn't like chrysanthemums?" I said, trying to sound witty.

"And the card?" Hugh waved the orange envelope, which he'd opened. "A pug peeking out of a pumpkin? Seriously?" He tossed the bouquet and card onto a nearby folding chair and sidled closer. "I'm a *man*, little lamb. I don't like pugs. And anyway—" He was really, really close. I could see every bristle of his sparse designer stubble. "—don't you think flowers make a pretty lame gift?"

*Gross.* What did he expect, that I'd kiss him or something to butter up the Peeper Prize judge?

I dodged to the side. "Well, Hugh, I'm sorry you don't like the card and flowers, which of course were more of a ceremonial symbol than a gift to you. Good thing they're recyclable and compostable! And since you made it pretty clear that town business owners should stay away from you, and since I help run the Stagecoach Inn, well, I guess I'd better dash." *There* was my bag and coffee. I snatched them up and darted away.

* * *

I hadn't gone more than ten yards when I found myself face-to-face with Effie and the gaggle.

Effie beamed. "Wonderful speech, Agnes! Simply wonderful!"

"And now it's party time," Chester said. "I'm entered in the pie-eating contest, which starts in five minutes." He smooshed a handful of caramel corn in his mouth.

"Don't you want to save room for pie?" I asked him.

"This is my warm-up."

I turned to Lo. "What was the deal about you yelling to the crowd that I'm single?"

"Only trying to help, honey." Lo sounded hurt. "Don't forget, he kissed you *on the top of your head*."

Chester said, "Haven't you heard of guerrilla matchmaking, Agnes? It's all the rage."

"I don't need matchmaking, because I . . ." My voice trailed off as my eyes fell on Otis, talking to Delilah in front of her shop. She was passing out miniature cupcakes. He was smiling.

Maybe I *should* have Lo play matchmaker . . . and match me up with own flipping almost-boyfriend.

* * *

Honestly, I *tried* to have a good time with Effie, Chester, and Co. I made an effort and stubbornly ate my way through caramel corn, a caramel apple, and a Zweigle's hot dog in an attempt to forget Otis smiling at Delilah.

The ensuing stomachache did take my mind off it. Sort of. Except for the time I saw Delilah shrieking, clapping, and jumping up and down with delight because she'd won the binoculars raffle at the outdoor gear store.

What was this, *The Price Is Right*? And, as a local business owner, was she even supposed to have *entered* that raffle? I kinda doubted it. But evidently, that's how Delilah rolled. She just helped herself.

I didn't see Otis again. I thought about texting him and asking to talk, but didn't. I just kept eating instead.

Meanwhile, Effie and the gaggle buzzed around like bugs, tasting samples, buying souvenirs, and trying their hands at the games. We cheered on Chester as he competed in the pie-eating contest. He came in third, behind a waifish teenage girl and a guy who was called—I am not kidding—Anaconda.

After the pie-eating contest, I got separated from Effie and the gaggle. The crowd was really thick, and everyone was wandering around with corn dogs and cider doughnuts, and the hot caramel corn truck was pumping out fragrant smoke.

I searched all three floors of Doug's Fine Antiques. No gaggle. I checked in the bakery, the coffee shop, and the bookstore. No sign of them.

Where were they? I kept stopping and turning around in slow circles on Main Street, peering into the crowd. I had the spooky sense that I was being watched, but I brushed it off as a sort of residual paranoid feeling, left over from having had to make that stupid welcome speech.

All I wanted was to change out those pinching boots and

that dress with its gastric-bypassing belt. I stopped in front of the BOBBING FOR APPLES! tent in a far corner of Fountain Square, which was unoccupied now. I dug out my phone, dialed Aunt Effie's cell, and listened to it ring.

The apple bobbing seemed to be done for the day. Puddles shone on the brick pavement. A scattering of apples gleamed red on the ground. A tent flap fluttered in the breeze. I picked my way around the puddles, pushed the tent flap aside, and peered in.

Empty. Nothing but crates of apples and a big tub of water right in front of me. A couple of apples floated in the dark water.

Aunt Effie's phone went to voicemail, so I punched END CALL. She never retrieved voicemails.

Suddenly, I was grabbed by the arms from behind and, in the same powerful motion, shoved headfirst into the tub of water. It was icy and dark and the very definition of panic. The hands holding my arms—*man*, they were strong.

I tried to buck my head.

Stabbing neck pain. Sloshing water.

I tried to scream.

Gurgles.

I don't know how long I was held under—long enough for my contacts to dislodge and my lungs to burn and the little voice inside my head to say, *Welp, I guess this is it, then. Too bad about all those unrealized dreams. You never did try an apple-pie milkshake. Or have a family.*

Then suddenly the pressure on my arms was gone.

I swept my head out of the water and stood there for a minute, dripping, gasping for air, and making choky splutters that I couldn't believe were coming from me. My attacker had left throbbing, fingertip-sized dots of pain on my arms. I was only vaguely aware of footsteps tapping away.

Only when enough oxygen squeaked back into my brain did I swing around. There was motion on the other side of the fountain. But since my contacts were now floating in the apple tub, all I could see was a round bobbly orange thing on top of a reddish blur of plaid.

*A Headless Horseman mask.*

"Hey!" I tried to shout, but it came out limp, and water trickled out of my nose.

I was standing there shaking and trying to force my brain to come up with a plan when I heard Chester and Effie's voices.

Effie: "Goodness, Agnes! You look like a drowned rat!"

Chester: "It's not a wet T-shirt contest, Agnes."

Effie: "Shush, Chester—look, she's upset." Then they were beside me. "Agnes! What happened?"

"What happened?" I smeared water out of my eyes. "I think someone just tried to kill me."

# Chapter 10

Effie rushed away to find a policeman, leaving me with Chester. He was noisily eating a caramel apple.

"How are you eating a caramel apple after participating in the pie-eating contest?" I asked, alarmed at the quaver in my voice.

"I need some fresh fruit."

"Wait," I said. "Where's my bag?" I stumbled around a little. "Chester, do you see my shoulder bag? I lost my contacts—"

"Nope."

"That psycho jerk stole my bag! My wallet was in there!" I spotted the white blur of my phone on the pavement beside the apple barrel and snatched it up. Thank goodness I'd been holding it when that creep came up behind me.

"Then that means whoever dunked you was possibly trying to *mug* you, Agnes." Chester took another crunchy bite. "Not murder you because you're such an awesome sleuth that you should have been recruited by the CIA in the seventh grade."

"They wanted to kill me. I think." I lowered myself shakily onto a stool inside the apple-bobbing tent. Chester untied the sweatshirt from his waist and passed it to me. I took it gratefully and put it on.

The thing was, I was no longer convinced it was a drowning attempt. I'd been wired with pumpkin spice latte, snappy with adrenaline left over from my welcome speech, and weirded out about Otis and Delilah. Maybe my imagination was getting carried away.

"Did you see anyone?" Chester sat on a stool next to me.

"Yes. But I'm pretty sure they were wearing one of those Headless Horseman pumpkin masks that Harries Stationery has been hawking."

"Cu-reepy."

"I know. I also saw plaid. A blur of plaid, with some red in it. Running away. I think."

"Plaid is the unofficial fall uniform of Naneda, so that could've been approximately half of the people currently roaming downtown."

"Clifford Prentiss was wearing plaid today," I said, wiping a trickle of water out of my ear. "He always wears plaid."

"Hey, wasn't Otis wearing plaid today?" Chester tipped his head to strategically gnaw caramel.

"How can you even *suggest*—"

"I'm not suggesting anything, Agnes, I'm merely saying that your plaid clue isn't very useful. In fact, didn't you see all the plaid hunting jackets for sale at the Army Navy Surplus? But you *could* go and find out who purchased a Headless Horseman mask."

"That's actually a pretty good idea."

"Stick around. I'm full of them."

"Oh, and whoever dunked me had pretty small hands. Small-ish, but strong." Those fingerprint-dots of pain still throbbed on my upper arms. I felt so *violated*.

"A woman?"

"Well, yeah, I guess it could've been a woman. A strong one. Or a dude with little mitts."

After a few minutes, Effie showed up with some policemen, who took a statement. I sat there, hair dripping, shivering in Chester's sweatshirt, and told the police about the dunking and how my bag had been stolen.

"All righty," one of the policemen said. "We'll do what we can."

"You don't seem overly concerned," Effie said.

"We are concerned, ma'am." The officer wiggled his hat. "It's just that we can't exactly send out an alert for all our forces to look for—" He glanced down at his notebook. "—a pumpkin mask and a 'blur of plaid.'"

"Told you," Chester whispered to me.

"Shut *up*," I told him through clenched teeth.

\* \* \*

Effie, Chester, and I walked to Harries Stationery, where all but one Headless Horseman mask had been sold. I elbowed, still dripping water, through the shoppers inside, and spoke to the cashier. "Excuse me, but can you describe to me every person who purchased a Headless Horseman mask this afternoon?"

The cashier snapped her gum. Because I had lost my contacts, I couldn't see her too well, but I did see that she had pink hair. "No. What happened to you? You're getting water everywhere."

I ignored her question. "Why not?"

"Number one, do you see how insane it is in here today? And number two, I heard from my manager that one of those masks was shoplifted about an hour ago."

Well, it had been worth a shot.

\*   \*   \*

We found the gaggle and Effie drove us back to the inn in the Dustbuster. Chester was driving the Caddy back. Since I was dripping water, I had no choice but to explain what had happened to everyone as we went.

"A mugger?" Lo gasped. "*Upstate?*"

"What," Myron said, "you think there's no crime upstate?"

"I doubt it was a mugger," Hank said from the third row. "You don't look wealthy."

"Um, thanks?" I said.

Hank went on, "It was probably the murderer."

"Brilliant thinking, Dr. Li," Dorothea said. She was buckled in the third row next to Hank.

"What?" I yelped.

"That's what *I* thought, too," Effie said, rolling through a stop sign.

"Why?"

"Obviously, you spooked the murderer," Hank said, "going around asking questions and intruding in people's personal space."

I guess it had crossed my mind that Mikey Brown's murder and my dunking could be connected. Of course it had. But I hadn't had time to think it through, and hearing it said aloud made me feel icy cold. "You think the *murderer* dunked me?" I asked Hank over my shoulder.

"Who else?"

Good question.

The dunker had had small hands. Clifford Prentiss fit the bill. So did Randy Rice, for that matter. Belinda Prentiss was surely too frail and wimpy. Karen Brown and Alexa Rice weren't. And then there was Delilah Fortune . . . But Delilah ran her cupcake shop single-handedly. She wouldn't have left it unattended.

It was around five o'clock when Effie parked the Dustbuster in front of the inn. The Bermans were going to meet their Tom Clancy–reading friends for dinner at the Thai place, and the rest of us agreed that hearty Italian food at six thirty sounded like an excellent plan.

I got my bathrobe from my room, went down to Aunt Effie's bathroom, undressed (boy, was I glad to take off that belted dress and those pinching boots), and took a long, hot shower. It took three shampoos to get out all the Aqua Net.

After that, I plodded wearily back up to the attic. I stood in the bathroom doorway and looked sadly at the original-yet-rotted floorboards. I could see it, now, a splotchy sponginess that made the wood grain look fragile.

*You know, those boards would be a cinch to pry up with a crow-bar*, a little voice said in the back of my mind. It wasn't the pompous bug-voice of my conscience. It was a new voice, as bubbly and go-get-'em as a gymnastics coach: *Do it! Do it! Do it!*

I turned away from the bathroom. I didn't have time to go ripping up wood floors. Although there *was* a crowbar in the tool shed . . . nah.

As I was pulling on my jeans, my phone buzzed with a text message. I shoved on my glasses.

Otis: MEET ME FOR DINNER? A COLLEGE BUDDY OF MINE IS IN TOWN. YOU'LL LIKE HIM.

Okay, so it wasn't exactly a romantic date if Mr. College Buddy was in the mix, but hadn't I agreed to have dinner with Aunt Effie, Chester, Hank, and Dorothea anyway?

**Me:** SURE, AS LONG AS I CAN BRING THE GAGGLE. HOW ABOUT THAT'S ITALIANO?

**Otis:** GREAT. WHAT TIME?

**Me:** SIX THIRTY?

**Otis:** SEE YOU THEN.

He wasn't going to mention the thing about Lo saying I was single, then. Maybe everything would be okay.

Or maybe he wanted to talk about it in person.

I spent the next hour canceling my stolen credit cards and ordering a replacement driver's license online. Fortunately, I hadn't had more than fifteen or twenty bucks cash in my wallet, but what *really* ground my gears was that my Black Drop punch card had been in there. I had been just one punch shy of a free sixteen-ounce pumpkin spice latte.

I dug around in my cardboard boxes until I found the thick navy-blue wool cardigan I wanted. I pulled it on, applied some tinted lip balm and subtle eyeliner, and replaced my glasses, which were a thick-framed tortoiseshell pair that Chester said made me look like Austin Powers but made me feel grounded. I had a backup pair of contact lenses, but I didn't feel like dealing with them. Not after what had happened to the first pair.

I went downstairs.

The inn was hushed. I found Aunt Effie in the laundry room, which was off the short passage that connected the bottom of the servants' stairs to the kitchen. She was folding towels, which looked incongruous with her black pantsuit and heels. Also incongruous: the martini with extra olives sitting on the shelf between the liquid detergent and the bleach.

"There you are, Agnes. Feeling all right?"

"Yeah. Just . . . shaken up. And *pissed*."

"I don't blame you." She placed a folded towel inside a basket and pulled another out of the dryer. Our washer and dryer were brand-new, gorgeous, and ultraefficient. Granted, they looked out of place against the faux wood paneling someone had misguidedly installed in the laundry room a few decades back.

*Which, incidentally, would be a ton of fun to rip out with a crowbar.*

I pulled a towel out of the dryer, too. "Do you think Hank was right? Do you think the *murderer* dunked me?"

"I'm going to go out on a limb and guess that it was either the murderer or someone else our questions have made feel threatened. You know, someone with something rotten to hide. Either way, *I* don't feel inclined to stop sleuthing, but then, I'm not the one who was assaulted."

"You could be next."

"Bring it on. I lived through the Jazzercise craze. I'm not afraid of anything."

Despite the awfulness of the situation, I laughed as I placed the folded towel in the basket. "Okay, well, if the murderer is spooked, does that mean that one of the people we talked to today is the murderer?" *What an icky thought.*

"One of them, yes, or someone else who knows what we talked about with the people we questioned."

"Like a spouse."

"Mm. It means *something* we discovered was on the right track. We just don't know what that something is." Effie set the last towel in the basket, picked up her martini, and sipped.

"How did this thing get so out of control so quickly?" I said. "I mean, we were just trying to learn more about Mikey, and we stumbled upon his killer?"

"Why not? It's a small town. You look like you need a drink."

"No, I don't. Plus, presumably I'm the designated driver tonight."

"Fabulous." Another deep sip.

I pulled the lint trap from the dryer, peeled off a grayish puffy sheet of lint, and tossed it in the trash can. "Okay. We talked to Karen, Clifford and Belinda Prentiss, Delilah Fortune, and Alexa. So *these* are our suspects?" It was mind-bending to picture any one of them bludgeoning Mikey to death with a wrench.

"I suppose they are, with the addition of their spouses and anyone else they may have told about our conversations."

"The spouses are Karen's clean-freak husband—whatever his name was—and Randy—I met him briefly. Man, was he in a surly mood."

"Hold on, don't you remember that according to Karen, her husband—Mark was his name—was camping in Canada with their son Scootch over the weekend?"

"Oh, yeah."

"So he can be ruled out."

Not for the first time, I wondered what Aunt Effie's secret to such a spry seventy-something brain was. I'd asked her before, and she'd said something about taking fish oil supplements, but I hoped that fantastic genes *I* might possess were also a factor.

I elaborated to Effie about Randy's simmering rage when he was waiting for Alexa at the coffee shop and how Alexa seemed a little scared of her husband.

"Ugh. I absolutely loathe that sort of man," Effie said. "Angry and bullying and controlling. And they always seem to be able to find women willing to play their game."

"Yeah. Omigosh, and I totally forgot what *else* Alexa told me. She said that a few weeks ago, Mikey started throwing cash around, buying expensive stuff that he normally could never have afforded."

"How does she know that?"

"I guess because Mikey and Randy were best frenemies? I don't know. Alexa said Randy's and Mikey's moms were best friends, so through childhood they were basically forced to spend time together even though they didn't particularly like each other. Anyway, I was thinking, if there was cash involved—*serious* cash—well, could that have been the motive for Mikey's death? The money disappeared. The police told Alexa as much."

"Well, well, well." Effie's eyes were glittering. "Now we're getting somewhere. Excellent work, Agnes. My husband Freddy—the New York State attorney general?—"

I nodded, even though I had never heard of Freddy before, since Aunt Effie had been married an unspecified number of times over a span of nearly sixty years.

"—*he* always said, 'Follow the money.'"

"Follow the money." I opened the washing machine. "Can all this stuff go in the dryer?"

"Mm."

I started throwing wet laundry into the dryer. *Thunk. Thunk.* "Except, how exactly do we follow the money? Go back to this list of suspects and ask questions about Mikey's purported cash?"

"Yes. And we should find out about everyone's alibis while we're at it."

"Good point. Alibis." *Thunk* went another wet laundry ball.

"Did Mikey steal that cash? Was someone paying him off? Did he sell something valuable that, maybe, someone thought he shouldn't have? Was he, heck, I don't know, working as a gigolo?"

"*Please*, Agnes. Don't make me ill."

"*Follow the money*," I murmured, mostly to myself. I looked at Effie. "I should've taken Clifford and Belinda's unopened bills when I had the chance. Why didn't I?"

"You were playing it safe, darling. Luckily, this is easily remedied. We can pop by there later tonight and grab them."

"Okay. But . . . we should be careful, Aunt Effie."

"What does being careful entail?"

"I don't know. But everyone knows where we live."

"I'm not scared. I *refuse* to be scared."

I wasn't as seasoned as Aunt Effie, but I was old enough to know that fear-based decisions are for the birds. So I took a deep breath and willed every last speck of fear from my mind.

It mostly worked.

# Chapter 11

I drove everyone back downtown in the Dustbuster. Lo and Myron would be joining their Tom Clancy pals for dinner, but they needed a ride. It was a clear, crisp evening, with stars twinkling overhead and a bite of wood smoke in the air.

It was the kind of night to be strolling hand-in-hand with your sweetie, not cruising around in the world's junkiest minivan with your cousin and a bunch of senior citizens made noisy by cocktails in the library.

Downtown was bright with streetlamps, strings of bulbs draped over Main Street, and light from busy restaurants, Polly's Ice Cream Parlor, and a few still-open shops. I found a spot in front of the bookstore and parked.

"Oh, goodie," Lo said, unbuckling. "This spot is perfect because I want to check and see who won Gourd Queen. They said the winner's name would be posted in the window."

I exchanged a look with Effie. Because *c'mon*. Did Lo really think she could've won Gourd Queen? The thought was so pathetic it made my stomach cramp.

The metal pumpkin was still in front of the bookstore, but it wasn't revolving. Although the bookstore was closed, the display window was all lit up. Children's picture books shared real estate with historical novels, thrillers, bird-watching guides, and color-ful cozy mysteries. And smack in the center of this was an orange sign on an easel that said:

CONGRATULATIONS TO THIS YEAR'S
HARVEST PARADE ROYALTY WINNERS!
GOURD QUEEN· AGNES BLYTHE
PUMPKIN PRINCESS· DELILAH FORTUNE
* SPONSORED BY DICKENS NEW AND USED BOOKS *

Shut. The. Door.

"You won!" Lo screamed, grabbing my arm. "You won Gourd Queen!"

I stared blankly at the sign as Lo shook me like a rag doll. "How is that possible?" I finally said. "Who voted for me?"

"Most of the people, apparently!"

Chester was smirking. Not a good combo with the smarmy little mustache.

"That nice young lady from the cupcake store came in sec-ond," Myron said. "She'll look real pretty in one of those beauty queen dresses."

*Delilah* had won Pumpkin Princess. We would have to ride on the float together. *Theoretically*, I mean. Because I was back-ing out of this thing ASAP.

Although—and I know, it is so immature and absurd and everything—I couldn't help indulging in a smug little glow.

I had gotten more votes than Delilah. Haha*ha*.

"Aren't you going to thank Lo?" Chester asked me.

"For what?"

"For spending about an hour writing your name on ballots? You must've gotten five hundred votes. I'm surprised the people who tallied them up didn't notice that every ballot had the same handwriting."

I rounded on Lo. "*You? Why?*"

"To get you the exposure you need, honey."

"Exposure?" My mind conjured up words like *windburn* and *pants falling down*.

"In the town dating scene. All the bachelors out there need to know what they're missing."

"I'm not doing it," I said.

"Oh, come on, Agnes, be a sport," Effie said. She was standing a few paces off, smoking.

"Why not?" Hank said. "Nothing ventured, nothing gained."

"*Why not?*" I cried. "Maybe because I'll feel embarrassed standing on that float in a big poofy dress and waving? I find enough ways to embarrass myself accidentally. I don't need to deliberately sign up for surefire routes to humiliation."

"You must stop being so very cynical, Agnes," Effie said.

"I'm not cynical! I'm *sane*. There's a difference!"

"I gave up being cynical when I was in my thirties," Effie said. "It was so liberating. Being cynical is simply a way to protect yourself from pain, but it also prevents you from fully immersing yourself in life—"

"I am in no mood to listen to Effie Winters's Philosophy Hour, okay?" I said. "Who runs the Gourd Queen thing, anyway? I need to tell them I'm out."

"The Harvest Festival Parade Committee," Effie said, billowing smoke like Mount Kilauea. "You'd want to talk to the chairperson, Elaine Cruz, about backing out—but I don't think you should."

"Elaine Cruz?"

"She owns the bookstore," Chester said.

"Well, I think you'd be an inspiration up on that float," Lo said, hooking her arm through Myron's. "We'll take a taxi back tonight, okay? You enjoy yourselves." They set off toward the Thai restaurant.

I trailed after the others in the other direction, feeling way hotter and sweatier than the weather warranted. Oh, I'd been in parades before. Playing my clarinet in the high school marching band.

Gourd Queen? Me? *Snort.*

\* \* \*

That's Italiano was warm inside, with a gentle hubbub, accordion music, and simmering tomato and melty, cheesy aromas that made my mouth water. Otis was already seated at one of the white-and-red checked tables. Across the table from him, my best friend Lauren was deep in conversation with a dark-haired guy I assumed was Otis's college buddy.

What was Lauren doing here? And why was she in full Vintage Amazon battle regalia—i.e., Marilyn Monroe lipstick, winged eyeliner, and a wiggle dress?

"Go ahead and sit with your friends," Aunt Effie whispered to Chester and me. "I'll manage the oldsters." She said this in a way that made clear she didn't consider *herself* an "oldster."

"Thanks," I said.

"Why didn't you tell me Lauren would be here?" Chester whispered to me ferociously as we wove our way through the tables.

"Because I didn't *know*," I whispered back. "Trust me, I would've let you know so you could've put on a better outfit."

"Like you should talk!" Chester whisper-snarled, ripping off his terry cloth sweatband. "Anyway, I find Lauren's addiction to epic fantasy novels a bit cloying."

"Uh-huh."

"And all that red lipstick . . . how could you even kiss her?" Chester flushed blotchily.

"Ew, no fantasizing about kissing my best friend."

Loudly, to Lauren, he said, "Hello. Hi. How are you? I'm great! I'm—" *Cough.* "—I'm great. Doing some pretty heavy-duty demo at the inn. With a sledgehammer."

This was untrue.

Lauren looked bored as she sipped water through a straw. "Hey, Chester."

"Hi," I said to Otis, my hands dangling.

Basically, Chester and I were the Awkward Nerd Brigade. What was *up* with the Blythe gene pool, anyway?

"Hey," Otis said to me. A warm smile, but no kiss. Not even on the top of my head.

Why couldn't I just reach out and touch him? It wasn't like that was against the rules—this wasn't an Edith Wharton novel, for gosh sakes.

But I just . . . couldn't. It was like Otis had this new, impenetrable force field around him. I figured he hadn't heard about my Gourd Queen (pseudo) victory yet. I decided to leave him in the dark.

I sank into the chair beside him. Chester took the head of the table, kind of far away from the rest of us, his bugging eyes glued on Lauren.

Otis introduced the dark-haired guy as Jake Barbosa, a friend from college. Jake looked like one of those smooth, bronze, body-hair-less dudes from the designer underpants ads.

"How do you know Otis?" I asked Jake.

"We met at RIT—I'm originally from Rhode Island, though."

Rochester Institute of Technology was a pretty prestigious alma mater. Otis had majored in engineering there, but he needed to work with his hands and hated desk work, which is why he had taken over the family automotive shop.

"Jake's a brain surgeon in Syracuse," Lauren said to me with shining eyes. "Otis introduced us this afternoon at the Kick-Off."

"Lauren's shop is great," Jake said. "Really neat."

"He bought that seventies windbreaker with the rainbow patch," Lauren gushed. "It looks perfect on him."

Since when had Lauren been interested in doctors with Hollywood-grade teeth who said "neat"? She had always insisted that her dream man had a sensitive artist's soul, first-edition Tolkiens, and was good with parrots.

Lauren, Jake, and Chester started a conversation about CrossFit, which was apparently how Jake whiled away the hours when he wasn't saving lives and stuff.

"I wanted to ask you about something," I said to Otis. "Earlier today, I happened to, uh, run into Karen Brown, Mikey Brown's sister-in-law—did you know she lives right across the street from your Grandma Bee?"

"Of course."

"Uh-huh, and she said something weird about your grandma. She said that your grandma has been acting . . ." I swallowed. "Crazy."

"Crazy?" Otis frowned. "Grandma's not crazy."

"I know, I know—I don't want to upset you. I just wanted to tell you, in case you need to . . . Your grandma is getting up there in years, so if a neighbor has seen anything that suggests maybe someone needs to go over to check on her more often . . ."

"Oh my gosh." Otis raked a hand through his hair, which

stood up and didn't lay back down. "I guess I always thought Grandma Bee, of all people, would keep her wits about her forever. Did Karen say what Grandma did?"

"No, and I didn't want to press her. Karen's family is going through a tough time, so—"

"Hold on. Why were you at Karen's house?"

"Um."

"Why?"

Did I feel crummy? Why, yes. Yes, I did. Was I going to tell Otis the unvarnished truth? Heck, no. He had specifically asked me not to meddle, so it would strain our relationship if he knew I was ignoring his wishes.

The annoying little bug-voice in the back of my head said, *This is* already *straining your relationship, you twerp!*

I wanted to take a can of Raid to that voice.

"It was about Chamber of Commerce things," I said. "The Harvest Festival and all that. Remember I gave the welcome speech to the Peeper Prize judge this afternoon?"

"Oh. Right. Where that lady for some strange reason yelled to everyone that you're single?"

"Uh-huh." This was a whisper.

Thankfully, at that moment the waiter arrived.

Everyone ordered dinner. I ordered the eggplant parmesan, one of That's Italiano's famed specialties and, I hoped, a piping hot dish of comfort. When the basket of breadsticks arrived, I got down to it. So did Chester, who sort of hunkered over his bread as he watched Lauren and Jake flirt.

"So, I, uh, I saw you with Delilah this afternoon," I said to Otis.

"I was helping her move some shelving in the back of her shop. Is . . . is that a problem?"

"A problem? What? Ha!" I slapped my thigh.

Otis was watching me closely. "You aren't . . . jealous of Delilah, are you?"

"What? *No.*" I scoffed. "Well okay, maybe I'm a little jealous about how she gets to eat buttercream frosting all day *as her job*, but otherwise, no. And I mean, you're free to do whoever—I mean, *whatever*—you want."

*Cool, Agnes. Real cool.*

"Okay," Otis said, "because I agreed to help because Delilah doesn't know many people in town."

"How do *you* know her?"

"She's my cupcake supplier. Don't tell the cops. She makes the best German chocolate, even better than Grandma Bee's, actually."

I wanted to kick something *so badly*. Instead, I reached for a second breadstick, ripped off a chunk, and stuffed it in my mouth.

"Have you, um, heard anything more from the police?" I asked Otis after I'd chewed, swallowed, and released more carb-triggered endorphins into my bloodstream.

"They brought me in for more questioning."

"Are you serious? Why?"

"Well, they figured out the time of death and wanted to see if I had an alibi or not. The coroner examined the body, and it turns out that Mikey died between ten AM and one yesterday—hours before I got there. What he was doing at the shop at that time on a Sunday, I have no idea." A flicker of something passed across Otis's eyes.

He *did* have an idea what Mikey had been doing at the shop off-hours. But I didn't feel super comfy about grilling him in front of the others.

"I was shopping at the mall in Lucerne with Grandma Bee

at the time of Mikey's death," Otis said. "I take her once a month."

"You're such a nice grandson," I said.

"Who said anything about nice? I *love* mall walking." Otis chuckled. "So basically I have an airtight alibi—jeez, I can't believe I'm talking about this kind of thing."

"But that's great news!" I said. Was Otis really off the hook so tidily? Could I go back to life-as-usual so soon? "If you have an airtight alibi, then you're free to leave town, right? We can still go on our Adirondacks trip next—"

"Nope."

"What? Why not?"

Otis sighed. He rubbed the back of his neck. He lowered his voice. "Okay, well, the thing is, a witness overheard me having a . . . a heated argument with Mikey about money the day before yesterday."

*Money.* It felt as if a steel clamp had tightened around my ribs. Because hadn't Aunt Effie and I just agreed to follow the money?

"What money?" I asked. "*Who* heard you?" It wasn't like Otis to argue with anyone about anything, honestly, and— heated? I just couldn't picture it.

"I noticed that a few hundred bucks were missing at the shop. From the lockbox. And since Mikey, Grandpa, and I were the only ones with access to the lockbox, I decided I had to ask Mikey about it. He got defensive, I got frustrated, he started guilting me about being suspicious of him, and that's when I noticed that Sharleen Kowalski was standing there in the garage doorway, hanging on to every word."

"Sharleen Kowalski? That lady from the gardening shop?"

"Uh-huh. She was there to pick up her car. Apparently she

told the police about the argument—I can't really blame her—so despite my taking-Grandma-to-the-mall alibi, I'm still not off the hook. I got the impression Detective Albright is going to try to verify my alibi."

"With Grandma Bee."

"Yeah."

*With Grandma Bee, who Karen said is a few sticks of gum short of a pack. Great.*

"And . . . there's more," Otis said.

"No."

"Yep. According to the coroner, the locations of the wrench wounds to Mikey's head suggest that he was *not* fleeing his assailant."

"So he knew his killer?"

"Maybe. Or, if the killer was not known to him, that he had a high level of comfort around the killer and didn't expect to be hit. Naturally, Detective Albright has latched on to option one—that Mikey knew his killer, because his killer was me. Don't worry. This will all fizzle out once my alibi is verified by Grandma. I hate the idea of her having to talk to the police, but she's tough."

"Right," I said, my belly knotting. "Hey, where did Mikey work before you hired him last month?"

"Well, he had been unemployed for a few months, but before that he worked at the Speedy Lube in Lucerne."

"Did they fire him?"

"Uh . . . yeah. For being late all the time. I can tell you're wondering why *I* hired him."

"Maybe."

"I guess I just felt kind of sorry for him, you know? He had just turned forty and he was still living like he was twenty-one and with all the time in the world to get his life together. Mikey was the star quarterback at Naneda High twenty-some years ago—that was actually on his résumé, believe it or not—and I guess he just never got over it. After high school, he dropped out of community college after one semester, and then he had this long string of unskilled jobs until by some miracle he got on-the-job training at an automotive repair shop in Syracuse. Plus, I know Karen, and I knew how much Mikey drove her nuts. When I hired Mikey, I just wanted to . . . help. Can we talk about something else?"

"Sure."

"Have you unpacked your boxes yet?"

"What boxes?"

"You know what boxes."

"I haven't had time."

Otis kept bugging me about those unpacked boxes in my room at the inn. I wasn't sure why, since he wasn't controlling, nor was he especially domestic. His own little bungalow on A Street was tidy but bare-bones. I figured that bringing up my unpacked boxes was just him trying to make conversation.

# Chapter 12

The talk at our table at That's Italiano turned to other topics. Lauren and Jake kept flirting, Chester tried to outshine Jake by quoting Wordsworth poems between bites of lasagna (didn't work), Otis acted a little depressed, and I gave my eggplant parmesan my full attention since Otis was acting so withdrawn.

I couldn't stop obsessing about how (a) Effie and I had agreed to "follow the money" and (b), lo and behold, Otis had had an argument with Mikey *about money*.

Not. Good.

Needless to say, I barely tasted the eggplant parmesan, and suddenly my plate was empty.

When Chester started trying to convince Jake and Lauren that he was now "technically a fitness instructor" since he taught a calisthenics class at the inn "every morning," I signaled for the check.

We were out on the sidewalk, waiting for Aunt Effie, Hank, and Dorothea to finish paying their own check, when Otis, Jake, and Chester got involved in a conversation about cars. Even Chester could talk cars, since his beyond-crappy Datsun required as much maintenance as a ninety-year-old showgirl.

"So what's with Mr. Brain Surgeon CrossFit?" I whispered

to Lauren. "I noticed he was really enjoying his spinach leaf dinner."

"He's eating low-carb," she whispered back. "He follows the Paleo Diet."

"What, he personally runs down and kills his own mastodon burgers when he's not foraging for berries and nuts?"

"Hey, if not eating carbs is what gave him a six-pack, I'm not complaining."

Aw. Poor, poor lovesick Chester. He and I both have precisely *one* pack, which sort of obscures the snap on our jeans.

"Since when do you care about six-packs?" I whispered. "And how do you even know he *has* one?"

"Come on. Look at him. Anyway, Agnes, you should talk about liking hot guys."

"That's not why I like Otis." *That's not why I love him. Even though he shuts me out and eats other ladies' cupcakes.*

"Agnes, it's time for us dorky girls to reach out and grab what we want. Just because we're smart and not into spray tanning doesn't mean we shouldn't have our pick of the crop. What's with Otis?" Lauren's eyes flicked to Otis. "He seems . . . depressed. So do you."

"I'll tell you later. Suffice it to say that things have gone from zero to cray-cray in one day. Oh—and I need to dry-clean that dress you lent me before I give it back."

"Okaaaay."

Jake pulled Lauren into the conversation, and then Otis was next to me.

"You look tired," he said.

"*You* look tired." I hadn't told Otis about being apple-bobbed, obviously, since that would entail telling him I had, y'know, gone and spooked the killer. But the money argument he'd told me about was still bugging me. Maybe if I was blunt and got everything out in the open, this miserable awkwardness would go away.

"So," I said in my most casual, friendly voice, "earlier today I was talking to Alexa Rice, and she told me Mikey had this big influx of cash a few weeks ago, and I'm starting to get worried because you said you had that argument. With Mikey. About money . . ." My voice trailed off. I hugged my cardigan around myself.

Otis's mouth was tight. "Listen, Agnes," he said softly, so that the others wouldn't hear. "I'm just going to come right out and say this. First, you tell me that you just *happened* to be at Karen's house, where she made that comment about my grandma being crazy, and now you're saying you just *happened* to fall into conversation with Alexa, the wife of Mikey's best friend?"

"Wait—Mikey and Randy *were* friends?"

"What difference does it make? The point is, I know you're sleuthing, and I think it's a really bad idea. Number one, it's dangerous, and number two, you could tick off the police, and, frankly, the fact that you keep lying to me is ticking *me* off, too."

"What?" My eyes grew wide.

Otis had never once been mad at me before. Of course, we had only been sorta-dating for about a month, and there's a first time for everything.

"Don't look at me like that, Agnes."

"Like what?"

"Like some kind of Precious Moments figurine. Listen, I'm sorry. It's . . ." He pushed a hand through his hair, messing it up. "Listen, I just don't want you to . . . Focus on helping the Chamber make the harvest festival go great—Naneda really needs it, especially with the news of Mikey making it to some of the big regional news shows and newspapers. Plus, you've got your work cut out for you, what with hiring an architect for the inn renovation, and—" Otis made a lopsided smile. "—finally unpacking those boxes of yours."

"Ugh." The thought of all those unpacked cardboard boxes suddenly felt like a dead weight sucking me down. "Honestly, I'm considering just dumping them in one of those storage pods or something."

Otis's face suddenly shuttered. "A storage pod. So they'll be all ready to go for your next move."

"I can't deal with unpacking boxes right now. Deciding what to keep and what to get rid of—how can I even know, when where I'm living is temporary?"

"Huh." Otis turned to the others. "Listen, I've gotta go." He went to Jake and gave him a hug and a slap on the back. "Great seeing you, man." He turned to Lauren and Chester. "Don't get Jake into any trouble, okay?" Last, Otis turned to me. "Good night, Agnes." No hug. No kiss. No smile. Then he said softly, so the others wouldn't hear, "I think we need to take a break."

I reared back. "*What?*"

"I just . . . I need some space, okay? To be alone and . . . and deal with all this. Okay?"

"No, it is *not* okay."

"I'm sorry, Agnes." Otis turned and set off down the lamplit sidewalk.

I watched him go, my lungs tight and my eyeballs hot.

What had just happened?

Wait. I'd meant that living at the inn felt temporary, but Otis must've thought I meant my living in *Naneda* was temporary. Which it was . . . maybe. Because applying to grad school suddenly seemed like more of a possibility.

"Everything okay, Agnes?" Lauren said.

I couldn't answer.

* * *

After the gaggle had been delivered to the inn and Chester had gone home, Effie and I got into her Cadillac and drove through the night to Birch Grove B and B.

Believe me, with Otis saying he wanted to "take a break," I was in no mood to go poking around in other people's recycling bins. I was in the mood to eat Ben & Jerry's and watch a mopey movie while wearing sweatpants. Otis said he needed a break to deal with what was happening in his life, but we both knew that was only kinda true. He also needed a break because I wouldn't stop snooping. But, talk about a catch-22, as long as Otis was a murder suspect who could, theoretically, be wrongfully imprisoned, I was all over this investigation like white on rice.

Hopefully I wasn't making the biggest mistake of my life.

Effie rolled to a stop at the curb across the street from Birch Grove.

"Tons of lights are on," I whispered, staring at the house's facade.

"It's only about ten o'clock. Go on. You'll be fine. Channel your inner panther. I'll wait here so we can make a quick getaway." *Snick* went Effie's lighter as she fired up a ciggy.

I got out and tiptoed across the shadowy lawn to the side of the house.

When I reached the recycling bins, they were empty.

* * *

Later, up in my room, I sat down on my bed with my phone, found the number for Dickens New and Used Books, and dialed. After suffering through their recorded spiel about fall hours and toddler story time and punching 2 a couple of times, I got through to Elaine Cruz's personal mailbox. I left a message telling her I was the Gourd Queen winner and that I needed to discuss the situation with her so could she please call me back.

Sometimes I can't believe the sentences that come out of my own mouth.

Then, just for kicks, I went to the bathroom doorway and looked at the rotten floorboards. It would feel really good—no, *amazing*—to pry those up. Get rid of the rot. Set that floor on the path to recovery. It wasn't terribly late. I could remove a few boards, right?

I laced my sneakers back on, went downstairs, and headed out to the toolshed. I yanked a string to switch on the lightbulb. There it was, sturdy and unassuming, leaning in a dim corner next to a shovel: the crowbar.

I smiled.

*   *   *

Twoish hours later, untidy stacks of cracked, stinky, 150-year-old floorboards filled the attic hallway. Antique nails, charming in their irregularity, lay scattered everywhere. The bathroom floorboards had come up without much protest, although it hadn't been as easy as I'd imagined. On HGTV, demolition happens in a montage with a sprightly soundtrack.

This, however, wasn't pretty. The rotten boards were spongy, even powdery in spots, but the boards that weren't rotten had been harder to pry up. I'd braced the curve of the crowbar on the joists below and shimmied until the nails squeaked and popped free.

*Yeah.* I might not be able to hang onto a sorta-boyfriend, but I could demolish a floor. So there.

What remained was a grid of floor joists and a few pipes, below which were the lath and plaster that made up the ceiling of the floor below. I had to walk on the joists like a tightrope walker; one wrong step and I'd go crashing through.

I was breathless, sweaty, grimy, buzzing with exhaustion, and I had the disgusting suspicion that my hair was now harboring millions of wet rot fungus spores. But I had done it. The floor was gone.

What came next, I wasn't sure. But hey, you know what they say about hitting rock bottom: there's nowhere to go but up.

\* \* \*

The next day was Tuesday. I dragged myself out of bed before dawn and dressed in leggings, an oversized sweatshirt, sneakers, and my glasses. Because I'd taken a late-night shower and gone to sleep with wet hair, I looked like road kill. Even though I'd worn gloves the previous night, my palms were raw from all that crowbarring. Bad hair, sore hands . . . those were still no match for the Otis-induced ache in my heart.

I climbed into the Dustbuster and made the sojourn to Flour Girl Bakery. I had agreed to do this so Chester could get some extra sleep. After all, he had to work the janitorial night shift at the middle school on weekdays.

As I sat in the bakery waiting for my order, I picked up the latest *Naneda Gazer*.

Aaaaand . . . there I was on the front page in grainy black and white, standing on the stage in Fountain Square and awkwardly holding out the bouquet for Hugh Simonian. Hugh looked slim and attractive in his jeans and plaid jacket. I, on the other hand, looked like a brunette Barbie caught on a wide-angle lens. Why had Aunt Effie made my hair so *huge*?

"*Great* picture," someone said.

I jumped, rattling the newspaper, and looked up.

"Delilah," I said. "I didn't even hear you."

"I'm light on my feet." She flashed her dimple. "I took a lot of dance classes as a kid. Ballet, tap, you name it. I was obsessed with Shirley Temple. I wanted to *be* her."

"Where did you grow up?"

"Indiana. I'm just a little midwestern girl." Delilah sipped from her to-go coffee cup.

"And what brought you to Naneda?" I was just making polite conversation. All I really wanted was to get away from Delilah. She had this sparkly gloating thing going on—and who wore that much mascara at six in the morning, anyway?

"I came here for a long weekend once with my boyfriend— that was when I was living in New York City, going to pastry school—"

*Pastry* school? Had I ever missed my calling.

"—before I moved back to Indiana, and I totally fell in love with Naneda on that trip. It's such a cute town! I told myself if I ever had the chance, I'd set up a cupcake store here. It feels like stepping back in time. The pace is slower, people are friendlier, and it seems like the perfect place to put down roots. I always wanted to live in a small town. I was raised by a single dad in the suburbs—the yucky suburbs, not the pretty ones—"

"Wait—you have a boyfriend?"

"*Ex.*" Delilah gave me a smile as fakey as a chimpanzee's. I assumed she was thinking about Otis and how she was in the process of stealing him.

I held her gaze. Neither of us was willing to lose the staring contest. My right eyelid started to twitch. *Hold on, Agnes, hold ON.*

I was spared from having to look away when the barista chirped, "Pumpkin spice latte on the bar!"

"Anyhoo," Delilah said, "congrats on winning Gourd Queen. We're going to have *so* much fun up on that float, aren't we? Oh, and isn't it great that we discovered that superimportant new clue that Mikey had a bunch of cash?"

"You . . . know about that?"

"Thought you were one step ahead of me, dincha? Nope, Agnes, you're going to have to try a little harder than that to be one step ahead of little ol' me! Why are looking at me like that?"

"Like what?"

"I hate to rain on your suspicion parade, Agnes, but I have an airtight alibi. Otis told me what the coroner said about Mikey's time of death—does that bug you?—and on Sunday, before I went in to work at the shop, I was with Alexa between ten and one. In Brighton, as a matter of fact, visiting her grandpa at his nursing home. He has dementia. Luckily, I was a candy striper in high school, so he finds my presence super soothing."

Aw, rats. Alexa had already mentioned that she and Delilah were together that day, and *that* meant Delilah couldn't be the murderer. Not that she even had a motive or anything. But I realized that, in the back of my mind, I had been hoping she'd get thrown in the slammer for murder, keeping Otis forever out of her reach.

"Here's my cappuccino," Delilah said. "I have to caffeinate before I start making today's batch of German chocolate cupcakes. I don't know why, but I just can't keep them in stock. Gotta go!" She swanned out of the bakery.

It occurred to me that maybe, just *maybe*, it wouldn't be so bad if I accepted the title of Gourd Queen, after all. Just to prove . . . well, to prove *something*.

Nah.

\* \* \*

When I shoved into the inn's kitchen with an armload of white paper bags, Chester and Aunt Effie were in a huddle at the table. They both looked up.

"Did you get sticky buns?" Chester asked.

I tossed him one of the sacks. "Why do you guys look like Act Three of *The Shining*?"

"Late last night Hank pounded on my door and woke me up to inform me that he heard mice in his wall," Effie said. Under her luminous makeup, she looked tired.

"Oh, no," I said. "Maybe he heard me ripping up the rotten floorboards in the attic bathroom last night."

"Ripping up floors at night?" Effie said. "Agnes, you need your beauty rest."

"You don't mind?" I asked her. "About the floor? I should have run it by you, but I was just itching to get those rotten boards out—"

"Mind?" Effie said. "Of course I don't mind. This is your project, too. Besides, the attic is your private space, to do with as you wish."

"Yeah, it's my project, but it's *your* inn."

"Tell me, what are you going to replace the floor with, wood or tile?"

"I was thinking vintage-style tile. Black and white mini hexagons?"

"I adore those."

"You need a subfloor first," Chester said through a mouthful of sticky bun. "Lined with a moisture barrier."

I had no idea what that meant, but I said, "Yeah, I know."

"Chester knows how to do carpentry," Effie said to me. "He'll cut the subfloor pieces for you."

"I will?" he said.

"Yes," Effie said, "because that's the kind of cousin you are."

"By the way, there *are* mice in the walls," Chester said through another bite of sticky bun. "They skitter around like a *Lawrence Welk Show* finale."

"I've heard them, too," I said, setting the rest of the bakery bags on the counter. "In the ceiling right above my bed. Chewing."

"Ugh! Why didn't you tell me?" Effie cried. "I told Hank he was surely mistaken."

"I assumed you knew," Chester said. "Hey, at least it's not rats. Rats smell disgusting."

"We'll get some mousetraps," Effie said.

"If you set mousetraps anywhere Hank can see them, you can't keep telling him he's delusional," Chester said.

"Why don't we let Tiger Boy inside?" I said. "He'll kill the mice, or at least scare them away—"

"He comes into the kitchen for food," Effie said, "but I've never set him loose in the rest of the inn. He's feral . . . although, on the plus side, I did see him killing a bird the other day."

"Not a plus for the North American songbird population," Chester said.

"He doesn't even have to be good at hunting mice," I said. "The mice just need to *smell* a cat, and then they'll move out."

"Get him a collar so he doesn't look like such a derelict," Chester said. "There's nothing you can do about all those notches in his ears, though, or the way he makes that face with one squinty eye like a boxer with an eye swollen shut."

This was all true. Tiger Boy looked tough.

"It's a plan, then," Effie said. "Invite the stray cat to live in the inn. Fabulous. Now, who moved my cigarettes?"

# Chapter 13

Fact: every hotel maid in the world deserves a Medal of Valor for her service. What. A. Job.

The gaggle weren't even as dirty as I imagine folks in, like, Vegas, can get. They didn't party. They weren't eating room-service barbecue ribs. They weren't sneaking indoor cigars or using the mattresses for Zumba practice. Still, making beds is an athletic undertaking, and scrubbing other people's toothpaste and hair out of sinks is an existential crisis.

Chester was exercising the gaggle out on the lawn. I could see them through the windows, with Tiger Boy looking on, flicking his tail, and the blue, blue lake beyond.

As I made up Dorothea's bed, I told Effie about my conversation with Delilah at the bakery. Effie wasn't helping with bed making. She had said something about osteoporosis and her lower back being in danger of snapping in half if she bent at the waist. Privately, I thought it was because if she bent at the knees, her skintight black jeans would rupture a seam.

"I have to say, I'm disappointed by this alibi Delilah has," Effie said.

"Join the club. But keep in mind, Alexa and Delilah could be covering for each other."

"Why?"

"Who knows? Also, how the heck did *she* figure out that Mikey had that influx of cash?"

"Alexa might have told her. Or perhaps Mikey bragged about the money to her."

"She *did* say Mikey was always going in to her shop to salivate over her and her strawberry cupcakes."

"She's the kind of gal who thinks the lamppost is making a pass at her if she bumps into it, Agnes. Some people are just like that."

"Conceited?"

"Well, on the surface. The reality is, they're tragically insecure."

What could Delilah possibly have to be insecure about? Not reaching her stolen-boyfriends quota for the week? "The point is, I can't let Delilah cut me off at the pass. If she figures out who killed Mikey before I do . . ."

"Otis might run away to a cabin in the woods with her?"

I scowled.

"I very much doubt that, Agnes. That man adores you."

"Yeah, right," I muttered, now tucking the sheet double time. "That's why he's completely blowing me off."

"Agnes, you aren't very experienced with men, are you?"

"I'm not going to answer that."

"Allow me, as one who has had an abundance of experience with men, to pass on a little tidbit of wisdom: when men feel stress, they act aloof. *Always.* And as a murder suspect, your scrumptious mechanic is under great stress. So, I might add, are his shirt sleeves with those *muscles*—"

"Aunt Effie!"

"Darling, I only aim to speak the truth. Now, what you

ought to do is put on some mascara and a low-cut dress, buy some cookies, and take them to his house. Mother Nature will take care of the rest."

"Omigod. Are you serious?" Actually, Otis did like cookies, especially oatmeal chocolate chip, but if I tried out the seductress-with-baked-goods routine on him *and it didn't work*, I would never, ever be able to look him in the eye again. Besides, how could I compete with Delilah's German chocolate cupcakes? "I think I'll stick to using my own personality," I said, "since Jessica Rabbit's is already taken."

"Suit yourself. But the method is tried and true, although sometimes one swaps out the cookies for rib eye."

"I am getting *way* too much relationship interference from women over the age of sixty! First Lo, now you—"

"We speak from a combined century of experience."

"Help me shake out this duvet," I grumbled.

\* \* \*

At a quarter to ten, Effie led Chester, the gaggle, and me into Lilting Waves Day Spa.

Karen was standing behind the front desk talking with the receptionist, and her eyes flared slightly before she beamed and said, "Welcome!"

I knew what she was thinking. Aunt Effie had enough filler and Botox to qualify as legally embalmed in some states, but Karen didn't have the fruit acid, salt scrub, and essential oil to even make a dent in the rest of us.

But spas peddle hope, and we'd signed up to be seasonally pampered, darnit. So Karen led us back to the changing rooms, and then Myron and Lo were whisked away by a white-smocked masseuse for their Couple's Cinnamon Massage. The rest of us were instructed to loiter in the softly lit relaxation area, reading magazines and sipping herbal tea in pink robes and slippers.

Dorothea was led away first. She was signed up for a pedicure.

Chester showed up in his pink robe, his heels hanging several inches out the backs of the slippers.

"They don't have men's size slippers," he said, helping himself to granola nuggets from a dish beside the tea stuff. "In case you were wondering."

"I assume you're getting the leg wax?" I joked, leafing through my *Self* magazine.

Chester munched granola, peering over my shoulder. "Those models are so photoshopped, they look like they're made out of some kind of Plasticine modeling compound."

"I know," I said. "They look like they'd melt if they stood too close to a radiator."

"What treatment are you having?"

"Pumpkin peel facial and brow shaping." Effie had insisted that if I didn't get my brows done, I was in imminent danger of being mistaken for an Ewok. And since Delilah had perfect eyebrows (so Otis was clearly into that), I needed perfect eyebrows, too. "You?"

"Nothing."

"Seriously, what?"

Chester muttered something, coughing at the same time.

"What?"

"He said *back wax*, darling," Effie said, gliding into the relaxation area in her pink robe.

"Aunt *Effie*," Chester yelped. "Can't I have *any* privacy?"

"No, dear. Not with your family."

"I dunno, Chester," I said, sipping my tea. "I think Lauren once told me that she's into cavemen."

"This has nothing to do with Lauren," Chester said, too loudly.

"Sure."

A spa technician appeared in the doorway. "Chester?" she said.

"Just close your eyes and think of Britain," I said to him as he got up to go.

He gave me a squinchy look over his shoulder.

After Chester left, Effie and I were alone. Effie asked me, "What time is your appointment?"

I looked at the clock on the wall. "In fifteen minutes."

"Oh, good, mine too." She stood. "Come on."

"Um . . . where are we going?"

Effie lowered her voice to a whisper. "To have a look at Karen's accounts."

"Are you crazy?" I whispered back.

"Come on. We'll lose our chance. I poked around a bit and stumbled upon Karen's office, and she's giving Hank his body scrub at the moment."

I burst into nervous laughter. "Hank? Body scrub?"

"He says he has a thyroid condition that prevents his skin from sloughing off properly."

"Okay, yuck, *no*, don't tell me more."

I followed Effie out of the relaxation room.

*   *   *

Karen's office was on the third story, way at the top of the quirkily laid out turn-of-the-century building.

"Um . . . how was it that you quote-unquote 'stumbled' upon this?" I asked Effie as, breathless, we emerged in the office. It was a pleasant space, with soft blush walls, skylights, and a sleek white desk forming an L shape. Windows overlooked an alleyway with dumpsters.

The desktop was uncluttered, with stacks of papers—spa-specials leaflets, it looked like—an open laptop, and—"It's her phone!" I whispered to Effie. A smartphone in a pink plastic case sat next to the computer.

"Well, what are you waiting for?" Effie said, jabbing a key on the laptop. The screen flashed to life.

"I can't—"

"It may be password protected, anyway."

I picked up the phone and swiped it on. "It isn't. I'm on the home screen."

Effie was clickety-clacking on the laptop. "This doesn't seem to be password protected, either. Oooh, looks like someone is addicted to eBay."

Feeling like a really crappy human being, I located the text-messaging icon on Karen's phone.

This was wrong. This was really, really wrong, and it went against everything I believed about people's right to privacy. Not to mention I'd once read that the virus and bacteria load on cell phones is catastrophic.

And yet . . . Karen might've murdered Mikey. Karen might've dunked me in that cold, dank, apple-bobbing water.

I opened her text messages.

A chain of texts between Karen and someone named Mark appeared.

"Who is Mark?" I whispered to Effie.

She was scrolling through what looked like an Excel file. "The husband. Remember, the one who was doing the OCD vacuuming?"

"Oh, right." I turned back to Karen's phone.

**Mark:** You left a towel on the bed again.

**Karen:** Sorry.

**Mark:** Apology accepted.

**Mark (a few hours later):** Could you PLEASE empty the crumb tray on the toaster after you use it?

No reply from Karen.

So Karen's husband was a clean freak. Granted, a little odd. And who empties the crumb tray on their toaster? I owned my toaster for, like, two years before I *accidentally* discovered the crumb tray.

I navigated my way to the list of all recent texts, and something else caught my eye. It was an exchange from Wednesday, between Karen and her son Scootch, whom we'd briefly met the day before.

**Karen:** Got another call from the principal's office.

**Scootch:** (Eye roll emoji)

**Karen (that evening):** Where are you? You are still grounded!

No answer from Scootch.

**Karen:** Officer Torres came by and said you and Duncan were seen smashing pumpkins on Oak Street. You are in BIG TROUBLE. I'm going to tell your father. The Canada camping trip is OFF.

No answer from Scootch.

And people think smartphones will help them keep tabs on their teenagers. Ha.

I scrolled up to read earlier messages between Karen and Scootch. There was a text from the previous Thursday at 7:32 PM.

**Karen:** DUNCAN'S MOM TOLD ME YOU THINK YOU'RE GOING WITH UNCLE MIKEY SUNDAY TO MEET RANDY AT GARAGE? THE ANSWER IS NO. YOU ARE GOING CAMPING WITH YOUR FATHER AFTER ALL IF IT IS THE LAST THING I DO.

No answer from Scootch.

Hold up. Mikey planning to meet Randy? At the *garage*?

Someone behind Aunt Effie and me cried, "Ex*cuse* me?"

I dropped the phone like it was hot. Effie straightened. We turned.

Karen was standing in the doorway, her face hot pink and contorted with fury. "What in the *hell* are you doing in my office?"

Effie and I looked at each other, then looked back at Karen.

"Oh," I said, "we just, um, needed to check our email."

"In my *private office*? What is the matter with you? People told me you're both crazy, but I didn't believe it till now." Karen pushed past Effie, slammed the laptop shut, and then snatched up her phone. "What, are you guys seriously *sleuthing*?"

"What?" I said, scoffing.

"The only sleuthing I do is into my subconscious," Effie said. "It's an absolute labyrinth. No, as my niece said, we merely wished to check our email—we're expecting important news—and we were under the impression that the computer here was available for spa clients' use."

"Well, it's not," Karen said, "so please go to the relaxation room." Her voice shook, and I couldn't tell if she was on the verge of tears or of blowing a gasket.

Effie and I slunk out.

When we had made it to the stairs, I whispered, "Did you see anything?"

"Yes. You?"

"Yep."

The relaxation room was unoccupied, so we sat down and, whispering, compared notes. I told Effie about the text messages—"I knew her son Scootch looked naughty," Effie said—and she told me what she'd seen on the computer.

"The first screen was Karen's eBay account. She has a dozen open bids on used designer shoes."

"Weird."

"I know. I love a bargain as much as the next person, but I draw the line at used shoes. Other people's foot odor?" Effie shuddered. "Anyway, I pulled up accounting sheets in Excel for the last two months."

"And?"

"The spa is just barely squeaking by. It's a wonder she's been able to keep her staff."

"Money," I said. "Everything keeps coming back to *money*."

"Agnes?" a spa technician said, appearing in the doorway.

\* \* \*

My facial was administered by a technician named Portia who was plump, almond-eyed, bleach blonde, and rocking a tan the color of a teak patio set. She greeted me so kindly, I assumed that Karen hadn't told her about the spying incident.

She started in with the cleansing and scrubbing and massaging. Just when I was beginning to doze off, she covered my eyes with cotton pads and painted something on my face that smelled like pumpkin pie and tingled. A lot.

"This is the peel," she said in her soothing, self-hypnosis-CD voice. She aimed a steady blast of warm steam on my face. "We'll let it sit for a few minutes."

"A few minutes?" I said. "I don't know if I can last that long." The tingle was becoming a burn.

"It's the enzymes," Portia said. "They gobble up all the dead skin just like Pac-Man, and your face will be as smooth as a baby's bottom. Some of my clients who are way older than you have just the nicest skin because they come in for one of these peels once a month, religiously."

"It . . . hurts," was all I could manage.

"Like, my client Alexa? She just turned forty, but her skin is radiant."

I forgot that my face felt like a marshmallow over open flame. "Alexa Rice?"

"Yeah. Do you know her?"

"Uh-huh."

"Doesn't she look amazing? Of course, she'll do anything to look younger." Portia's voice lapsed into a hush-hush, gossipy register. "She'll do anything to *feel* young again, too, and I mean *a-ny-thing.*"

"Anything? Like drink kefir?"

Silence.

"Wear SPF one hundred?"

No answer.

"Do that thing where Japanese fish nibble the dead skin off your feet?"

"Why are you so curious about Alexa?"

"I'm not," I lied. "I just want to know the secret of staying young."

"Okay, well, maybe I should've said, she would do . . . any*one*."

Wait. What? My eyes struggled to open underneath the cotton pads. I gave up. "Are you saying—?"

"I don't talk about my clients," Portia said in a prim voice. "That's the very first thing they teach you at beauty school: never talk about your clients."

"Right," I said. "Makes sense." A pause. "*But . . . ?*"

"Well . . . since you *know* her . . ." Dramatic pause. "Alexa is having an affair."

"Are you sure?"

"She told me so herself. She said it makes her feel young again. Hooking up in back seats, sneaking around, all the stuff she used to do back in high school. I guess she was one naughty girl. She said she was superpopular, cheer captain and all that, but now she's just stuck working at the orchard. I don't blame her for looking for thrills."

"Um . . . do you know who she's having the affair with?"

"No."

"What about her husband?" I asked. "Randy. Does he know about this?"

"Of course not! Omigosh, he would be *so mad*. He has the worst temper ever—not violent or anything, but she says sometimes he just *snaps*. Anyhoo, like I said, I don't really talk about my clients." Portia wiped the pumpkin peel off my face, put on mist and serum and lotion and SPF, and then said, "Okay, I'm all done with your facial." She got to her feet.

"Thanks," I said. "But what about my brows?" I wasn't going to admit it aloud, but I had started to get pretty psyched about having movie-star eyebrows.

"Oh, Karen does all the brow waxes," Portia said. "She's amazing at brows."

"Karen?" I said weakly.

"Yeah! I'll just go and get her."

"But—" I fell silent. Portia was gone.

# Chapter 14

I lay there on the spa table, weighing the pros and cons of having my brows waxed by Karen.

> Pros: I could try to make nice with her about spying on her text messages, or at least try to convince her that my motives had been good. (Unlikely.) Also, she was purportedly talented at shaping eyebrows.
> Cons: Hot wax. On my face.

Karen came in, all fakey smiles and generic small talk. She wasn't going to mention the Incident in Her Office.

Fine by me.

"Ding-dong *Sally*," she said, when she rolled her seat over and switched the white-hot torture chamber light on over my face. "We haven't had our brows done in a while, have we?"

I assumed "we" meant me.

"Not for a little while," I said. I think the last time had been before my college graduation, over six years before. Long enough for a complete reforestation. Heck, long enough for old growth.

Karen smeared hot wax in the space between my eyebrows.

"Wow," I said nervously, "that's not as hot as I thought it would be."

"Oh, I wouldn't burn you," Karen said tightly. "Not with you being the Peeper Prize liaison, and the Lake Club Masquerade being tomorrow and—is this true?—you being Gourd Queen on Saturday?"

"Um," was all I said. Elaine Cruz had yet to call me back, and I didn't feel like explaining to Karen, who was exuding electric aggression, that I was planning on backing out of the parade.

The warm wax actually felt relaxing, and the ripping part wasn't as unpleasant as it could've been, and before I knew it, Karen chirped, "Okay! All done! Mason will take care of you up front." She got up and left.

I struggled upright, drank a glass of cucumber water, and found my way back to the women's changing room, where I got dressed. A few minutes later, I emerged into the front waiting area, carrying the hot-pink leather bag Aunt Effie had loaned me since my shoulder bag had been stolen.

By a killer.

I actually kinda liked the hot-pink bag, although it probably had cost as much as a used car and made the rest of me look slightly slobby by comparison.

I spotted Myron and Lo reading magazines and looking fresh and relaxed.

"Hi," I said, sitting down beside Lo. "How was the massage?"

"Oh, honey." Lo shook her head, hand over her mouth. "Oh, *no*."

"What?" I touched my cheek. Had the pumpkin peel turned me into beet slaw?

"Your skin looks wonderful," Lo said, "but . . ."

Myron looked up from his *Popular Mechanics*. "It's your eye-brows, kid. They're kinda . . ."

"Sparse," Lo said.

Myron said, "I was gonna say cockeyed, but yeah, they're sparse, too."

I ran to a mirror on the wall. At first, I didn't even recognize myself because so much of my eyebrows had been removed. It was like seeing your house after the furniture has been hauled away.

"Omigod," I choked out.

It would've been one thing if Karen had botched both eye-brows in the same way. But they were two different lengths, and the left one was thicker on the inner corner, like a caterpillar head. They were both razor thin—like, Greta Garbo thin—and arched. "I look like a freak!"

"Hel-lo," Effie called, breezing into the waiting room.

I spun around.

Effie stopped short. "Oh, *diddle*, Agnes. What have you *done*?"

"*I* didn't do it! It was Karen."

"Oh, dear. Well, there is no *fixing* those—"

"What do you *mean*?"

"—but you should ask for a full refund. It's odd, because I heard Karen did the best brows in town."

I lowered my voice to a hot whisper. "Don't you see what's going on here? Karen butchered my eyebrows on purpose. As *revenge*."

"Is there some kind of problem?" Mason the receptionist asked, walking in and settling himself at his desk.

I turned to Mason.

His jaw went slack. "Oh."

"I need to speak with Karen," I said, trying to sound calm but fully aware of the way my voice shook.

"Karen? She just left."

"I didn't see her."

"She always parks out back."

I jogged into the spa's inner sanctum, passing the relaxation room and the stairs, and burst out a rear door into the alleyway.

A black SUV was just turning at the end of the alley. It disappeared.

*Argh!*

I turned and stormed back into the spa.

Mason refunded my fifteen dollars for the bad brows, but that hardly seemed like appropriate compensation for having to go around for six weeks looking like I'd been attacked by a Weedwacker.

"Here," Effie said. "Wear these." She passed me her ginormous lemur sunglasses, which went with the hot-pink bag but not the rest of my overall look. I breathed a sigh of relief when I saw in the mirror that the sunglasses hid the place where my eyebrows once had been.

*   *   *

We took the gaggle to the Cup 'n' Clatter for lunch. Sadly, no amount of biscuits and gravy could distract me from my bad eyebrows. It seemed as if people were staring at them in horrified fascination. Maybe I was just being paranoid.

"Honey, you're never gonna fit into your Gourd Queen gown if you keep at those biscuits," Lo said.

I got it. She was being motherly, in a circa-1963 way. Still, I snapped, "Maybe that's the point."

Effie said, "She'll fit into it just fine. The worst-case scenario is she wears a few pairs of Spanx."

"I'm not wearing Spanx! I wore them once and my left leg almost got gangrene."

"She's exaggerating," Effie said to Lo. "She only got pins and needles."

"There will be no Gourd Queen gown," I said, "because I'm not accepting the title."

This fell on deaf ears, apparently.

"Well, I'm just saying that you'll be up there on that float for all the men in town to see," Lo said, "and you want to look your best. It could be your last chance. We'll have to draw on some new eyebrows for you. I have a Mary Kay brow definer pencil in my makeup kit back at the inn."

I resisted the urge to bang my forehead on the tabletop.

\* \* \*

After lunch, Chester took the gaggle out to one of the wineries for a tasting and Effie and I went to the hardware store.

"We need to talk to Scootch," I said to Effie as we walked up and down the aisles of lumber out back. "We need to ask him about this meeting at the garage between Mikey and Randy on Sunday. That could be the key to everything." I peered at a cryptic lumber label. "What kind of wood do you use to build a subfloor?"

"Scootch is probably at school right now," Effie said, "and what's more, we can't very well corner and interrogate a teenage boy. That could have serious legal ramifications."

"Yeah. You're right. Why don't we confront Karen, then?"

"After what she did to your brows?"

"*Because* of what she did to my brows. I'm mad enough to

cage fight her! And anyway, we never asked about her alibi on Sunday."

"I don't think this will go over well."

"I don't care." I spotted a hardware store employee and waved.

Twenty minutes later, we had four huge sheets of plywood, a roll of moisture barrier, a roll of crack-suppression membrane, an electric radiant heating kit with wire grids, and tubes of construction adhesive crammed onto the folded-down rear seats of the Dustbuster. I wasn't sure what I was going to do with all that stuff, but that's what cousins and YouTube are for.

Next, Effie and I drove to Karen's house.

No cars in the driveway. When we rang the doorbell, no one answered.

As we were driving away, though, a curtain twitched in an upstairs window.

Creepy.

\* \* \*

The gaggle came home from the winery thoroughly drunk, and after trying out the antique billiards table Boyd had delivered the day before, they all went up to bed.

I hauled the rotted floorboards from the attic to the rent-a-dumpster, took a shower, and turned in early. I hadn't heard from Otis, of course, since we were "taking a break." I refused to even think about that. All the not-thinking made my stomach hurt.

Out of sheer curiosity—I swear—on my smartphone I looked up the university in Seattle where my friend Charlotte was attending graduate school. The campus was gorgeous, and Seattle, ringed by blue water, green fir trees, and snowcapped mountains, looked like some magical realm, as far from upstate New York as could be.

Then I went to the anthropology department's web page. Yep. All of the materials I'd used to apply to Naneda University's program the previous year would still work. Applying would be easy-peasy. To heck with Otis not really being mine, and the inn not really being mine, and Naneda being, well, *Naneda*. I could just . . . *go*.

I lay there in my bed under the eaves for a long time, listening to the mice chewing inside the ceiling, staring at my heap of cardboard boxes and wondering if I would ever find the right time and place to unpack them.

\*　\*　\*

The next morning, Chester helped me unload the floor-building supplies from the back of the Dustbuster.

"I'll cut the subfloor pieces for you," he said, "but you'll have to help me carry them up to the attic later, okay?"

"Sure. Thanks." Power-saw usage wasn't in my skillset, but Chester was a pretty good carpenter. He'd worked as a set-builder for a Shakespeare company during summers in college.

"I still can't believe you're undertaking this project in the middle of everything else that's going on," he said.

"Me neither."

The gaggle had Riesling hangovers, so we didn't leave the inn until lunchtime. Aunt Effie and I took them back to the Cup 'n' Clatter, since they all had expressed a desire for greasy, carby dishes.

While we were eating, the Peeper Prize Judge Hugh Simonian came in and was seated at a table by himself. He ordered dish after dish, taking only a bite or two of each and tapping at a computer tablet as he did so.

I loved the Cup 'n' Clatter with a passion. Seeing someone

just—just *judge* it in cold blood, made indignation surge in my heart. But that was silly. Judges gotta judge.

After lunch, we walked down the street to Lauren's shop, Retro Rags, to search for things to wear at the Lake Club Harvest Masquerade that evening. Everyone wanted to go (even, weirdly, Hank), and tickets would be available for purchase at the door.

"Everyone stay far, far away from those Headless Horseman masks they're peddling," I said as we passed Harries Stationery. "They give me the creeps."

"Hi!" Lauren said when we poured into her small shop. She put down a doorstop-sized novel with a sorcerer on the cover. "How can I help you?"

"Oh, we're just browsing," Lo said. "Myron, just look at this blue blazer! I haven't seen lapels that big since our wedding day."

"Goodness me," Dorothea said, "wouldn't that look handsome on Hank." She blushed a little.

"Who, me?" Hank said, confused.

While the gaggle and Effie browsed, I went over to Lauren at the counter.

She clapped a hand over her mouth. "What happened to your eyebrows?"

"There are consequences to poking your nose in other people's business."

"Meaning?"

I took a deep breath and spilled. It took a solid five minutes, and I didn't even mention the part about Otis and me taking a break, or how I was toying with the idea of applying to grad school in Seattle. That stuff was too sensitive to share. Also, I knew Lauren would be upset about the possibility of me moving away.

"I don't get why you feel like you have to find the murderer, Agnes," Lauren said when I'd finished. "Everyone knows Otis wouldn't kill someone. The police will figure that out soon enough."

"What if they don't?" My voice was shriller than I would've liked. "What if they arrest him? And anyway, what's wrong with helping someone you care about? Because that's all I was trying to do! *Help*—"

"Otis is crazy about you Agnes. You don't have to make some grand gesture to prove anything to him."

"He's not."

"Not what?"

"Crazy about me."

Lauren snorted. "Are you blind? No. Never mind. Don't answer that. You *are* blind."

How could I say aloud, even to my best friend, that I couldn't understand what Otis saw in me? He was just about perfect. He was kind, ridiculously handsome, with a great body, smarts, and an easy self-confidence. Next to him, I felt . . . flawed. Dumpy. Angsty.

I felt as if no one could understand why he'd want to be with me.

Over the past weeks, our new relationship had felt like a fragile, enchanted bubble. I had made sure not to get too comfortable, because if I got comfortable, settled in, made myself at home, it would hurt that much more when the bubble inevitably popped.

"All I'm saying," Lauren said, "is that maybe your sleuthing is . . . overkill. I mean, someone dunked you in a barrel of water? You could've been killed."

"The police said it was a mugging."

"That's stupid."

"See?" I threw my hands wide. "They're getting it wrong!"

"I guess I see your point. Well, if I were you, I would keep trying to talk to Karen Brown. Anyone who would savage someone's eyebrows like that is not thinking straight, plus, that text about her son going with Uncle Mikey to meet Randy at the garage? Completely fishy. Oh, and I'd also make sure Alexa and Delilah's joint alibi holds water."

"Yeah, that's definitely something I need to look into."

Lauren nodded. "Alexa seems nice enough, but she's not exactly a stable person, you know? And Delilah . . . even though she looks and acts like some kind of cute Japanese anime character, something about her bugs me. Anyway, are you still going to the Lake Club Masquerade tonight?"

"Yeah. And I know Aunt Effie roped you into being in the bachelorette auction."

"Nothing like selling yourself off like livestock."

"It's not selling *yourself*. Just your time."

"Maybe Jake will come. I'd give *him* all my time for free."

# Chapter 15

The gaggle decided to keep shopping downtown while Effie and I ran some errands. We had an appointment with another architect who had a proposal for the Stagecoach Inn renovation, and then we needed to go shopping for odds and ends. We planned to pick the gaggle up at four o'clock at Fountain Square and bring them back to the inn.

While Effie and I were making our way to the place we'd parked the Dustbuster, I caught sight of Belinda Prentiss through the big plate-glass windows of Lakeside Fitness. Behind a row of furiously pedaling, ellipting, and treadmilling citizens, she was talking to a guy at a desk.

"Psst," I said. "Aunt Effie." I tipped my head in Belinda's direction. "Belinda Prentiss *at the gym.*"

"So?"

"Strong hands? Dragging corpses? Holding people's heads underwater in bobbing-for-apples barrels?"

"*No.* Really? Doesn't she look like she'd stick to exercising with those rubber fitness balls? You know, the ones that make people look like they're doing Sea World tricks?"

"Let's go and see."

"Fine."

Inside, pop music blasted tinnily over grinding cardio equipment. Belinda was just disappearing into the women's locker room at the back, so I stopped. I said to Effie, "I do *not* want to confront her back there. What do we do? Loiter until she comes out?"

"Let's ask questions," Effie said.

A guy was approaching us, with muscles so bulky and taut it looked as if he were trapped inside a beefcake suit. "Can I help you?" he asked in a surprisingly high-pitched voice.

"That woman who just came in," Effie said. "Belinda Prentiss. What class is she taking?"

"Excuse me?" Beefcake said. "We don't talk about our clients."

Effie twiddled her fingers. "That's what everyone says."

"No, we really don't talk about our clients. Now, I could help you with something else, except you really look like you should be taking the seniors' aquarobics class at the community center."

Effie recoiled. "Seniors' . . . aquarobics?" she said delicately, as though trying out a new phrase in Swahili.

I took her arm and steered her away from Beefcake. I could tell it wouldn't end well.

Someone chirped, "Hey! Over here!"

Avi Gupta, D.D.S., was dismounting a stair-climbing machine. He came over and he and Effie did the double air-smooch thing. They had met soon after Effie had arrived in town the month before and, discovering their shared interests in snarkiness and fashion, had become fast friends.

"I haven't seen you in *ages*, sweetie," Avi gushed. "You look as stunning as ever."

"So do you," Effie told him. "Where did you get this marvelous ensemble?"

"This old thing?" Avi glanced with feigned modesty down at his slim, seemingly boneless body, clad in small orange shorts, a tank top with a graphic of shooting stars, and electric turquoise sneakers. "Are you going to the Lake Club Masquerade tonight?"

"Are we *going*," Effie said. "We're going to *own* it."

"*We*?" Avi said. His luminous brown eyes swiveled to me, or, rather, to my eyebrows. He gasped, and touched a hand to his throat. "Oh. Agnes. I didn't even see you there. Wow. You look . . . different."

"Avi," I said, "Do you know who Belinda Prentiss is?" This was a rhetorical question. Avi Gupta is a dentist whose not-so-secret superpower is being a bottomless font of gossip.

"Sure. In fact, I saw her come in a minute ago."

"So she works out a lot?" I asked.

"All the time."

"Is it restorative yoga?" Effie asked.

"Yoga, yes, but not restorative. Level-five power yoga."

"Goodness," Effie said.

"She can do the Wounded Peacock pose," Avi said.

"What's that?" I asked.

"The one where you balance your entire body on one arm while the rest of your body basically looks like it's doing a swan dive."

"How terrifying," Effie said.

If this was true, then Belinda was surely much stronger than she looked. Strong enough to kill a man and load his body into the back of a minivan. Strong enough to have held me underwater without much effort. And all this time, I had written off Belinda as a suspect, assuming she was too frail to have pulled it off.

Avi sidled closer. "That's only one of the ways Belinda wears the pants in that marriage."

"Mm," Effie said. "I did get the impression that her husband, Clifford, is a little, shall we say, *downtrodden*."

"That's not the half of it." Avi's eyes glowed. "Our little train engineer in chinos signed a prenup."

Effie made a disgusted noise. "The kiss of death."

"Why would he do that?" I asked.

"Because Belinda *made* him, that's why," Avi said. "She was the one with the bucks when they got married, not him. She inherited that big old house and a bunch of cash from her parents—before the marriage—and I heard that Belinda and Clifford have just about drained the well keeping that B and B running. *I'd* bet, since Clifford obviously married Belinda for her money and she won't be able to keep him in plaid shirts and choo-choo trains any longer, he wants out."

"You mean a divorce?" I whispered.

"What else?"

It crossed my mind that Clifford could simply *murder* Belinda. Yeah, that's where my head was.

"Couldn't Clifford get a job?" Effie asked.

"He *could*, but he doesn't want to. He's basically a kept husband. All he's done for the last ten years is work at the B and B, and since we all know they have, like, one guest a month and no one ever comes back because they either have an asthma attack from all the dust or they get creeped out by the electric trains, that means Clifford has been living a life of leisure. It would be hard to go back to work after loafing for a decade. Besides, he has no skills. When Clifford and Belinda got married, he was working in a hobby shop, but that went out of business."

At that moment, I caught sight of a green-and-blonde blob out of the corner of my eye. I turned to see Delilah Fortune in a matchy-matchy green Spandex workout outfit, complete with a tank top that said WILL WORK OUT FOR LUCKY CHARMS accompanied by the breakfast cereal's leprechaun logo.

Vomit.

"Look at those eyebrows," Delilah cooed to me, flashing her dimple. "I didn't know they were having a two-for-one special at the bait-and-tackle shop."

"And *I* didn't know that Mattel made Fitness Barbie clothes in grown-up sizes," I said.

"Come on, Agnes, don't be bitter. It'll give you jowls."

"Don't you have to run your shop?"

"It is *so* worth it to close for a half hour to get some cardio in. Hey, fun fact—did you know that cardio makes people look way less like crabby librarians?"

"Ladies, *ladies*," Avi said, "what's the problem?" He looked avidly between Delilah and me, and I knew his Juicy Gossip Radar was dialed up to maximum.

"You know what?" I said, bugging my eyes meaningfully at Aunt Effie. "We've got to go. See you guys at the dance tonight." I headed for the door, leaving Effie and Avi to air-smooch bye-bye.

As I stepped onto the sidewalk, my phone buzzed inside the hot-pink bag. I pulled it out to see its screen glowing with an unfamiliar local number. I punched ANSWER.

"Hello?"

"Is this Agnes?" a woman said.

"Yeah."

"This is Elaine Cruz. You left me a message about the Gourd Queen the day before yesterday? I'm so sorry I took so long to get back to you—parade preparation is just hectic and now we're behind schedule—which reminds me, we've got to get you in for a gown fitting."

"Oh." I cleared my throat. "I was actually calling about possibly . . . withdrawing."

Stony silence. Then, "We haven't had a Gourd Queen withdraw from the parade since 2001, and that was only because Becky Halpert's triplets were born a week early. But I certainly can't *force* you to ride in the float. What will happen is, the Pumpkin Princess will be promoted to Gourd Queen—"

"Wait. What?"

"Delilah Fortune, the Pumpkin Princess, will fill your shoes."

No. No, no, *no*. I was not going to let that unpleasant carton of cupcakes take *this* away from me, too.

"You know what, Elaine?" I said. "Never mind. I would love to be Gourd Queen. I was just struggling with a little stage fright, but that's nothing a little Xanax can't fix, right?"

"Wonderful. Will you be able to come in for the gown fitting tomorrow morning at, say, ten o'clock? The gowns are stored backstage at the Community Theater."

"That should work, yeah." *I'll be done with scrubbing the toilet by then.*

"Excellent. Meet me in the wardrobe room."

\* \* \*

Effie and I drove to the Green Apple Supermarket and stocked up on "clean cotton"–scented air freshener spray, coffee, tea, half-and-half, maraschino cherries, and cocktail olives. The bare necessities, people.

Next, we stopped by Tiles 'n' More. They happened to have the perfect mini hexagons in stock and—get this—*on sale*, because someone had returned a special order.

"See?" Effie said. "It was meant to be."

Then we drove to the downtown offices of Patricia P. Montagu, Architect, and walked upstairs to her suite overlooking Fountain Square. The brick pavement had been cleared of all traces of the Harvest Festival Kick-Off. No stage. No sound equipment. No potentially lethal apple-bobbing equipment.

Ugh.

"Good afternoon," the receptionist said with a big smile. "You're Mrs. Winters and Ms. Blythe, right?" She was a pretty, forty-something woman of *very* considerable proportions, with chocolate-brown skin and abundant glossy-black curls, wearing a floral blouse and tasteful makeup.

"Yes," I said.

"I'm Lally. Ms. Montagu is ready to see you." Lally leaned forward. "I have to say, I am *so* excited that you guys are renovating the Stagecoach Inn. I just love that place. When I was a little girl, back when that place was a boarding house, my uncle lived there for a while when he was going through a divorce. My brothers and I would jump at the chance to visit him there with Mom, just so we could run wild in the back stairs and attic and cellar, looking for a secret passageway." Lally laughed. "Someone told us the inn might've been a stop on the Underground Railroad back in the eighteen hundreds, so we were convinced there were secret rooms and tunnels *somewhere*. Never did find any, though. Bringing that place back to life, my oh my, that will be an accomplishment! And it would be good for Naneda, too. Good for you, girls. Good for you."

I liked Lally already, if for no other reason than she hadn't commented on my mangled eyebrows.

However, despite Lally's enthusiasm, twenty minutes later I emerged from Patricia P. Montagu's office completely deflated and disgusted.

"How'd it go?" Lally asked brightly, looking up from her computer.

"We'll have to think about it," Effie said.

"Oh." Lally's face fell.

"I can't believe Ms. Montagu, too, has a problem with us pitching in with the renovations," I whispered to Effie as we pushed out of the suite.

"She went to the Harvard Graduate School of Design, darling."

"So?"

"Oh, I don't know. Perhaps she's simply a purist."

We were starting down the stairs when Lally emerged from the suite door behind us.

"Hey," she whispered.

Effie and I stopped on the stairs and turned.

Lally's cheeks were flushed, and she spoke in a whisper. "I, um, I just wanted to say, I overheard a little of your conversation with Ms. Montagu—how she isn't into you guys helping out with the renovations—and I'm completely on your side."

"Thank you," Effie said, sliding on her sunglasses and turning to go.

"Wait." Lally glanced over her shoulder. "I've been doing some interior decorating on the side for a while—mostly stuff for friends of friends and whatnot—but I've been going to night school to pick up my architect's degree. It's not gonna be from Harvard, obviously, and I don't have tons of experience, but, well . . . I could take on your project. I'd let you guys help as much as you want. It should be a labor of love."

"We'll think about it," Effie said.

"That's what you just said about Ms. Montagu."

"We have one more candidate's proposal to review," Effie said.

"Do you have a portfolio we could take a look at?" I asked Lally.

"Just my web portfolio that I made for my design course-work, but . . . Okay. I get it." Lally's hopeful expression evaporated. "Well, best of luck." She turned and went back into the suite.

"We could at least *consider* someone who doesn't have a fancy Ivy League degree," I said to Effie as we got back in the Dustbuster. "And Lally seemed . . . she seemed like she cared. Like she *gets* it."

"Gets what?"

"That the inn is more than just a building. That it means something to our family."

\* \* \*

The next stop would be Pet Junction at the minimall on the edge of town. As we drove, Effie and I tried to list everything we knew about our suspects. This basically boiled down to:

- Delilah Fortune is a hideous, cupcake-baking demon who is stealing my man. (Motive: unclear. Plus, possible alibi.)
- Karen is hurting for $$. (Motive: protect son from Mikey's bad influence?? A dicey motive at best. Alibi?? Husband and son supposedly camping in Canada that weekend.)
- Clifford and Belinda are also hurting for $$. (Motive: get rid of Mikey because he's ruining their B and B's online reviews. Alibi: ??)
- Plus, Clifford allegedly signed a prenup, but what would that have to do with Mikey's death?

- Randy is a bad-tempered jerk. (Motive: ?? But he of all the suspects appears to have the temperament to bludgeon someone to death with a wrench.)

In a nutshell: We knew diddly-squat.

# Chapter 16

At the minimall, I ran into the dry cleaner's to drop off the dress Lauren had lent me for the speech a couple of days before. It was still damp with apple-bobbing water, and the dank smell made my skin crawl all over again.

"Why are you looking at me like that?" the guy behind the counter asked.

"Like what?"

"Like you're angry or surprised about something."

"I'm not angry or surprised. It's just my eyebrows."

"Oh."

In Pet Junction, Effie selected a pink collar with a bell and rhinestones for Tiger Boy.

"Isn't that kind of froufrou?" I said. "Tiger Boy is macho. Is that collar even big enough for him?"

"Hank is going to object to the cat. We can count on that. We need to disguise the fact that Tiger Boy is feral with the most domestic-looking collar we can find."

I eyed the sparkly collar. "It might just enhance his wildness by contrast."

Effie picked out some cans of organic cat food and a couple of cat toys.

"A turquoise plush mouse?" I said. "Tiger Boy isn't going to go for that. He looks like he plays with nunchakus."

"I *know*, Agnes. This is all for show."

"To trick Hank into thinking the cat is sweet and cuddly while said cat secretly goes all ninja on the mice?"

"Exactly."

Effie paid, and we walked back to the Dustbuster.

I was buckling my seat belt when I caught sight of Clifford. I froze. He was coming out of the UPS store.

"Look," I said to Effie. "Clifford."

We watched as he got into his Subaru station wagon, which was piled with bags and boxes.

"What *is* all that?" I said.

"I can't tell from here."

Clifford backed out of his parking spot.

I switched on the Dustbuster's engine.

"We're following him?" Effie asked.

"Looks that way," I said.

\*   \*   \*

We followed Clifford two cars back. He didn't go back toward the town center but out to Route 14B.

Seven miles of foliage and farmland later, we entered the town of Lucerne. At the first intersection, he turned right, drove a few blocks, and then pulled into the parking lot of *another* minimall.

It was midday, and the minimall parking lot was buzzing with cars going in and out, so we decided it was safe to follow. We parked at a discreet distance from Clifford and watched.

He got out, beeped his car locked, walked along the mini-mall sidewalk to White Glove Dry Cleaning, and went inside.

"*Dry cleaning?*" I said. "But there was a dry cleaner's at the minimall in Naneda."

Effie lit up a Benson & Hedges.

I scrounged around the console and, finding nothing but a container of orange Tic Tacs, stress-ate some. "You said you were going to switch to electronic cigarettes," I said. "What happened to that?"

"I'm working up to it."

"How?"

"Okay, fine, I'm not working up to it. I'm simply indulging myself in the real thing until the inn is actually licensed and I *have* to switch."

"Listen, if you want to destroy yourself, be my guest. This is just a friendly reminder that those things will kill you."

"We're all killing ourselves, Agnes. Our personalities contain the seeds of our own destruction."

I crunched on Tic Tacs, wondering what the seeds of my own destruction were. Insecurities, maybe. But aren't we *all* totally insecure?

After a few minutes, Clifford came out of the dry cleaner's with a few garments on hangers and sheathed in plastic.

"Clifford is picking up dry cleaning miles away from home, even though there is a perfectly good dry cleaner's near his house," Effie said, puffing smoke. "Are you thinking bloodstains?"

"Yep."

"Should we keep following him?"

"Heck, yeah."

We followed Clifford on Route 14B back in the direction of Naneda. But he passed the exit that would take us closest to downtown and Birch Grove B and B and, a mile later, exited onto one of the back roads.

"This is the road that passes by Hatch Automotive," I said. My belly was twisting.

"You look like you're considering ducking down," Effie said.

"Well, yeah. If Otis sees me driving by, he'll think I'm stalking him."

"Could I make a request? Please don't duck down while you have your foot on the gas, m-kay? Anyway, it's lunchtime. Otis may not be there."

This was true. Otis usually went into town for lunch.

As we drew closer to the shop, I noticed his motorcycle wasn't parked in its usual spot. "Phew. Otis isn't there."

"Oh, my," Effie said. "Lookee here."

Clifford was turning into the Hatch Automotive parking lot.

"I'm going to have to keep driving," I said. "If I stop now, he'll know we've been following him."

We rolled past the shop, and then I twisted my neck to see Clifford's Subaru stop perpendicular to the row of parked cars waiting to be serviced. Then I had to look at the road in front of me.

"He's getting out," Effie said. "Slow down a little—he's taking the dry cleaning out of his car—he's opening the back of another vehicle—a beige van, one of those Volkswagen camping things—a Vanagon—he's putting the dry cleaning inside—diddle. I can't see him anymore—those trees are blocking my view."

"Should I turn back?"

"No. Too risky. There isn't much traffic on this road. He'll notice. Anyway, haven't we seen enough? He picked up *dry cleaning*—from another town—and put it in a van. A van not at his home, but out here." Effie was scrabbling in her handbag for a fresh cigarette.

"He's obviously up to something weird. Pass me the Tic Tacs, would you? Do you think that Volkswagen belongs to him?"

"Couldn't you simply ask Otis?"

"No *way*. He's . . . he's really upset with me because of our snooping. If he knew I was *still* snooping, I don't . . ."

"I see. You're holding out hope that you'll crack the case, Otis will see the folly of his ways, realize what a brilliant sleuth you are, sweep you into his arms, apologize, and whisk you away to the Adirondacks."

*YES! Yes, exactly this!*

"Please," I said.

\* \* \*

I kept going back and forth in my mind about whether I should call Detective Albright and drop hints about Clifford Prentiss being up to something odd. After all, I had Albright's private cell number stored in the contacts on my phone. There were two problems with calling him, though. First, I would have to explain *how* we had learned about the dry cleaning and the Volkswagen van. Admitting to stalking my fellow townsperson = not good. Second, it is not even bragging for me to say that Sinclair Albright had a thing for me, and calling his cell would overstep the boundary I had so painstakingly drawn.

When Effie and I arrived back at the inn, Dorothea and Hank were sitting on Adirondack chairs on the lawn overlooking the lake, talking. A big white storage pod was sitting beside the rent-a-dumpster out by the garage.

"What's that?" Effie asked.

"More room to store antiques while we're renovating," I said.

"Genius!"

When we went inside through the kitchen door, Chester was making coffee on the state-of-the-art espresso maker Effie had splurged on. Behind Chester's back, Tiger Boy was on a counter-top eating Chester's sandwich.

"Perfect," Effie said to me. "We'll put Tiger Boy's collar on now and I'll take him straight up to Hanks's room for a mouse-scaring session, and then, when I see Hank heading back inside, I'll simply go and fetch him."

"Sounds like a totally normal thing to do," I said.

Chester told me he had cut the plywood into pieces that would fit the bathroom floor. "I even cut holes for the bathtub and toilet plumbing."

I thanked him, and we carefully hauled the pieces up to the attic and leaned them against the wall in the hallway.

"Do you want me to help you glue and nail those down?" Chester asked, wiping his sweaty forehead with his T-shirt hem.

"No, actually. I think I want to do it myself."

"For practice?"

"Yeah."

Honestly, I didn't know why I wanted to install the floor by myself. I just did.

*   *   *

For dinner, Chester ordered a huge takeout feast from Bengal Palace. We ate at Effie's recently acquired, castle-sized dining room table, sitting on antique chairs whose upholstered seats were still covered in protective plastic wrap. Somewhere between my samosa and my chicken tikka masala, I decided that, if I happened to run into Detective Albright at the Lake Club

Masquerade later, I'd drop hints about Clifford. It was probably my civic duty. But mostly, I wanted to corner Clifford and Belinda *myself* and demand some answers.

After helping Chester and Effie with the cleanup, I turned to go upstairs and get ready.

"Wait, Agnes," Effie said. "Let me fix your eyebrows."

"They're fixable? Why didn't you tell me?"

"Only temporarily, and in a water-resistant but not water*proof* way. Sit back down. I'll be back in a jiff." Effie stubbed out her cigarette and went off somewhere. After a few minutes she returned with what looked like a fishing tackle box and plunked it on the kitchen table. Inside were an incomprehensible number of blushers, eyeliners, lipsticks, and mascara tubes.

"Jeez, auntie, you could set up shop getting every last kid in town ready for Halloween."

"There's a thought." She was unscrewing the cap of a little glass jar. "Bear with me—I haven't done someone else's brows since ex-hubby number three decided that a full face was more his style than the corporate businessman look." With a tiny brush she dabbed at my eyebrows until I thought I was going to scream with impatience. Finally, she capped the jar of eyebrow gunk and passed me a mirror compact to see.

"Oh. My. Gawd," I said, or, possibly, moaned.

"You look fantastic!"

"I look like a female impersonator."

"Those are Sophia Loren eyebrows."

"These brows are wearing *me*."

I couldn't look away from my reflection. The brows Effie had painted on were mesmerizingly symmetrical, lush, tapering tributes to Effie's modeling career. They didn't look bad at *all*.

They actually looked terrific. It's just that they didn't go with the rest of me.

"I know you have an allergy to looking like you're trying too hard, Agnes, but it's either these brows or looking like you were almost pecked to death by Peregrine falcons."

*　*　*

The Naneda Lake Club sits about a mile south of town, a rambling, crouched 1930s lodge kind of thing on the lakeshore. It's about as swanky as it gets in Naneda, which is to say, not especially. It used to be *the* place to hold a "classy" function, although in recent years, converted barns and vineyard tasting rooms have taken away some of its party and wedding traffic. It has lakefront lawns and a beautifully restored wooden boathouse, from which club members launch rowboats in nice weather.

When I braked the Dustbuster at the VALET sandwich board in the clubhouse's front drive, the windows were glowing and rock music floated out.

"I can't wait to dance, Myronie," Lo said, clambering out of the back seat. She and Myron hadn't wanted to shell out for costumes they'd never use again, so she was wearing a black velour tracksuit heavily embellished with rhinestones and a small silver masquerade mask with an elastic strap that she'd gotten at Harries Stationery. Myron was in slacks and a blazer, with a silver mask that matched Lo's. They linked arms and headed toward the club's open doors.

Hank got out next, wearing a scarecrow costume that his scrawny body was *made* for, and then he turned to give Dorothea, in a Dorothy from *The Wizard of Oz* costume, a hand. Then *they* linked arms and headed toward the door, their heads bent close.

I looked at Aunt Effie. "What in the world?"

"Love is in the air, Agnes. Love is in the air."

"Not for everyone," I said darkly.

"What would the hills of a romance be without the valleys?" Effie got out, and so did I. She was in a black sheath dress, spiky black heels, and a mask made of peacock feathers.

I had gone with a black jersey wrap dress that could be dressed up or down. Effie had informed me that I had gone with "down." I wore no jewelry (unless you counted my glasses) and black ballet flats. My costume consisted of a headband from which two bobbling plastic pumpkins sprouted from springs. Understated elegance, no?

As I was handing my keys to the valet, a Datsun hatchback stuttered to a stop behind the Dustbuster. Chester climbed out from behind the wheel wearing a capacious, orange plush pumpkin suit.

"Evening, ladies," he said, tossing his keys to the gawking valet.

The Lake Club's interior was all exposed wood beams, oil paintings, stone fireplaces, and clusters of brass-studded club chairs. Antique oars and framed sailing flags decorated the walls. You could just picture Teddy Roosevelt striding around in there with a scotch and soda. Tonight it brimmed with costumed Nanedans in a festive mood.

Chester bumped—literally—into a friend, so Effie and I left him behind as we made a circuit of the oak-paneled ballroom.

"The auction begins in about forty-five minutes," Effie said over the cover band, "so we have until then to ask questions. Remember, be subtle."

"I'm always subtle."

Effie eyed my sproingy pumpkin antennae. "M-kay."

She swiped two flutes of bubbly from a passing tray and passed me one. We stood there, sipping and inspecting the crowd. Up on stage, the band was plowing through a peppy version of "Billie Jean." Couples rocked and twirled in the middle of the room, and lots more were mingling at the peripheries, drinking, eating, and laughing.

"It looks like a wild success," said Effie. "I hope the bachelorette auction goes just as well. The proceeds are for the county literacy program."

"After the jet-setting life you've led, I'm surprised you can stand this kind of party out in the sticks," I said.

"Oh, but you see, there really *is* no bigger, better life somewhere far away. That's an illusion. True, some parties have better *clothes* than others"—she was looking at a guy in a used-car-salesman-style checked sports coat—"but tonight Naneda is just as much at the center of the universe as anywhere else. It's simply a matter of perspective."

"You really believe that?" I couldn't help it; I was thinking about Seattle.

"I do. Coming back to Naneda has been a revelation for me, Agnes, an absolute revelation. It feels wonderful to be rooted to a spot, not to be—to be *searching* for something anymore. Oh, look. Alexa and Randy Rice have arrived. What is Alexa dressed as?"

"Um . . . oh, there she is. She's a black cat."

"Of *course* she is."

"She looks like she may be tipsy already, the way she's clinging to Randy for balance. I was thinking of asking her about her alibi, but maybe tonight isn't the night."

"Randy cleaned up nicely, didn't he?"

"He still looks angry."

"Mm."

Randy wasn't in a costume but a navy-blue suit. His face was flushed, and he was scanning the ballroom as though itching to pick a fight.

Effie jabbed me with a sharp elbow. "Look. There's Clifford, over at the nibbles table, going at the prosciutto like there's no tomorrow."

"And there's Belinda, right next to him. Looks like she's costumed as a gypsy."

It looked as if Belinda was quietly chewing Clifford out, actually, by the way her head was dipped low and her lips were working like a rubber band.

"Let's go ask them about the dry cleaning and the Volkswagen, shall we?" Effie said.

"I can't think of anything I'd like to do more."

# Chapter 17

I followed Effie around the crowd in the ballroom to the hors d'oeuvres table. We got really close to Clifford and Belinda without them noticing us in the hubbub. I heard Belinda say, "—and would you lay off the snacks? You're starting to look like a marshmallow stuffed into that suit. That used to fit you *perfectly*."

I'm not one to talk, but the seams of Clifford's navy-blue suit did look as if they were on the verge of giving up.

Clifford ostentatiously stuffed two prosciutto canapés into his mouth at once and chewed slowly, without taking his eyes from Belinda's face. Then he polished off a glass of wine in one swallow.

"Stop it," Belinda whispered. "*Stop it!* Where is your costume, anyway?"

"I left it in the car."

"Go get it."

"I don't feel like it, Belinda *dear*."

"What has gotten into you, Cliff? Besides several dozen cupcakes, that is. You're acting crazy."

"What's gotten into me?" Clifford said. "I'll tell you what's gotten into me, Belinda *dearest*. I'm done."

Belinda's shoulders tensed. "Done?"

"That's right, *done*." Clifford speared a cube of cheddar with a toothpick and popped it into his mouth. "Things have changed for me—changed in a *huge* way—and now I'm free. You know where I think I'll go first? *By myself?* The San Diego Model Railroad Museum."

"What are you talking about?" Belinda snapped. "How do you think you're going to get there? May I remind you that you're afraid of flying and that we don't have the money for plane tickets?"

Something made Belinda turn her head.

"Oh, hello!" Effie trilled, as though we'd suddenly come upon them. "How are the nibbles? They look exquisite. Are you enjoying yourselves? Have you danced yet? You two look like you could compete with Fred and Ginger in the airy department."

"Airy?" Belinda said. "Cliff? That's a joke. Oh, he gets the steps right—*on my feet*."

"What do you want?" Clifford asked. His words were slightly slurred and he was craning his neck. "Where's that darn waiter with the wine?"

"More wine is the last thing you need," Belinda snapped.

I cut in. "Actually, I was going to ask you guys about cars."

Clifford stiffened.

I went on, "I'm thinking of buying a new car and I've narrowed it down to a few different models. I noticed you guys drive a Subaru station wagon—one of my top choices—and so I wanted to ask, um, how you like it, and how it compares to your Volkswagen Vanagon."

Clifford's face turned the color of used dishwater.

Belinda was watching me closely. "You're really weird, you know that?"

"Yup." I beamed, hoping she'd continue.

She did. "The Subaru is fine—even though Cliff has destroyed the clutch about ten times. We don't have a Volkswagen Vanagon—where did you get that idea? We can't afford to insure two vehicles! And you know what? I'm sick of you two and your bizarre questions. Come on, Clifford." Belinda stepped away.

Clifford lurched in the opposite direction.

"They don't have a Volkswagen?" I whispered to Effie. "Are you sure you saw—"

"I'm positive."

"Then what the hey was that Volkswagen Vanagon at Hatch Automotive?"

"That's obvious, darling. It's Clifford's little secret. Maybe he uses it to store things he doesn't want Belinda to see. Maybe he uses it to take secret jaunts. Or—and I don't expect you to know this since you weren't around in the seventies—those sorts of vans are *ideal* for trysts. Perhaps Cliff has been meeting a lover in the back."

"Ew." *Alexa's affair.* Could Alexa and *Clifford . . . ?* "I'm thinking he's planning on driving it to San Diego. To see that model train museum. Except, what about the dry cleaning?"

"There *is* that. Any way you look at it, though, those two are on the express to splitsville. Oh, look." Effie made wiggly fingers up high. "It's that little darling, Mr. Solomon. I'm just going to pop over and say hello—you'll be all right, won't you, Agnes? And go and get yourself a drink, because Otis Hatch just walked in, and my, my, my does he look delicious tonight. I've never seen him in a suit. James Bond has nothing on that swagger."

My heart fluttered. "What? Where?"

Effie was gone.

Then I saw Otis. Dreamy in a black suit and white shirt open at the neck, he was looking around the ballroom searchingly.

I was on tiptoe and lifting my hand to wave at him when I saw the bouncy blonde curls beside him.

Delilah.

My hand fell to my side.

She wore a clingy white dress, with a silver halo trembling over her head and feathery angel wings.

Cheese suddenly sounded like a great idea.

I had only been grazing at the cheese platter for about a minute when Lauren appeared beside me in a pale gold 1960s sheath dress. Her hair was a full-on *Bewitched* flip, complete with headband.

"Hey," she said.

"Hey." I swallowed pepper jack. "Why do you sound like that?"

"Like what?"

"Like you feel sorry for me . . . wait. You saw Otis. With the Frosting Floozy."

"Uh-huh."

I speared a cube of Gouda with a toothpick. A lump was gathering in my throat.

"The good news is, I have some intelligence to pass your way," Lauren said.

"Okay." I popped the Gouda in my mouth and chewed. I barely tasted it.

"I stopped by my sister's house for dinner tonight."

Lauren's sister Lucy has a great husband, two Jack Russells, and three small kids who worship their auntie.

She leaned in. "Lucy saw Delilah Fortune on a date with Mikey Brown sometime last week."

"*No.*" My pulse ticked up.

"Yes. We were talking about the murder—everyone has

182

been—and she was saying it was so weird to have just seen him alive, full of life and everything—"

"Wait. Lucy knew Mikey?"

"Uh-huh. Same class in high school."

"Maybe I should talk to her."

"Be my guest. Anyway, she said she saw Mikey at a restaurant in Lucerne with someone she called 'that cupcake store chick.' Delilah."

"Delilah dating Mikey? No way. I just can't picture it. At *all.* Maybe it wasn't a date. Maybe it was, like, a business meeting, or maybe they're second cousins."

Lauren shrugged. "Ask Lucy about it. Anyway, I have to go. I'm supposed to help set stuff up for the bachelorette auction." Lauren gave my hand a squeeze. "Hang in there, Agnes. And by the way—your eyebrows look beautiful."

She was gone.

I turned back to the cheese platter and found myself face-to-face with the Peeper Prize judge, Hugh Simonian. He was holding his large smartphone like a holy relic and wearing a skinny-cut suit and a cravat.

He peered hard at my face. "Do I know you?"

"Not really."

"I *do* know you . . . do you work at the minimart by the highway?"

"Nope."

"Oh, wait. I know. You're the chick from the Chamber of Commerce. I didn't recognize you in those glasses. And your eyebrows are—"

"First of all, don't call me 'chick' unless I get to call you 'snoogums'—"

"I like your wit," Hugh said. "It's relatively quick."

Omigosh. I *hated* this guy. "—and second of all, I was under the impression that the Peeper Prize judge wasn't supposed to fraternize or consort with business owners."

"You've read the rulebook. Cute."

I unclamped my teeth. "What I'm trying to say, Hugh, is that we shouldn't be talking."

"It's okay. No one will know."

"Literally *anyone* could see!" I swept an arm around the ballroom. Not that anyone seemed to be paying any attention to Hugh and me.

Except for Karen Brown, that is.

She was standing at the hors d'oeuvres table in a farmer's costume of denim overalls, a plaid shirt, and a straw hat. She was watching Hugh with wide eyes.

Wait. Did Karen even *know* Hugh? And did she have a crush on him or something? Because she looked riveted.

"Listen," Hugh said in a lower tone. "You're not really . . . my type. But I'm flattered that you're interested—"

My mouth fell open like a trapdoor. If there's anything I can't stand, it's being pitied. Especially by some arrogant hipster dude I barely even knew.

"—and like I said, you're fairly witty. In New York City, the dating scene is big league. I date *models*."

"Hand or foot?"

"What? Oh. Runway models. Obviously."

"Do you have to carry a stepstool when you go out?"

"I like that you're trying to make me laugh, Agnes. It's fun. So what I'm going to do is tell you that as soon as this contest is over, we can go out for a drink."

"Um, I think there's been some sort of misunderstanding . . ." My voice trailed off, because I'd just caught a fleeting glimpse of a pumpkinhead in the churn of the dance floor. My heart kicked into high gear. "Sorry, Hugh, gotta go."

"But—"

I wasn't going to waste time explaining myself to Hugh. A pumpkinhead had dunked me. A pumpkinhead was likely Mikey Brown's killer. So if there was even the slightest possibility this was the same pumpkinhead, I was going to unmask them or sprain something trying.

"Excuse me," I mumbled, elbowing through the crowd. "Oops! Sorry about your—excuse me—whoa, watch that sword, dude—excuse me—"

I burst out of the ballroom into the lobby.

Empty, except for the valet flirting with the coat-check girl. Two hallways stretched out from the lobby, one to the left, one to the right. Pumpkinhead was speed-walking down the right-hand hallway in a navy-blue suit.

*A navy-blue suit.* So it was a guy.

"Hey!" I called, heading after him. "Hey, Pumpkinhead, wait!"

He sped up.

I broke into a jog.

"Hey!" I called, breathless. "We have some stuff to talk about, don't you think?"

We passed the men's room, the ladies' room, the kitchen, and then Pumpkinhead shoved open a door leading outside. Cold air gusted in.

I did *not* want to follow this creep out into the night. But I did it anyway. I had to know who he was.

Outside, wind spun off the lake and the stars were out in shimmering splashes. Across the lake, the dark hills looked like slumbering dinosaurs.

And there was Pumpkinhead, disappearing into the boat-house. The boathouse that looked like a big black tunnel to the underworld.

On the plus side, if I went after him, he'd be trapped, right?

I ran down the path, slowing to a walk as I drew near the boathouse entrance. I stopped.

"Pumpkinhead," I called. My voice echoed inside the wooden structure. Down below, lake water slopped. "Don't be a coward. Show your face."

No answer.

What the heck was he doing in there?

I stepped into the boathouse. My eyes were adjusting, and I could distinguish between charcoal and black. I saw the bulbous shape of the pumpkinhead mask over in the far corner. He wasn't moving.

*RUN!* Every last nerve in my body shrieked. *Are you INSANE?*

But this was my adrenaline talking, so along with the urge to flee was an irrational, pumped-up feeling. I *would* find out who he was, dangit.

I stalked closer.

He didn't move.

Closer.

I heard him breathing inside the mask, sounding for all the world like Darth Vader.

"Why did you do it?" I asked, whispering now. "Why did you dunk me? Was it because I was getting too close to the truth?"

He was still just standing there, arms dangling.

"Are you . . . are you scared, Pumpkinhead?" I whispered. "Scared of a girl?"

A fresh burst of adrenaline shot through my system.

I reached out, grabbed the sides of the pumpkinhead mask, and yanked. Pumpkinhead doubled over from the force—the mask was on pretty tight.

I wrenched harder, the mask popped off, and I staggered backward with the mask in my hands.

I looked up to see . . . Clifford Prentiss.

"*Clifford?*" I said, wheezing from exertion. "It was you? You dunked me? Did you—did *you* kill Mikey Brown? Is that what you meant when you told your wife that things have changed for you in a huge way?"

"Get away from me, you crazed dork," Clifford snarled. He lurched to go past me.

I stepped in his path. "I want answers."

"Well, too flipping bad!" Clifford yelled, and he was reaching out, shoving me hard—

I spiraled my arms to keep my balance. I was falling backward. Down, down. I hit the icy water, and it rushed to cover me. I burst to the surface, choking and gasping and thrashing my arms.

Pounding footsteps retreated.

I had lost my glasses. Everything was black and wet. Coughing on stale water, I dog-paddled until I crashed into the dock. I gripped the edge and tried to hoist myself. No go. Low center of gravity. I tried again and finally heaved myself up, crashing face first onto the wooden dock, where I lay for a second, soaking, chilled, and panting.

I got up. I felt as if I'd gone twice through the Turbo-Kleen cycle at the automatic car wash. I went back into the clubhouse through that same side door, dripping water as I went. I needed to find someone—Effie, Detective Albright, heck, even

Dad—and tell them that Clifford was Pumpkinhead, and that Pumpkinhead was probably the murderer.

"Agnes!" This was Chester's voice. A big blur of orange was coming toward me. "What in the—did you fall in the lake?"

"Nope. Dunked again."

"Who?"

"Clifford Prentiss?"

"Why?"

"Because I tore off his mask."

"Um, okay, that sounds like a fascinating story, Agnes, but Aunt Effie is freaking out because the bachelorette auction is starting and the Hansen twins didn't show. She told me to go and get you."

"Why?"

"Because you need to get on the auction block or there won't be enough dates for Effie to hit her goal. She was counting on the Hansen twins to tip her over. They're the closest thing Naneda has to Coors beer spokesmodels."

"I have *so many* questions and objections to this, Chester, the foremost one being, I am currently dripping wet and blind, and I have possibly just identified Mikey Brown's murderer."

"I hate to break it to you, but the fact that Clifford was wearing a pumpkin mask in no way proves anything."

My feet suddenly felt like cement blocks. Chester was right. I had no proof of anything, and with the adrenaline leaving my system, I was starting to feel bummed out.

"Why don't you ask Delilah Fortune to do the auction?" I said. "She'll love being the center of attention."

"Oh. Yeah." Chester scratched his head.

"What?"

"I did ask her, and she said . . ."

"*What?*"

"She said she's not a bachelorette because she's dating . . ."

"Otis?" This was a croaky whisper.

"Uh, yeah. Sorry."

I started shivering. That did it. My mind was made up. I was reapplying to grad school. In Seattle. I couldn't live in the same town as Otis if he was leaving me behind. It would kill me, one little cut at a time.

"You should change," Chester said. "Here. You can wear my costume. I have slacks and a black turtleneck on underneath."

"I cannot do this."

"You have to."

"No, I don't."

"You do. Because there's something else I haven't told you."

"I can't deal with this stuff right now!"

"I kind of told Detective Albright that you'll be in the auction, and he got all excited about it and said he was going to bid on you since you won't accept any of his date invitations—"

"What?" I yelled.

"—and Aunt Effie—she was listening in like she does—told me to tell you that you *have* to go on a date with Albright. She said something about squeezing him for info regarding your quote-unquote *case*."

"How does Aunt Effie create these insane situations?"

"No offense, but you seem to be pretty good at creating them, too."

If I hadn't been dripping lake water onto the floor, I would have objected.

"And how did so much stuff happen in, like, fifteen minutes?" I said.

"Because it's the freaking Naneda Lake Club Harvest Masquerade, baby."

\* \* \*

Twenty minutes later, I was standing beside the stage in the ballroom in Chester's puffy orange pumpkin costume. All of the other bachelorettes had been auctioned off, including Aunt Effie, who had been won by Mr. Solomon, and Lauren, who had been won by Skeeter Miller, the balding guy who owns the shooting range. I guess Jake hadn't showed.

My plastic pumpkin antennae trembled with every move I made. My hair was wet, although I had crouched under the hand dryer in the women's bathroom for a few minutes. My plunge in the lake had ruined my artistically painted eyebrows, so I had rubbed what was left of them off with paper towels. My butchered eyebrows were exposed to the world, but since I had eaten seven cheesecake bites and drunk one and a half glasses of local Riesling, I was past caring.

"And now, ladies and gentlemen," Effie said into the microphone, "our next date is the beautiful, brilliant Agnes Blythe!"

A splatter of applause.

I walked up onto the stage, my ballet flats squelching with water. I turned to face the audience.

"Isn't Agnes's pumpkin costume just *darling*?" Effie cooed. "Agnes is just a boatload of fun!"

I tried to smile. Didn't work. The silver lining was that without my glasses, the audience was just a big blur. Were Otis and Delilah out there? Would her hand be on his arm?

"The bidding starts at two hundred dollars. Two hundred,

anyone? Ah, I see you, Detective Albright. Anyone else? Can I get two-fifty for a one-on-one date with Agnes Blythe, Naneda's most eligible bachelorette? Anyone? No?"

Silence.

I wanted to evaporate. I wanted to run. I needed more cheesecake bites and wine.

"Then two hundred it is to Detective Albright. Going once—going twice—sold!"

Indifferent applause.

Then a man staggered into the ballroom through the double doors. "Someone call the police," he cried, gasping for breath. "It's Clifford Prentiss. He's dead."

# Chapter 18

It was pushing midnight when I was ushered into a room at the Naneda Police Station to give a statement about my encounter with Clifford Prentiss in the boathouse. Effie, Chester, and the gaggle had been questioned already and were on their way home stuffed in Chester's Datsun. Even though I had lost my glasses in the boathouse dunking and my vision was blurred, I would be driving myself home in the Dustbuster. Slowly.

"Hello, Agnes," Detective Albright said. In his midthirties, wearing a baggy suit and thick glasses, he had brown skin, a conservative haircut, and goldfish eyes. I happened to know his hobbies included bowling and playing the tuba, and there wasn't a bigger Star Trek fan in the entire universe. A woman officer with red hair sat beside him.

"Hi," I said, sitting. My pumpkin antennae boinged. I hadn't bothered to take them or Chester's plush pumpkin suit off. It just seemed like too much effort. My heart was broken, my optimism was in the gutter, and I had no clue what I was doing with my life.

The officer switched on a digital recording device.

"Agnes Blythe, I understand that you were one of the last people to speak to Clifford before he was killed," Albright said.

"So he was *killed*. Like, murdered. Someone said something about an oar, but I didn't know what to believe."

"He was bludgeoned to death with one of the decorative oars that hang on the walls at the Lake Club."

"Bludgeoned. Just like Mikey Brown."

"Yes."

"So do you think it was . . . the same person?" Too late, I remembered that Albright suspected Otis of having killed Mikey.

"It could be. Walk me through your encounter with Clifford."

I took a deep breath and launched into the story of how I had chased down Pumpkinhead, determined to unmask him because he was wearing the same mask as the person who had dunked me at the Kick-Off on Monday.

I omitted the part about having been convinced that Clifford was the murderer. Now that theory seemed incredibly stupid. Clifford was dead.

I needed to tell Albright about Clifford's secret van, though. It could be a break for the police investigation, and there *was* a double murderer out there. So I described how Aunt Effie and I had followed Clifford to the dry cleaner's in Lucerne and then to the Volkswagen Vanagon at Hatch Automotive.

When I said *Hatch Automotive*, Albright leaned forward in his chair. "So Clifford was running away from you because he didn't want to deal with your snooping, is that it?"

My cheeks went hot. "I think the important part of this is that Clifford was obviously *hiding* that van at Hatch Automotive—"

"The police will decide what's important and what's not, Agnes."

"There's something else," I said. "Something really weird. My aunt and I happened to, uh, overhear Clifford saying to his wife, Belinda, that he was done—"

"Done?"

"With their marriage, I think—and that things had changed for him in a huge way, and that now he was free, and that he planned to go—by himself—to some model railroad museum in San Diego."

"Noted." Albright actually looked interested.

Heartened, I said, "I think he was planning on driving to San Diego in that van. My aunt and I figured out some other stuff, too, about other people who—"

Albright put up a hand. "Agnes, please. No more snooping. Just get some rest, okay? This concludes your statement."

The woman police officer pushed a button on the digital recorder.

I went to the door, and Albright followed me out into the hallway. He lowered his voice. "I'll call you about—" He cleared his throat. "—*you* know."

Ugh. Our date that he'd won at the bachelorette auction.

"Oh," I said. "Yeah. Great."

\* \* \*

I drove slowly back to the inn through serene, dark streets. Naneda appeared snug, but violence and death were twisting like withered vines around the heart of this community.

I parked the Dustbuster at the back of the inn and went up the kitchen steps—

I slipped on something and thumped to the concrete walkway. Pain zinged up my back and down my legs.

I lifted my hand to see it in the glow of the porch light. *Stringy pumpkin goo.*

I looked around. I couldn't see that well without my glasses, but without a doubt, shattered pumpkin pieces littered the drive and the porch.

I scrambled to my feet, clutched by panic, hurried up the steps, through the screened-in porch, unlocked the kitchen door, and slammed inside. I just stood there for a minute in the dark kitchen, breathing hard.

Slowly, I calmed down. Good golly, it was only a smashed pumpkin. Smashing pumpkins in other people's yards was a teenage boy rite of passage, at least in Naneda. No biggie.

Even if it was, say, Scootch Brown who had done the smashing, that would only be a coincidence, right?

It seemed that Effie and the gaggle were already asleep, but I ran into Tiger Boy on the back stairs, his new rhinestone collar glittering in the dim light.

"Hey," I whispered to him. "Hunting mice?"

He made a throaty chirrup and kept going. He looked as if he had a full agenda.

Up in my attic room, I didn't turn on the light right away. First, I found my backup glasses and put them on. Then I crept to the window, pulled the curtain aside, and peered down into the shadowy yard.

I don't know what I expected to see. Maybe someone in a glow-in-the-dark shirt reading I AM THE KILLER would've been helpful.

No one. Just a few silhouetted leaves fluttering from the big trees and the pewter glint of the lake.

When I finally fell asleep, it was to dream about a jumbo jack-o'-lantern with legs, chasing me with an oar.

\* \* \*

I survived the night and was woken by the buzz of my phone. I pushed on my backup glasses and looked at the screen.

One text.

Otis: WE NEED TO TALK.

My throat constricted and my heart sped up.

*No.*

I dropped the phone on the floor. No. I could *not* deal with a formal, face-to-face dumping. Not today. Maybe next week. Better yet, I could move to Seattle ASAP and avoid it altogether.

I rolled over, my hip throbbing dully. I got out of bed and peeled the side of my pajama bottoms down. A saucer-sized bruise bloomed at the back of my hip, where I had fallen on it after slipping on pumpkin goo.

I got dressed in jeans, a T-shirt, a hoodie, and sneakers, brushed my teeth, pulled my hair back into a stubby ponytail, and went downstairs the back way to the kitchen.

I took a deep breath and cracked the back door. Fresh morning air gusted in. The goopy pumpkin carnage on the steps was still there, turning brown and crusty. I would have to clean that up. But first, coffee.

Maybe caffeine would get rid of this gross violated feeling. I mean, someone—possibly *a double murderer*—had trespassed onto the grounds of the Stagecoach Inn to smash that pumpkin. Jerk!

The territorial feeling that surged up in my chest was unexpected. And weird. This was Effie's property. Not mine.

I was just pouring myself a cup of coffee when shouting broke out in the entry hall.

I rushed out of the kitchen.

Hank was standing at the bottom of the main staircase, shoulders hunched, face red, shaking a fist at Effie and at Chester, who was frozen in the front doorway with an armload of bakery bags. Further up the stairs, the Bermans hovered.

"I'm telling you, that mangy cat has fleas!" Hank was yelling. "Why do you have an obviously feral cat inside the inn, anyway?" He paused to spastically scratch his neck.

Effie caught sight of me. "Oh, good morning, Agnes. I was just explaining to Hank that Tiger Boy is most assuredly *not* feral, and that he does *not* have fleas."

Hank swung to face me. "That cat was running up and down the upstairs hall all night, his stupid bell ringing like crazy. Of course, the reason he was running around in the first place is because this place is infested with mice. He finally goes away, but the next thing I know it's morning and my door is open and I have fleabites." More neck-scratching. "I think that mangy cat was sleeping on my pillow!"

"Little Tiggy-Wiggy Boy does love to cuddle," Effie said.

Chester added, "Everyone knows cats like to cuddle with the people who hate them most. They're passive-aggressive." He looked at me. "I got apple-cinnamon crullers."

"I've just about had it with this place!" Hank roared. "It's unacceptable!"

"Please, Hank," Effie said in a soothing tone. "Allow us to make it up to you. What would you like to do? Hike? Drive to the casino? Eat pie?"

"*We* wanted to go to Mikey Brown's funeral," Lo said. "We think the murderer will be there. People at the dance last night said the funeral is today at one o'clock at Blanshard's Funeral Home."

"Cheap thrills," Myron said.

Effie looked at Hank. "How does that sound? It's not often that you can attend a murder victim's funeral."

"Fine," Hank said. "But you have to do something about those fleas."

\* \* \*

I hosed the pumpkin goop off the back steps and threw the pieces of pumpkin shell in the compost bin. While I ate breakfast in the kitchen, I pulled up the graduate school application forms on my smartphone and sent them to the inn's printer, which was in Aunt Effie's office next to her bedroom.

I wasn't super psyched about the idea of returning to academia, but I figured that was just because I'd spent so much time away. I had loved college. I *was* psyched about getting out of Naneda, once I figured out who the murderer was and cleared Otis's name. Even if he was dating Delilah, and even if I couldn't bear to see him again, I still cared about him and knew he was innocent. Oh, and I'd need to find someone else to help Aunt Effie and Chester with the inn renovations. I mean, I didn't even have any construction skills. I would be way better off attending seminars and writing papers about gift-exchange cultures.

Next, I did the whole housekeeping thing in a hurry, because I had a Gourd Queen gown-fitting appointment to keep. Effie was downstairs working on the breakfast cleanup, and Chester was leading the gaggle through their stretches out on the lawn.

As I vacuumed and changed towels and scrubbed the inevitable toothpaste blobs from the sink, I couldn't really remember why I had agreed to go through with being in the parade. Something about wiping the smug look off Delilah Fortune's face, I guess. But it was starting to look as if that would be impossible. Her last name said it all: fortune smiled on her.

Except—wait a second. In all the insanity, I had totally forgotten about what Lauren had told me the previous night: her sister Lucy had seen Delilah out on a date with Mikey Brown.

"Agnes?" Effie had appeared in the bathroom doorway. "Wonderful—the place is sparkling. Take off those rubber gloves and put the Ajax away. It's time for your gown fitting."

While Effie drove us to the community center in her Caddy, I dialed Lauren's sister Lucy's number. She picked up after a half-dozen rings. "Yeah?" She sounded breathless, and at least one small child was squalling in the background.

"Hey, it's Agnes Blythe." I told her that Lauren had mentioned she'd seen Delilah Fortune out with Mikey Brown. Possibly on a date.

"Oh, yeah. I did. And it was unquestionably a date. It seemed like no big deal at the time—although they were pretty mismatched. But after Mikey was . . ."

I racked my brain for a child-friendly euphemism for murder. "Iced?"

"Sure. Iced—"

"Mommy, I want ice cream!" a childish voice screamed.

Whoops.

Lucy raised her voice over the whining. "After that, I started thinking about it more. You know, if maybe Delilah had killed him."

"She has an alibi," I said. "Supposedly."

"Oh, too bad. She rubs me the wrong way. The hubs is always raving about her coconut lemon cupcakes."

"My Aunt Effie always says men aren't very good about seeing past a layer of makeup, and with cupcakes in the equation—"

"Seriously. Anyway, I saw them at the Mill House. The hubs and I were out for my birthday." The Mill House is a pricey restaurant out in the countryside toward Lucerne. Think free-range chops, organic micro greens, and local wines.

"When was this?" I asked.

"This past Saturday night."

The night before Mikey was killed.

"Mikey was dressed in a button-down shirt, which was weird, since he usually went around in sweats," Lucy said, "and Delilah was doing all the flirty stuff girls do with their hair—hold *on*, Jeremy! Mommy wants to—oh, I give up. My point is, it was *definitely* a date. Listen, Agnes, I gotta go. I'll be rooting for you at the parade on Saturday!" Lucy hung up.

I stashed my phone in my bag and filled in the details for Effie.

She blew a stream of smoke out her cracked window. "It's all becoming clear. Delilah is a digger."

"A what?"

"A gold digger."

"What? With *Mikey*?"

"His *cash*, darling. Delilah went on a date with him only *after* he began flaunting money, correct?"

"Well, yeah."

"There you are. Trust me, I know a digger when I see one."

I wasn't going to argue with that. "You'd think she would've been a little more upset about his death if she'd dated him."

"Oh, the innocence. You don't *understand*, Agnes. Diggers don't care about the men they date."

"Oh." How depressing. "Wait. If she's a digger, then what's she doing chasing after Otis? He has a very modest income."

"Even if she's a digger, darling, she's not *blind*. Otis is the most—"

"*Stop.*" I sighed. "I'm burned out. I'm fried. Two murders,

Aunt Effie. *Two*." I looked out at the town whizzing past in a blur of autumn gold. "And here we are ferreting around in people's dirty laundry with nothing to show for it. *This* is what I destroyed my relationship with Otis for?"

"Once this all blows over, he'll be back. And if you can score the winning point that lands the real killer in police custody, why, you'll have the moral high ground *and* the delicious man-treat."

"I don't want the moral high ground."

"Of course you do. Now. What else do we know?"

I threw my hands up. "Nothing! I mean, we know about people's horrid little secrets, but who doesn't have horrid little secrets?"

"I know *I* do," Effie said serenely.

Actually, I didn't have any horrid little secrets. This apparently made me an anomaly in Naneda. "I was so sure that we were going to nail Clifford for killing Mikey, and it turns out we were completely off track. Maybe he wouldn't even be dead if we had done a better job figuring stuff out."

"Don't be so hard on yourself—"

"I'm being hard on *us*."

"The police haven't figured out the murderer's identity, either."

"Because Albright is obsessed with pinning this on Otis. My point is, we're not making any connections."

"Maybe that's because we aren't going about it the right way."

"There is only so much we can do. We aren't the police. We aren't detectives. Heck, we aren't even amateur journalists. We're just two wannabe innkeepers who the whole town thinks are crazy."

"Number one, don't underestimate the crazy card, Agnes. It can come in handy—"

"*Pfft.*" I slouched in the passenger seat.

"—and number two, we do have a lead."

"What?"

"Do you recall how Avi Gupta claimed that Clifford Prentiss had signed a prenuptial agreement?"

"Yeah."

"And you recall Clifford's cryptic statements last night, about things changing for him and so forth?"

"Uh-huh."

"And you also recall how Mr. Solomon, of Solomon and Fitch, Attorneys at Law, was the highest bidder for a date with me at the bachelorette auction last night? He had some stiff competition, too—"

"Fast-forward to the good part."

"Well, I already arranged my date with Mr. Solomon. We're attending—" Effie swallowed as though she were queasy. "—senior aquarobics together this morning. Apparently Mr. Solomon goes three times a week. He claims it keeps him spry. I myself shudder at the thought of submerging myself—not to mention my Tory Burch swimsuit—in that chlorine and bacteria broth they call the community swimming pool, but this just may lead to a break in our investigation."

"That sounds . . . tenuous."

"You're welcome."

# Chapter 19

We parked in the lot at the community center and went inside. We passed a kung fu class, a watercolor class, and a fierce game of girls' basketball, and pushed through double doors into the half-lit backstage area of the auditorium.

After a little exploring, we found Elaine Cruz in a room stuffed with wardrobe racks and tables heaped with theater props. A shelf on one wall held white polystyrene heads wearing hats and wigs.

"Hi!" Elaine said, looking up from a dress she was fluffing on a garment rack. She was an attractive, dark-haired forty-something in jeans and a white button-down. "You're a little late, but I have time to squeeze you in"—her eyes flicked to my middle—"before the Pumpkin Princess arrives for her fitting."

"You mean Delilah Fortune," Effie said.

"Yes. She's due at ten thirty."

Fist pump. As much as I loathed Delilah's presence, this was a plum opportunity to question her about her date with Mikey.

"It's just terrible about these murders," Elaine said. "I don't know what's happened to this town. Such a shame. It used to be so safe. And with that Peeper Prize judge in town? Yesterday he was in my bookstore, looking like he was tallying up scores or something on a computer tablet. I feel like he's going to hold the murders against us. Here. Go ahead and try this one on behind the divider there." She passed me a gown on a hanger. "It hasn't been worn by the Gourd Queen since 1998."

"I can see why," Effie said.

I held it up. "I thought parade-queen gowns were supposed to be poofy. This is basically an orange tube."

"That was the fashion in 1998." Effie draped herself on a chair.

"Don't you have anything more . . ." I searched for the word.

"More princessy?" Elaine said in a sarcastic tone. "We generally save the princessy gowns for our *younger* Gourd Queens."

"What am I, Betty White?" Actually, I would kill to be Betty White.

"Please, I'm on a tight schedule. Let's just find a dress that fits, okay?"

"No alterations will be made?" Effie asked.

"Are you kidding?" Elaine said. "This is Naneda, not Paris."

I took the orange dress behind the room divider and pulled off my hoodie. The wall back there was decorated with framed color photographs of the casts of past Naneda Musical Theater productions. There was *Carousel*, *Kiss Me, Kate*, *L'il Abner*, and *Annie*.

Something about the *Kiss Me, Kate* photo caught my eye. The female lead had a cascade of red curls, and standing next to her was . . . Randy Rice.

Seriously? *He* was into theater? I never would've guessed it, but then, maybe it provided a vent for his little rage problem.

Randy. I had yet to learn more about the meeting Mikey

might have been setting up with him at the garage for Sunday, the one Scootch had been banned from per his mom's text.

I shimmied the Gourd Queen gown up over my jeans and T-shirt. I didn't bother with the zipper. The gown didn't flare until my ankles, which meant I had to waddle like a penguin to show Elaine and Effie.

Effie tipped her head. Elaine held her chin between thumb and forefinger.

"I can't wear this," I said. "I'll break my neck."

"Take tiny steps," Effie said.

"You won't really need to *walk*," Elaine said. "You'll be up on the float, sitting on your throne. Mainly you'll be waving, and the dress is strapless, so . . ."

The *throne*. I'd forgotten about that. I was trying to recall— yet again—exactly why I had agreed to do this when Delilah walked in and refreshed my memory.

She beamed when she saw me. "Wow, Agnes, you look *fantastic*." She put a hand on her waist. "Gosh, I don't know why, but for some reason I'm suddenly super hungry for a mondo burrito."

My impulse to kick something was thwarted by the tight dress around my knees. "*I'm* super in the mood to watch that Oprah episode about passive-aggressive people."

"You should." Delilah's dimple flashed like a danger signal. "You could learn a lot!" She turned to Elaine. "Where's my gown?"

Elaine was all smiles as she mounded three or four dresses into Delilah's arms. "Here you go—you pick. You have such a flair for fashion."

"Thanks, Elaine." Delilah went behind the room divider.

I followed.

Believe me, I did not relish the idea of being in a confined space with Delilah. It felt like climbing inside the tarantula exhibit at the zoo. But number one, I was on a mission, and number two, I needed to peel off the orange tube so I could take a full breath again.

Oh—and thank goodness I was fully dressed under the gown so Delilah couldn't mock my underwear choices.

Delilah was arranging the gowns Elaine had given her on a rack.

"Oh, hey," she said casually. "You need help with that? I've always been really good at peeling bananas."

"Makes sense, since your chimp warfare instincts are hyperdeveloped."

"Jeez, Agnes, I try to lighten the mood, and you get all *mean*? What is with you? Is it because Otis dumped you? He told me all about it last night." She smiled sweetly. "*Late* last night. After Clifford's body was discovered at the dance, I was just too shaken up to be by myself. Otis was *really* comforting."

"You know what you are?" I said, peeling the gown down over my jeans. "You're mean. *And* you're an opportunist."

"I would've assumed, with *those* shoes, that you were a feminist, Agnes. But here you are calling me icky names. Opportunist?"

"I know you went on a date with Mikey Brown. But only *after* he started flashing cash."

For the tiniest fraction of a second, Delilah's eyes rounded in surprise. Then her face was all bemusement. "It was a surprisingly fun date."

"You're not denying it?"

"Why would I? I can date whoever I want, Agnes." Her eyes glittered. "Obviously."

"But you told me he was always asking you out. You said you were out of his league."

"Sure, but I didn't say I never went out with him. He *was* always asking me out. But I told him I wasn't going to go unless he could pony up for a dinner at the Mill House. So he did. I figured that's why he got the cash in the first place—so I'd go out with him. I assumed he sold off a big-screen TV or something."

"You're pretty vain."

"Wouldn't *you* be?"

"Is everything okay back there?" Elaine called.

"Yes!" I shouted.

I heard Effie say, "She's just nervous about the parade."

Delilah was studying the *Kiss Me, Kate* cast photograph. "Look, it's Randy Rice. Alexa told me he's an actor. I guess that explains why he has such a good poker face. And look at this gal in the curly red wig. People have *no* sense of what is flattering on them." She looked at me with sad-puppy eyes. "That seems to be a chronic problem in this town."

"Back up," I said. "What's this about Randy having a good poker face?"

"Whoops. I shouldn't have said that."

"But you did."

"I don't like spreading gossip."

"What happened to investigating?"

"Oh, I'm still doing that. Are you?"

"Of course."

"I just wasn't sure because, you know, it doesn't seem like you're making any progress."

I forced myself to breathe. In. Out. In. Out. *She's just baiting me.*

"Let's do another trade," I said, softly now. Effie and Elaine were chatting, so I didn't think they could overhear. "If I give you something good, you tell me what you were about to say about Randy's poker face."

"Sure thing. Whaddaya got?"

I did a quick mental scan of Things I Knew. Alas, it was mostly speculation.

"I heard Clifford and Belinda Prentiss might've had a prenup," I said.

"So? That's not a clue. Lots of people have prenups."

"Well, in the light of their financial problems, maybe it *is* a clue."

"I know all about their financial issues. Don't you remember I was the one who told you about their horrible reviews on countryinns.net?"

"Okay, how about that Karen Brown's spa is *also* having financial problems."

"How do you know that?"

"I have to protect my sources and methods."

"Get real."

Delilah was trying to sound flip, but I could tell I had startled her with that tidbit about Karen's money woes. For once, I was one step ahead of the Cupcake Kiss-Up.

"Now tell me what you were about to say about Randy," I said.

Delilah tossed a blonde curl over her shoulder. "Well, at a poker game last week—"

"A what?"

"There's a regular Thursday night poker game at Charlie Morel's house, and I got invited—the only woman, of course, because guys have an easy time talking to me, I guess. Anyway,

Randy was there, and he was so incredibly cutthroat about the game. Like, when there was maybe five hundred dollars in the pot, he started getting all competitive and—this is Randy Rice we're talking about—*angry*."

"That's it?" I said. "Your info for me is that Randy has anger issues? Because I already figured that out."

"It's not the anger part that's so interesting. It's the gambling part."

"What do you mean?"

"I mean, I think Randy might have a gambling problem."

"Maybe he's just competitive."

"Okay, then how do you explain this?" Delilah dug into her bag and produced a silver plastic card the size and shape of a library or credit card. She passed it to me.

"Lakewinds Casino Players Club?" I said, reading the card.

"Yeppers."

"You stole this from Randy?"

"Gosh, no!" Delilah pressed a hand to her heart. "He dropped it in my shop the other day when he came in for a cupcake. I just haven't had a chance to return it." She took the card from me and tucked it back in her bag. "My point is, with all this money stuff swirling around, I wonder if Randy was hurting so badly for money because of his little gambling problem, he might've . . ."

Delilah didn't need to finish the thought. I already knew: Randy might've killed Mikey for his cash.

What Delilah still didn't know (I hoped) was that Mikey and Randy had had a meeting set up at the garage the very afternoon Mikey was killed. How Clifford might have factored into all this, I wasn't sure.

"Now, if you don't mind, I need to change?" Delilah said.

"Go for it." I kicked the mound of orange gown off my feet, snatched it up, grabbed my hoodie, and went back around the room divider. Effie took the gown from me and hung it up.

"Bye, Agnes!" Delilah called.

Elaine beamed. "That Delilah is such a sweetheart."

* * *

I told Effie about Delilah's report as we walked down the hallway. "Why haven't we been more aggressive about investigating Randy? He suddenly seems so suspicious."

"We've been busy."

"And we need to make sure the police know about Randy's meeting with Mikey at the garage. And—"

"You really should make your date with *your* high bidder," Effie said. "Go on, call Albright."

"Do I have to?"

"His infatuation with you gives you—gives *us*—a clear advantage over Delilah. Something tells me Albright is not one to be taken in by the likes of her. He likes dorks."

"Gee, thanks."

"It's a compliment, darling. Now. Go on. If you don't want Delilah Fortune to head you off at the pass, crack the case, and rescue Otis—subsequently whisking him away for a weekend celebration in, oh, I don't know, *a cabin in the Adirondacks*—then *call Albright*."

"You're mean." I hadn't told Aunt Effie about how Otis wanted to "talk." That was something I refused to even think about, let alone discuss.

"I'm realistic. Men can be very confused creatures, Agnes. They can't help it. And with Delilah's *cupcakes* in her arsenal—"

"Okay, fine."

"I'd say, put on your sultry voice, but I think Albright would prefer it if you spoke in Klingon." Effie glanced at her wristwatch. "I must go to the locker room and change for aquarobics. Remind me to buy a preemptive tube of athlete's foot cream. Meet me after."

\* \* \*

The Naneda community center is only two blocks behind Main Street, so I decided to walk to the Black Drop and get a coffee while I called Albright.

I dialed his cell number. To my dismay, he picked up right away.

"Agnes," he said. "Good morning."

"Hi." I cleared my throat.

"Everything okay?"

"Yeah! Of course. I mean, except for the fact that Clifford Prentiss was, you know, bludgeoned to death last night . . ." *Oh, the things that come out of my mouth.* "Listen, I'm calling to ask if you wanted to set up that date you bid on last night."

"Sure. Want to go bowling next week?"

*No.* "I kind of, um, pulled my back. While emptying the dishwasher, so—"

"I did that once. Even we nerds need to stretch, Agnes. Hey, how about I take you to the movies tomorrow? I'll be ready for a breather from work by then. Things are pretty crazy here at the station, what with what happened at the Lake Club last night."

"Do you . . . have a suspect?"

"I'm just glad you saw the light and broke up with that meathead, Otis Hatch."

"Who told you that?"

"Everyone knows."

*Bloop bloop* went my stomach acid. "Are you saying you suspect *Otis* of killing Clifford?"

"I can't discuss the case with you, Agnes. Listen. *Headless Horseman III* is playing downtown. I've been dying to see it. The special effects are supposed to be incredible. Meet you there a little before four tomorrow?"

"Yup," I said dully.

"Cool beans!"

I punched END CALL.

# Chapter 20

It pretty much sums up the weird and quasi-crappy plane on which my life had landed to say that I spent the next forty-five minutes sitting in the poolside bleachers of Naneda community swim center eating a muffin from a white paper bag, washing it down with pumpkin latte, and watching senior citizens flop around in the water.

I don't want to complain too much. Feeling sorry for yourself isn't healthy, and anyway, things could've been worse. It wasn't like I was milking horses in Mongolia for a living.

Mr. Solomon, wearing prescription goggles and woefully inadequate Euro swim trunks, was right up in the front row. He looked like a hairy species of tree frog. When Effie, a little late to class, slid into the pool in her chic black-and-white swimsuit, she waded over to his side with a toothy smile on her face.

Mr. Solomon looked delighted to see her. He came up to the level of her earlobes.

The class got started, led by a perky young man with a spray tan and a habit of saying "Work it, people!"

Effie whispered stuff to Mr. Solomon, and he whispered back, until the instructor blew a whistle and said, "*All* right, you two! Are we here to chitchat, or are we here to get fit?"

"A little of both, I suppose," Effie said.

The class finally ended, and, after what seemed like an eternity, Effie emerged from the women's locker room looking ready for her close-up.

"Well?" I said. "Was there really a prenup?"

"I'll tell you in the car. It's sensitive. You drive." She tossed me her keys. "I need a post-workout ciggy."

Once I was steering the Caddy out of the community center parking lot and Effie was puffing a Benson and Hedges, she turned to me, eyes bright, and said, "Clifford *did* sign a prenup, because he came to his marriage with nothing but credit card debt, whereas Belinda had recently inherited the house as well as a moderate inheritance from her parents. But that isn't the juicy part. And, by the way, I deserve kudos for this, because I had to kiss Mr. Solomon to get it."

"Yuck!"

"On the cheek, darling. The cheek. And anyway, he's really very sweet, and he smells like the most expensive aftershave money can buy. Maybe a little like Bengay, too, but it isn't overpowering. Now listen. You recall what Clifford was ranting about at the dance last night?"

"Of course. Saying stuff about how everything had changed for him, big time, and all that?"

"Mm. Well, it turns out that was no exaggeration. He had just come into an inheritance of his own. Fifty thousand cool ones."

"*What?*"

"Yes. From an uncle. About three weeks ago."

"Omigosh."

"So, Clifford went to Mr. Solomon for help in managing the legal ramifications. Clifford wanted to make certain Belinda didn't have any right to his money when he asked for a divorce.

Which probably wasn't going to work because New York is an equitable-distribution state."

"So he *was* going to ask for a divorce?"

"Yes."

"What's Mr. Solomon's first name, anyway?"

"Why, I never thought to ask."

"You were kissing him in the locker room and calling him *Mr. Solomon*?"

"He seemed to like it."

"No. Ew. *Stop*."

"The police may know more about Clifford's inheritance money. Did you set up your date with Detective Albright?"

"We're going to the movies tomorrow afternoon."

"You couldn't set up anything sooner?"

"Nope."

"Ah, well, that's thirtyish hours of eyebrow regrowth."

"You said they look fine!"

"They *do*, darling." Effie flicked ash out her cracked window.

We returned to the Stagecoach Inn to find Chester, Hank, and the Bermans dressed all in black and eager to head to Blanshard's Funeral Home. Dorothea was in her room doing some work for her motor coach business on the computer. Effie and I went to our rooms to change into black, too.

"This is great," Myron said to Lo as we all piled into the Dustbuster. "We can do a little comparison shopping on caskets."

Lo gave a muffled shriek and elbowed him.

Ten minutes later, we were squeezing into the back row of the chapel at Blanshard's. The lighting was low and soothing. The chairs were comfy. The casket was closed. The place was packed.

Not packed, I calculated, because Mikey had been popular,

but because murder was in the air and people wanted to gawk. I saw the darting eyes as the minister droned the eulogy up at his podium. Everyone was looking for the killer in the chapel, because everyone with a subscription to basic cable knows killers like to go to their victims' funerals.

What had become of my sweet hometown? I wasn't sure if I wanted to live there forever, but I sure as heck wanted it to stay safe, gentle, and picturesque forever. Naneda wasn't supposed to be like this! People didn't even lock their doors. At least, they didn't used to.

In the front row, Karen Brown sat between her son Scooch and her husband, Mark. I had a pretty good view of the family, since the chairs were arranged in a crescent. The three of them were red-eyed. Karen stared ahead, expressionless, her hair lank and her black dress rumpled. Mark kept dabbing his nose with a balled-up Kleenex. His hair was tightly combed and his suit pressed. Scooch slouched low in his chair, oversized sneakers thrust forward, head slung low.

Man, what I wouldn't have given to ask that kid about his Uncle Mikey's meeting with Randy at the garage. Would it really be so awful to interrogate a grief-stricken teen? Even one who might've smashed pumpkins on my back porch?

Well, yeah. It would.

Anyway, Alexa and Randy Rice were there, too. And Randy was now my numero uno suspect. I just needed to figure out how to ask him about that meeting without him, say, karate-chopping my shins.

Alexa looked stricken and pale, with black eyeliner smudged under her eyes, her blonde ponytail looking greasy, and her dark roots showing. Beside her, Randy leaned forward, elbows on knees, staring at the floor. Every so often he'd shake his head as though angered by something the minister had said. Except the minister uttered only the blandest Biblical soothers.

No Belinda at the funeral.

No Otis. No Delilah.

Other faces I recognized from around town. Cordelia, Dad's housekeeper. Dirk Vargo, the manager of the Green Apple Supermarket. The Banerjees who owned Bengal Palace. Professor Morel, Dad's neighbor and an English lit professor at Naneda University—

*The Dude.*

My pulse ticked up.

The Dude I'd seen at the Harvest Festival Kick-Off sat on the other side of the chapel, but I recognized him, all right. The black Adidas tracksuit. The stringy neck. The potbelly. The oily, thinning, back-combed hair. He sat back, manspreading his legs, arms crossed high and tight on his chest. Just like the previous times I'd seen him, he was obviously looking for someone in the crowd.

What the *what*?

The service ended, and everyone got up and migrated to the reception room, where a long table was laid with cookies, electric percolators, napkins, and paper cups. The air smelled of lilies and weak coffee.

Lo and Myron were the first to hit the cookies, and they piled their plates so high, I realized we were in it for the long haul.

I got a cup of coffee and then slowly inched myself closer to where Randy stood talking with the funeral director. The reception room was packed, so it was easy to loiter behind them unseen as they made small talk. The second the funeral director excused himself, I wedged myself in front of Randy.

"Hi!" I said.

Randy looked at me with unmasked disgust. "Hi." He was wearing cords and a streaky purple-and-brown Cosby sweater. His acne-scarred face was flushed, and his bushy hair needed to be combed. He wasn't much taller than me, and I was in my ballet flats.

"Agnes Blythe," I said, proffering my hand.

Randy didn't take it. "I know who you are. You're the nut who's been bugging everyone about Mikey's death."

"I'm really sorry for your loss," I said. "I understand that you and Mikey knew each other since you were babies. You must feel . . . awful."

To my surprise, tears welled up in Randy's eyes. He pinched them away with forefinger and thumb. "I can't say that I *liked* the jerk, but he was a fixture." Randy's eyebrows jutted down. "But you know what? Mikey finally got what was coming to him. He was a taker. And for the first half of his life, everything was just handed to him on a silver platter. His mom thought he was God's gift to humanity. Our moms were best friends—they were both young single moms—so Mikey and his brother Mark and me were forced to play together all the time, although *playing* usually consisted of Mikey giving me noogies and wedgies and locking me in the basement, and then if I told on him, my mom would laugh and his mom would act like I was making it up. Mikey never got in trouble. It was ridiculous. And it was always just take, take, take. He stole my favorite Teenage Mutant Ninja Turtle toy when we were six. He always stole my Halloween candy by force. And you know what happened in high school?"

"No," I said. "What happened?"

"I caught him kissing my girlfriend! Not because he liked her—no, just to take something else from me. I could've *killed* him!"

Two women in black dresses looked over at Randy, askance. He didn't seem to notice.

"Well, the joke's on Mikey," Randy said, "because obviously someone got sick of all his taking, and now he's dead."

"I heard a rumor about him having a bunch of cash suddenly, which disappeared when he d—"

"What's your problem, anyway, asking me this stuff?" Randy snarled. "Why don't you mind your own business?"

"Problem? No problem." I took a sip of coffee and burned my tongue. "If it seems like I'm asking about Mikey's death, well, that's just a coincidence. Because what I'm really trying to do is just be really, um, active in the Chamber of Commerce."

Randy's Adam's apple joggled up and down.

Interesting.

"I want to be one of the gang, you know?" I said.

"No."

"For instance, I heard there's a regular Thursday night poker game that some of the Chamber people go to? I'd love to join in. I play a mean hand." A lie. "Is the game happening tonight?"

"You're not invited."

"Oh. Darn. Is it high stakes?"

"Get a life, okay?" Randy elbowed away, leaving me alone with my coffee.

Only about a minute later, I overheard an exchange between Karen Brown and Bitsy Horton. Bitsy and her sister, Lily, run Naneda Realty with an iron fist, so don't let the JCPenney pantsuits and blue eye shadow fool you.

Karen (passing something tiny to Bitsy): Here you go. Mark had a spare.

Bitsy: Wonderful! And the . . . the police are finished in there?

Karen: They gave us the go-ahead.

Bitsy: Do you think there is anything of value for an estate sa—

Karen: (Snorts loudly.) Are you kidding me? Maybe his video game setup could be eBayed, but you can send every last thing in that house to the dump. Bulldoze it for all I care.

Bitsy: Then I don't suppose you want to read this literature on local estate sale services? (Holds out a folder.)

Karen: Puh-leez.

Bitsy: (Purses lips.) Okeydokey, then.

*Omigosh.* Where was Aunt Effie? I had to tell her about this. Ah. There she was, laughing uproariously between two silver foxes in suits.

I went over and pulled her away. "We need to talk," I whispered.

"Good-bye, boys," Effie said to the men over her shoulder. "You're both hilarious!" She turned to me. "What is it, Agnes?"

I dropped my voice to a whisper only Effie would be able to hear. "Karen Brown has a possible financial motive for killing Mikey."

"Which is?"

"His house. It looks like she and her husband inherited Mikey's house—"

"Makes sense."

"—and now they're having Bitsy Horton sell it off. Karen just gave her the key."

"But surely that dump couldn't be worth enough to warrant *murder*, Agnes."

"That would depend on how desperate Karen is. You saw the spreadsheets in her office. You said she was in the red."

"Mm. True. But what happened to being totally sure Randy is our man?"

"Well, *I* don't know! But opportunity knocks, right?"

"Mrs. Winters," someone said.

Effie and I turned to see none other than Bitsy Horton, still holding her folder and, pinched under her thumb against the folder, the key to Mikey's house.

"How *wonderful* to see you." Bitsy's tone suggested that seeing Aunt Effie was about as wonderful as an ingrown nostril hair.

"Likewise."

"How are things at the old deathtrap?"

"If you are referring to the beautiful, historic Stagecoach Inn, Bitsy, the answer is *fabulously*."

"That's not what I heard."

"And what did you hear?"

"That you have a rodent problem."

"Only when my niece wears her Minnie Mouse bedroom slippers."

"Isn't it *great*-niece?"

"You only feel as old as your oldest pantsuit, darling."

Bitsy flushed. "If you want my professional opinion—"

"Not especially."

"—I suggest you sell that place before you dig yourself too far into the hole. All of the value is in the land, and you know it.

Let me take it off your hands, and you'll have a nice chunk of change to buy yourself a brand-new condo."

"I'd rather die."

"Why are you Blythes so stubborn?"

"Just good genes, I suppose."

"The real estate inventory in the town is stagnating because people like you are holding on to worthless properties."

"Oh? I heard there's a property on D Street that'll hit the market soon."

Bitsy pinched the key a little harder with her thumb. "Another property where all the value is in the land. That one's going to be a nightmare to clean up, too."

"Maybe you could make a game of it," Effie said.

Bitsy scoffed. "What are you talking about?"

"Like that television show *Trading Spaces*." As Effie said *Trading Spaces*, she caught my eye, then bugged her own eyes at Bitsy's key. "*You* know, where next-door neighbors renovate each other's homes? I think *Trading Spaces*"—more buggy eyes at the key—"would be *such* fun. Nothing like the *old switcheroo.*"

What the hey? *Trading Spaces?* The old switcheroo? Oh. Wait. Switcheroo. As in, *key switcheroo.*

Um, how did Effie think I was going to pull *that* off? I'm no magician. My all-time best magic trick was hiding broccoli under a napkin and then feeding it to my dog under the table when I was a kid.

On the other hand, getting our hands on that key, *sneaking into Mikey's house* . . . Whoa. This could be the break in the case we so desperately needed.

"Back in a second," I mumbled to Effie and Bitsy. They didn't respond, because Effie was still gushing about *Trading Spaces* and Bitsy was glazing over.

# Chapter 21

Was I really going to do this?

Yes. Yes, I was.

I edged through the funeral reception crowd, pulled my keys out of my bag, selected one that was the same size and brass color as Bitsy's key, and pried it off the ring. I wasn't even sure what this key was for. Possibly the door to the apartment I'd shared with my ex-fiancé Roger. Whatever it was, it was out of circulation and expendable.

I put my keys back in my bag and approached Effie and Bitsy.

I felt bad about this. I really did.

I bumped my arm into Bitsy's back and gave an extra little shove.

She squealed and stumbled forward, and her folder and key flew out of her grasp. Papers billowed. The key hit the carpet.

*I* hit the carpet, on hands and knees.

Bystanders gasped, and two people rushed forward to help steady Bitsy.

With feet and legs churning all around me, I dropped my key on the floor, snatched up Bitsy's key, and slid it into my cardigan pocket. Then I gathered up the flurry of papers, the folder, and the other key, and got to my feet.

"Well if it isn't Princess Grace," Bitsy said, dusting off her sleeve. "What did you do that for?"

"Sorry," I said, stuffing papers into the folder. "I tripped."

Bitsy grabbed the folder from me.

"Oh, and there's this," I said. I held out the key.

"For Pete's sake." Bitsy snatched the key, wheeled around, and was gone.

Effie was hovering a step back. "Well?" she whispered.

"Score," I whispered back.

"Then let's round up the gaggle and get out of here."

"Okay—but first I have to use the restroom. Back in a second." Too much funeral home coffee.

I waded through the cookie eaters and coffee drinkers—giving Karen Brown, who was watching me closely, a wide berth—and made my way down the hallway toward the restroom.

The Dude loped out of the single-occupancy restroom and, without really looking at me, passed in a smog of cheap cologne.

I went into the restroom.

A black Adidas track jacket hung on a hook beside the sink.

The *Dude's* track jacket.

I stole a look over my shoulder. He was entering the reception room.

I shut the restroom door. I felt in the track jacket's right pocket.

Empty.

Left pocket.

Also empty.

My heart was hammering like Jessica Fletcher's typewriter.

I twisted the jacket around. There was an inner zippered

pocket with something weighty inside. I unzipped it and pulled out a worn leather wallet.

My fingers shook as I flipped it open and . . . *bingo*. The Dude's driver's license was right on top. I slid it out.

Darrell Dvorak. Height 6'3, weight 175. Address: 102 Meigs Street #2, Rochester, New York.

The door swung open.

I jumped.

"What the eff are you doing?" someone said.

I looked up to see the Dude—Darrell—standing in the doorway. His shoulders were hunched, his jaw was thrust forward, and he held a small black gun tight to his side. Aimed at me.

My brain short-circuited.

"I *said*, what the eff are you doing?" Darrell growled.

I commanded my mouth to say something really, really convincing, but all that came out was "Uhhhhh." I couldn't take my eyes off that gun. It had mesmerized me, like a snake.

"Okay." Darrel's voice had gone from angry to menacing. "Then I guess I'll have to make you talk." He took a step forward.

"No!" I yelped. I darted back, hitting the sink hard with the back of my hip.

*Ow.* Right on my pumpkin-slipping bruise.

"Tell me what you're doing going through my wallet, or you're gonna be sorry." He adjusted his grip on the gun. "You plainclothes?"

"Police? Me? *No.*"

*Why doesn't anyone need to use the restroom right now? HELP.*

"Yeah, I didn't think so. You don't look like you've done a sit-up in your life."

"What?" I said. I forgot all about the fact that Darrell was aiming his creepy gun at me. "Like you should talk, *Darrell*. And I know we all have a 'driver's license weight'"—I made air quotes—"but come *on*. A buck seventy-five?"

"Work has been real stressful lately. Quit trying to sidetrack me. I wanna know what you were doing in my wallet."

"And *I* want to know who you're looking for in Naneda."

"Not gonna tell you."

"So you *are* looking for someone." *Score.*

Darrell stepped closer.

Instinct kicked in. Sadly, not the instinct of a superhero ninja warrior. The instinct of a hamster.

I dropped the wallet, shoved past him, and took off jogging down the hallway.

"Hey!" Darrell shouted. Footsteps pounded behind me.

At the doorway to the reception room, I hesitated.

The footsteps were almost upon me.

There was Effie, with Lo and Myron beside the cookie table. I zigzagged through the crowd toward them with the garbled idea that I'd scoop them up and we'd all head to the minivan and zoom off and leave this armed weirdo in the dust.

Then I stumbled against someone—Karen Brown—and her coffee went spraying everywhere. People cried out.

"What in the heck, Agnes Blythe?" Karen shrieked. "Don't you have even a drop of respect? Running at a funeral?"

"It's the Dude—"

Karen's eyes slitted. "The Dude."

"—and he has a gun—"

"Gun?" Karen craned her neck. "I don't know what you're

talking about, but I do know that I want you and your ragtag pals to get. The heck. *Out.*"

"But he's—"

"*Now.* Or I'm calling the police." Karen was pulling a phone out of her purse.

"Okay, okay," I said. "Sorry. It's just . . . if you see a guy in a black Adidas tracksuit, he has a gun, okay?"

Karen rolled her eyes. "Yeah. Okay. *Sure*, Agnes."

I collected the gaggle, Aunt Effie, and Chester, whispering that we had been banned from the reception and that I'd explain later. I didn't see Darrell anywhere. Had he left, or was he hiding?

We went out into the bright parking lot.

"So," Myron said, "what's the big deal? I was enjoying those pecan sandies."

"Oh, it's—um, Karen Brown said we were no longer welcome," I said.

"But why?" Myron asked.

"*I* think it's because she's jealous of our Agnes," Lo said. "Agnes is looking so glamorous with her new eyebrows."

"Yeah," I said. "Something like that. Anyway, it's lunchtime. Who's hungry?"

As we drew closer to the Dustbuster, I vaguely wondered why the hood and windshield looked lumpy and orange . . .

Then I froze.

"That's pumpkin," Myron said. "I have carved my share of jack-o'-lanterns. Three kids and seven grandkids."

"I'm getting sick of this," I said.

"That's going to wreck your windshield wipers," Hank said, sliding the side door open. He climbed in.

"Oh, my," Effie said, rooting through her purse. She pulled out her Benson and Hedges and her lighter.

Lo, Myron, and I clustered around the hood.

"Looks like two or three pumpkins," Myron said. "I'll go get a garbage bag from the funeral home."

While we waited for Myron, Lo got into the minivan with Hank, and I stood on the pavement with Effie. I kept scanning the parking lot for Darrell, Karen, and, yes, the police.

"I'm going to assume this wasn't a coincidence," I said.

"That sounds reasonable." Effie billowed smoke.

"And I'm going to assume that the murderer did it."

"Also reasonable."

"Which means that the murderer is keeping track of our whereabouts."

"Evidently."

I threw my hands in the air. "Well, that's absolutely creepy!"

A few minutes later, Myron returned with a black garbage bag, into which we tossed the larger chunks of pumpkin. He had also brought a newspaper, and I used this to wipe away the stringy, seedy pumpkin goo. The end result was orange smears and a few random seeds. Myron went to the dumpster behind the funeral home and disposed of the garbage bag and newspaper.

We drove the few blocks to Main Street in silence. I think we were all pretty rattled, except for Hank.

"Can't you drive faster?" he whined. "Didn't you hear me when I said I was hungry?"

"Pass him a sippy cup and some Cheerios," I muttered.

"I heard that!"

The Bermans snickered.

I parked, and we all got out and headed down the sidewalk.

Tourists strolled past with ice cream cones, coffees, and shopping bags. However, Crumble+Fluff was dark, and the curlicued pink-and-white CLOSED sign hung in the door. In the display window, the tiered trays were empty.

"That's weird," I said. "Delilah's missing out on some serious trade today."

The nasty little voice in the back of my head said, *Gee, maybe Delilah didn't come in to work today for the same reason Otis didn't show up to Mikey's funeral.*

"Shut *up*," I muttered.

"What was that, dear?" Lo said.

"Nothing."

\* \* \*

I didn't tell Effie that I had seen the Dude's driver's license until we were in the sandwich shop. Lo, Myron, and Hank were still up at the counter, driving the employees nuts with persnickety requests. Effie, of course, hadn't gotten anything, and I was in no mood to eat after being chased by a dude with a gun. Go figure.

"Isn't it weird that Darrell's first suspicion was that I was a plainclothes cop?" I said softly. "I mean, wouldn't most people automatically assume I was just a *thief*?"

"What are you getting at?"

"I think he's a criminal. He's had run-ins with plainclothes police before, or at the very least, he's up to something that makes him think a plainclothes cop might search his things. And let's not forget he had a *gun*. Wait. I should Google him." I dug my phone out of my bag, poked the Internet icon, and typed in DARRELL DVORAK ROCHESTER.

Nothing. I tried Facebook. Still nothing.

"Do you remember the address on his driver's license?"

"Yes. One-oh-two Meigs Street number two, in Rochester."

"Well, Google that."

I did. It was one of the floors of a dumpy converted Victorian on the edge of downtown.

"I don't know where to go with this," I said. "What do we do? Drive to Rochester and break into his apartment?"

"That sounds a little rash. You'll think of something."

"Why do you always say that?" I wailed.

"Because it's true. Ooh! I nearly forgot." Effie got out her own phone. "Remember Lally Douglass, the receptionist at that snotty architectural firm?"

"Yeah."

"She emailed me a portfolio of some of her past interior design work, and it is *gorgeous*." Effie tapped something on her phone, then slid it across the table to me.

I studied an image of a stunning kitchen with dove-gray cabinetry and marble countertops. "Wow," I said. I checked out another image of a restored historic staircase, one of a library with rich-toned furnishings and built-in bookcases, and another of a sweet, vintage-style bathroom, complete with authentic claw-foot tub and black and white hexagonal tiles. "This is what we want, Aunt Effie." I looked up. "This is exactly what we want."

"But is Lally up to the task? She may be a talented interior decorator, but she's untried as an architect and we have remodeling that must be done."

"Maybe that's just a risk we'll have to take—I mean, that *you'll* have to take. Since it's your inn."

Why did it hurt just a smidge to say that? Weird.

Just as we were leaving the sandwich shop, Hugh Simonian, the Peeper Prize judge, strolled in with a messenger bag strapped over his thin shoulder.

"Hi," I said.

"I'm sorry, Agnes, but I'm here to judge the sandwich shop," he said with a flutter of the eyelids. "I really can't consort with townsfolk."

"Ok*ay*, then," I said.

After that, I ran into the drugstore while the others waited in the Dustbuster. First, I selected a box of size-medium disposable latex exam gloves. In an attempt to make the purchase look less suspicious than it actually was, I threw a bag of gummy worms into my shopping basket. Passing the pet section, I remembered the fiasco with Tiger Boy possibly getting fleas in Hank's bed. I picked out a canister of lavender-scented flea-and-tick carpet powder that claimed to kill all four life stages of the flea.

The thrills just never stop.

Effie and I drove the gaggle (minus Dorothea, who was still back at the inn and, she told Effie on the phone, now printing out letters of apology to her stranded motor coach customers) up to Naneda Lake State Park to see the falls, and then we cruised around the glowy golden landscape to let them peep at some prime leaves.

Was that Peeper Prize Judge Hugh Simonian *blind*? Couldn't he tell that Naneda blew every other leaf-peeping town out of the water when it came to quaint, cute, and picturesque? Jeez.

As we drove past Naneda Orchards, the rows of apple trees were alive with moving bodies. A tractor-drawn hayride was just pulling out of the gravel parking lot. Families with wheelbarrows roamed the pumpkin patch, and scarecrows studded a golden-stubbled slope. The big white farmhouse overlooked the lake, and several outbuildings—barn, garage, sheds—were scattered amid lawns and brassy-leafed trees.

"Oooh," Lo said, "let's go *there* tomorrow! It looks just like a postcard."

Effie and I exchanged a look. I was thinking, *We* do *need another shot at talking with Randy about his planned meeting at the garage with Mikey*, and I was sure Effie was, too.

"Yeah," I said over my shoulder to Lo. "We should."

*   *   *

We arrived back at the inn just in time for predinner drinkie-poos in the library. The entire gaggle was going out that evening to celebrate Lo and Myron's anniversary.

Which, of course, would leave Effie and me free to commit crimes with our stolen key.

After putting in a load of laundry, I tiptoed upstairs with the lavender-scented flea-and-tick powder. The coast was clear. I sneaked into Hank's room and lightly sprinkled the powder on his pillow, blanket, and folded bath towels. I sprinkled a little more on the floor for good measure.

Skulking away down the hallway, I ran into Tiger Boy. He was walking purposefully in the direction of Hank's room.

"Hi," I said.

Tiger Boy gave his tail an extra swish, but he didn't slow down.

*   *   *

I spent the evening installing the plywood subfloor in the attic bathroom. It was not easy wielding those boards alone, and I came close to punching my foot through the ceiling below. Following the instructions I found on an online tutorial, I glued the plywood pieces to the floor joists with stinky construction adhesive and nailed them down tight. And then . . . I had a floor! I took a celebratory stroll around the bathroom.

Tears sprang to my eyes as I inspected my handiwork. Tears

I didn't understand, because at first I thought I was crying—finally—about how Otis had asked for a break, only to turn around and start dating Delilah the Sprinkles Succubus. But I also felt like I was, well, *crying about the floor.*

Construction adhesive fumes. That had to be it. I opened the bathroom window wider.

# Chapter 22

A little before ten o'clock that night, Effie and I rolled through Naneda's quiet, dark streets in the Caddy. Effie was in head-to-toe black, including a slouchy beret with a huge pom-pom that I privately thought looked more cat *toy* than cat *burglar*. I was in sneakers, dark-wash jeans, and, since the night was nippy, my black puffer jacket. The key to Mikey's house was in my right-hand jacket pocket, and a pair of latex gloves and a small flashlight were in my left. Effie had gloves and a flashlight, too.

We went down Birch Street, passing the lit-up B and B.

"I wonder how Belinda is doing," I said.

"She loathed Clifford."

"Yeah, well, it would still be pretty freaky to have your spouse murdered. And to learn that he was keeping a bunch of money secret from you. Not to mention a secret Volkswagen van. Do you think Belinda has found out about *that* yet?"

"I have no idea."

"I feel bad for her."

"She could be the murderer, Agnes."

Oh, yeah.

Effie turned onto D Street.

"Let's park further up," I said. "It will look suspicious if we're right out in front of Mikey's house."

Effie stopped in front of the next house, switched off the engine, and took a last drag of her cigarette. The orange tip crackled and glowed.

"I was thinking of buying you a present," I said. "An electronic cigarette."

"Just as soon as we catch this murderer."

"Way to put the pressure on."

"I can't quit my Bensons when I'm under strain."

"Then you're never going to quit."

"I *am*." She stubbed out the cigarette in the ashtray. "I've tried before, you know. Countless times. Back in my modeling days, each time I quit for a while, I'd put on a few pounds and have photographers and fitters and agents yelling at me to start smoking again."

"That's awful!"

"I know. Nowadays people point to women's figures from earlier decades and howl about how women didn't use to be so very fat, how they were so much more virtuous—but guess what? We all smoked. Same with French women even nowadays. People write entire books about Frenchwomen's wonderful lifestyles that keep them slim, but walking down any sidewalk in France is like walking into a hookah parlor. Their secret to slimness isn't *joie de vivre*. It's Gauloises."

"So you're smoking to stay skinny." I snapped on my latex gloves.

"Not really. But I do have many, many thousands of dollars' worth of designer apparel that's just one plate of rigatoni away from not fitting." Effie was pulling on her own gloves. "It would be a shame to waste them."

I opened my door. "Your shoes would still fit."

We walked slowly down the sidewalk. Butterflies flitted in my stomach, and I held the key tight in my gloved fist.

This was insane, right? Totally insane.

Obviously, the porch light at Mikey's wasn't on, but there was a streetlamp on the corner that lit things up fairly well. If someone in the house across the street happened to look out their window, they'd see us.

We'd have to take that chance.

Effie and went up the saggy steps. I opened the screen door and, my pulse racing, put the key to the deadbolt. At first, it seemed as if it wasn't going to fit, but then it slid home. I twisted, and the door was opening.

We darted inside and shut the door behind us.

"It smells like dirty socks in here," Effie whispered.

"I'm picking up on more of a Hot Pockets odor," I whispered back.

"What about the key?"

"Oh. Well, let's just leave it in the lock. We have to lock up before we go, right?"

"That's efficient, I suppose."

We both dug out our flashlights and switched them on. The beams swung around a combination living/dining room, which was open to a small kitchen on one side. A hallway branched off on the other side of the dining table.

"What a pigsty," Effie said. "What's all this white stuff?"

"Fingerprint powder. The police have already been over everything." I felt pretty proud that I knew what fingerprint powder was, and that I'd thought to buy us the gloves. Gold star!

"What are we looking for, exactly?" Effie whispered.

"I don't know. *Something.*"

"I'll search this room, then. You can take whatever is down that hallway."

"Don't forget the garbage in the kitchen."

"What a disgusting thought."

"That's what detectives do. They look through the trash."

"Oh, fine."

Effie went over to the living area, which consisted of a massive flat-screen TV with various gaming consoles enshrined in front of it, and one of those squashy black faux leather couches that seem to be requisite in any bachelor pad.

I took a deep breath and walked slowly toward the hallway. I couldn't get rid of the feeling of *being watched*. But all the curtains were closed.

The hallway led to a laundry closet, two small bedrooms, and a tiny bathroom. One of the bedrooms was chock full of exercise equipment—a treadmill, an Olympic barbell set—off of which dangled towels and sweatshirts. The other bedroom was taken up by a king-size mattress on the floor.

I knew I was supposed to go *in* these rooms and look through Mikey's stuff. That was the plan. But it was freaky to be in a dead man's house, and my heart was tripping over its own beat.

I forced myself to step into Mikey's bedroom. It was pretty bare-bones. There was the low, tangly bed that smelled, shall we say, *unlaundered*, and crushed Genesee beer cans were scattered across the wall-to-wall carpet. The closet's sliding doors were open to reveal a pile of dirty clothes and, up on the closet shelf, glimmery gold objects.

My flashlight beam illuminated a row of athletic trophies, their little figurines frozen in the act of catching footballs or wrestling. I stepped closer. MIKEY BROWN was engraved on the plaques along with NANEDA HIGH SCHOOL, or REGIONAL

CHAMPIONSHIPS, or ALL-STATE, as well as dates that corresponded to when Mikey had been in high school.

Sadness hit me. Mikey had peaked in high school. To me, high school had felt like a rodeo holding pen more than anything else. For Mikey, that had been *it*. And now he was dead.

I poked the toe of my sneaker around in the dirty clothes pile before I realized that the police must have already picked through it. Maybe this snooping mission wasn't going to bear fruit.

I crossed the hallway and went into the bathroom. My flashlight beam caught a filthy toilet with a stack of *Sports Illustrated* beside it. The window above the toilet had crooked miniblinds that were only half down. Light from a streetlamp hit the blinds' slats with a weird orange glow.

Aaaand . . . there it was again: the tingly feeling of *being watched*.

There was a flesh-tone shower/tub combo with a yellow curtain and a vinyl-topped vanity. I glimpsed a pale face and gasped, adrenaline shooting into my veins, then realized that the apparition with the patchy eyebrows was my own reflection in the medicine cabinet mirror.

Okay, then. On the plus side, I was all ready for Halloween.

I opened the medicine cabinet. It was sparsely occupied by a bottle of Tylenol, a bottle of NyQuil, a crunched tube of antifungal cream, and Gold Bond Medicated Powder. There was also an unopened box of toothpaste, which seemed like a surprising stroke of foresight on Mikey's part. A worn-down toothbrush and a twisted tube of Colgate lay on top of the vanity.

I was closing the medicine cabinet when I saw something else behind the box of toothpaste. Something black.

I opened the cabinet again and nudged the toothpaste box aside.

The black thing was a hair elastic.

I stared at it for a couple seconds. A *hair elastic*. Mikey had had short hair.

I picked up the elastic between by gloved thumb and forefinger. I shone the flashlight beam.

A long hair—a long *blonde* hair—was tangled up in the elastic.

Holy hollandaise sauce, Batman. Because who had *long blonde hair*? Delilah Fortune, that's who.

There was a *thunk* outside the bathroom window.

*Zing* went the adrenaline into my veins again. I fumbled the flashlight off.

A pumpkinhead was staring in the window, streetlamp glow bouncing off the bulbous side of its head. Its triangular eyes and jagged, leering mouth were deep black pits.

I screamed and backed out of the bathroom, stumbling on my own feet and slamming my shoulder into the doorframe.

"Agnes?" Effie called from the living room. "Agnes, what's wrong?"

I staggered down the hallway, my body humming with horror and my thoughts pinging haphazardly like electrons.

"Agnes, what is it?"

"Turn off your flashlight!" I croaked.

Effie switched it off, plunging us into darkness.

*Crud. This is way worse.*

"What's the matter?" she whispered.

"There's someone outside," I whispered. My voice quavered. "Someone looking in through the window. A pumpkinhead."

239

"A what?"

"Someone with one of those Headless Horseman masks on."

"Oh my lord." A pause, during which I knew with one hundred percent confidence that Effie was thinking about cigarettes. Then she whispered, "What do we do?"

"Obviously, we can't call the police."

"Probably not."

"So we have two options. Stay in here and wait it out, or run."

A pause. Then we both said at the same time, "*Run.*"

We went to the front door and slipped out into the cool night. My heart was hammering so hard, I couldn't hear much else. I swung my head to the corner of the house, fully expecting to see Pumpkinhead peering around.

Nope.

Effie and I skittered down the porch steps and along the sidewalk to the Caddy and leapt in. While Effie was fumbling the car keys into the ignition, I peered into my side view mirror.

Nothing.

What if . . . what if I had only *imagined* the pumpkinhead peering in through the window? Maybe I was just cracking up. Maybe the strain of having wrecked my relationship with Otis before it even got started, coupled with the Stagecoach Inn drama and all this stupid, *stupid* sleuthing, had made me go insane—

Effie gassed the Caddy out into the street.

"Slow down," I cried, clawing the dashboard. "The last thing we need is a traffic stop."

Effie slowed up a notch. "Where to?"

"The inn, I guess. We should get some sleep."

Yeah, right. Sleep was unimaginable with the amount of adrenaline frolicking through my system.

"Uh-oh," I said. "We left the key in the lock."

"What!"

"Sorry."

"Oh, diddle. Well, I'll turn around. We can't leave it there. It'll have some of your fingerprints on it, won't it?"

Oh, *no.* "Yeah," I said. "It will. I was holding it before I put my gloves on. Turn around."

Effie pulled into someone's driveway, reversed with a squeal of rubber, and we were heading back toward Mikey's house.

"This is the moment in the horror movie when people in the audience smear their fingers down their cheeks and groan, *Don't do it!*" I said.

"Nonsense. It would be more unwise by far to leave that key in the lock for someone to find. And if there was someone watching you through the window"—she slid me a sidelong look—"they're probably gone by now."

"You don't believe me, do you?" I said.

"Of *course* I believe you."

"You don't."

"I—"

"No, no, it's fine." I held up a hand. "Honestly, *I'm* starting to wonder if I imagined it."

Effie slid the Caddy to a stop in front of Mikey's house.

Feeling exposed and all creepy-crawly, I got out, trotted up the front walk, up the front steps, opened the screen door . . .

The key was gone.

I twirled around, stampeded back to the Caddy, and dumped myself in. "Drive!" I yelped.

"What—"

"*Go.*"

241

Effie lurched into drive.

We hadn't gone more than a third of a block when lights flared up in the rearview mirror. I twisted around. A car, head-lamps blazing, was coming after us.

"Omigosh," I breathed. "Someone's following us!"

"Calm down, Agnes. It could be a coincidence."

"But the key wasn't in the lock! There *was* someone watch-ing me—and I bet that's them following us right now!"

"In that case—" Effie fumbled a cigarette from the pack next to the parking brake. "—light this for me, darling."

I rolled my eyes, but I put the cigarette to my lips and, with shaking fingers, lit it. I don't like to be an enabler. However, Effie focused best while smoking, Effie was behind the wheel, and those headlights were getting bigger and brighter by the second. Lung disease wasn't exactly number one on my list of concerns that very second.

I passed her the lit cig.

"Perhaps we should drive to the police station," Effie said once she'd taken a drag. "We could run in and say we're frightened."

"Um, *no*? Whoever is in that car saw us trespassing in Mikey's house. They have the door key that has my fingerprints on it, and do I need to remind you that the Naneda Police Department just so happens to have a complete set of prints from both of us after that craziness last month?"

"Well then, we'll simply have to evade them." Effie stepped harder on the gas. The headlights in the mirror shrank, but then grew larger again as our pursuer sped up, too.

"We should just drive back to the inn," I said. "That creep won't dare park in our driveway and get out." *I hope.* "They're trying to intimidate us, that's all."

"Fine." Effie turned onto Main Street. There was more

traffic here, and more light. The vehicle right behind us was a black SUV, with a puffy-haired lady behind the wheel.

"That can't be who was following us," I said.

"It isn't," Effie said. "That SUV just turned out from a side street. Our charming stalker is in a white Buick."

"*What?* Are you sure?"

"I got a pretty good look at it. I'd know that make and model anywhere. A Buick LeSabre. I once drove across Mexico in one of those. Don't ask."

"I only know one person who drives a white Buick LeSabre," I said, feeling sick. "Otis's Grandma Bee."

"She can't be the only person in town who owns one."

I craned my neck, struggling to get a better look at the Buick behind the SUV, but I couldn't.

We left the downtown blocks, with their storefronts, plentiful streetlamps, and four-way stops, and then Main Street's speed limit went up to twenty-five miles per hour and we were passing old houses with big trees set well back from the road. Our headlights flashed on white picket fences and leaf-blanketed front lawns.

A pair of headlights was rapidly advancing behind us.

More adrenaline. At this rate, I was going to run out. Something to look forward to.

The headlights were bigger. Bigger.

"What are they *doing*?" I cried. "They must be going fifty miles an hour! Effie, be careful! Pull over or something!"

"I can't pull over here—the ditch is too deep!"

"Then turn into someone's driveway or something! Hurry! Omigosh, they're—"

The car behind us roared up so close, its headlamps flooded the Caddy's interior with retina-scorching whiteness.

Effie, her cigarette dangling from her lips, panicked and veered off to the right. We didn't plunge into the ditch because there just so happened to be a driveway there. And a big tree.

Effie slammed on the brakes.

The other car was passing us, and I swung my head just in time to catch the briefest glimpse of the car sailing past, behind the wheel of which was someone with a big, round pumpkin head.

We hit the tree with a sickening smash. My spine did a Slinky maneuver. The airbags poofed up. Something was hissing. Wait—that was my lungs.

I punched the airbag away from my face. My nerves jangled like a xylophone. "Effie! Are you okay?"

"Mm. Yes. I believe so." A pause. "I'll probably need to visit the chiropractor tomorrow, though."

We disentangled ourselves from airbags and seat belts and got out.

The Caddy's hood was sort of wrapped around the tree trunk.

"Poor tree," I said stupidly. "That's gotta hurt."

"Hey!" someone yelled. A figure was running down the driveway from the direction of the house. "Is everyone okay?"

"What's the story?" I whispered to Effie.

"Did you see who was in that car?"

"Pumpkinhead. You know—the person who knows we broke into Mikey's house?"

"Diddle."

"Yeah."

We would either have to lie about the accident or lie about how and why that pumpkinhead freak had followed us in the first place. Plus, if Pumpkinhead really had been tooling around in Grandma Bee's Buick, that would give the police yet another reason to be suspicious of Otis.

Effie read my mind. "Let's go with single-car accident," she said.

\* \* \*

We had to do the whole police report thing, lying through our teeth, although Officer Torres seemed to believe every word of Effie's story about how she'd dropped hot cigarette ash on her leg, causing her to crash the car into the tree. Lucky for us, Officer Torres didn't ask to see the fictitious burn on Effie's slacks.

"Seniors like you gotta get your eyes checked if you want to keep driving," Officer Torres said.

"*Senior?*" Effie said it like you'd say *goose poop*. "I'll have you know, I very recently had laser surgery on my eyes, and I've got the eyesight of a hawk."

"Okay, okay." Officer Torres chuckled. "Say, you two should go to the hospital and get checked out."

Effie looked at me.

"I'm okay," I said. "Except I have a couple extra inches between my neck vertebrae now."

"We'll go to the chiropractor tomorrow," Effie said to Officer Torres.

"You sure?"

"Positive."

Officer Torres finished filling out his report, the tow truck showed up, and then Effie and I started walking the half mile to the Stagecoach Inn.

"I'm going to miss that car," Effie said. "What should I buy next?"

"I don't know, an armored tank?"

As we walked down the inn's rutted drive, I had an idea.

"Let's drive to Grandma Bee's house in the Dustbuster," I said.

"Surely we shouldn't confront the poor woman."

"No, I just want to see if her car is there or not."

"Oh, all right."

So, without even going into the inn first, I drove us in the Dustbuster through the dark town. My fingers quivered with after-jitters.

As we approached Grandma Bee's house, I saw her white Buick LeSabre in the driveway where it always was.

"Maybe Pumpkinhead *wasn't* using her car," I said, driving slowly past.

"Stop," Effie said.

"What?"

"Just stop."

I braked.

Effie got out, trotted over to the Buick, and laid a hand on the hood. Then she got back in the Dustbuster. "The hood is warm."

Crud.

# Chapter 23

Back at the inn once again, laughter and The Beatles emanated from somewhere inside. We found Chester glugging liquor into a cocktail shaker in the library and Myron and Lo dancing. Lo's face was shining, and Myron was surprisingly nimble in his loafers. They smiled and waved when they saw us but kept dancing.

I went over to the bar. "Private dance party?" I said to Chester.

"Yup. They're loving it. They said this is the best anniversary they've had in at least a decade."

"Where are Hank and Dorothea?" I asked, thinking of the flea issue. "Hank didn't—"

"Hank came down with a terrible migraine. He said his room reeks of lavender all of a sudden—"

That would be the lavender-scented flea-and-tick powder.

"—and lavender is a migraine trigger for him."

"Did he . . . leave?"

"Nope. It gets better. He's sleeping in Dorothea's room. With Dorothea. Apparently, she gives really good migraine-relieving head massages or something."

"Are you serious?"

"Would I joke about Hank and Dorothea cuddling it up? Anyway, what happened to you and Aunt Effie?" Chester put the lid on the cocktail shaker. "You look like you just got back from a rave."

"Nothing much," I said. "Stalked by a psycho in a pumpkin-head mask. Brief car chase. Totaled the Caddy."

"Whoa." Chester clacked the shaker and then winced.

"What's the matter?" I asked.

"Oh, just a little sore." He puffed out his chest. "You know, from my workout."

"Should I ask?"

"I downloaded a strength-training app on my phone. It's awesome. All you do is crank out a few dozen pushups and sit-ups and stuff, and before long you look like a Navy SEAL." Chester poured an icy pink concoction into two waiting glasses.

Effie sidled up to the bar. "You look like you need a double vodka, Agnes."

"I should, after what just happened. What are we going to do? Pumpkinhead . . ." I shivered. "It has to be the murderer." *Driving Grandma Bee's Buick.*

"I actually have to take off for my shift at the middle school," Chester said. "I'll see you guys bright and early."

"Okay," I said. "Stay away from any and all pumpkins and Buicks."

"Good night, Chester," Effie said.

We watched Chester carry the pink drinks to a table near the stereo so Lo and Myron could sip between dances. He appeared to be limping slightly as he walked out of the library.

"The poor fellow," Effie said to me. "I don't know how he gets any sleep between working here and at the middle school. And did you see? He's *limping!*"

"That's from his workout."

"Oh." Effie poured vodka into two glasses and nudged one over to me.

I'm not much of a drinker, but I needed something to calm me down, and an aromatherapy candle wasn't going to cut it. I clinked glasses with Effie, and we both took long sips. Effie sighed. I coughed.

The Beatles' "I've Got a Feeling" came on.

"As for what to do next," Effie said, "well, what *can* we do? We've already lied to the police about our little accident—I shudder to think what that's going to do to my insurance premiums, by the way."

"Plus, Pumpkinhead apparently now has a key with my fingerprints all over it."

"Look on the bright side. That means the police *don't* have it."

Paul McCartney crooned, "Everybody had a good year, everybody let their hair down . . ."

"Everybody let their hair down," I blurted.

"Mm," Effie said, swirling her drink, "1970, I believe. Everybody's hair *was* down. Head hair, underarm hair—"

"Ew. No. I mean, I totally forgot that I found what is possibly a clue. In Mikey's medicine cabinet."

"Let's see it."

"I didn't take it. But I found a hair elastic behind some toothpaste. Maybe the police missed it. I mean, the Naneda police can't be used to doing meticulous crime scene investigations."

"A hair elastic?"

"A black one. With a long blonde hair snarled in it." I lifted my eyebrows, waiting for Effie to connect the dots and say *Delilah Fortune.*

But she didn't. "Alexa Rice," she said.

I frowned. "Alexa?"

"You've seen her roots, darling. Under that blonde hair, she's a natural brunette."

"But why would Alexa's hair elastic be in Mikey's medicine cabinet? Delilah is the one who went on a date with him, remember, and if her hair elastic was in his medicine cabinet, then she was doing more than just *dining* with him, if you know what I mean."

Effie was shaking her head. "I'd bet a sizable sum of money that it's Alexa's."

"How can you be so sure?"

"Two reasons. First of all, it's a black hair elastic. Blondes buy beige hair elastics."

"Not always. Black ones are way more common."

"Yes, but a vain woman like Delilah Fortune would buy hair elastics that match her hair."

"Alexa is vain, too."

"Oh, I know. But since her natural hair color is dark, she might own black hair elastics, left over from a time when her hair was darker."

"I'm not buying it."

"No? Well, I have more. You never asked me if *I* came across any clues in Mikey's house."

"Did you?"

"Mm. The only books on the bookshelf—if you aren't counting electronics user's manuals, I mean—were his high school yearbooks."

"Yeah, I saw his high school athletics trophies in his closet. Evidently a good stretch for Mikey."

"*The* good stretch. His yearbooks suggest that he was

Mr. Popularity. Not only that, but in the prom section of his senior yearbook, he was depicted in a white tuxedo with none other than Alexa—with brunette mall bangs, by the way—on his arm."

"Seriously?"

"Yes. And she'd scrawled a profession of her undying love in pink marker next to the picture. She'd dotted her I's with hearts, too."

"Always a reliable indicator of true love," I said. "So you think, what? That Alexa and Mikey secretly stayed together all these years, despite the fact that Alexa married Randy?"

"Think about Alexa. Her rebel-chick outfits. Her devotion to the day spa. The tears in her eyes when she remembers she's about to turn forty. *She wants to be young again.* And what did she do in the glory days of her youth?"

"Head the cheerleading squad and get drunk at keggers in the woods?"

"Yes, that. And, she slept with Mikey Brown. I don't have *proof* of this—call it a flash of intuition—but mark my words, she took up an affair with him—who knows when—as just another method of trying not to feel forty."

Portia at the day spa *had* hinted at this.

"Here's my theory," Effie said. "Randy, whose relationship with Mikey we know was always strained, learned of the affair. He tipped over the brink. He set up the appointment at the garage with Mikey under some pretense or other. Then, fueled by jealous rage, he killed him."

"Okay. And what about Clifford?"

"Clifford knew too much. Maybe he was even hidden in his Volkswagen van at the garage and witnessed the murder, and somehow Randy found out."

"Hey, that's actually a pretty good idea. But wait—what about Mikey's missing money?"

"Stolen to mislead the police. Or perhaps Randy stole it because it happened to be *there* and, well, why not?"

"Huh." I had to admit that Aunt Effie's theory possibly added up. "So what do we do next?"

"We speak with Alexa, tell her we know about her affair, ask her if she'd like to say anything in her defense, and try to get more information about Randy's movements at the time of both murders."

"Sounds safe."

"Don't be sarcastic."

"Wait. What about Randy? Did you see *him* in the yearbooks?"

"Oh, yes. Puny, pimply little fellow with Coke-bottle glasses and braces. He seemed to be quite active in marching band and drama club."

"The refuges of high school nerds," I said.

\* \* \*

In the morning, I woke up with a medium-grade hangover and two text messages from Aunt Effie on my phone. The first one was to inform me that she'd made us both chiropractic appointments for nine thirty in the morning and that she was texting me because she didn't feel like walking all the way up to the attic. The second one—from 9:10 AM—was to tell me that she had taken care of the gaggle's breakfast, done a quick housekeeping check, and it was time to leave for our appointments.

It was 9:15.

"No," I moaned into my pillow. I forced myself out of bed.

The good news was, neither of us had whiplash, and we got great adjustments. The bad news was, my hastily penciled on eyebrows got fifty percent smeared off on the sanitary tissue while I was lying facedown on the chiropractor's table.

"Better?" Effie asked me. I was steering us out of the chiropractor's parking lot in the Dustbuster.

"My neck feels amazing, but I need coffee desperately. Why did you give me three vodkas last night?"

"Don't be dramatic, Agnes. You only drank two and a half. And, *give you*? You sound like some sort of rodent in a cage at MIT, not a woman with her own free will."

"I'm not talking to anyone until I've had coffee." I aimed the Dustbuster in the direction of the Black Drop.

A little later, I had a jumbo to-go coffee in my cup caddy. Usually, caffeine means an uptick of optimism. Today, however, each sip only brought a more focused sense of doom.

Pumpkinhead.

In Grandma Bee's Buick.

Running us off the road.

Otis, the love of my life . . . gone.

On the other hand, Effie and I were inching closer to solving this thing. Maybe. We had Alexa's hair elastic from Mikey's medicine cabinet, right? Maybe if we confirmed that affair, I could tell Detective Albright that angry Randy had an excellent murder motive.

It kind of felt as if I was clinging to that hair elastic for dear life.

\* \* \*

Effie and I swung by the inn to pick up the gaggle, and then we were on our way to Naneda Orchards.

"Say, what happened to your Cadillac?" Myron asked. "I didn't see it at the inn."

"It's in the shop," Effie said breezily.

"Not Hatch Automotive, I hope," Lo said.

"No, another one." Effie was the master of being convincingly vague.

When we pulled into the gravel parking lot of Naneda Orchards, the festivities were already in full swing. Morning sunlight washed the landscape with a Hallmark-special haze.

"Is that Karen Brown on the hayride?" Effie said, peering over the tops of her sunglasses.

"Yeah," I said. "It is. With her husband and her son."

"Quality family time," Effie said.

"Except that Scootch is slouched so low on that hay bale he looks like he's in danger of falling off."

"Mm. And Mark looks as though he's already planning to wash their clothes with color-safe bleach when they get back home."

I parked, switched off the engine, and turned to the gaggle. "What first?"

"I want to press apple cider," Lo said. "I've always wanted to do that."

"I wouldn't mind trying the corn maze," Myron said.

"Oh, honey, you'll get lost in there," Lo said.

"Maybe I want to get lost."

"The pumpkin patch might be enjoyable," Dorothea said.

Privately, I wanted nothing to do with pumpkins.

"I may have worn the wrong shoes," Effie said, peering out onto the vista of gravel, dirt, and hayfield.

"You always wear the wrong shoes," I said.

"These shoes may *look* frivolous," Effie said, "but I'll have you know they're keeping my ankles as strong as a Russian gymnast's. Use it or lose it."

We all unloaded from the minivan and went straight to the rust-red wooden building with a sign that said FARMSTAND. Plump apples and pears were heaped high in crates, and rustic wooden tables held big glass jugs of apple cider.

Randy Rice was straightening the jugs, scowling.

"Look," I whispered to Effie, "there's Randy."

"He looks as though he'd like to throttle those jugs of cider."

"And there's Alexa."

"Where?"

"Behind the counter."

Alexa was working the till like a pro. She'd swapped out her usual rebel-chick attire for jeans and a white T-shirt printed with a huge red apple.

"Why don't you have a look around?" Effie said to Lo and Myron. Hank had already disappeared, presumably to the restroom. "Agnes and I will purchase apple-picking passes, m-kay?"

"Sure," Lo said. "Myron's eyeing those caramel apples. I've got to stop him before he pries his dentures out."

Effie and I got in line. There was only one person ahead of us.

"What's the plan?" I whispered.

"Ask her about the hair elastic, darling."

"In front of everyone? It's pretty crowded in here—"

We were up.

"Hello, Alexa," Effie said, sliding a platinum credit card across the countertop. "Six day passes, please."

"Hi." Alexa took the credit card, her eyes cast down.

"I have to compliment you on how well you're holding up despite . . . everything," Effie said. "Even your hair looks perky."

Alexa's hand froze mid–credit card swipe. She looked up. Her eyes flicked over to Randy with his cider jugs, then back to us. "What do you mean, *despite everything*?"

Effie smiled kindly. "*I* lost a lover once—an absolutely scrumptious Scotsman with these big burly *Outlander*-type muscles and an accent to die for. I couldn't understand a word he said, honestly. Not that we did much *talking*."

Alexa looked confused. "What happened to him?"

"Freak bagpipe accident," I cut in. "Look, Alexa, could we talk in private?"

Another eye-flick to Randy. "No. Can't you see I'm busy? You're holding up the line."

"I'm waiting for you to swipe my card, darling," Effie said.

"Oh." Alexa swiped the card. The machine starting spitting out receipts.

"We want to discuss the matter of *lovers*," Effie said softly.

Alexa tensed. "I don't know what you're talking about. I'm married to the love of my life. Randy is all the man I could ever want."

The three of us looked over at Randy. He was rooting around in his ear with a pinky.

Effie reached out and patted Alexa's hand. "Of *course* he is, darling."

I was in a throw-caution-to-the-wind mood. I was sick and tired of liars, sneaks, and that goldarn Pumpkinhead creep, and I was done with being subtle. "I found a hair elastic of yours," I said. "In Mikey Brown's bathroom."

Alexa blanched beneath her sparkly bronzing powder. "What." Her voice was flat.

"Which is why we need to talk," I said. "In private."

"Okay." Alexa's hands shook as she shoved the credit card,

receipts, and a pen at Effie. "Okay, fine. In fifteen minutes. Up on the porch at the house."

"What's the holdup?" A man behind us complained.

Effie signed, took her receipt and credit card, and we stepped away from the counter.

# Chapter 24

The plan was to pick apples ("a bushel," Lo said, but I don't think any of us knew how much a bushel was) and then take them to the cider-press room.

We set out into the sweetly fragrant orchard, beneath deep red apples against a bright blue sky. The lake sparkled. The distant vineyards glowed. The rolling forests were knock-your-socks-off orange and pink today, and the fields glinted like twenty-four-karat gold.

We found a tree laden with fruit and got the gaggle started with picking.

I noticed that Hank held a bucket for Dorothea.

"We'll be back in a bit," Effie said to them.

"What, do you have a lead in the murder case?" Myron asked loudly. "We saw you grilling that Alexa gal like a bratwurst."

"*Shh*," I said. "And *no*, we're, um, we're looking into planting a few fruit trees at the inn and we're getting advice from her. That's all."

"Uh-huh," Myron said, reaching for an apple.

Effie and I made our way back through the orchard, across the crowded parking lot, and up the sloped lawn to the farmhouse.

Alexa was pacing on the wraparound porch, hugging her elbows. When she saw us, she stopped.

Effie and I went up the porch steps. Inside the house, a dog barked.

"Let's be quick," Alexa snapped. "What were you saying about a hair elastic?"

"I found one," I said. "In Mikey Brown's medicine cabinet. With your hair on it."

"How do you know it's mine?"

"I just do."

"Why were you in Mikey's bathroom?"

"Why were *you*?"

Alexa slitted her eyes. "Why don't you just come right out and say it? You think I'm a killer."

"Of course not," Effie cooed.

"Well," I said, "you claim to have an alibi . . ."

"Okay, fine!" Alexa pulled a mobile phone from her jeans pocket. "You win. I'm going to call Walnut Manor and confirm that I was there on Sunday when Mikey was killed."

"With Delilah," I said.

"That's right." Alexa was scrolling through the contacts on her phone. "With Delilah." She punched one of the contacts, set the phone on speaker, and it was ringing.

Someone picked up. "Walnut Manor, where seniors live life to the very fullest," a woman's voice droned.

"Hi, Patsy, this is Alexa Rice, Morton's granddaughter?"

"Oh, hi, Alexa." Patsy was still droning, but it sounded as though she liked Alexa.

"Hi. Say, remember when my friend and I were in on Sunday to have lunch in the dining room with Grandpa Morton?"

"Sure do—"

Alexa shot Effie and me an I-told-you-so look.

"—and your friend was just as cute as a button!"

"You mean Delilah?"

"Yes, Delilah. Such pretty eyes!"

Puke.

"Anyway, Patsy, did anyone see a pair of sunglasses in the dining room? I lost a pair."

"Not that I know of, hon, but I can check."

"Thanks! See you the Sunday after next, Patsy." Alexa punched her phone off. "Satisfied?"

"Yeah," I said, feeling like rained-on laundry. I guess that was it, then. Alexa and Delilah were both, beyond a shadow of a doubt, nonsuspects. At least for Mikey's murder.

I hadn't realized how much I'd been clinging to the hope that Delilah was the killer. Apparently I had some serious jealousy issues to work through.

Later.

On the positive side, this meant we were closing in on Randy as the only suspect. Progress, folks.

"Now that that's all sorted out," Effie said, "about the hair elastic. How long were you and Mikey seeing each other, Alexa dear?"

I thought Alexa was going to get angry. Instead, she burst into tears. "I can't believe he's g-gone," she sobbed. "He was *my* age! That's too young to d-d-die!" She hunkered down on a porch swing, her body racked with sobs.

Great. Now I felt guilty.

Aunt Effie produced a travel-size packet of Kleenex from her handbag and passed it to Alexa. "There, there," she said. "It'll be all right." A tactful pause. "Did Randy know about your fling?"

Alexa sounded choked. "I—I don't know, actually. But I'm . . . I'm afraid."

"Afraid?" Effie said. "For your safety?"

"No, no." Alexa shook her head. "Randy loves me—he's devoted to me. I was an idiot to start something again with Mikey. It was the biggest mistake of my life. It's just that I've been so depressed. And believe me, no pills the doctor gave me could make it stop. I've tried every single kind. I just . . . I just needed something to make me feel good again. Even if it was just for a little bit. In high school, Mikey and I dated from the summer before senior year till we left for college. We broke up when Mikey went to Finger Lakes Community College and I went away to school in Pittsburg. I feel like I've wasted my life! It's half over—*half over!*—and what do I have to show for it? Nothing. Poor Randy. I don't deserve him."

"Of course you do," Effie said.

"Well, okay, I guess I do. Randy had always . . . it sounds vain to say it, but he's always just worshiped the ground I walk on. He always has, ever since we were forced to be study partners in health-and-hygiene class during sophomore year. I was failing, so the teacher paired me up with the best student, Randy."

"How romantic," Effie murmured.

"I know, right?" Alexa blew her nose.

"Back up," I said. "You said you were afraid?"

Alexa swallowed. "I'm afraid that Randy might've—*you* know."

"Killed Mikey?" I said.

Alexa's voice was a whisper. "Yeah."

I knew it.

"Out of jealousy, you know," Alexa said. "If he knew about me and Mikey's fling. Randy has just an *awful* temper. He loses

261

it—and I mean *loses it*—if someone, like, cuts in line at the supermarket, or forgets to use their turn signal, or drives too slow in the fast lane."

"Road rage?" I said, sliding my eyes to Effie.

She'd caught on already. Because remember who else had a bad case of road rage? *Pumpkinhead*, cruising around in the Buick LeSabre.

"Um, Alexa," I said, "what was Randy doing last night?"

"Last night?" Her expression closed. "He was with his buddies, same as every Thursday night. Poker at his friend Charlie's."

"Uh-huh."

"Randy hated Mikey—just *hated* him. He couldn't forgive him for kissing his girlfriend one time back when they were in high school. If he somehow found out that Mikey and I were—you know—he would've gone ballistic."

Effie said, "Is there any reason your husband might've wanted Clifford Prentiss dead?"

"Clifford?" Alexa rubbed her nose. "No. We barely knew him and Belinda, and that was just through the Chamber of Commerce, you know?"

Still, if Randy was the killer, he might've killed Clifford just because Clifford knew too much. Happens all the time on PBS *Mystery!*.

"If you truly believe Randy could be the killer," Effie said, "don't you think you should mention it to the police?"

"I did," Alexa said.

"Oh?" Effie and I exchanged a look.

*Did Alexa throw her husband under the bus?*

"Yeah," Alexa said. "I mentioned Randy's rage about Mikey to Detective Albright. But he said they have a prime suspect already and it's only a matter of time before they nail him."

My belly twisted. "Great."

"Alexa dear," Effie said, "I don't wish to cause you any more pain, but are you aware that Mikey and Delilah Fortune went on a date last Saturday?"

"Yeah." Alexa shrugged. "So?"

"Didn't that . . . bother you?"

Alexa snorted. "Um, I'm *married*? How could I have a problem with it?"

"So it *did* bother you," Effie said.

"Whatever."

I said, "You mentioned that Mikey had a mysterious influx of cash in the weeks before he died."

"Yeah."

"Delilah told us that's why she consented to going out with him—

"Consented?" Alexa narrowed her eyes. "Is *that* what she said?"

"More or less."

"I thought we could be friends, but I am so sick of her! She waltzes into town and just grab, grab, grabs. She's a narcissist, you know. I saw a Dr. Phil about them."

"I'm going to have to agree with you on that one," I said.

Alexa slid me a look. "I hear she stole *your* man, too."

"*Anyway*," I said, "do you have any more insight about where Mikey's influx of cash might've come from?"

I had already asked Alexa and other people that question a bunch of times to no avail, so I was shocked when she whispered, "Yeah."

"You do?"

"Yeah." Alexa shifted in the porch swing. "He . . . found it."

"Really? Where?"

"In a ziplock baggie. In a . . . a car he was working on at Hatch Automotive."

"Whose car?" Effie asked.

"No idea. Some car he was working on a few weeks back. He bragged about it to me. Pillow talk, you know. Mikey liked stealing stuff. He liked the thrill of it."

Right. Like stealing other men's wives.

"What . . . what did you do with that hair elastic you found?" Alexa asked. Her eyes had gone flinty.

"Um . . ." I said. I had actually left it in Mikey's medicine cabinet.

"If you turn that over to the police," Alexa said, "I'll tell them you were snooping in Mikey's house."

"Deal," I said quickly. "We stay mum if you do, too."

"Great. Okay, I have to go fix my makeup and get back to work."

"She certainly drives a hard bargain," Effie said as we walked back to the orchard.

"Can we talk about the bigger issue here?" I said. "Mikey Brown *found* that money. In a car he was working on."

"Yes, Agnes. I heard her."

"Don't you see what this means? If we figure out which car he found it in, we could really be on to something. I mean, maybe someone killed him just to get their money back."

"How can we figure out which car he found it in without looking at Hatch Automotive's records?—which, I must point out, would entail speaking to Otis about our investigation, something you have hands down refused to do."

I didn't answer.

"Let's stop at the farm stand," Effie said. "I need a bottle of water."

"Sure. I'm going to run to the restroom. Meet you back here."

I saw a sign for the restrooms and headed down a hallway at the rear of the farm stand.

Up ahead, I caught sight of none other than Karen Brown. Seeing she was about to look over her shoulder, I darted behind a stack of apple crates. I waited a few beats. I peeked out.

Karen was disappearing through a door.

I tiptoed after her.

As I drew closer, I realized she hadn't gone into the restroom, but into some kind of storeroom.

The storeroom door was half open. Whispering floated out.

I edged close to the doorway and strained my ears.

"Ten tonight, right?" Karen whispered. "At your garage?"

"Yeah," a man said. This was definitely Randy. "Why can't you remember anything?"

Stop the presses. Were *Karen and Randy* having an affair? What was going *on* in this town? Jeez. It was starting to seem like a prime-time soap opera.

Hearing footsteps, I hurried on to the restroom, my brain buzzing.

*Your* garage, Karen had said. Not *the* garage.

Had I misinterpreted those texts I had seen on Karen's phone? Karen had texted her son Scootch saying he was not allowed to go with Uncle Mikey to meet Randy at a garage. All along, I'd been assuming the garage in question was Hatch Automotive.

Had Mikey and Randy actually been planning to meet on Saturday at *Randy's garage at Naneda Orchards*?

And now Randy was setting up a meeting with Karen Brown. That was something I did *not* want to miss.

When I passed the storeroom on the way out, Karen and Randy had gone.

* * *

Effie was waiting for me in front of the farm stand with a bottle of spring water.

"You're not going to believe what I just heard," I whispered. "Walk and talk."

We headed back into the apple orchard, and I summarized what I'd overheard.

"All I know his, Randy is looking bad," I said. "Really, really bad." I ticked it off on my fingers. "He has a rage problem. He *hated* Mikey—who was having an affair with his wife. And now he's setting up clandestine meetings with another woman. This stinks to high heaven."

"We should check on Randy's alibi for last night," Effie said. "Alexa said he was playing poker at his friend's house."

"Yes," I said, "we should. Charlie Morel was the friend. He's my dad's neighbor. He teaches English lit at the university. And we *also* have to show up tonight at ten at Randy's garage."

We looked across the fields to the garage. It was a newer-looking red building with two shut vehicle-sized doors and one regular door. No windows. Its corrugated metal roof glinted in the sunlight.

"Not many places to hide," Effie said.

"Nope."

An enormous pumpkin patch stretched away from one side of the garage, a stubble field on the other. No trees. No shrubs. A couple of grinning scarecrows in plaid shirts and floppy hats studded the field.

"It'll be dark, though," Effie said in an optimistic tone. "And we'll be wearing black."

"I think I might have a better idea," I said.

\* \* \*

The gaggle managed to pick and press only a half gallon of cider, yet by the time they were done, they were overheated, sweaty, hungry, and sticky with apple juice.

"Lunchtime!" Effie trilled.

I drove us into town, and we disembarked in front of That's Italiano. The fact that they offered senior lunch specials was a big selling point.

After lunch, we headed back to the inn. I had about half an hour to get ready for my date with Albright. But first: call Professor Charlie Morel and verify that Randy had been at the poker game the previous night.

Sitting at the kitchen table, I looked up his number in the white pages and dialed.

He didn't answer. No answering machine picked up. Shucks.

After that, Effie volunteered to do my eyebrows.

"Now remember, use your feminine wiles with Albright, Agnes," she said, dabbing the makeup brush across my brow bones. "It's your prerogative as a woman."

"Gross."

"No, really. You have them. Let them come out and play."

"What's wrong with being honest?"

"In this case, everything. We can't have Albright know we're snooping, dear. There. Today you're less Sophia Loren and more Audrey Hepburn."

"So we're adding another half inch of thickness. Fab. By the way, why are *you* all gussied up?" Effie had changed from slacks and a blouse to a formfitting plum dress, and her makeup had been redone.

"Mr. Solomon is coming over for a drink."

"He just can't get enough, huh?"

Effie's smiled. "We have things to discuss."

"I'll bet you do."

"Knock-knock," Dorothea said, standing in the kitchen doorway.

"Oh, hello," Effie said. "Would you like a cup of tea? Or, it's not too early for a drink—?"

"No, thank you." Dorothea waved some papers in her hand. "I'm afraid someone else's papers got mixed up with mine in the printer—they look like some sort of university application forms?"

"Oh." I hurried over and took the forms. "Thanks."

Dorothea left. Effie was opening the window over the sink, lighting up a cigarette.

"Aren't you going to ask me about the application forms?" I said.

Effie blew a thin stream of smoke through the screen and turned to me. "You do what you need to do, Agnes."

"Are you . . . upset?"

"How could I be? You're young, you're exploring your options. I know that you'll keep me updated on a need-to-know basis, m-kay?"

"Okay." Feeling vaguely like a jerk, I stashed the application forms on the pile of junk mail and takeout menus on the kitchen counter. I'd deal with them, just as I was apparently dealing with everything else in my life, *later*.

I drove myself downtown, since everyone was planning on spending the afternoon at the inn anyway. Effie had impulse-bought a croquet set at an estate sale a few weeks before and had triumphantly wheeled it out, much to the gaggle's delight. They were whacking wooden balls around on the lawn when I left.

# Chapter 25

"Wow," Detective Albright said when I found him waiting on the sidewalk in front of the movie theater at 3:59. "You look great! Are those new glasses?"

"Hi. Thanks. These are my backup glasses. I keep losing eyewear. Sorry I'm late."

Albright was wearing saggy jeans, a too-tight windbreaker, and approximately one gallon of cheap aftershave. All for my benefit.

Man, I felt like a jerk, leading him on. On the other hand, he knew stuff that I wanted to know, and wasn't as if going to one movie with a guy means you're going to marry him. Besides, Albright didn't really deserve my pity. Not when he was trying to get Otis thrown in the slammer.

At my insistence, we bought our own tickets for *Headless Horseman III* at the window, and went in. At the concession stand, Albright bought an extra-large buttered popcorn and Coke, and I bought a jumbo Junior Mints. Silent ads were flashing on the screen when we shuffled into a couple of free seats.

"So," I said, after what I hoped had been a reasonable amount of time, and also because I couldn't stand the sound of

Albright's adenoidal breathing. "How's that crazy murder case going?"

"You know I can't talk about my work," Albright said with all the husky mysteriousness of Batman.

"Yeah, I know . . . but a murderer, still at large." I gave a mock shiver. "It's pretty scary."

"Don't be scared," Albright said, and to my total horror he raised one of his stubby windbreakered arms and *put it around my shoulder.*

Oh, no. Ugh. No, no, *no.*

Aunt Effie's voice echoed in my skull: *Use your feminine wiles, Agnes. It's your prerogative as a woman.*

I didn't remove Albright's arm. It was like a slug. A limp, clammy, nylon-covered slug. I mustered what I hoped was a sweet-and-frightened tone. "Um, about Clifford Prentiss's secret van parked at Hatch Automotive . . . have you looked into that?"

"Yeah, it's true. He had a 1987 Volkswagen Vanagon . . . recently purchased with cash from Hatch Automotive."

I swallowed thickly. "Oh."

"Clifford was keeping the van a secret from his wife, it seems. She knew nothing about it, and it wasn't registered or insured. I'm thinking he was planning on taking off in that thing, leaving his life behind, as soon as the time was right." Albright sighed and stuffed a handful of popcorn in his mouth. A few pieces dribbled onto his lap. "But he didn't make it out alive. This is the thing that just kills me about cases like this. Unhappy people wading through life and then—poof—their lives are over and they'll never have another chance to make things better for themselves. Sure makes you think, doesn't it?"

"Uh-huh." I shrank incrementally away from Albright's arm.

"I'm thinking Clifford was planning on using that money to

fund his new life wherever he was going in that van," Albright said. "Start over fresh. Make himself a new home."

"But now Belinda is going to get the inheritance money."

Albright's fingers paused in the popcorn carton.

"What?" I said.

"Well, no, she isn't going to get it."

"What do you mean?"

"Agnes, I shouldn't be telling you all this."

*Feminine wiles, Agnes. Feminine wiles!*

"I'm just curious," I said in what I hoped was a sultry voice. "All this stuff is as minding-bending as, I don't know, an episode of *Battlestar Galactica* or something."

*Battlestar Galatica* is the equivalent of *Open Sesame* to a nerd.

Albright sighed. "Okay. Clifford had recently opened a bank account with the entire inheritance—about fifty thousand dollars."

"A joint account with his wife?"

"No. She knew nothing of the account. He used a chunk of the inheritance to buy that Volkswagen two weeks ago, and then he turned right around and cashed out the remainder of the account on Wednesday morning. He was murdered Wednesday night. But no one knows what happened to the remaining forty-odd grand in cash."

Whoa. This was big. This meant *the killer wanted money in both cases*. The motive was never personal. It was all about the ka-ching.

"No one knows where Clifford's keys are, either," Albright said. "He had driven himself and Belinda to the Lake Club Masquerade, but the keys weren't on his body."

"Belinda didn't have them?"

"No."

"Have you considered Belinda Prentiss as a murder suspect?" I asked.

"Belinda? Why?"

"I happen to know that she hated Mikey and thought he was ruining her B and B business, and, also, she can't keep up with her bills."

Albright was peering at me closely.

I kept my eyes glued to the silent advertisements on the movie screen.

"How do you know about Belinda's bills?" Albright asked.

I shrugged. "People gossip. And then there's Randy Rice. Have you talked to him?"

"No. Who's he?"

"The guy who owns Naneda Orchards. He was really close to Mikey. It sounds like they had a pretty . . . intense relationship." I stopped there. Revealing more about Randy would mean revealing how I had spied on Karen's text messages and eavesdropped at the orchard storeroom.

Holding back like this was starting to feel slippery.

"*Otis Hatch* was aware of Clifford's van and, very likely, his secret money," Albright said, "since that's what Clifford used to pay for the van. As far as I can tell, Otis is the *only* person who knew about those things. And . . . I'm sorry Agnes, I know you were attached to the guy . . ."

"What." I swear my heart stopped.

"Well, the thing is, we found Clifford Prentiss's wallet in the storage compartment of Otis's motorcycle."

*Omigosh.*

"That doesn't mean anything," I said, my voice shrill. "It could've been planted."

"Okay, then how do you explain how no one can account for

Otis's whereabouts at the Lake Club dance around the time Clifford was killed in the bathroom—"

"Really?"

"—or how he doesn't have an alibi for when Mikey Brown was killed?"

"He told me he did. He said he was at the mall in Lucerne with his Grandma Bee."

"I talked to Bee."

"And?"

"She backed him up—"

"See?"

"—but I have reason to believe that Bee isn't . . . I'll put it this way, she isn't as sharp as she might've once been."

*Karen.* Karen Brown had told him that.

"You're bending over backward to keep believing in Otis, Agnes." Albright shook his head. "Why do nice girls like you always go after the bad ones?"

The lights went down, and the Coming Attractions started in a gush of sound and rapid-fire imagery. More people shuffled in and scooched into seats.

I plotted how to get Albright's condescending sluglike arm off my shoulders. Should I pretend to drop something on the floor and then bend to pick it up? Yeah. That could work. I'd drop a Junior Mint.

As soon as the final credits were rolling, I extricated myself from Albright's offer of ice cream or coffee and made a beeline to the Dustbuster.

*      *      *

"Do you realize what all this *means*?" I exclaimed to Aunt Effie and Chester in the inn's kitchen a while later. I had told them

273

everything, pacing back and forth. Tiger Boy watched me from a chair, tail flicking. "It means all this stuff we've learned, this personal stuff, is completely meaningless. The murderer wants money. That's it. Not revenge. Not to shut somebody up or because they're jealous about an affair or whatever. We've been totally wasting our time! All along it was about money. You said it yourself, Aunt Effie—*follow the money*. Why did we let ourselves get sidetracked?"

"Live and learn," Effie said. She was standing at the kitchen sink with another cigarette.

"Next time, you guys should make a spreadsheet or something," Chester said. He was unwrapping a bodybuilder's cookies 'n' cream protein bar. "Maybe use a whiteboard?" He bit into the bar.

"We've been blind," I said. "And there will be no next time! I am never, ever, ever, *ever* getting mixed up with murder again."

"We've been figuring things out," Effie said. "And now you've figured this out. Thanks to your feminine wiles. Did you end up speaking Klingon at all?"

"No. But I did mention *Battlestar Galactica*."

"You wanton, you," Chester said.

I was suddenly exhausted. It was as if I'd hit a brick wall. I sank into one of the chairs at the kitchen table. "I just . . . I just can't bear it that Albright is still investigating Otis. That he's assembling a *case* against Otis. It's not right. And Clifford's wallet in Otis's motorcycle can only mean one thing: the killer is trying to frame him."

"We're going to crack this thing, Agnes," Effie said. "You're going to save Otis."

I snapped my fingers. "The Dude! Darrell Dvorak!"

"Go on," Effie said.

"He's been looking for someone in town, right?"

"Mm."

"Well, what if he has something to do with all this money stuff? Like, what if he works for, I don't know, a mob boss or something, and he's in town to collect?"

"A mob boss?" Effie said. "In Naneda? *Darling.*"

"Yeah." My shoulders slumped. "Never mind."

"You have Darrell's address, right?" Chester asked around a mouthful of protein bar. "From his driver's license?"

"Yeah," I said. "It's in Rochester. One-oh-two Meigs Street, number two."

"I'll go stake him out. Figure out what his deal is. I'll go tonight."

"But don't you have to go to work?"

Chester shrugged. "I'll go in late. And anyway, it's not like the middle school will cease to exist if I don't empty the waste-bins for one day."

"Maybe not, but you could get fired."

"Fired? No way. They love me there. I write lines from famous poems on the chalkboards every night."

Okaaay.

"I'm doing it," Chester said. "I want to help. And man, I feel pumped." He threw the balled-up protein bar wrapper at the garbage can, and missed.

\* \* \*

At seven o'clock that evening, Dorothea and Hank announced that they were going out to dinner. Alone.

When they drove off in a taxi, I was pretty sure they were holding hands in the back seat.

"Whew," Myron said, watching with me from the front

275

porch. "My Lo may not be a good matchmaker, but that cat of yours sure is."

I concentrated on watering the hanging pots of chrysanthemums. "What do you mean?"

"C'mon. The cat thrust them together. Sure, he had a little help from his fleas and your flea powder—"

"You know about that?"

"We all do. But you know what I think? I think that cat of yours is a cupid." Chuckling, Myron went back inside.

Cupid? Tiger Boy?

The rest of us went out for Mexican food at Mariachi. I texted Lauren, and she met us there. Myron and Lo both hit the margaritas pretty hard, but I limited myself to hitting the chips and salsa hard. I needed to keep my wits about me for the night ahead.

Chester was halfway through his combo plate when he let slip to Myron that he was going to stake out Darrell the Dude's apartment in Rochester.

"Sounds dangerous," Myron said. "Didn't Agnes say that man is armed? I'll come with you."

I clapped a hand on my forehead.

"Myron was in the Navy," Lo said, flushed from tequila. "He's still got some moves."

"Sure," Chester said. "You're welcome to come."

"I'll come too," Lo said.

"No," Myron said. "Too dangerous."

"I'm coming, Myron," Lo said with a steely smile.

"Okay, okay," Myron said.

I guess Lo still had some moves, too.

"What's this about a stakeout?" Lauren asked.

Lo and Myron filled her in. Chester blushed and forklifted enchilada into his mouth.

"Oooh, I want to come," Lauren said. "Is there room in the car?"

"Yeah," Chester said in a slightly choked voice. "We'll be taking my Datsun."

"Cool," Lauren said.

"I thought you were meeting Jake tonight," I whispered to Lauren.

She shrugged. "I'll cancel. This sounds way more fun."

After dinner, Chester, Lauren, Lo, and Myron got into Chester's Datsun hatchback, which sagged to the pavement under their combined weight.

"Good luck," I said, bending to see them through the open window.

"We don't need luck," Myron said. "We've got skills."

They puttered away into the night.

\* \* \*

Effie and I went back to the inn and got to work on our disguises. Then, with our hats in our laps, I drove the Dustbuster to a side road abutting Naneda Orchards. The sky had clouded over and a brisk wind had kicked up. When I turned off the headlights and switched off the engine, the night seemed too big.

Also, our plan seemed crazy, but I was getting used to that.

Because there was no place to hide in the vicinity of Randy's garage, we had disguised ourselves as scarecrows in floppy-brimmed hats from Effie's closet, plaid shirts from Carson's Outdoor Emporium, and alfalfa hay purchased at the feed store. The hay had come in a bag with a picture of a guinea pig on it.

"Are you sure you want to go ahead with this?" I whispered.

"The hay is giving me a rash."

"Yeah, the hay under our shirts may have been sort of overkill."

"You already said that Agnes, but what if someone comes up close for some reason?"

"Um, they're probably going to wonder why one of the scarecrows is wearing sweatpants"—that would be me—"and why one of the scarecrows is wearing pointy high-heeled boots."

Effie was opening her door. "For the tenth time, Agnes, I don't *own* flat shoes."

"By the way," I said, "do me a favor and don't light up until you're out of your disguise, okay? This hay is flammable."

# Chapter 26

We hobbled across the ditch, through the barbed wire fence, and then we were in the stubble field. We picked our way along. Fields always look smooth from a distance. You picture yourself running through them in full *The Sound of Music* mode. But in my experience, walking through fields is actually hard. They're rutted. There are dirt clods. There are rustling rodents and, worse, snakes.

Below us, rustling lines of apple trees sprawled to the lake. There was the dark farm stand, the empty parking lot, the cider house, and the main house, in which a single upstairs window glowed.

And there was the garage, a silhouette hulked at the edge of the stubble field.

We were out in the open, just a stone's throw away from the garage, when light a blinked on, filtered by apple trees.

Effie and I froze in our tracks.

A door slammed.

"He's early," I whispered.

I heard a man saying something, his voice garbled by the wind. Then—Arf! Arf!

Crud. A dog.

I stood still as a statue. Okay, still as a scarecrow.

Effie did the same.

And then a short dog bounded out from the apple trees, its white ruffly neck fur glinting in the sparse moonlight. The corgi.

It was barking and running straight at me.

I stopped breathing.

Now here was Randy, loping out from the apple trees. "Grace!" he shouted. "Come!"

Grace ignored him. She was squiggling right up to me, snorfling and wagging her tail. I held my breath as she reached me and started sniffing my sneakers and whining.

*Oh crud oh crud oh crud.*

But Randy wasn't paying attention. He had gone up to the garage, taken a key out of his pocket, and was unlocking the door. He pushed the door open, then turned around and shouted, "Grace! Come, you stupid dog. *Come.*"

Grace had abandoned me to go and sniff Effie's feet. Ever so gently, Effie tried to nudge Grace away with her boot. Apparently, that got Grace in the mood to play, because she went into downward dog pose, wagging her tail.

"Dammit," Randy shouted, peering in our direction. "Grace, come!"

I channeled scarecrowness.

Then I heard a small trickling sound. Grace was peeing on Effie's foot.

"Grace!" Randy roared.

Grace finished up and bounded over to Randy.

"You damn dog! Forget it. You're going back to the house." Randy bent, grabbed Grace's collar, and ushered her into the orchard.

He'd left the garage unlocked.

"Psst!" I whispered to Effie. "Let's go have a look. We have maybe a minute or two."

"That dog ruined my boot!" Effie half whispered, half sobbed.

"You can wash it off."

"It's *suede*."

"We don't have much time!" I did the G.I. Joe hunker-run to the garage. Alfalfa hay dribbled in my wake.

Effie was right behind me. "These are handmade boots, one of a kind," she whispered.

We stepped through the open door into the garage. I squinted around in the pitch darkness. "Well, why did you wear them on a spying mission?"

"They go with the slacks."

"It's too dark in here." I reached into my sweatpants pocket and pulled out my phone. "We're going to have to risk it."

"Agnes, no! He'll be back any second!"

"Then we have a couple of seconds." I switched on the flashlight app on my phone. A narrow, bluish-white beam shot out onto a concrete floor. I swung it around. The beam bounced off the shiny, candy-apple-red wheel well of the antique pickup I had seen earlier in the parking lot. Its bed was piled with hay bales, a blue plastic tarp tied over them.

I squeezed around the pickup. There was the tractor with the hayride wagon hitched to it. And on the other side of that, a low, lollipop-yellow sports car.

"Look," I whispered. "A Camaro."

"So Randy owns a frivolous boy toy," Effie whispered back. "No surprise there. All of my husbands had sports cars that they lavished with affection—oh, wait, all except Narid." Narid, Effie's—what was it? third? sixth?—husband, had been a nuclear physics professor. "But," Effie continued, "he had his atom smasher, which really amounts to the same thing, don't you think?"

"Don't you remember? The text message from Karen to her son Scootch about meeting at Randy's garage? Now I get it! Karen said Mikey mentioned buying a Chevrolet Camaro, but she thought he was just bragging to impress Scootch. Then Alexa mentioned that Randy bought a midlife-crisis sports car that he never even drives. Don't you see? Mikey was going to buy Randy's Camaro. *This* Camaro. That's why they were setting up that meeting. That's why Mikey invited Scootch along— to impress him. Only, Karen wouldn't let Scootch go, so he went camping in Canada instead, and . . . Mikey never made it here to buy the Camaro. He was killed before he got here. And you know what? If he stopped at Hatch Automotive with the plan to continue on here and purchase the Camaro, he might've had cash for the car on him."

"Oh, my. That does make sense—although, why would Randy be secretive about it?"

"Because he's embarrassed about needing the money, maybe. He didn't want to sell the sports car. He *had* to sell it. What I don't get is, why is Karen meeting up with Randy, now? It doesn't make any sense."

"Maybe *she* wants to purchase the sports car. For Scootch."

"Doubtful."

"He's coming!"

I tapped off the flashlight app.

"Quick!" Effie whispered. "Up here!"

"Where?" I whispered back. I couldn't see a darned thing, but I heard rustling and crunching. Then I realized Effie was climbing into the back of the flatbed pickup and getting underneath the tarp.

Sounded good to me.

I climbed up and collapsed onto the pickup bed. Effie was crouched beside me. The tarp clung to the top of my head.

Good thing I wasn't *super* claustrophobic.

The garage door thunked open and someone was coming in. And . . . there were voices.

I squeezed my eyes shut. *Oh please oh please oh please don't get anything out of the back of the pickup.*

Randy didn't. And he didn't switch on the garage light, either.

Effie and I had gone to Randy's garage that night with the expectation that he was going to meet up with Karen Brown. Except that wasn't Karen he was talking to.

It was Belinda Prentiss.

Belinda was whispering, but I heard the words *time* and *hurry.* Randy's response was unintelligible, but he sounded annoyed.

In slo-mo, I inched to the edge of the flatbed and, veeeerrrry slowly, lifted a piece of the tarp to make a one-inch crack. I peeked out.

The only light was a shaft of gray coming from the open door.

More footsteps, whispers, shuffling.

*Just how many people are in here?*

"Everyone here?" a woman said. It was—omigosh—*Delilah.* "It is so super creepy to be doing this in the dark. It's not like anyone is going to see us way out here in the sticks."

"This is hardly the sticks." This was Randy, in a surly voice. "And my wife is watching TV right over there in the house."

"Stop complaining, Delilah." This was Belinda, full of scorn.

"If you think this is creepy, Delilah, try a night in jail." That was—*whoa*—Karen Brown.

"Jail?" This was the contemptuous voice of Hugh, the Peeper Prize judge. "You small-town folk sure have a taste for intrigue. Come on, people, this isn't *Days of Our Lives*."

Karen. Delilah. Randy. Belinda. Hugh.

Was it possible that they, working together, had *colluded* to murder Mikey and Clifford? Like some kind of weirdo conspiracy?

"Let's get this over with," Belinda said. "I need my sleep. I have yoga at six tomorrow morning."

Not *My husband was murdered and I'm freaked out*?

Effie poked me. "*Record them*," she whispered, almost inaudibly.

Oh. Yeah. Good idea.

I was still holding my phone. I swiped it on. The flashlight app flared, blinding me. I pressed it against my chest to hide the light.

Yikes.

For an agonizing second I was sure they'd seen my phone flash on.

But then Delilah said, "Well? Why did you call this *emergency meeting*, Karen?" I could hear the air quotes. "So much drama."

Shielding the lit-up screen with my cupped hand, I found the voice memo app on my phone and pushed RECORD. Then I dimmed the screen as far as it would go and turned the phone's microphone hole in the direction of the conversation.

"So much drama?" Karen said. "Um, do you even realize the pile of doo-doo we're in? Not to mention the fact that all that money is just *gone*? I never should've let you in on the deal, Delilah."

"And *I* never should've taken you up on it," Delilah snapped. "It was supposed to be a straightforward thing, and it's turned out to be a total disaster, with gross dead bodies and the police bugging us, and my investment—do you realize how hard it was for me to scrape together five thousand bucks?—*stolen*. You know what, Karen? I think this is all *your* fault."

"All my fault," Karen repeated in an expressionless voice. "And how is that, Miss Priss?"

"Miss Priss?" Delilah gave a mock giggle. "Do you think I haven't heard that before? Mainly from washed-up hags like you who can't stand the sight of a *feminine* woman—"

"What about me?" Hugh cut in. "Did you ever think of that? You guys *promised* me that money, but then I come to town and that sardonic Agnes chick passes me a stupid card with a pug dog on it, and no money inside?"

*Omigosh. A bribe conspiracy!*

"That was *not* the deal," Hugh said.

"Let me get this straight," Belinda snapped. "We're supposed to think about how you've been inconvenienced when two people—including my husband—have been murdered? Give me a break!"

"Cut it out!" Randy said. "We can't be fighting like this. Get a little perspective. We could be in serious trouble."

"That's exactly why I called this meeting," Karen said. "I want to make sure nobody is saying anything that they shouldn't to the police."

"Seriously?" Delilah said. "*This* is why we had to come all the way out here? To get a lecture on the most obvious thing in the world?"

"You know what?" Hugh said. "None of this is my problem. I'm out of here. You guys are a bunch of Podunk losers. I'll tell you one thing, though—you'll be sorry you messed this up. I was counting on that money." Stompy footsteps. Slamming door.

"Great," Randy said. "Now Hugh is angry—"

"Who cares?" Karen said. "He's not going to say anything to the police. If he did, he'd have to incriminate himself."

"Listen." This was Belinda. "The money that was stolen from Mikey Brown when he was killed was *our money*. That means the longer the police poke around into his death, the more likely it is that they catch on to what we were doing."

Randy said, "What we were doing wasn't even *illegal*."

"Maybe not," Belinda said, "but it was a violation of the Peeper Prize rules."

"So what?" Delilah said.

"So *what?*" Karen scoffed. "Maybe *you* don't care about Naneda—you just came waltzing in last summer, and I doubt you'll even last till *next* summer before one of your customers' wives runs you out of town—but *we* care about this town. Our families depend on the tourists who come here to visit. If it gets out that we were planning on bribing a Peeper Prize judge, then Naneda will be disqualified from the contest forever."

"It'll ruin our town's reputation," Belinda added.

"It'll ruin our *personal* reputations," Randy said. "The money is missing and there's nothing we can do about that, but at the very least we can triage the situation by making sure we all keep quiet about the money—"

"That's exactly why this is all Karen's fault," Delilah said. "Can't you guys *see* that? She was supposed to hide the money in a safe place, and now it's gone. I'm starting to wonder if Karen set all this up to keep that money for herself. Gee, maybe *she* killed Mikey and Clifford."

There was shocked silence, punctuated by a rattle of wind across the roof.

"I'd watch my mouth if I were you," Karen said.

"I'm just pointing out the obvious," Delilah said. "The money was given to you because you said you could keep it safe, and the next thing we know, it's gone?"

"How was I to know that old bat was going to take her car into the shop?" Karen cried. "She never, and I mean *never*, drives that thing, and suddenly she's taking it in for a tune-up?"

They had to be talking about the car in which Mikey had, according to Alexa, found cash in a ziplock baggie. Two puzzle pieces snapped together in my mind: the car with the money in the ziplock was *Grandma Bee's Buick LeSabre.*

"We trusted you," Belinda said.

"It's not my fault!" Karen exploded.

"Tell me again why you didn't keep it in your house," Randy said. "Like any normal person would have."

Belinda said, "Because her husband is a certifiable clean freak."

"Watch your mouth," Karen snarled.

"Well, he is," Belinda said. "She was afraid he'd find the money since he obsessively cleans and organizes their house twenty-four/seven."

"At least he isn't planning on secretly running away from me because I'm such a domineering shrew," Karen said.

"You take that back!" Belinda shouted. "Have a little respect for the dead!"

"Stop!" Randy bellowed.

One thing was for certain: coconspirators though they were, this group wouldn't hesitate to betray each other. No sirree, Bob.

"Well, I resent this," Karen said in a lower tone. "I went out on a limb, being the one responsible for looking after the money, and this is the thanks I get? It was a total fluke that Bee took her car into the shop when she did—she never drives that thing!—and it was a total fluke that that idiot Mikey found the money. It should've been a foolproof plan. God, I stare at that stupid Buick every time I wash dishes in my kitchen sink. It never goes *anywhere*."

"You need to own up to this, Karen," Randy said. "Now we've got that Peeper Prize jerk Hugh on our cases, whining about the money—"

"He threatened to remove Birch Grove B and B from his app!" Belinda shrilled.

"He threatened to do that to Lilting Waves, too," Karen said. "He uses that app like a weapon. We have to do something about it."

"Like what?" Delilah said, syrupy sweet. "*Kill* him, Karen?"

"That's it. I'm leaving," Karen said. "Keep your traps shut, people. The future of our town is at stake."

Aunt Effie was really twitchy—nicotine fit, I figured. Meanwhile, I had developed a cramp in my foot. We both shifted position at the exact same time, so I wasn't totally sure which one of us rustled the tarp.

"Hold on," Belinda whispered. "What was that?"

"What?" Randy said.

"I heard something. Over there. Someone switch on the light."

"No light!" Randy said. "I don't want Alexa to know we're out here."

"Who has a flashlight?" Delilah asked. "Anyone?"

"I do." That was Randy.

*Click.* A beam of light swung across the tarp.

Footsteps.

With a crumpling whoosh, the tarp was ripped off from Effie's and my hiding spot. A flashlight blinded me.

I held up my arm to shield my eyes.

"It's you goddamn snoops!" Randy bellowed.

"Get her phone!" Karen shrieked. "She recorded us! Omigod, *she recorded us!*"

Randy lunged at me.

I reared back, crashed into Effie, and my phone flew out of my hand, over the side of the pickup, and clattered somewhere in the darkness.

"You're disguised as *scarecrows*?" Karen said with a nasty laugh. "You really are a couple pieces of work, you know that?"

Effie had climbed over the side of the pickup. She edged toward the garage door.

"Oh, no," Belinda said, blocking her path. "Not before you hand over *your* phone."

"Phone?" Delilah said. "We should be calling the cops. Randy, they're trespassing on your private property!"

"I don't. Want. Alexa. To. Know," Randy said through gritted teeth.

Effie said, "I don't suppose you want the police to know about this little meeting either, mm? How would it look, a clandestine meeting under cover of darkness, discussing a bribe?"

"We did nothing illegal," Karen said.

"That's right," Belinda said.

"Even so," Effie said, "it just doesn't look *wholesome*. Come on, Agnes."

"I need to get my—" I stopped in my tracks.

Randy was blocking my way, holding a pitchfork.

"Never mind," I said.

Effie and I rushed out the garage door. I felt as if someone was going to tackle me or trip me or grab my ponytail, but we scurried into the field without anybody stopping us.

"God, I need a cigarette," Effie said breathlessly as we stumbled along.

I almost needed one myself.

The night was chilly, but I was panting and sweaty. We reached the fence. I held open the barbed wire for Effie to climb through, and then she held it open for me. We threw ourselves into the Dustbuster, I jammed the key into the ignition, and we spluttered away as only people in a used minivan can.

# Chapter 27

Neither Effie nor I said a word until I had driven about a mile toward town.

"Crud." I smacked the steering wheel. "Crud! That recording was our only proof of their conspiracy! We could've taken that to the police and—and—"

"And what?" Effie was rummaging in her purse, presumably for her cigarettes. "It's proof of their plot to bribe the Peeper Prize judge, but it hardly proves who the murderer is."

"Sure, yeah, but maybe that recording would've forced the police to take those guys more seriously as murder suspects. Plus, now they're on to us! All of our suspects are on to us!"

"They already were, Agnes. From the start."

"Okay, sure, but this makes it official."

"Drive to the minimart," Effie said.

"What?"

"I don't know how it happened, but I seem to have left my cigarettes at home and I need one. Now."

"Okay, okay." I turned left, heading toward the twenty-four-hour minimart at the gas station by the main highway. "I cannot *believe* that Karen, Randy, Delilah, and Belinda pooled money to bribe Hugh. Were they really that desperate to push Naneda to the top of the foliage tourism list?"

Effie didn't answer because she was busy drumming her fingers on her knee.

"And second of all," I said, "I'm mad—*furious*, actually—that those jerks are putting the entire town of Naneda's future at risk! A scandal like bribing the Peeper Prize judge could blacklist us for years to come. Our tourist economy could take a serious blow."

"Us? *Our?* Agnes, darling, are you saying you're a real Nanedan now?"

"Yes! Yes, I am a real Nanedan. And I'm *pissed*!"

"Well, don't take it out on the gas pedal."

Effie's phoned jingled. She dug it out of her purse and looked at the screen.

"Who is it?" I asked.

"No idea. Local number." She tapped ANSWER. "Hello? Oh, hello Detective Albright. How are you?"

Just great.

"Mm," Effie said, listening. "I see. Yes, yes of course. Driving? No, no. Agnes is driving . . . mm. All right. Tomorrow. After the parade, of course—you may recall that Agnes is Gourd Queen? Mm. Oh, I *know*. She'll be the belle of the ball . . . really? I'll tell her to leave her glasses on, then. Well, we'll see you soon, then, and have a wonderful evening. Goodbye." She tapped the phone off. "*Diddle.*"

"Care to fill me in?" I said.

"I really need a cigarette. And a drink."

"TELL ME!"

"Earlier this evening, Detective Albright got an anonymous

tip that we were seen snooping around Mikey Brown's house last night—"

Oh.

"—and that a key was found in the lock."

"That means Pumpkinhead—who's probably the *murderer*—put the key *back in the lock*!"

"Slow *down*, Agnes."

I slowed down fractionally.

"More importantly," Effie said, "your fingerprints could be on that key. Naneda Police Department has both our fingerprints, and Albright said we must go down to the station for questioning. On the record."

"*Cheese and rice.*"

"My thoughts exactly."

"When are we supposed to go?"

"Tomorrow. After the parade."

"Great." We had reached the gas station. I turned into the parking lot. "I need some Tums."

I parked, and Effie and I went into the minimart. I selected a bottle of Tums and a Snickers bar and placed them on the checkout counter.

"Rough night?" the cashier asked. His crooked nametag said DARIUS and he had tired, kind-looking dark eyes.

"Yeah."

"May I interest you in a scratch card?" He tapped the Plexiglas on the counter, beneath which were displayed a colorful assortment of scratch cards. "Perhaps it will cheer you up."

"No, thanks," I said. "I have bad luck."

I paid, gathered up my purchases, and found Effie, who was still perusing the bottled-water case.

"Could I borrow your phone?" I asked.

She passed it over.

I went outside into the cold night. Under the garish lights of the gas station roof, I dialed Otis's number. As the phone rang, I peeled the SEALED FOR YOUR PROTECTION thingy off the Tums bottle.

He picked up on the fourth ring. "Hello?" His voice was fuzzed with sleep.

"Hi."

"Agnes? Are you okay?"

"Um. More or less." I unscrewed the lid of the Tums.

"It's—" Rustling. "It's almost midnight. Can it wait till morning? This was the first real sleep I've gotten all week."

"Sorry." Holding the phone between my shoulder and ear, I shook five Tums into my cupped palm. I wasn't totally sure why I was calling Otis at this hour, and after all that had happened. I needed to hear his voice, I guess. Even if we were through. "I just found out some really . . . startling information."

Otis sighed heavily. "You and your aunt are out messing around again, aren't you? Listen. I'm glad you called, because you haven't responded to my message. We need to talk."

*I can't do this.*

My hand shaking, I popped the handful of Tums into my mouth and chewed. "Talk?" I mumbled through the disgusting chalky sweetness. "Okay. Let's talk."

"I stopped by the inn earlier this evening—"

"You did?"

"—and I get what's going on."

"Really? Because I sure don't."

"I saw the storage pod out back—"

"That's for—"

"I know what it's for, Agnes. It's for your boxes of stuff that you never bothered to unpack because you weren't really ever planning on staying in Naneda—"

"It's—"

"Don't try to sugarcoat it, okay? I thought someone might be home, so I went into the kitchen—the door was unlocked—and I saw your application forms on the counter. For graduate school in anthropology. In Seattle. Sure would've been nice if you'd told me your plans."

I didn't answer. Otis had it wrong about the storage pod, but the grad school applications? There was no spinning that. I'd been seriously considering applying.

I felt as if I was going to puke Tums.

"No answer?" Otis said. He sounded weary and sad. "Okay. Well, I need to get some sleep, so—"

"Wait! I can—"

"I really cared about you. Heck, I even fooled myself into thinking I was just as in love with you this time around as I was back in high school. Joke's on me, I guess. It's over, Agnes."

"Wait!" I cried.

But Otis had already hung up.

I lowered myself shakily to the curb. The fluorescent lights buzzed overhead. My stomach acid seemed to have taken the Tums as a challenge to produce even *more* stomach acid.

My heart was cracking in half.

Behind me, the minimart's electronic door signal went *bee-bong*, and then Effie was handing me a bottle of water. "I noticed you bought antacids without buying water. That's a no-no. I'd sit next to you, but after that flatbed pickup, my joints have gone on strike."

I uncapped the water bottle and took a swig. "I hate this town."

"No, you don't. You're hating yourself. It'll pass." She pulled the little red string to unseal the plastic wrapping around her pack of cigarettes.

"You can't smoke at a gas station," I said. "The entire thing will blow up."

"Then we'd better get going."

I stood. I felt dizzy. "Does every single speck of plooey have to hit the fan at the exact same time?"

"Apparently."

We were climbing into the Dustbuster when Effie's phone, still in my hands, rang. My heart juddered. *Otis! Otis was calling back to say he'd made a huge mistake and he still loves me!*

I knocked the phone in the abyss between the seat and the door, and I had to open the door to fish it out.

But when I saw the screen, it wasn't Otis calling.

I pushed ANSWER. "Hello? Chester?"

"Agnes!" A tinny, excited woman's voice said with a lot of road noise in the background.

"Lo?"

"Yes, bubbeleh, it's Lo, and I'm in the car with Chester—"

"And her husband!" Myron cried in the background. "Even though I'm pretty sure she wishes it was Josh Groban—"

"*Shush*," Lo said, sounding as if she'd put a hand over the phone. Then, louder, "We're tailing the mark."

"Who's Mark?" This was too much for my brain, already overloaded with adrenaline and grief.

"Not Mark," Lo said impatiently. "*The* mark."

"Start at the beginning," I said. "Weren't you going to stake out Darrell Dvorak's apartment in Rochester?"

"We were," Lo said. "I mean, we *did*. And we saw him come

out, get into his car, and start driving. He went all the way out to an all-night diner at a truck stop on the Thruway."

"Okaaay," I said.

"It gets better, don't worry," Lo said. "By the way, are you in bed?"

"No, I'm actually sitting here in the minivan at a gas station with Aunt Effie. Why?"

"Perfect! Start driving while I talk."

"Start *driving*?"

"Toward the Thruway. Believe me. You'll want to."

"Okay, sure." Why not? Heck, the night had already reached Looney Tunes levels of ridiculous, so why stop now? I put the phone on speaker, turned up the volume, and put it on the console. Then I pushed the key into the ignition, and we were off. Effie didn't protest; she was complacently smoking.

"Okay," I said to Lo, loud enough to be heard over the *vroom* of the Dustbuster's engine. "Keep going."

"Well, that awful man had a tall stack of pancakes, sausages, and three—no, maybe four—cups of coffee," Lo said.

"Made my bladder hurt just watching him," Myron said.

"Can we fast-forward to the part where I find out why I'm driving to the Thruway in the middle of the night?" I said.

There was some rustling, possibly some cursing, and then Lauren was on the line. "Agnes," she said briskly, "Hi. Here's the thing. Darrell had some kind of business meeting with a really sketch-looking guy at the all-night diner during which an envelope changed hands, and now he is this very second pulling into the Lakewinds Casino parking garage."

"Lakewinds Casino?" I said.

"Oh, my," Effie murmured.

"He's either a compulsive gambler," Lauren said, "or he works at the casino. We thought you'd want to know. We can keep track of him until you and Effie get here. Call us when you do. Got it?"

"Uh—"

"Great." Lauren hung up.

"It seems as though we might be about to find out what Darrell was doing in Naneda," Effie said.

"Guess so." I stepped harder on the gas.

* * *

It was 11:51 when I pulled into the parking garage of Lakewinds Casino. As Effie and I rode the parking garage elevator down to the casino entrance, I dialed Chester's number.

"Yeah?" Chester said. It sounded as if he was eating something.

"We're here."

"Great. We're in the Spirit Rock Lounge. Don't ask. There's nothing spiritual about it except for the liquor fumes."

"And Darrell?"

"He's tending the bar."

*Fist pump!* "There in a minute."

Effie and I went through a side entrance into a vast, gaudily carpeted, low-ceilinged room filled with blinking, bleeping slot machines. I saw only two people playing—if you could call that slack-faced, robotic punching of touchscreens "play." It looked more like garden-variety compulsive despair to me.

Speaking of compulsive despair . . . I needed carbs. Like, *now.*

Next, we passed through a slightly less depressing room full of blackjack and poker tables. There was only one of each game going. The rest of the tables sat empty. This wasn't Vegas.

Effie took big sucks of the air. "I just *adore* casino air."

"Because you don't even have to light up to get a nicotine rush?"

"No, because they pump oxygen in."

"Really?"

"Mm. Keeps you feeling great. They want you to feel great so they can keep taking your money. It's a win-win."

We went out into a shopping atrium area, complete with naturalistic fountains. All the shops—selling jewelry, techno gadgets, and tart-wear—were closed, with metal grills pulled down tight. We studied the directory next to the all-glass elevator.

"There," I said, pointing to the map. "Spirit Rock Lounge. Mezzanine level."

Up we went. My heart was pounding in anticipation of talking to Darrell Dvorak. I couldn't stop picturing the gun he'd pulled on me at the funeral home.

We entered the bar, which was dim, pulsating pop music, and smelling faintly of bleach. Only a few tables were occupied, and we found Lauren, Chester, Myron, and Lo at a table under a curve of faux rock.

"Where is he?" I said softly.

Lauren tipped her head in the direction of the bar.

I turned.

My belly did a triple Salchow.

Darrell stood behind the bar, wearing a black mandarin-collared shirt with a name tag on it, pouring liquor into a jigger. A male barfly was draped on a stool nearby.

"Go get 'im, slugger," Chester said.

"Yes, do," Effie said, sliding into a chair next to Lo. "And while you're at it, would you order me an extra-dry vodka martini, extra olives? Oh—and see if they have potato vodka. I'm going gluten free."

"I'm doing this alone?" I said.

"I think that would be best," Effie said. "So he doesn't feel bullied, you know."

For the love of Mike. "Okay, fine. Anyone else want a drink?"

I'd meant that to be sarcastic, but Lauren said, "Yeah, a lemon drop," and Chester said, "I'm good. I'm the designated driver." He puffed his chest in Lauren's direction. "Also, I'm training."

"For what?" she said. "A poetry slam?"

I walked slowly to the bar. I leaned against it and cleared my throat.

"Help you?" Darrell said, not looking up from his mixing.

"I, um, need . . . we need to talk."

"Thas what my ex-wife is always thaying," the barfly slurred.

Darrell looked up and squinched his eyes at me. "Wait a minute—do I know you?"

"Sort of."

"You're the weirdo who was going through my wallet!"

"And *you're* the weirdo who pulled a gun on me."

"You deserved it."

"We have some unfinished business."

"That right?" Darrell plopped a drink in front of the barfly, and liquor sloshed.

I fully expected Darrell to try to intimidate me. Instead, he strode in the opposite direction, passing the shelves of liquor, and shoved through a swinging door.

If this were an action film, I would've vaulted over the bar and chased him down. Alas, although my sweatpants might've been able to handle such a feat, my body said forget it.

Darrell was getting away.

"Can I help you, hon?" someone said.

I turned to see a female bartender approaching from the other direction. She had an aggressive push-up bra, wrinkles between her tanning salon–ravaged cleavage, a moussed blonde updo, and loops of thick black eyeliner around faded eyes. She could've been thirty or sixty. Her name tag said BRITT.

"Oh," I said. "Yeah. I, um—I wanted to talk to Darrell."

"What, you one of his exes? Don't you gals know better than to come to a man's place of work and give him the shakedown? If he's a deadbeat dad, talk to a lawyer."

"No, it's not—I'm not one of his exes."

Britt looked me over. "Yeah, I guess you don't really look like Darrell's type."

As if my night couldn't get any worse, now I wasn't even up to nasty, probably-criminal Darrell's standards? Jeez.

"Darrell wasn't in to work yesterday, was he?" I said.

"Nope. Said he was *sick*."

"You don't believe he was?"

"Let's just say that he has a side business."

*Well, well, well.* "Which is?"

"Can't say."

"I'm a good tipper," I said.

"Oh, yeah? *How* good?"

"Um—" I burrowed into my bag. Keys, Tums, Snickers bar, eyebrow pencils galore, wallet. I took out my wallet and unzipped it. "All I have is two dollars in cash—but I could credit card it."

"How about you give me that Snickers, and we'll call it a deal? I'm starved."

I thunked the Snickers on the bar. It disappeared into Britt's apron pocket. Her eyes roved the bar, settling briefly on the barfly. I guess she decided that the barfly was too drunk to eavesdrop, because she leaned closer and whispered, "I heard Darrell's a twister."

I frowned. "A twister?" I pictured Darrell playing Twister with Britt. Not pretty. "What do you mean?"

"I *mean*, he gets paid to twist peoples' arms."

"What people?"

"People who owe his boss money."

Oh. *Oh.*

"You mean . . . his boss here at the casino?"

"No, I mean his boss the loan shark."

That took a second to sink in. "A loan shark who loans money to . . . gamblers?"

Britt shook her head. "You sure are one little greeny, aren't you? Yeah. Loan sharks loan to gamblers. At ten percent interest a week, I hear, and if you don't pay up, well, that can be a *problem*, if you know what I mean."

I had been toying with the idea of still trying to corner Darrell. But, what with his gun, the loan shark, and his twister side hustle, that was now seeming like an exceptionally bad idea.

"How come you're checking up on Darrell, anyway?" Britt asked.

"I'm a private detective."

Britt laughed. "You? In those sweatpants? Sweetheart."

"I need a lemon drop and an extra-dry gluten-free vodka martini," I said stiffly.

# Chapter 28

After I carried the drinks back to the table, in a hushed voice I filled everyone in on what Britt had told me about Darrell Dvorak. "Theory," I said. "Someone in Naneda has a gambling problem. They borrowed money from a loan shark and didn't pay him back, so the loan shark sent in their twister to breathe down their neck."

"Clarification: the *killer* has a gambling problem," Chester said. "The killer took Mikey's cash. The killer likely took Clifford's cash."

"That's easy, then," Myron said. "Which one of your murder suspects has a gambling problem?"

"Randy plays poker," I said. "Then there's Belinda. Could she be a compulsive gambler?"

"Hard to picture," Effie said. She tamped out her cigarette and in the same fluid motion, pulled another from the pack and stuck it between her lips. *Snick* went the lighter. "Then there is Karen and eBay."

"What?" I said. "eBay?"

"We know she's obsessed with bidding on used designer shoes on eBay, right?"

"Yeah."

"Isn't that a kind of gambling? The thrill of the clock running out, escalating the bid at the last second, and so forth?"

"Kinda sounds like you at an estate sale, Aunt Effie," Chester said.

I said, "That the killer is a gambler makes sense, too, since, you know, bludgeoning people to death is risky behavior." I waved smoke out of my face. "I want to get out of here. We've learned what we came here to find out, and"—I glanced over at the bar—"I don't want to run into Darrell, like, ever again."

"Don't you want to stop by the all-you-can-eat buffet?" Lo asked. "It's open."

"Nope."

"I heard they have great curly fries and General Tso's chicken."

Normally I make detours for curly fries, but this loan shark stuff had killed my appetite. "Let's *go*."

* * *

On the road, Effie and I didn't talk much. Between learning about the Peeper Prize bribe conspiracy, that Darrell Dvorak was a twister, and that the killer was very likely a gambler who was in over their head, we had a lot to process.

And, despite knowing all that juicy stuff, I just felt . . . sad. Deflated. I just wanted to quit investigating, yet how the heck could I quit without first clearing Otis's name?

Even though he had dumped me. The reality of that was so excruciating, it didn't even fully register. Maybe I was in shock.

"What's next?" I asked Aunt Effie as I turned onto the Naneda exit.

"Figure out which one of our suspects is a compulsive gambler."

"How?"

"Oh, I don't know. Ask their families if they frequent the casinos, I suppose? We'll figure it out in the morning."

"We're running out of time. We're supposed to go to the police station tomorrow right after the parade."

"I'm well aware of that. But we must get some sleep."

\* \* \*

I tossed and turned in bed. Tiger Boy had inexplicably joined me, and he curled at my feet, purring like a chainsaw. I hoped the fleas would keep to their end of the bed.

I had just about given up on sleeping, my digital alarm clock glowing 4:56, when I must've fallen asleep, because the next thing I knew, it was bleeping me awake. I slammed it off and sat blearily up.

Three hours of sleep. I was in hell.

And yet, my day of hamming it up on a pumpkin float, desperately trying to unmask a compulsively gambling killer, being shunned by the love of my life, and possibly being arrested for breaking and entering had just begun.

I needed coffee and carbs, STAT. Good thing it was my turn to go to the Flour Girl Bakery to pick up brekkie for everyone.

I went out into the chilly dawn, bundled in my puffer jacket and wearing my backup glasses. The lenses were a little scratched, making the misty morning look even fuzzier. The Dustbuster was icy inside, and I hunkered behind the steering wheel.

When I turned onto the road, I noticed a blue Prius parked beside the hedge, but I couldn't see who was behind the wheel, and I didn't much care.

I drove toward downtown.

The Prius followed.

I sped up a little.

So did the Prius.

Okay. Someone was stalking me. Great. I was so sick of the whole thing, I didn't feel panicked or frightened so much as weary.

I pulled into a spot in front of Flour Girl.

The Prius rolled past. I peered into my rearview mirror but still couldn't make out who was behind the wheel.

And anyway, they were gone. Maybe the whole following thing had been a coincidence.

I was sitting at a table in the bakery, sipping my latte and waiting for the rest of my order, when someone sank into the chair opposite me. I looked up from the newspaper I'd been leafing through.

It was Hugh Simonian, the Peeper Prize judge, with a smattering of stubble, a slept-in-looking plaid shirt, and a down vest.

"Well, hello, little lamb," he drawled.

"Hello, snoogums." Hugh had left Randy's garage the previous night before Effie and I had been discovered, so this probably wasn't about that. I slapped the newspaper shut. "That was you in the Prius, I assume. What is it this time?"

Hugh snorted. "That's rich. Cool as a cucumber, aren't you? Why aren't you returning my calls?"

"I have no idea what you're talking about, but if this is about that date that you so kindly offered me, the answer is no thanks."

"Is that what this is all about?" Hugh said. "The fact that you're just not my type?"

"*What?*"

"Indulging in a little revenge? Yeah. Okay. I get it."

"Why are you following me?" I cried. "I am *so sick* of shenanigans!"

"Shenanigans?" Hugh leaned in and lowered his voice. "You blackmail me for seven grand and then get all cute on me?"

Hold on just one ever-lovin' minute. *Blackmail?*

Hugh slouched back in his chair and folded his arms. "Don't worry. We're still on for nine fifty at the community pool—yeah, I can tell by the look on your face that you're worried about the bargain—"

He could?

"—and I need a little more time to get the funds together, but I wanted to clarify something before you go and get too high on your own cleverness."

"Uh-huh," I said.

Hugh sneered. "Tough as nails, huh? No one would know it by looking at you. Well, joke's on you, because I have technology on my side, and tech always wins. You listen up." He stabbed a finger at me. "After I give that stupid speech right after the parade today, I'm outta there. I'm due at the opening ceremony for the foliage festival in Montpelier, Vermont, and I don't want to make the hippies impatient. A lot of them are Wiccans."

"Okaaaay," I said.

"I'm warning you, if there are any other copies of that file—even if I find out you emailed it to yourself—this town is toast."

"Toast?"

"You may be squeezing me for cash, little lamb, but I've got insurance. *I* engineered North America's number one leaf-peeping app. If it turns out any copies of that recording remain, or if you breathed a word about it to anyone, I destroy Naneda with my app."

"Like . . . a doomsday device?" I gave a nervous laugh.

"It's not funny!"

"Well, *actually*—"

"I could make sure every last business in Naneda has a one-star review average or—yeah, I like this one even better—I could just not even have Naneda on the app at all. It'll be like Naneda never even existed as a tourist destination. Got it?" Hugh stood. "I'm not messing around. Any of this gets out, Naneda is done for." He stalked away, shoved out the bakery door, and disappeared.

I sat there, stunned. The espresso machine hissed and gurgled in the background.

This could mean only one thing. Whoever had picked up my phone in Randy's garage last night had sent Hugh a text message. About the recording I had made of the bribe conspiracy.

That person was blackmailing Hugh for cash.

And who committed crimes because they were desperate for cash?

The murderer.

*　*　*

"It's obvious what must be done," Aunt Effie said, once I had returned to the inn and told her about my conversation with Hugh. "A sting operation. With the police."

I took a deep breath. "Okay. Yeah, I think it's finally time to bring in the police."

"Here." Effie passed me her phone. "You call Detective Albright. I've got to finish putting out breakfast. I hear stirring upstairs."

Even though it was still really early, Albright picked up on the first ring, and he listened in silence as I explained my conversation with Hugh. Then *that* entailed backing up and explaining

how Effie and I had just so happened to record the bribe con-
spirators' conversation the night before.

"Where was that?" Albright asked.

"Oh, um . . . in Randy Rice's garage."

"Why were you there?"

"It's not important. What I was thinking was that if we
intercept Hugh and the blackmailer at the community pool at
nine fifty and catch them in the act of exchanging the phone for
the money, we will have the murderer. Piece of cake."

A long pause.

"Hello?" I said, checking the phone's screen to make sure I
still had a connection.

"Agnes," Albright said, "this sounds crazy. Are you *mostly*
using logic? Yes. But you have this—this chain of inferences
and, let's face it, straight-up guesses that are pretty darn shaky.
It's like a house of cards."

"This could be your chance to nab the killer!"

"*If* everything adds up the way you claim it does. Which
is . . . unlikely. Could it be that you're just nervy about being in
the parade? Because you'll do great—"

"Please." I hated the desperation in my voice.

"And then there's the problem of how you've been shame-
lessly meddling in a police investigation. I'm starting to think
maybe you *did* trespass in Mikey Brown's house—"

"*Please.* I think this could be our big chance."

A heavy sigh. "Okay, Agnes. You got me. I'll be there at the
pool with an officer or two at nine fifty. But I don't have high
hopes, and the department has a lot on its plate what with the
parade detail, so we won't be able to stick around for long."

"Thanks."

"But I want you to stay out of it, understand?"

"Yes, sir." I punched END CALL.

* * *

By nine fifteen, Effie had applied enough makeup and hairspray on me to coat the entire cast of *Dancing With the Stars*.

"Whoa," Chester said, eating his third cinnamon roll. "I didn't recognize you, Agnes. You look like a high-end call girl."

"Shut up," I said, but I didn't frown, for fear of cracking the layers of primer, foundation, blush, bronzer, and pearlescent highlighter on my face.

"Call girl?" Effie said, tipping her head to study her handiwork. "Mm. Yes, I suppose I can see that." She rearranged one of the bouncy curls on my shoulder. Because I was too tired to fight it, I'd allowed her to clip temporary hair extensions under my own hair, so now I had flowing chestnut waves worthy of a Pantene commercial. I had even put in contact lenses for the first time in days. Fancy schmancy.

We drove to the community center, where the parade was slated to start. I planned to change there, since that's where my Gourd Queen gown was.

We slid into the last available spot in the parking lot, which was teeming with people getting out of cars and carrying stuff around. The adjacent street was blocked off and lined with parked floats and parade vehicles—an old-time Model T, a truck carrying one monstrously huge pumpkin that was definitely going to give me nightmares, a vintage convertible, and—there it was—the Gourd Queen's float. It resembled Cinderella's pumpkin coach, except it was open on four sides, had a golden flag flapping on top, and was hitched to a Dodge Ram pickup.

Inside, the wardrobe room was blessedly unoccupied. While

Aunt Effie fidgeted, I went behind the divider screen and boogied myself into my orange polyester tube of dress. I managed to zip it up, and the hem just covered the toes of my sneakers. In a full-length mirror, I crowned myself with the faux-gold crown.

I went around the screen. "I look like a twenty-something sweet-sixteen impersonator."

"You look marvelous, Agnes. Truly."

I stuffed my regular clothes in one of the lockers in the costume room and checked the clock.

Nine thirty-nine.

"Time to roll," I said.

"I need to smoke."

"And miss all the action? Smoke *after* the murderer is busted."

We walked through the community center toward the aquatic center. With each step, the odor of chlorine intensified, and so did the butterfly bonanza in my stomach.

We reached the stairs leading up to the observation balcony over the pool. At the top, we paused in the shadows. Down below us, the turquoise surface of the water was as smooth as glass. The only light came from high windows on one wall.

"No one's here," I whispered.

"Surely the police are hiding," Effie whispered back.

We waited. And waited. The second hand on some unseen clock started to sound like a snare drum.

Nine fifty came and went.

My heart was sinking slowly, slowly.

"The parade starts in two minutes," Effie finally whispered. "And it looks as though we've failed."

Down below, two men emerged from one of the locker rooms: Detective Albright and a uniformed police officer.

Albright was not going to be happy with me. To make matters worse, in order to set up this failed sting operation, I had filled him in about much of Aunt Effie's and my potentially unlawful snooping.

We'd have puh-lenty to discuss at the police station later.

"Did Hugh trick me?" I asked Effie as we walked down the stairs. "Or is there some other community pool I'm not aware of?"

Effie shook her head. "I don't know what happened."

I had missed the Big Chance, and now . . . what? The killer had made off with a bunch of blackmail money and Hugh was going to go on his merry way to Montpelier?

It didn't seem right.

# Chapter 29

I split up with Effie outside the community center, since she was hankering for a nicotine wand. In my orange dress, I minced across the parking lot to the parade staging area, which by this time was a swarming mass of an oompah band in lederhosen, fire trucks, preschoolers in owl and apple costumes, flags, and Chihuahuas in hats. Silver clouds had come rolling in from the hills beyond the lake. I shivered. It wasn't exactly weather for a strapless gown.

"Look, Daddy, the Gourd Queen!" a little girl cried, pointing.

I smiled and waved at her.

"That can't be the Gourd Queen, sweetie," the dad said gently. "She's too old."

My smile slipped off.

I wended my way to the pumpkin float. Delilah was already up there on one of the thrones, peering into a compact and patting powder on her nose.

"Hi," I said to her, trying to hoist a foot onto the lowest rung of the ladder on the side of the float.

She snapped her compact shut. "Oh, hey. You know, you

look *just* like a walking ad for the mother-of-the-bride out-fits at Bargain Bridal Barn. Wow, with hair extensions and *everything*."

"Better the Bargain Bridal Barn than the 1982 Mrs. Bul-garia Pageant."

Delilah's eyes slitted.

One point for me. I guess. Scoring points against Delilah had lost its luster.

I managed to winch myself onto the float by yanking my skirt up to my knees and then going up the ladder sideways. At the top, I settled my skirt back around my ankles, shuffled over to my throne, and sank into it.

"You're out of breath," Delilah said. "Maybe you should start working out. I had the *best* workout this morning." She flashed her dimple. "With Otis."

My heart did a somersault. "At the gym?" Otis didn't belong to a gym. He had some mismatched weights in his garage.

"Something like that."

"You ladies ready?" a guy in a baseball cap asked, looking up at us from the side of the float.

"I guess," I said.

"Sure am!" Delilah said. "And thank you so much for pull-ing the float, Allan. You're such a sweetie."

Allan, who appeared to be pushing eighty, gave his cap a wiggle. "Anytime, Delilah. Maybe you can pay me back with one of those maple cupcakes later. I had a dream about those last night."

"Deal." Delilah giggled.

Allan got in the truck. Up ahead, the high school marching band was assembling.

"Daddy, Daddy!" This was the little girl who had pointed

me out minutes earlier, except now she was pointing at Delilah. "Is that the Gourd Queen?"

"Sure looks like it, honey," the dad said.

Allan started the engine, and we were off.

Just like every parade in Naneda for as long as I could remember, this year's Harvest Festival parade would go two blocks from the community center and then turn onto Main Street. It would traverse the length of the business district and then make a right on Maple, go two more blocks, and end at City Park. There, at the band shell, would be the closing ceremonies, including Hugh's speech.

And then, apparently Hugh was going to use his leaf-peeping app to make certain Naneda was toast.

We turned onto Main Street. Cheering crowds lined the sidewalks on either side. The marching band honked out a jaunty rendition of "Stars and Stripes Forever."

"It's show time, Agnes!" Delilah said. "Wave!"

"Oh. Right." I waved at the crowd. And waved some more. It felt insincere.

I saw people I knew in the crowd, people I had known for my whole life. My third-grade teacher, Mrs. Neely. The librarian from the public library, Chris McCavity. Lauren, standing in the crowd next to—wow—next to Chester. Alexa Rice, in dark sunglasses, holding the leash of her corgi, who was eating something off the sidewalk. The gaggle. Other people, whom I had seen a million and one times, at the supermarket, the post office, the farmer's market, but had never officially met. Everyone looked so happy. So relaxed.

That I'd failed to catch the murderer, and that Hugh Simonian might destroy our town's popularity with his leaf-peeping app, made my throat ache.

The whole parade came to a wobbly halt.

"What's the problem?" Delilah said with a princessy frown.

I craned my neck around the side of our float. "It's just that the front of the parade is starting its turn onto Maple. That's always a little rocky."

"'Naneda is always this, Naneda is always that,'" Delilah said in a mocking, singsong tone, smiling and waving to the crowd all the while. "You don't *own* the town just because your daddy happens to be mayor, Agnes."

"Um, where is this coming from?" I asked.

Delilah didn't answer because a man approached the float, pushing a tiny, pig-tailed girl in a stroller. He looked familiar. Oh, right. He was the clerk from the all-night minimart at the gas station.

He looked up at Delilah. "Hello," he called up to her over the noise of the marching band and the crowd. "Did you win?"

Delilah recoiled, steadying her tiara with one hand. "What?"

"The Wild Cash. Did you win? I thought you might have a good shot with those fifty cards you bought."

"I don't know you," Delilah said. "And I have no idea what you're talking about."

Then the parade was rolling again, and we left the guy behind.

"What was that all about?" I asked. An idea was stirring in the back of my brain, but I had slept for only a few hours . . .

"I get approached by crazy guys *all* the time."

"So you say."

We rode along for a bit, smiling and waving.

Then my tired brain spit out the idea. And man, it was a doozy.

"Scratch cards," I whispered. "Wild Cash cards are *lottery scratch cards.*"

Delilah kept on smiling and waving, but she said out of the corner of her mouth, "What?"

"You play the scratch cards. Like, big-time. Fifty Wild Cash cards from the minimart? And at the Kick-Off, you entered the raffle for those binoculars, and I saw you going nuts when you won. Oh—and you go to Charlie Morel's weekly poker game. You're a gambler . . ." My heart pumped hard. My palms started to sweat. "You're the *murderer.*"

Delilah didn't look at me. She just kept waving to the crowd. But her smile suddenly looked petrified.

"You desperately needed money—money to give to your loan shark—so when Mikey told you about the cash he'd found in a ziplock bag at the automotive shop, you killed him for it. And Clifford—Clifford stupidly confided in you about his inheritance money and his plans to leave town. Did he tell you he'd hidden his cash in his Vanagon? You kept telling me how people confide in you. I should've listened. You killed Clifford, stole his keys, let yourself into the Vanagon, and took the cash. Oh—and you also stole his wallet and planted it in Otis's motorcycle."

"Bless your soul, Agnes, making up stories. Why, you could give Nora Roberts a run for her money, couldn't you?" Delilah giggled as a man in the crowd blew her a kiss.

"And your alibi . . ." I shook my head. "How could I have been so dumb? You and Alexa had a deal of mutually assured destruction. She lied for you, saying you were with her at her grandpa's nursing home, and in return . . . in return, you didn't tell anyone about Alexa and Mikey's affair."

I realized all of a sudden how Alexa had tricked me about

their alibi. She had brought her *corgi* to the nursing home. Not Delilah. She had mentioned "a friend" when she called the nursing home in front of Aunt Effie and me. The receptionist had said the friend—the corgi—was as cute as a button, and Alexa had bluffed and said the corgi was named Delilah.

Risky, but pretty clever.

"Did Mikey tell you about his affair with Alexa?" I asked. "You suck people in with your cupcakes and your cutesy routine, don't you? I know about you blackmailing Hugh Simonian with that audio file, by the way. I almost had you. But you changed the meeting time."

"It's the first rule of blackmail, sweetie. Always change up the meeting time and place."

"So you've done it before."

"Maybe." Delilah kept on smiling and waving with her right hand, but her left-hand fingers pinched hard around the gold satin clutch purse in her lap.

"One thing I can't figure out," I said, "is how come Darrell, the loan shark's twister, was having a hard time finding you in Naneda."

"That's easy. Because I avoid him. When I see him coming, I turn off the shop lights, lock the door, and flip the sign to CLOSED."

"Is that what happened when you dunked me in the apple-bobbing tub?"

"Maybe."

"Who are you, anyway? Where did you come from? I thought you were like a character out of some romantic comedy movie, but really you're just . . . creepy. Is Delilah Fortune even your real name?"

"Don't you see what's happened here, Agnes? Look around.

This town loves me. I can do no wrong. I make them *cupcakes*, for goodness' sake." Smile. Wave. Dimples and a hair toss. "What have *you* ever done for them? Look at you. You won't even smile and wave at them. I keep trying to tell you: nobody likes a Debbie Downer. This is my town, now, Agnes, and Otis is my boyfriend. By the way, Grandma Bee thinks I'm great, too, even though I beat her at Clue the other night."

"You went to Grandma Bee's house? Is that when you stole the keys to her Buick LeSabre so you could go cruising around town in that freaky pumpkinhead mask?"

Delilah ignored that. "Heck, even your dad and his housekeeper just *love* me." A nasty giggle. "Maybe *I* can be their daughter when you're gone."

"Gone?"

"Oh, didn't you realize? I'm going to kill you, too."

Fear sizzled down my spine. "You're crazy."

"Am I? The talk around town is that *you're* the crazy one, Agnes. You and your weird old aunt. Yeah, I think getting rid of both of you is definitely the way to go. I won't say exactly how or when, but you're dead."

"You won't get away with it."

"I'm on a winning streak. And you'll never be able to pin anything on me."

We rumbled along Main Street. I felt as if I might puke.

I loved this town. Omigosh, I *loved* it. No way was I going to let some psycho murderer like Delilah move in like a hermit crab and call it her own.

I eyed the clutch purse in Delilah's lap. "How is the town going to feel about you when they find out you're a compulsive gambler, a blackmailer, and a murderer?"

"They aren't going to find out."

"Oh, no? Not even up here on this float, with everyone watching and taking pictures—and oh, look, there's the camera crew from Shore 7 News." I leaned over, snatched Delilah's clutch purse from her hands, and stood up shakily on the float. "Look, everyone!" I shouted, waving the purse in the air.

Gasps and shouts from the crowd.

"You know what's here in Delilah Fortune's purse?" I cried. "I'm guessing seven thousand bucks of blackmail money!"

"You're embarrassing yourself, Agnes," Delilah said softly.

"She's the murderer!" I shouted. "She's a money-hungry gambler who killed Mikey Brown and Clifford Prentiss for cash, and I can prove it!"

A ripple of gasps and murmurs. The float kept on rolling along, but all eyes were on me. Someone was weaving quickly through the sidewalk crowd toward us. *Otis.* And from the other direction I saw Aunt Effie's big round lemur sunglasses bobbling our way.

With shaking fingers, I unsnapped the purse. I opened it and looked inside.

The was nothing but a lone tube of lip gloss inside.

"Like I said," Delilah snarled in an undertone, *"you're embarrassing yourself."* She stood up shakily and snatched at the purse.

I swooped it out of her grasp.

"Give it to me!" she shrieked. She grabbed my hair extensions and yanked.

With a scalp-searing rip, the extensions were gone—

The crowd sucked in a collective breath.

—and Delilah held them up like some dead animal, giggling wildly.

"Be careful, Agnes!" This was Otis, only a few yards off. "Agnes, get away from her!"

"You're nuts!" I shouted at Delilah, rubbing my burning scalp.

"*I'm* nuts? You're the one going around accusing everyone of murder, Agnes Blythe. You need to be on meds."

The pumpkin float stopped hard.

I lurched toward Delilah, arms outstretched.

Delilah whipped out a pistol from somewhere—her puffy sleeve? Her pageant-sized hair?—and aimed it at me.

I recoiled.

"*Agnes!*" Otis shouted, really close by.

I teetered in my tube dress.

Delilah crashed into me and—*CRACK!*—the gun went off. A hole popped open in the papier-mâché pumpkin coach ceiling above us.

Screams from the crowd. Someone cried, "Police! Help! Police!"

Delilah and I both thumped to the floor of the float in a tangle of polyester satin.

A billow of cash poofed out of Delilah's bodice.

People in the crowd screamed some more, now with a mixture of fear and excitement. Kids darted forward, hands outstretched to the fluttering, twirling green money. Parents rushed frantically forward, trying to grab their kids. And there was Otis, his face drained of color, his eyes huge, vaulting up onto the float, curling a protective arm around me as I peeled myself upright.

Delilah sat up, too, pink lip gloss streaked across her cheek and her tiara askew.

I snatched her pistol and passed it to Otis. "Huh," I said, panting. "I guess you win some and you lose some, Delilah."

# Chapter 30

The rest of that day was a blur.

What happened to Delilah? Well, the parade stopped in its tracks, but the video cameras and camera phones whirred away. A couple of the cops on parade detail hurried forward and broke up the kids who were grabbing the fluttering cash, and while they were doing that, Delilah hitched up her skirts and tried to make a break for it. One of the cops stopped her and said she was going to have to make a statement about the cash and the gun. Then he told me *I* was going to have to make a statement, too. Otis offered to go with me; I said no thanks, but I'd call him later. This was all really awkward and rushed, and we didn't look each other straight in the eye.

Apparently, this wasn't a feel-good movie where everything gets magically resolved.

At the police station, feeling stressed out and itchy in my Gourd Queen gown, I spilled everything I knew about Delilah, the murders, and the blackmail. On tape.

Detective Albright listened, his face growing more and more serious.

"Hugh Simonian will have my phone," I said. "And if you look on Delilah's smartphone or computer, I'll bet you'll find more copies of the audio file I made last night. I'll bet if you look in Delilah's apartment, you'll find a Headless Horseman mask. She's probably up to her ears in debt, too. Wherever she came from—she said it was somewhere in Indiana—there might be blackmails, thefts, and even unsolved murders in her wake."

Once Albright had finally stopped the digital recorder, he said to me, "Off the record, Agnes . . . does all this mean that you only went out to the movies with me to further your investigation?"

"No," I said. "That was because you won a date with me fair and square at the bachelorette auction."

His face fell.

Guilt punched me. "And . . . well, even though I'm mad that you were so obsessed with pinning the murders on Otis, I still think you're . . . you're a good guy."

"You mean that?"

"Sure."

"So . . . want to go bowling?"

Mental face plant.

*　*　*

Dad was waiting for me at the police station.

He gave me a big bear hug. "Honey," he said, "how do you get into these situations?"

"No idea, Dad. No idea."

He gave me a ride to the Stagecoach Inn, and although he was going to stick around to see Aunt Effie, I desperately needed a shower. I was exhausted, too, but napping was out of the question. I was too amped up.

I went up to Aunt Effie's bathroom and took a long shower, washing away layers of makeup, hairspray, and stress. I brushed my teeth, moisturized, bundled myself in my bathrobe, and, thinking about calling Otis, climbed the stairs to my attic room.

Otis was waiting for me, sitting on the edge of the bed, elbows on knees, hands clasped.

He straightened when he saw me. "Hi," he said, sounding a little shy.

"Hi." I stopped in the doorway.

"Things have been happening to your bathroom floor."

"Yeah."

"Looks great."

"Thanks."

"But I see you still haven't moved your boxes."

"That storage pod down in the yard isn't for my stuff," I said. "It's for Aunt Effie's antiques."

Otis's face clouded with confusion. "Okay . . ."

"You're thinking about the grad school applications you saw, and yeah, I was thinking about applying. Why shouldn't I? Nothing is holding me here in Naneda. You wanted a break—whatever *that* means—and this inn isn't even mine—"

"You have your family here."

I threw my arms wide. "So I'll come and visit on Thanksgiving and Christmas! I need a life—my *own* life—with a—a deliberate foundation. Not just a series of accidents and coincidences that keep me in my hometown by default. And I sure as heck can't stand *sort of* dating the man I love. I want something real. Something solid."

"Agnes. Calm down." Otis was in front of me, placing his hands gently on my shoulders.

"Why should I calm down? You let yourself be seduced by a psycho cupcake hussy."

Otis flinched. "What? No, I didn't."

"But Delilah said—"

"Haven't you realized what a monster she is, Agnes? She stirs up trouble and manipulates people wherever she goes. I saw it from a mile away—"

"No, you didn't. You ate her German chocolate cupcakes. Gross!"

"Okay, okay, I admit that I didn't catch on immediately. Blame the baked goods. But the minute she started saying nasty little things about you, I steered clear. I could tell she was jealous. Didn't bank on her being a *murderer*, though."

Delilah? Jealous of *me*?

"Anyway, she had nothing to do with why I wanted to take a break. I just needed to deal with being accused of murder privately. It was embarrassing and, well, *painful*, and I didn't want to make you have to go through all that." Otis swallowed. "Especially since I still haven't figured out if you're planning on . . . sticking around."

"I didn't know my long-term plans even mattered," I said, "because I wasn't sure if we were, you know, dating or . . . *dating*."

"You mean, were we a couple?"

"Right." A pause. "So. Were we?"

"I guess not."

"And . . . should we be?" I tried to sound rational and detached. Too bad my voice wobbled.

"I don't know."

"*O*kay, gotta go!" I wriggled under his hands.

Otis held my shoulders firmly. He edged closer so that our hearts were touching. "Stop," he whispered. "Listen."

I fell still. I felt his heartbeat pumping through my robe and his T-shirt, smelled his laundry detergent and his warm skin.

"I thought I was reading too much into it," Otis said. "Into us . . . hanging out. I mean, it was less than two months ago that you broke up with the guy you'd been with for several years. The guy you were going to *marry*. I wanted to take things slowly. To give you space."

A laugh bubbled up inside my chest, because at that moment in time there was no space whatsoever between us.

"You coming back to town, us getting back together . . ." Otis gently smoothed a wet strand of hair from my eyes. "It was kind of freaking me out, to be honest—"

"What?"

"No, no. In a good way. I guess. All these old feelings I had for you that I thought were just, you know, in the past, in a box on a shelf, were suddenly back, and real. I fell in love with you back in high school, and I guess the love maybe went dormant for a bunch of years, but it turns out it never died. You know?"

"Yeah," I whispered. "I know."

Otis cupped the side of my head. "Does this mean we can go away to the Adirondacks?"

"No," I whispered.

He pulled back. "What?"

"I have to finish that bathroom floor first."

Otis laughed. "Okay. Then, if you'll let me, I'll help you finish building that floor." He leaned down and touched his lips to mine.

\* \* \*

"Hello, darlings, don't *you* look all glowy," Aunt Effie said when Otis and I walked into the kitchen a while later. She was smoking at the open window over the sink.

"I don't know what you're hinting at," I said, "but we've been laying down crack-suppressing floor membrane. Hi, Dad."

"Hi, honey." Dad was at the kitchen table, nursing a mug of coffee. A small plate with nothing but crumbs on it sat beside the mug.

"Sit down, darlings," Effie said to Otis and me. "Could I make you a drink? Nibbles? Oh—and I have some wonderful news. I've hired Lally Douglass, and she starts tomorrow."

"Really?" I said. "That's great."

"Who's Lally Douglass?" Otis asked, walking to the refrigerator. "Agnes, want a sandwich?"

"Sure." I sank into a chair at the table, kitty-corner to Dad.

"Wonderful job, by the way, exposing Delilah like that," Effie said. "Everyone is thrilled that you landed that horrid creature in jail. Avi also wanted me to tell you thank you, because those cupcakes were of course diabolical sugar bombs that were giving the entire town cavities."

"Our Agnes is very brave," Dad said. "She's a town hero. Mark my words, she'll be mayor someday. Effie, when are you going to quit those filthy cigarettes? They'll kill you."

"All in good time." Effie turned to me. "Why don't you take a peek in that folder on the counter."

"What?" I looked over my shoulder to see a beige file folder sitting on the counter.

"Go on."

I went to the counter. I opened the folder.

Inside was a packet of legal-looking documents. I frowned. "What is this?"

"Mr. Solomon drew up the documents to provide you and Chester with shares in the general partnership of Stagecoach Inn Enterprises, LLC," Effie said.

I could only blink.

"If you choose to sign those documents—and of course think it over first—you, Chester, and I will be equal partners, each holding one-third of the shares, which, of course, since I registered an LLC, includes ownership of the property as well as the business."

I wanted to say thank you. Instead, I burst into tears.

Otis poked his head around the refrigerator door. "Whoa. Babe. What's—?"

"Aunt Effie?" Dad said. "She's crying."

"Oh, dear," Effie said. She ripped a bundle of paper towels from a roll, hurried over, and passed them to me.

"This is the nicest thing anyone has ever done for me!" I blubbered.

"Does that mean you're in?" Effie asked.

"Yeah," I said. I smeared my nose with the paper towels. "All in."